CRONAN THE LIBRARIAN

CRONAN
THE LIBRARIAN

Book two of the
Black Dragon Trilogy

STEVE WESTCOTT

FrontList Books

Published by FrontList Books.
An imprint of Soft Editions Ltd,
Gullane, East Lothian, Scotland.

Copyright © Steve Westcott 2007.

Steve Westcott has asserted his right
under the Copyright, Designs and
Patents Act, 1988, to be identified
as the Author of this Work.

All rights reserved.
No part of this publication may
be reproduced, stored in a retrieval
system, or transmitted in any form
without the prior written permission
of Soft Editions Ltd.

A catalogue record for this book is available from
the British Library.

ISBN: 1-84350-102-3

ISBN 13: 9781843501022

This book is sold subject to the
condition that it shall not, by way
of trade or otherwise, be lent,
resold, hired out or otherwise
circulated without the publisher's
prior consent in any form of
binding or cover other than that in
which it is published and without a
similar condition including this
condition being imposed on the
subsequent purchaser.

CRONAN THE LIBRARIAN

Steve Westcott and his family live in an old farmhouse on the picturesque Isle of Man, where they have resided these past thirteen years. He fits his writing in and around his day job, when he can find the time to scribble down notes for later translation. For more information visit Steve's website at:

www.stevewestcott.com

This book is dedicated with love to Carole, Samantha and Michael Westcott. Without your support, this tome would never have been written.

As translated by Cronan, the librarian.

... and so it shall come to pass that on the fiftieth day in the one thousandth year from crossover — give or take a day or two, the working out of sums not being one of my stronger points — the skies above Tiernan Og shall be rent by turmoil. When the storm doth reach its zenith, the roiling clouds shall be ripped asunder and a second sun will appear. A black sun, not bright like our own, and it may be slightly oval instead of round, but a sun it shall be. And from this sun, like a swarm of stingy things, will emerge the horde of Snor'kel. And then shall the dark ones be driven from their foul nests, rendered impotent by Snor'kel's divine fury, given a right good shafting. Only then shall our brave new world know true peace.

Book of Prophesies, by Nostra-Ogmus
(Written this five mill... six mi... Bugger it! Written this seven hundredth year since crossover)

Chapter One

There is one thing that can be guaranteed to bite faster than a striking snake, gather pace more quickly than a falling rock, spread more rapidly than an outbreak of strep throat in an old folks home — bad news. The worse the news, the quicker it spreads, infecting everyone who hears it with impending doom. And this news was the worst possible. It infiltrated the labyrinthine tunnels, caverns and vaults of the mountain stronghold of Hope like a plague, carried from person to person in hushed tones. The last bastion of the Ogmus was awash with the ill tidings.

The book had been stolen! Not just any book, but *the* book. The book that held the future of the Ogmus within its carefully bound pages. The Book of Prophesies. It had been taken from the safety of the library grotto while Cronan the librarian took forty winks.

Nostra, the famed seer of the Ogmus, had devoted his short, opiate-dependant life to writing the book. Its cryptic contents provided clues of what was to transpire for future generations, if one could understand his inane musings.

Sadly, as is often the case with drugs, the abuse of Nostra's body eventually killed him. At the tender age of twenty-six, while walking a mountain ledge when totally out of it on concentrated poppy juice, he failed to foresee the savage, body-rending attack from the black dragon that claimed his life. His untimely death had shocked the small community of Ogmus, and led to the creation of the oft-quoted saying: 'Me? Take drugs? Are you out of your nostra? I'd sooner chase the dragon, mate.'

And now his book was missing, presumed stolen. It was a disaster. It was a nightmare. It would prove to be a real headache for the poor sod who had taken it when he tried to make sense of the gibberish that Nostra had written. Most of the verses made sense after the events they foretold had actually happened. But trying to interpret and link them to the future? Tricky.

The painstaking process of translating the verses into plain, understandable Ogmus had kept Cronan busy for the past forty years, and he had only just got to the stage where he was working on the important ones; those dealing with the future. It was only twenty days into the future, mind, but it was a start. His reasoning for beginning so far back was so that he could get a feel for the way in which Nostra hid the meanings, which should then help him when it came to foretelling future events.

What he hadn't taken into account, however, was how long it would take him to work out the past. Nostra's obvious penchant for narcotics had rendered the later verses all but indecipherable. Cronan had given up entirely on the bits that referred to flying lime-green snugglebunnies.

But worse still, not only had the book gone, so had Cronan's scribbled notes of what was prophesied to happen in just twenty days time. Completely taken aback by the theft, he sat at his desk in the centre of the small, fifteen foot by fifteen foot, vaulted cell that housed the library of the Ogmus. Although given the distinct lack of books, library would appear to be something of a misnomer. With the room's single bookshelf remarkably devoid of the one book that had given the grotto the entitlement to call itself a library, 'bookshelf room' would now be more apt.

In all of his fifty-five years, Cronan had never felt so miserable. He ran a slender hand through his thinning grey hair and stared at the vacant spot on the shelf, willing the book to reappear. But the blank rock wall stared impassively back at him, almost seeming to smirk in the light of the room's single glow-globe.

Ever since he was a young lad he'd had a way with cryptic clues and had become a master at solving the most obscure problems well before he'd left Rock-School. So much so that his ability came to the attention of the Wing Commander, Volgen, who immediately commandeered him to work on Nostra's book. Convinced that the answer to defeating the Dark Ones lay hidden in its pages, Volgen instructed Cronan to find it. None of the previous Wing Commanders had given the cryptic tome much credence, but Volgen thought differently.

Cronan gave a heavy sigh, leaned his elbows on the desk and cradled his head in his hands. He stared at the scarred desktop in despair. What would Volgen say when he found out the book was missing? The Wing Commander was irascible at the best of times, and this news would set him off on one of his rants. Of that Cronan was sure.

After centuries of the Ogmus hiding in their mountain retreat, Volgen wanted to be the Wing Commander that led the last of them out. Back into the world of sunlight, blue skies and green fields; and to bring back the good dragons. He was convinced the answer was concealed in Nostra's scribblings and, two days ago, Cronan had found it — probably.

"Master?"

Not having heard young Tobias enter the room, Cronan looked up in surprise at the sound of the voice. He spotted his apprentice standing before the desk, hands clasped loosely in front of him and hazel eyes filled with concern.

"Is it true?"

The smile that tried to force its way onto Cronan's face gave up and fled in defeat. He nodded in solemn confirmation. "It's true."

Tobias's eyes widened, the spattering of freckles on his nose seeming to stand out more starkly against his pallid complexion. "The thieving b—"

"Tobias!" snapped Cronan, scraping back the chair and rising to his feet. "I will not have profanities used in my presence."

"I was only going to say booknappers," Tobias retorted. His face reddened to match the colour of his mop of wiry hair.

Cronan pursed his lips and shook his head, then sat back down. He chuckled. "Somehow what I thought you were going to say might have been more apt."

Tobias half smiled. "Any idea who took it?"

"Humph! If I knew that I wouldn't be sitting here pulling the remains of my hair out, trying to figure out the very same thing." He looked up and met Tobias's concerned gaze. "But it has to be an agent of those Blackabbots. May their souls rot in the bowels of eternal hell."

Tobias nodded, his expression grim. "And just when we were getting to the interesting part. The return of the good dragons."

"Return of the good dragons? Whatever makes you think the verse referred to their return?"

A frown formed on Tobias's face. "B-b-but it said that Snor'kel and his horde would emerge like a swarm of stingy things and rid us of the Dark Ones. Nostra had to mean it was the good dragons, didn't he?"

Cronan gave a wry smile. "Have you learned nothing during your years with me? About how he worked his cryptic clues?"

Tobias flushed with embarrassment and stared down at Cronan, arms folded across his scrawny chest, his foot nervously tapping the floor. "What did it mean, then?" His brow furrowed in puzzlement.

"It meant …" Cronan sighed. He'd jumped to the same conclusion as Tobias when they'd first translated it, but deep inside he suspected that the verse did not contain all of the information they needed. Such as where Snor'kel would appear, for starters. Tiernan Og was a big place, according to the few crudely drawn maps the library possessed. More so when you were confined to living inside a mountain and didn't have a clue what the outside world actually looked like beyond the rocky ledges.

As Cronan had found with most of Nostra's verses, you had to have two or three of them worked out to get the whole picture. But without the book that would now be impossible. Part of him hoped Tobias was right. "It could well mean that, lad. Forgive a testy old goat. My patience is not what it should be."

Tobias relaxed, a small smile forming on his face. "So it could mean that the dragons and their riders are coming back?"

"It could," Cronan admitted. Tobias's infectious smile caused one to appear on his own face.

"I knew it!" said Tobias, punching the palm of his left hand.

"Knew what?" a deep voice demanded.

Cronan's chair toppled over with a clatter as he jumped to his feet. "W-W-Wing Commander." A nervous smile tugged at his lips. "Wh-what brings you here?"

Volgen strode into the small room, resplendent in his powder-blue leggings, tunic and cape. The soft soles of his powder-blue, pointy-toed flying boots barely made a sound on the hard floor. He stopped before Cronan's desk, folded his arms above his pot-belly and fixed Cronan with a steely gaze. Volgen's bushy grey beard bristled and writhed as he chewed at his lip. With his bald pate, he looked as if his head had been put on upside down.

Cronan broke his gaze and looked at the floor.

Volgen snorted in annoyance, then glanced to the side and saw Tobias. "You still here?"

Tobias gave a nervous smile.

"Well, bugger off!"

By the time Cronan looked up Tobias had fled the room. "There was no need for ..."

Volgen leaned forward and placed his hands on the desk, his eyes boring into Cronan's. "There was every piggin' need!"

Rather than flee to the safety of his room, Tobias ran far enough down the corridor to make Volgen think he had, then slid to a halt and silently retraced his steps. Once he reached the library he stood to the side of the entrance, his back against the craggy wall, straining to hear what was being said.

"How could you be so piggin' stupid?" he heard Volgen roar. "Leaving the damn book where any passing toerag could take it? And your damn translation too? Of all the ..."

"Half translation," Cronan's voice quietly interjected.

"WHAT?"

Tobias flinched at the volume of Volgen's shout.

"Er, I hadn't quite finished it," Cronan replied. "I fell asleep before I'd got that far."

"So that makes it all right, does it? You, you ..."

Tobias tiptoed away, wanting to get back to the safety of his room in the foundling's quarters. He'd heard enough. He loved Cronan like a father and didn't want to listen to any more of Volgen's ranting. The Wing Commander would calm down eventually, in a day or so. He usually did when something upset him. Mind you, nothing as bad as this had ever happened before. The gods alone knew if he would ever recover from this news.

Everyone in Hope knew Volgen's prime objective was to plot their escape from their mountain retreat, along with bringing back the dragons of the Ogmus that had mysteriously vanished from the face of Tiernan Og over three hundred years ago. Pretty soon after the birth of the six rogue blacks, in actual fact. Even though he had never seen a dragon, let alone ridden one, Volgen took umbrage at any attempt to thwart his plans. And the theft of the one book that could provide them with answers was a pretty serious thwarting in anyone's book. Or tome, as the case may be.

Tobias increased his pace, negotiating the twisting, turning tunnels and intersections of Hope with an ease born of familiarity. In a matter of minutes he reached the merchants' quarter, and paused at the entrance. The large amphitheatre was heaving. It seemed that most of Hope's population of some five hundred souls had chosen this day to do their shopping. With a wry grimace, Tobias wondered why. News of the stolen book, perhaps? He shook his head as he scanned the mass of bodies milling around the huge cavern, very few of whom seemed to be buying anything. Instead the populace stood in small groups, muttering amongst themselves and casting the odd, wary glance towards the tunnel Tobias was about to emerge from. The library tunnel.

Only the food stalls appeared to be doing a brisk trade. The smell of spit-roasted chicken and spices wafted enticingly through the air, tickling Tobias's nostrils, reminding him that he hadn't eaten for the past few hours. He shrugged the pangs of hunger aside and steeled himself to venture forth, knowing that as soon as he was spotted he would be accosted from all sides by people wanting to know if the news were true.

Not being of a mind to further fuel the rumours with idle gossip he ducked his head down, pulled the collar of his tunic up around his ears, shoved his hands in his pockets, and set off at a fast pace into the crowd. He strode forward, not looking up, nor left nor right, as his rapid strides carried him along the central avenue through the stalls. He murmured brief apologies to those he bumped into, but didn't slow.

When he was half way across, he allowed a small smile to grace his face. So far so good. He was nearing the safety of the tunnel leading to his rooms. Another couple of minutes and he would be there.

Unfortunately that was the point where his luck ran out. With his mop of red hair, a rarity amongst the Ogmus who were mostly dark, he stuck out like a boil on a sumo wrestler's backside. As there was only one person answering his description who was likely to be coming from the direction of the library tunnel, the cry was soon out.

Within moments Tobias was being buffeted, both verbally and physically, as people demanded answers:

"Is it true that the book's been stolen?"

"Has the Wing Commander murdered Cronan yet? If not, when will he?"

"Has the senile old duffer misplaced the book? Is he using it to prop up a table?"

"Is it the work of the Blackabbots?"

"Do you fancy a shag, big boy?"

That was the one that did it for Tobias. Until then he had politely declined to answer the questions and had been steadily forcing his way through towards the safety of the tunnel, although the press of bodies made it damned hard work. But when that question was asked, by probably the ugliest old crone Tobias had ever laid eyes on, and accompanied by a suggestive tongue movement, fear spurred him on. Not caring who he injured, he elbowed and kicked his way out of the melée, much to the disappointment of the aforementioned hag, who threw her walking-cane to the floor and glowered after the retreating figure in disgust.

After what seemed like an age, Tobias reached the tunnel and ran as fast as he could towards his rooms.

Not wanting to be too far away from the library when Volgen had finished with Cronan, few gave chase. Those who did soon gave up and settled for shouting abuse at Tobias's fleeing form.

As the final turn came into sight, Tobias breathed a sigh of relief and slowed. He was knackered. He hoped Jophrey, his roommate, was up and about. He was bursting to tell someone what had happened, and Jophrey was the only one he could trust with such news. His friend had no love of the Blackabbots, either.

Like Tobias, Jophrey was an orphan. He'd turned up at Hope's foundling annex two years ago, alone and bedraggled, his parents having been killed by Lord Blackbishop and Mandrake, his black dragon, while they were out on the mountainside. The poor lad had been traumatised, so it was only natural that Tobias should take him under his wing and look after him. With them both being fourteen cycles old at the time they had soon become firm friends, and had remained so ever since.

Tobias grinned. Jophrey was fascinated by the dragons — the ones that had vanished so many years before — and was as eager as he to know all about them. That was why Tobias kept him informed of how the translations were going.

Reaching their rooms Tobias paused in the doorway, his hands pressed against the jambs as he fought to catch his breath. "Jophrey! Jophrey! You in there?" No answer.

Tobias frowned and stepped into the living area. It was unlike Jophrey to not be up and about at this hour. Mind you, he had been working the late shift at Pies R Us, the fast food outlet, so he was probably still in bed.

Eager to tell his friend the morning's news, he moved across the small room, carefully negotiating the clutter of papers, cups, plates and dirty clothing that lay scattered on the floor and piled on the room's two chairs. He headed towards the door leading to the sleeping area. When he reached it he gently thumbed the latch and pushed the door open to poke his head through.

"Jophrey? You asleep?" Still no answer.

Tobias pushed the door fully open and stepped inside. The light coming from the room behind spilled in. Tobias's shadow stretched across the rug-covered floor towards Jophrey's rumpled bed. It was empty, devoid of anything remotely resembling the sleeping form of his friend.

A frown formed on Tobias's face as he raised a hand to switch on the glow-globe. A soft, pale light bathed the room. He sucked in his breath. The drawers of Jophrey's dresser were all pulled out and his clothes had gone.

Seeing some crumpled papers on the floor, Tobias moved across to inspect them. A terrible foreboding struck him as he stooped to pick them up and place them on the dresser-top. When he had smoothed them out the foreboding became a gut-clenching dread and his eyes widened. He recognised the neat, flowing script upon the paper. It was Cronan's handwriting; a translation of one of Nostra's earlier verses dealing with the rise to power of the black dragons.

Tobias stared at the papers in disbelief, his lips compressing into a thin line as he tried to make sense of what he had discovered. Mouthing an oath, he screwed up the papers and threw them to the floor in fury.

Jophrey was the thief. He must be an agent of the Dark Ones. During the past two years the double-dealing toerag had played them all for fools. The thieving little b—

Chapter Two

On another world entirely, Snorkel stood in the middle of the amphitheatre's sandy arena and tried to focus his mind on the task in hand. He gazed abstractedly at tier upon tier of stone seating that angled up and away from him. In the gloom that shrouded the upper levels, some seventy feet above, the seats seemed to merge with the rocky canopy of the cavern's ceiling. He wriggled his toes as the warmth from the volcano-heated sand permeated the soles of his little red boots, making his feet sweat. Damp patches had appeared under his arms and his tunic was stuck to his body like a love-struck leech.

An itch appeared under the thick tangle of beard that poked out of the sides of his red flying hat, causing his right eye to twitch. By the gods, he felt nervous. What if he opened a gateway to a world where they could not survive? Or had them appear in the middle of a rock, or beneath the sea, or ...

He pushed all negative thoughts aside and closed his eyes, mentally reciting the spell he would need to take them through to their new world. The world of Ogmus and dragons. Yet again Snorkel hoped that the instructions contained in his newfound lore were correct, that generations of passing the seed of the Ogmus down the dwarven line had not played tricks with the inherited memories.

"Are you ready yet?" a voice snapped from beside him.

Snorkel scowled, irritated by both the interruption to his preparations and the tone of the haughty young queen's voice. If it were not for her being a dragon who could literally eat him for breakfast, he would have told her where to go.

"Leave him be, Kraelin," another voice gently scolded. "He will let us know when he is finished."

Reizgoth! Snorkel snorted in amusement and stifled a smirk. It would appear that fully grown, big red dragons were as wary of the young queen as he was. Was it really only nine months since he and Reizgoth had first met? It seemed like a lifetime ago. Then again, maybe it was. In memory of his long deceased rider, whose bright red flying suit Snorkel now wore, Reizgoth insisted on calling him Galduran. Snorkel half smiled. He hoped that Galduran would have approved of the dragon's new rider.

The echoes of Kraelin's unamused 'harrumph' faded and the cavern was again silent. Snorkel closed his eyes and began the preparation spells, his arms outstretched as his deep voice recited the words that would take them to their brothers. And sisters, of course.

After a few moments the preliminaries were complete. All that was left to do was close the spell and the doorway would open. Wanting to savour the moment, he turned to face Kraelin and bowed, his hand skimming the warm sand as he gave an elaborate flourish. "Ready when you are, Your Majesty."

As Snorkel straightened, he gazed in admiration at her glowing bulk. It was amazing how fast she had developed. Although only five weeks old, she was already half as big as Reizgoth, who sat in the sand beside her. In contrast to Reizgoth's crimson, Kraelin's scaled skin was a deep, vibrant gold, and she had the prettiest yellow eyes Snorkel had ever seen; on a dragon anyway.

"It's about time," Kraelin said haughtily. "My people are waiting."

Snorkel grimaced. It was a shame her temperament was not as pleasant as her looks.

Reizgoth lowered his head and stretched his neck forward so that he could whisper in Snorkel's ear. "Forgive her, she is young. Her manners will improve."

"Like her eating habits?" Snorkel queried, raising an eyebrow, remembering how she had torn the goat carcass apart immediately after her hatching, and the way in which she had shredded every other meal that had been placed in front of her since.

"Some things take longer than others," Reizgoth replied, a long suffering expression on his face.

"Will you two come on," Kraelin's voice cut in. "And what are you whispering about?"

"Galduran and I were just deciding when would be the best time to undertake our journey, Kraelin," Reizgoth answered, dipping his long, sinuous neck in deference.

"Liar," whispered Snorkel.

The dragon turned his head and gave him an icy glare.

"Now sounds good to me," Kraelin retorted.

Reizgoth rolled his large eyes. "We'd better do as she says or we will get no peace," he murmured.

Snorkel gave a wry smile and turned to Meelan, his intended. If she would have him, that is. "Are you sure you still want to come with us?" he asked.

Meelan's face lit up with excitement. Her ten-past-two eyes brimmed with unshed tears as she squealed in delight and flew into his arms, crushing him with the force of her powerful embrace.

Snorkel grunted as the air rushed out of his body. Arms like hers could crush rocks. But at least he had his answer. It had been the happiest day of his life when, three months ago, Reizgoth had helped him to liberate her from her tribe[*] so she could accompany them on their travels. Aside from the pointy incisors, you would never know she had once been a cannibal.

At Kraelin's snort of displeasure Snorkel eased Meelan away, letting his hands slide down her arms to grasp her podgy fingers.

"I'll take that as a yes, shall I?"

"You try stop me, Norkel, I be ver' 'noyed."

Snorkel shook his head. He was the luckiest dwarf alive. He wished his father could see him now; he would be so proud. He grinned and kissed Meelan on the end of her flat nose. 'She must be keen,' he thought, 'she's even had a shave for the occasion.'

Another impatient snort intruded.

Giving Meelan a wink, Snorkel turned away and prepared to open the gateway. He closed his eyes, mentally reciting the spell before daring to speak it. A sudden feeling of something missing disturbed his concentration, and he paused to open his eyes. "Anyone seen Draco?" he asked, scanning the amphitheatre for the dragonet. The small, lime-green flying lizard had been his constant companion for a long time and he wasn't going anywhere without her.

"No!" snapped Kraelin. "Do get on with it. She is of no importance."

Snorkel opened his mouth to give a sharp retort, but Reizgoth

---

[*] As recounted in *Reluctant Heroes*. Still available from all reputable book stores.

interrupted. "Not since this morning when you began checking the spells, for the third time," rumbled the dragon, shooting Kraelin a warning look.

Snorkel frowned and turned to face the upper entrance. It was unlike the dragonet to go missing, especially at a time like this. "Draco!" he called.

'What's up, Mum?' her voice sounded in his head.

He sighed with relief. "Where are you? We are just about to open the gateway."

'We're nearly there,' Draco replied.

"We?"

The distant drone of happy squeaks and chirrups, intermingled with the odd woof and howl, started to intrude on Snorkel's awareness, growing louder as the source of the noise got closer. Suddenly the air was filled with the sound of hundreds of flying lizards as they erupted through the high entrance and flew into the underground amphitheatre, somersaulting and cavorting in happiness. Down the steps bounded a large, grey she-wolf, her woofs turning to yelps of pain as she jumped off the bottom stone tier and her feet touched the hot sand.

'We're here, Mum' mindspoke Draco, landing on Snorkel's shoulder and rubbing her head up and down his cheek affectionately.

Snorkel chuckled with pleasure and scratched her under the chin.

"Really!" snorted Kraelin. "If he thinks we are taking this rabble to meet our public, he has another think coming."

"Either they come or we all stay," snapped Snorkel, folding his arms and holding the young queen's gaze.

Flicking an anxious glance between them, Reizgoth looked at his queen. "Let them come," he urged in his most persuasive manner. "I am sure it is a big enough world for all of us. Look on the positive side; it means more subjects to worship you. They will be forever in your debt once they are through. Trust me, it is for the best."

The cavern quietened as the dragonets waited for the queen to decide their fate. Even the she-wolf stifled her yelps and hopped quietly from foot to foot.

Kraelin turned to look at the watching, expectant horde. "If they must," she sniffed, exuding an air of indifference.

The noise of the resultant jubilation nearly deafened Snorkel. "Tell them to shut up," he yelled to Draco, "or I'll not be able to concentrate and we won't be going anywhere!"

Within seconds the message had been relayed and quiet descended on the amphitheatre.

"That's better," grunted Snorkel. Closing his eyes he started the incantation that would open the gateway. As his voice recited the words of power a pale mist began to form before him. It started as a small ball, but steadily grew until it was thirty feet in diameter. Within the sphere the mist swirled, gradually moving faster and faster until it seemed to migrate to the edge, forming a circle. A dark tunnel stretched out before him.

"It's ready," shouted Snorkel, beads of perspiration forming on his forehead. "Hurry. I can't keep it open for long!"

Eager to be in her New World, Kraelin waddled quickly past him and into the tunnel beyond, with Reizgoth following closely behind. The she-wolf immediately bounded through after them.

Teeth clamped together, sweat pouring down his face, Snorkel fought to keep the gateway open. He opened his eyes and watched the steady flow of dragonets fly through. After the last one had entered, he grabbed Meelan's arm and hurtled after them before the portal closed. As soon as he entered the magic began to fade and the entrance shrank, rapidly getting smaller and smaller.

Safely concealed from prying eyes a tall, red, lizard-like figure with glowing eyes sprang from its hiding place and sprinted for the fast-closing gateway, just managing to throw itself through before it snapped shut. Chuckling to himself, Chrysothenalazm rose to his feet and dusted himself down. "You can't escape me," he chortled. "Wherever you wun, wherever you hide, Chrysothenalazm will be waiting, you little wunt."

* * * * *

The strange, pink, flesh-like substance of the tunnel quivered as they made their way along it, following the gently undulating and twisting path to the gods knew where. Escorted by the flight of dragonets the two dragons led the way, with Kraelin setting a fast pace, eager to see the New World. They had been walking for what seemed like hours and the end was nowhere in sight. With each step Snorkel's feet pressed lightly into the rubbery material and he was sure the tunnel pulsed as though affected by some other-worldly heartbeat. All it needed was for some semi-digested kippers washed down by ale to come surging at them and his suspicion that they were walking inside a huge intestinal tract would be confirmed.

Meelan sensed his unease and gently squeezed his hand. *'Relax!'* urged Draco from her position on his shoulder.

As Snorkel turned to give her a smile he spotted a movement out of the corner of his eye. He frowned and stopped to look back. But the tunnel was clear, and they continued on their way.

As they progressed Snorkel periodically glanced over his shoulder, convinced they were being followed. By what, he did not know, but he had an uncomfortable itch between his shoulder blades. When they rounded the next bend he stopped and gestured for Meelan to remain quiet.

'What's up, Mum?' asked Draco.

"I think we're being followed," Snorkel whispered.

Meelan's eyes widened and she raised a podgy fist to her mouth. "Vollowed?"

Snorkel squeezed her other hand and gave what he hoped was a confident smile. Urging her to silence, he knelt on the floor and poked his head around the bend. The floor of the tunnel gave slightly and was warm to the touch. Snorkel felt his gorge rise. He couldn't shake the feeling that the tunnel was alive. The sooner they reached their destination the better. He suppressed his feeling of nausea and, glancing back down the tunnel, spotted their pursuer.

Chrysothenalazm! The demon was trotting along, keeping close to the wall.

Snorkel pulled back and rose to his feet. "It's that demon I tricked when I rescued the wizard," he advised.

'Uh-oh!' said Draco, fixing Snorkel with her beady, yellow eyes.

A whimper of fear escaped past Meelan's hand.

Snorkel gripped her shoulders and gazed into her eyes. "Take

Draco and catch up with the others," he said. "Tell them I will be along shortly and not to worry. There is something I have to take care of."

Meelan shook her head and whimpered again.

"Go!" urged Snorkel, gripping her shoulders more tightly in his urgency. "Or we may not live to see the New World." Without waiting for her response, he spun her round and shoved her on her way. "I won't be long," he said, quietly adding, "I hope."

With one last look over her shoulder, Meelan fled down the tunnel.

"Go with her," Snorkel told Draco. "And don't let her try to come back."

The dragonet bobbed her head up and down. *'Sure thing, Mum.'* She stared intently at him. *'You sure you don't need any help?'*

Snorkel shook his head. "Only I can do what needs to be done. Go, my friend. I will join you shortly."

With a flap of her leathery wings Draco launched herself into the air and flew after Meelan. Snorkel massaged his shoulder where the dragonet's talons had left their imprint through the cloth of his tunic. He wished she wouldn't do that. It played havoc with his shoulder joint.

Still rubbing at his shoulder he set off down the tunnel after Meelan and Draco. He needed to gain some space between himself and the demon. It would not do to meet him before he had set his diversion. Snorkel grinned. It was time to get rid of Chrysothenalazm once and for all.

When he felt sure that enough distance separated him and his quarry he stopped and looked back. He caught a glimpse of something red ducking behind a twist in the tunnel, about two hundred paces back. He frowned. It would be a close call, but he should manage it.

He closed his eyes and began the incantation. It was nothing too difficult, according to his newfound knowledge. Merely creating another path in the tunnel between worlds. A detour, as it were. At the close of the spell, Snorkel clapped his hands and opened his eyes. He gaped in shock. Instead of a tunnel stretching before him a pink, fleshy wall blocked his view. The way back had disappeared. He'd closed it off. A smile formed on his face. "Let's see you get out of that one, smart-ass."

Still grinning, he turned and ran after the others. The New World awaited.

Chrysothenalazm poked his head out to check that the coast was clear before stepping out of concealment. That was close. He was sure the dwarf had spotted him. It would not do to face him just yet. When the final battle came Chrysothenalazm wanted it to be on his terms, not the magic-wielding dwarf's. He wanted the little runt to squirm before he died, not to make a fight of it.

Seeing that the dwarf had moved away, Chrysothenalazm loped on, and on, and on ...

After what seemed like an age spent following the tunnel he was growing concerned. It had been a long time since he'd last seen any sign of the funny little man in the red suit. Surely he couldn't have got that far ahead? The demon increased his pace until he was running at full pelt. He was still running like a demon possessed when the tunnel abruptly ended.

There was no warning, no sign, nothing. One minute he was surrounded by pale-pink walls, the next he was falling through storm lashed skies, wind and rain buffeting him as he tumbled. A long, drawn-out screech erupted from his mouth as he plummeted through the air. A long, drawn-out screech that was suddenly cut off as a rather large pair of jaws filled with exceptionally sharp, pointy, saliva-dripping fangs halted his fall and crushed away what little life remained in his body.

Chapter Three

An icy wind whipped through the mountain pass, lashing Jophrey's shoulder-length black hair across his face. Raising his free hand — the one not clutching Nostra's Book of Prophesies — he scraped the errant strands to one side, then peered up into the grey, roiling skies. He hoped Mandrake would appear before the clouds decided to shed their watery load. That would be all he needed, being soaked as well as frozen. It was bad enough feeling like an icicle, without looking like one too.

Pulling his fur-lined cape more tightly around himself, Jophrey ducked his head against the wind and continued up the narrow, precipitous mountain trail. He struggled against the elements for half an hour before he reached the small, boulder-strewn plateau where he had arranged to meet the dragon. The wind had increased in both force and ferocity by the time he got there, so he scurried across to take shelter behind an outcrop of rock. He leaned against the jagged surface and stared up at the craggy pinnacle looming above him, the mountain's lofty peak lost amongst fast moving, ever darkening clouds. A fat drop of ice-cold rain splashed onto his face. Jophrey sighed.

Impatient to be away from the mountains and once more enjoying the heady comforts of Mandragle Castle, he decided to contact his father's dragon with mind-speak. The one thing that had made his time at Hope more bearable had been his ability to converse with the beast.

'Mandrake, it is I, Jophrey. Are you nearly here? I'm freezing my butt off.'

The dragon's snort of amusement whispered in Jophrey's head, followed by the soft, deep tones of Mandrake's voice. *'Not much longer. Only another minute or two. I had to wait for your father to prepare me. You know what he is like.'*

Jophrey did. His father would not go anywhere unless he and his dragon were perfectly attired, perfectly scrubbed, perfectly perfect in every detail. In short, Lord Blackbishop could be a perfect pain in the ...

Rising over the roar of the wind, Mandrake's loud bugle heralded his arrival. Jophrey ducked and covered his face with his arm, prepared for the pebble-dashing caused by the dragon's wings when he used them to slow his descent. Jophrey had learned at an early age that to look up at a dragon when it was about to land could result in bodily harm.

When he was six years old he had rushed out, arms outstretched, to greet his father and Mandrake when they returned home from a successful hunt. As the dragon had flapped his leathery membranes to decelerate, Jophrey had been caught in the maelstrom of wind, dirt, pebbles and small rocks and had been catapulted backwards. When he had scrambled to his feet, tears of pain prickling his eyes, his face had resembled a smacked arse. It took weeks for the damage to heal. He'd never got that close since.

Jophrey waited for the rocks and debris to stop bouncing around the plateau before he edged out from behind the outcrop. Forty paces away from him squatted Mandrake's immense bulk, a dark shadow against a darker sky. Jophrey quickly stepped forward, a happy smile on his face, as Mandrake swung his huge head towards him.

'Was that quick enough?' Mandrake's amused voice whispered inside Jophrey's head.

'Perfect timing,' answered Jophrey. *'Any longer and my bollo—'*

"My boy!"

As soon as he heard the excited shout Jophrey stopped. He peered more closely at the dragon, his brow furrowed with a puzzled frown. "Father?"

A tall, skinny, black-garbed figure jumped nimbly from the saddle strapped to the base of Mandrake's long, sinuous neck.

Jophrey's eyes narrowed. It *was* his father.

Lord Blackbishop stood with legs splayed and raised his hands to lift his glass-fronted flying goggles over the peak of his flying cap. Once he had them settled, he turned his attention to his handlebar moustache. Twirling the ends to nice, neat little points, he tossed the loose-flapping folds of his black cloak over his shoulder, placed his hands on his hips and gave Jophrey a dazzling smile. If the sun had been shining it would have reflected with blinding brilliance from his gleaming white teeth.

Jophrey grimaced. "Hi, Father," he called, masking the disappointment he felt at not having Mandrake to himself, if only for a little while.

'One day,' Mandrake's voice reassured him.

Jophrey gave a half smile. *'Soon, I hope,'* he retorted.

"What's the matter, you young rapscallion? Not pleased to see your old dad after ..." Lord Blackbishop paused for a moment, "... er, a cycle or two?"

"Two cycles, Father."

"Ah, yes! After two cycles?"

Mandrake lowered his head to peer at Jophrey and rolled his eyes. *'He doesn't get any better, does he?'*

Jophrey chuckled. It was just as well that his father could not hear their private conversations or they would both be in trouble.

"Well, what are you waiting for? Come and give your old dad a ... No! Better not." He glanced down at his black riding leathers, and began to brush off particles of grit with his hands. "This is the latest Yarmani, and I don't want to get it fingered." He looked up and gave Jophrey an apologetic smile. "You know what I mean? Dirty fingers, grease and germs? This blasted rain and muck is bad enough, but ..." He left the implication hanging.

Jophrey knew exactly what he meant and stopped three paces away. His father avoided physical contact with anything or anyone. It always amazed Jophrey that he had managed to be conceived in the first place. He assumed his father must have found a way of performing sex by proxy.

Lord Blackbishop stepped forward and gave Jophrey a hug, without actually touching him, which was quite an achievement in Jophrey's mind. Stepping back, Blackbishop's eyes widened as he spotted the book under Jophrey's arm. He clapped his gauntleted hands together. "Excellent. You've got it. Well done you!" He went to punch Jophrey affectionately on the arm, but stopped short. "Yes, er, well done you."

Jophrey shook his head and eyed his father's black attire. "What's a Yarmani, then?"

Lord Blackbishop's jaw dropped. "What, dear boy? You've never heard of Yarmani?"

Jophrey slowly shook his head.

"He, young fellow-me-lad, is the most gifted clothes designer in Tiernan Og." He stepped back and did a twirl so that Jophrey could get a clearer look at his clothing. "Givus Yarmani is the latest, greatest designer ever. His designs are sought by all. But, sadly, can only be afforded by a few. Me to be precise." He gave a sly smile. "Can't have all the riff-raff wearing his stuff, can we? Where would the prestige be in that?" Jophrey shrugged, unimpressed.

"When you have quite finished," Mandrake said aloud, his voice a deep, gravelly baritone. "We have a thermal to catch."

"Ah, yes," said Lord Blackbishop, giving Mandrake a beaming smile. He turned his attention to Jophrey. "Come on, er ..."

"Jophrey," Jophrey prompted.

"I knew that," retorted Lord Blackbishop. He looked sideways at Mandrake and raised his eyebrows. "The past ..."

"Two cycles," said Mandrake.

"... must have addled his wits," continued Lord Blackbishop, oblivious of the pause. "As if I would forget my own son's name, hey?" He nodded at the dragon's rear end. "Your saddle awaits, down there, next to Mandrake's ar—"

"Tail!" boomed Mandrake.

"Make yourself lively, then," said Lord Blackbishop. He pulled his goggles into place, and putting a foot in the stirrup hoisted himself into the saddle. "We haven't got all day."

Jophrey pursed his lips, shook his head and walked the twenty paces to the saddle strapped to Mandrake's hindquarters.

'Welcome back, Jophrey.'

Jophrey smiled wryly. Judging by Mandrake's caustic tone the dragon wasn't impressed by Lord Blackbishop's manner either.

For a brief moment Jophrey felt a pang of remorse for the way he had tricked Tobias, the one person who had accepted him for what he was. Or, rather, for what Tobias thought he was. As he stepped into the saddle and settled the book across his lap, he swept the pang aside. *He* would be master of his own destiny. *He* would become a rider of a real, fire-breathing, black dragon, not some lesser species from fable. After all, his father couldn't live forever, could he? And who would ride Mandrake when he'd popped his clogs?

'Exactly,' confirmed Mandrake.

* * * * *

Realising Jophrey was the thief, Tobias grabbed the papers from where he had thrown them and ran back the way he had come. He didn't pause for anything or anyone in his eagerness to tell Volgen the news and divert the man's wrath from Cronan to the real culprit. When he neared the merchants' quarters he paused for a moment to catch his breath, a worried frown forming on his face.

Crowds of Ogmus blocked the way. He would have a devil of a job getting through that lot. Heaving a resigned sigh he readied himself, dipping his head and scrunching up his shoulders. Without pausing for breath he careened through the lot of them, bowling aside those unfortunate enough to be in his path. It was like playing skittles, only more painful. By the time he reached the relative safety of the library tunnel he was sure that by evening his body would be black and blue from the battering. Especially the left side of his ribcage, where the old crone with the big mouth had jabbed him with her walking cane.

As he neared the library grotto his breath came in ragged gasps, his tunic clung to his body and sweat ran freely down his forehead, stinging his eyes. Despite the heavy slap of his feet on the hard floor and the pounding of his heart, he could still hear Volgen's irate voice coming from the library.

Tobias scowled and wiped sweat from his eyes. Didn't the Wing Commander ever give up? As he slid through the doorway his frown changed to a look of shock. The floor inside the doorway was as slick as polished glass. Worn down by centuries of use, the rough-chiselled finish had been rendered smooth, and proved as slippery as a well-greased pig freshly prepared for a hog-wrestling bout. His feet went from under him and Tobias cried out in surprise, then pain as he slid into Volgen, knocking the man over mid-tirade. The breath rushed from his body as Volgen landed on top of him with a thud.

"My word," murmured Cronan, placing his hands on top of his desk and leaning over to look down at the two prostrate figures. "My word," he muttered again, spotting Tobias gasping for breath beneath Volgen.

"What the ruddy hell's going on here?" Volgen shouted, recovering from the shock of the assault. He rolled his portly form off Tobias and scrambled on to his hands and knees. "You!" His face reddened with anger. "I thought I told you to bugger off!"

Volgen levered himself to his feet, his face darkening to a weird purple colour. He appeared to be having difficulty speaking, for although his mouth moved no words came out. This seemed to make him angrier still, so he settled for wagging a finger at Tobias in righteous indignation.

Tobias shrank back. He had managed to divert Volgen's wrath from Cronan, but not quite in the direction he'd intended. His mind raced. How was he going to get out of this one? "I know who stole the book," he cried, scrambling backwards on elbows and buttocks. He stopped and winced when his head struck the rock wall. Yet another bruise to add to his rapidly growing collection.

Volgen grunted something indecipherable and stepped forward, rolling the sleeves of his flying-tunic up over his brawny forearms. Tobias felt what little colour he had drain from his face. He climbed to his feet, and standing with his back pressed firmly against the rocky wall he closed his eyes expectantly, waiting for the blow, as Volgen loomed over him.

"Hold!" shouted Cronan.

Tobias cracked open an eye. He saw Cronan move around his desk and shuffle across the room. He stepped between Volgen and Tobias. "The lad has news," he said, locking eyes with Volgen. "Didn't you hear him?"

Volgen gave a non-committal grunt and made to move Cronan out of the way.

Tobias seized the moment. "I know who stole the book!" he shouted.

Volgen lowered his hands, the merest hint of sanity returning to his eyes. Only the merest, however, and soon the madness made a successful counter-attack. He gripped Cronan's arms and heaved him to one side, sending him sprawling to the ground. "You what?" he demanded, foam flecking his lips as he glared down at Tobias.

"I know who stole the book," Tobias squeaked. "It was Jophrey."

"Who the hell's he?" growled Volgen, leaning menacingly forward.

"Jophrey?" queried Cronan, getting back to his feet and dusting himself down. "Your roommate in the foundling's quarters?"

Tobias nodded.

"Never heard of him!" growled Volgen.

"Wasn't he the lad who was orphaned when his parents were killed by Mandrake and Lord Blackbishop?"

"That's him," Tobias confirmed.

A furrow appeared on Volgen's forehead. Then a gleam of recognition lit his face and sanity ousted madness. "That Jophrey," he said. "Why didn't you say so?"

Cronan rolled his eyes.

"How do you know it was him?" Volgen demanded.

Tobias fished in his tunic pocket and pulled out the crumpled papers. "These," he answered. "And the fact that Jophrey is gone, along with his clothing and possessions."

Volgen scowled as he snatched the papers from Tobias's hand.

"Some of my early translations," murmured Cronan, recognising his handwriting as he peered over Volgen's shoulder. "I kept them in the back of Nostra's book. They must have fallen out when Jophrey made a run for it."

Volgen screwed up the papers and threw them to the floor, then turned and began to pace the small room, his hands clasped behind his back. "Jophrey," he murmured to himself. "What the devil does he want with the Book of Prophesies?"

Tobias gave Cronan a weak smile. Cronan winked, then moved to sit behind his desk, gesturing for Tobias to stand behind him with an inclination of his head. "Wing Commander," he called gently.

"Hmm?" Volgen stopped his pacing and turned to face Cronan.

"Did you ever check Jophrey's story? About who his parents were?"

Volgen's bushy beard bristled as he thrust out his chin. "What are you trying to suggest?" he demanded.

"Nothing, nothing at all," Cronan placated, holding his hands out, palms upward. "Only that, well, did anyone check that Jophrey's story was actually true?"

"There was no need!" growled Volgen. "I knew both his parents. And damned fine Ogmus they were too." He shook his head. "It was a sad day when Rufus and Charlie were killed."

"Charlie who? I remember Rufus, but never met his wife," said Cronan. "And I never knew he had a child."

Volgen frowned. "Charlie," he answered. "Charlie Vuntlewedge, the rocksmith."

Cronan snapped to his feet, his eyes wide in disbelief. His chair toppled over with a crash. "Charlie Vuntlewedge? But he was a man!"

Volgen puffed out his chest in indignation. "What of it?" he demanded. "We're an equal opportunities colony here, and one man's perversion is another man's preference. Okay, so Charlie may have liked to wear dresses, curled his hair and preferred to be called Charlene; but a finer rocksmith you would never hope to meet. I would've quite fancied him myself if I were that way inclined. Which I'm not," he hastily added.

"But he was a man," repeated Cronan.

Volgen frowned. "So?"

Cronan shook his head. "Rufus was a man." Volgen nodded. "Charlie was a man." Again Volgen nodded.

"So, correct me if I am wrong, but we have two men and one child."

Volgen frowned as he thought it over.

"How?" asked Cronan.

"How what?"

"How can two men have a child?"

Volgen's eyes widened as the realisation hit him. "Bloody hell," he murmured.

Cronan flicked a brief glance at the ceiling in relief.

Volgen shook his head in amazement and a wistful tone entered his voice. "You mean Charlie really was a woman?"

Tobias's hand flew to his mouth as he tried to suppress a snigger. Somehow he managed to keep his face straight.

"Er, not exactly," said Cronan with a sigh. He cast Tobias a warning look. "This whole business smacks of the Dark Ones. I am sure of it."

By the time Cronan had finished explaining what he meant and what he thought might have happened that fateful day, Volgen had slumped to the floor, his eyes gazing vacantly into space. "You mean to say that we've been conned?" he asked. "Taken for a piggin' ride? So that Lord Blackbishop could get hold of the book and the translations?"

From his perch on the corner of his desk, where he had moved when Volgen had shown the first signs of stupor, Cronan nodded. "It's my guess that Lord Blackbishop heard of the translations from some poor unfortunate that he had captured on the mountainside and hatched a plan to get one of his agents in here to steal Nostra's book. When he stumbled across Rufus and Charlie he must have assumed they were a happy couple out for a walk. He killed them, planting the boy as their poor, bereft son."

"But why steal the book now?" asked Volgen, peering up at Cronan with troubled eyes. "At this point in time?"

Cronan shrugged. "The boy had what he wanted: the translation regarding Snor'kel and the demise of the black dragons. He had the timing of when Snor'kel would arrive, so the Dark Ones could deal with the threat before the threat could deal with them."

"But how did he find out about the translations?"

Tobias slunk back, putting Cronan between himself and the Wing Commander.

"It's a small colony." Cronan shrugged. "On a more positive note, at least they will have the same problem as we have."

Volgen frowned. "What's that then?"

"The where."

"Ey?"

"I hadn't translated the verse pertaining to *where* Snor'kel would appear. So they will be as completely in the dark as we are, if you'll pardon the pun. They'll know the time, but not the place."

Volgen rose to his feet. "Well it's time we remedied that, isn't it?" The fire of determination shone from his eyes. "Come with me!" He turned towards the door, then paused. "And you!" he muttered over his shoulder. "Cronan will tell you all about it afterwards, so we might as well cut out the middle man."

With that Volgen strode from the room and turned right, towards the dead end of the library tunnel.

"Where is he taking us?" Tobias asked, running to catch up with Cronan.

The librarian shrugged. "I have no idea."

Chapter Four

A short while later they reached the dead end. A slab of rough-hewn rock blocked any further progress down the six-foot wide tunnel. Tobias frowned and looked at Cronan. The librarian shrugged and shook his head.

Sensing their confusion Volgen smiled craftily. Suddenly his eyes widened and he leaned to the side and peered at a point behind them. They both turned to see what he was looking at and scanned the corridor, completely baffled. It was deserted. A blast of warm, stale air swept past them. Tobias and Cronan spun back round at the same instant and stared into the dark maw of an unlit tunnel. The slab of rock that had previously blocked it rested against the wall.

"What the …" murmured Tobias.

Volgen gave a self-satisfied smirk and puffed out his chest. "Wing Commander's secret," he growled, giving them both a hard stare. "Until now."

He picked up a torch from its stand just inside the tunnel. Removing a fire-stick from his tunic pocket he struck it against the rock. He waited for the small stick to burst into life and touched it to the head of the torch. It caught with a splutter and black, oily smoke started to billow.

When Volgen had stopped the coughing brought on by the caustic fog that engulfed him, he wiped the tears from his eyes with the back of his hand and stepped further into the tunnel. "Get your sorry backsides in here," he croaked, gesturing for Cronan and Tobias to move forward with a flick of his hand. "And quick. Before anyone happens along and sees where we are going. It's bad enough you two knowing about the tunnel, without any other passing toerags copping a view." He started to cough again and tears streamed from his eyes.

As soon as Tobias and Cronan had stepped through the rock slab swung back into place. The small pool of light from Volgen's torch flickered in the draught from the slab's passage, causing grotesque shadows to dance on the craggy wall. Tobias had just done Rabbit Running From Fox and was on to Butterfly Flitting From Flower when Volgen's irked, if rather raspy voice intruded.

"If you've finished behaving like a prat, grab a torch and light it from mine."

With one last wiggle of his fingers, the silhouette of the butterfly flew off into the shadows and Tobias lowered his hands. Avoiding Volgen's gaze and bending to pick up a torch, he saw Cronan hastily lowering his own hands. Tobias chuckled quietly to himself as the librarian stooped down to take a torch, his face reddening at Tobias's querying glance. Tobias waited for Cronan to light his from the Wing Commander's before he, in turn, lit his own.

Volgen growled in annoyance, then set off at a fast pace. "We have a ways to travel, so we'd best get a move on. It's been a long time since I last ventured down here, and I don't fancy doing it in the piggin' dark," he called over his shoulder.

As Tobias made to follow, Cronan grabbed his arm, pulling him to a stop. He smiled mischievously. "Fancy a quicky before we go?"

Tobias grinned.

Soon the twin silhouettes of Swallows in Flight appeared on the wall. The shadows ducked and dived for a moment before Cronan gave a happy chuckle and lowered his hands. "Come. We'd better get a move on. Especially as we haven't the faintest idea where we are going."

The acrid smell of the torches accompanied them as they made their way swiftly down the steadily descending tunnel. To Tobias the smell of the pungent smoke was not dissimilar to that of burning boots. Rather niffy, well-used ones at that.

After nearly a candle-mark of walking, their destination was nowhere in sight. Given Volgen's refusal to answer any questions, Tobias had no idea how much further they had to go. He just hoped that whatever lay at the end of their trek would prove to be worthwhile. He wasn't sure whether he imagined it or not, but the temperature appeared to be rising the further they travelled. The tunnel was becoming warm and stuffy, and damp patches were starting to appear on his tunic around his armpits. Glancing across at Cronan he could see that his face had gone red, and similar damp patches had appeared under the arms of his brown jacket.

Tobias wiped a hand across his perspiring brow. Where were they going? To the very bowels of the earth? Fortunately he did not have too much longer to wait before he received the answers to his unasked questions. After roughly another three hundred paces Volgen halted.

Tobias and Cronan didn't, and bumped into the Wing Commander's back.

Stumbling forward Volgen turned, pursed his lips and cast them a withering look. He shook his head and gave a heavy sigh. "What you are about to see has not been seen by any other, aside from my predecessors, for centuries, and is not to be discussed with anyone when we get back to the main sanctuary of Hope." He gave Tobias a hard stare. "Understood?"

Tobias swallowed nervously and nodded.

"Good! Now wait here while I go and light some more of these god-awful torches." He dabbed at his watering eyes. "The stench of the damn things plays havoc with my sinuses. Bloody contraptions."

"Wh—" Cronan quieted Tobias with a shake of his head and a raised forefinger.

Tobias clamped his lips shut and watched as Volgen turned and wandered into the blackness. The yellow flame of his torch bobbed and weaved as he walked, leaving streamers of light in the darkness.

"I was only going to ask about glow-globes," Tobias whispered, once he was sure Volgen was out of earshot.

"All in good time," said Cronan. "For now we remain quiet and learn."

The bobbing torch halted thirty paces away, then rose in to the air. Shortly after another blob of flame danced in the darkness. Volgen continued, lighting torches as he walked. His path took him in an arc that led back to where Tobias and Cronan stood. With each torch that he lit the darkness retreated a little more and it soon became apparent that they were in an enormous amphitheatre, about two hundred paces in diameter.

Tobias and Cronan stood at the threshold of one of numerous tunnels leading off from a clear, central circle of sand. The tunnels varied in size and position. Some were at the level of the arena floor, some were a few feet off the ground, and others would require a ladder to gain access.

"Wh-what is this place?" murmured Tobias.

Cronan shook his head. "I have no idea," he replied, his voice pitched equally low.

"It is, or was going to be," corrected Volgen as he returned, "a birthing chamber."

"A what?" asked Tobias.

Volgen gave him a hard stare. "A birthing chamber. You gone deaf or something?"

A nervous laugh escaped Tobias's lips.

"For the dragons?" asked Cronan, gazing around in wonder.

"Of course for the dragons," snapped Volgen. "You don't think we'd send the womenfolk down here, do you?" His eyes took on a faraway look. "That is until those piggin' black dragons drove all the good ones off."

"Women?" asked Tobias with a frown.

"ARE YOU THICK AS WELL AS PIGGIN' DEAF?" Volgen yelled. His loud shout reverberated around the cavern, multiplying until it sounded as though thirty or forty Volgens had shouted. Tobias looked up and met the Wing Commander's incredulous gaze. "The piggin' dragons, you half-wit."

Tobias felt his face redden and looked at the floor in embarrassment.

"We don't know that," said Cronan.

"Know what?" asked Volgen.

"That the blacks drove off the other dragons."

A cold, hard glint entered Volgen's eyes. "Well, what else happened to them then?"

Cronan shrugged. "Is this what you were going to show us?" he asked, swiftly changing the subject.

Holding Cronan's gaze for a moment, Volgen answered. "Yes, and no. There is something else I want you to see. Something that might help you find where Snor'kel and his horde will emerge."

"Me? Find them?" The colour drained from Cronan's face.

"And him," Volgen answered, nodding towards Tobias.

"Find me?"

There was a moment of stunned silence as Volgen tried to work out what Tobias meant. Unfortunately for Tobias's eardrums it was a very brief moment. "THE PIGGIN' DRAGONS, YOU IDIOT!" he roared. "And you're going with him."

"Me?" Tobias cringed at the unnatural squeak that entered his voice.

"Why us?" asked Cronan. "Surely someone younger and fitter should look for them?"

"Aye." Volgen nodded his agreement. "That's why he's going with you." He stabbed a stubby digit towards Tobias. "Anyways, *you* lost the piggin' book, therefore *you* should go and find our saviours. Time is of the essence, as you piggin' well know, and we don't have any other options. So you're it."

Before Cronan could utter another word in protest, Volgen strode across the sand, entering one of the tunnels directly across from where they stood, his torch held aloft. "Bring your torches," he ordered. "You're going to need them."

His shoulders slumped in resignation Cronan followed, with Tobias close behind. Half way across Tobias realised that his feet were getting hot. The warmth was emanating from the sand, and on through the soles of his boots. By the time he reached the tunnel opposite he was sure that his toes would be baked. Once he was again standing on cooler rock he stopped and looked down at his footwear, half expecting to see his boots smouldering. But aside from a few particles of sand that clung to the edges of his soles, they appeared to be all right.

"Oy, carrot-top. You coming or what?"

At the sound of Volgen's voice, Tobias grimaced. He cast a puzzled look at the sand before hurrying to catch up.

The tunnel that they entered proved to be relatively short, and they soon reached the end. It opened in to a small twenty-pace square grotto. Volgen strode across the rocky floor and placed his torch in a sconce on the far wall, then gestured for Cronan and Tobias to place theirs in the sconces either side of the room.

With their torches safely secured Tobias and Cronan moved across to join Volgen, who was standing with his back to them, peering down at something.

"You have something to show us?" asked Cronan.

Volgen straightened, then turned. He stepped to his right and gestured towards a niche that he had been hiding from view. "What do you think of that then?"

Cronan frowned and stepped forward. "My word," he murmured, his voice tinged with awe. "Is that what I think it is?" Volgen nodded.

Unable to see properly, Tobias stepped forward and peered over Cronan's shoulder. His eyes narrowed, then widened with wonder. In all the days of his relatively short life he'd never seen the like before. "Is it real?" he asked.

"You betcha," said Volgen, folding his arms across his ample chest and nodding, a smug expression on his face. "You betcha piggin' ass it's real."

* * * * *

Like when wind breaks after a hearty fast, the worries will soon be over.
For out the sky, like a hornet's strike, will arrive the mighty Rover.
One thousand turns of our small world's wheel, plus fifty shorter trundles,
And out of a void, way up in the sky, will swarm some furless bundles.

Slightly misshaped, this void shall be, not round nor square nor slit.
Shape don't matter, the wise man say, it's what comes out of it.
Flying furies shall abound in the sky, to criss and cross the night.
But fearless shall our Rover be, and bad guys he shall smite.

But what shall we call this mighty one, who hails from lands afar?
John, Paul, Ringo, George, or something more bizarre?
Nay, I tell thee, we'll name him not. His name is his to tell.
But what the hell? Names can't hurt.
The dragon riding short-arse, shall go by the name Snor'kel.

(The author apologises for the non-conformist nature of the last stanza. By the way, who's nicked that damn poppy juice?)

Nostra-Ogmus

"Is that it?" Lord Blackbishop asked quietly, arching an eyebrow in puzzlement. He peered up at his manservant, who stood to his side, immaculate in his black leggings and frock coat, the white splash of his shirt marking a sharp contrast. "Nothing else? Nothing that would make the damn verse more ... more understandable?"

His manservant looked down and shook his head. The light from the glow-globes in the timber-clad ceiling of Lord Blackbishop's study reflected off his shaven head as he lowered The Book of Prophesies. "Would you like me to read it again, my Lord?" he asked, his dark, beady eyes peering at Lord Blackbishop over a large, hooked nose.

Lord Blackbishop leaned back in his leather-padded chair, steepled his fingers and closed his eyes. "One more time then, Wooster."

"As you wish, my Lord." Wooster eased the book open with his white-gloved hands and raised it to begin reading.

Seated on the other side of the small room on a low divan, Jophrey stifled a smirk. This would be the fifth time that Wooster had read the verse, and he doubted whether his father would be any the wiser after hearing it again. Should he tell him he had the translation in his tunic pocket? He grinned. He would wait a little longer. He quite enjoyed his father's confusion, even if he was getting a little bored with Wooster's renditions.

'You can be so cruel,' Mandrake's voice whispered in his head.

'I know,' Jophrey replied. *'But I'd forgotten how much of a pain my father can be.'*

The dragon's snort of amusement made Jophrey smile. He heard Wooster clear his throat and shifted in his seat to make himself more comfortable. One more time, then he would tell his father he had the translation.

"Like when wind breaks after a hearty fast, the worries will soon be over. For out of the sky, like a hornet's strike, will arrive the mighty Rover."

Lord Blackbishop nodded, tapping at his pursed lips with his forefingers. "Hmmm. So this Snor'kel will come from the skies."

"It would appear so, my Lord."

"And pretty damn quick, by the sound of things. But a Rover?" Lord Blackbishop shook his head, opened his eyes and peered at Wooster. "What's one of them?"

"I have no idea, my Lord. Shall I carry on?"

With a wave of his hand Lord Blackbishop indicated that he should do so, then he closed his eyes once more and leaned back in his chair.

Jophrey slowly scanned the oak-panelled walls of his father's study, growing ever more bored with it all. He had heard enough and was getting fed up with reading the titles of the books lining the shelves behind his father's leather-topped desk; studying the crude maps of Tiernan Og that were pinned to the walls, and trying to spot the merest particle of dust or dirt on the few items of furniture in the room. But it was a lost cause. Even the rug in front of his father's desk looked like new, and Jophrey knew it was at least as old as he was. He remembered playing on it as a child, until the day he puked all over it and his father had banned him from the study until he learned to be sick on his mother like normal kids.

His thoughts turned maudlin. He still missed her, after all these years. Even though she had left his father when Jophrey was only five, some things could never be replaced. To this day he didn't know why she'd gone, or where she'd gone to.

His thoughts drifting, he looked at his feet and the dainty paper slippers that he now wore, to be thrown in the bucket by the door after they'd been used. He shook his head. Sometimes his father went too far.

Wooster's cultured voice continued with the recitation. "One thousand turns of our small world's wheel, plus fifty shorter trundles, and out of a void, way up in the sky, will swarm some furless bundles."

"I've got it!" shouted Lord Blackbishop, jumping to his feet and slamming the top of his desk with the palms of his hands.

In his shock Wooster almost dropped the book, and Jophrey nearly jumped out of his seat.

"You have, my Lord?" queried Wooster.

Lord Blackbishop grinned. "It's obvious, Wooster."

"Really, my Lord?"

Jophrey scowled. It was getting to the point where he should own up about having the translation, before his father made a total prat of himself.

"Of course!" Lord Blackbishop twirled the ends of his moustache, a knowing grin on his face.

"Father!"

"Hmmm?" Lord Blackbishop gazed at Jophrey with dark eyes.

Jophrey rose to his feet. "There is something I think you should know."

"Not now," snapped Lord Blackbishop. "Can't you see I am on to something?"

Jophrey opened his mouth to speak, but his father motioned him to be quiet before he could utter a word. Knowing better than to cross him, Jophrey clamped his mouth shut.

"Now where was I?" Lord Blackbishop asked, of no one in particular.

"You have it, my Lord?" offered Wooster.

"I do?"

"So you said, my Lord."

"Ahhh! Have what, precisely?"

"The answer, my Lord?"

Lord Blackbishop frowned and shook his head. "No. Got me on that one, Wooster. The answer to what?"

Jophrey had had enough. "Father!"

"Not now, er … my boy, young fellow-me-lad. Can't you see that I am busy? Why don't you go off and play or something. Boys of your age are good at that sort of thing."

Jophrey stepped forward, trying to hold his anger in check. After being cooped up in a mountain for the past two cycles on a mission for his father, he was not about to be thrown aside like a used paper slipper. As he strode across the small room, he shoved a hand inside his tunic and pulled out the crumpled translation. He stopped short of the desk and thrust it forward. "Here!" he snapped.

The look of shock on Blackbishop's face faded, replaced by one of distaste, as he stared down at the tatty paper. "What is it?" he asked, giving it one last glance.

"Cronan's translation of the verse."

A cunning smile formed on Lord Blackbishop's face. "And you had it all along?" he purred, locking eyes with Jophrey.

Jophrey felt his face redden. "I know you can work the verse out," he retorted, thinking on his feet, "but I am tired and I need some sleep, so thought I would save you some time, even though I was eager to see your great mind working out such a difficult problem."

Lord Blackbishop looked up as he heard Wooster choke back a cough. "Are you well?" he asked, pulling a scented cloth from the top pocket of his flying-jacket and holding it over his nose.

"I am, thank you my Lord." Wooster gave a small smile. "Something must have caught in my throat."

"Yes, well. Can't be too careful," said Lord Blackbishop, shoving the cloth back into his pocket. "Get yourself off to that herb woman and get it checked out. Can't have any nasty germs floating around unchecked, can we?"

"No, my Lord. Right away, my Lord." He turned to leave.

"Not now, Wooster!" Lord Blackbishop nodded towards the paper still clutched in Jophrey's hand.

Wooster dipped his head in acknowledgement and moved around the desk to take the proffered translation. "Shall I read it, my Lord?"

"At your leisure, Wooster. At your leisure."

Lord Blackbishop sat back down in his chair and listened as Wooster read Cronan's translation, nodding in agreement as each line ended. When Wooster had finished, Lord Blackbishop looked up, a smile of satisfaction on his face. "Exactly what I was going to say," he said. "Almost to the word."

"And which word would that be?" Jophrey muttered under his breath.

'Jophrey!' Mandrake's voice whispered in warning.

"Did you say something?" Lord Blackbishop asked, switching his attention to Jophrey.

"I was only saying how much I applaud your acute acumen," Jophrey answered.

"My cute what?"

"He means intellect, my Lord," Wooster interjected.

"I knew that."

"Just making sure, my Lord."

Lord Blackbishop rose to his feet and gave Jophrey a dazzling smile. "Well done, my boy. Well done." He launched a playful punch at Jophrey's arm, which, of course, he pulled short. "Well don't just stand there, you young rapscallion. Go get yourself bathed and changed. Tonight we celebrate. I'll get Mandrake to send out the call and gather the Lords. It is time we made plans."

Jophrey turned to leave.

"Er …"

"Jophrey," Jophrey heard Wooster whisper.

"Jophrey." Jophrey turned to face his father.

"Don't forget to throw those …" he waved a hand in the direction of Jophrey's feet, "slipper things away, there's a good chap. The bucket's over there, by the door."

"I know, Father." After the door had closed on his exit, Jophrey leaned back against it, his head resting on the stout, timber panelling. Through the solid lump of oak he heard his father's muffled voice. "Just repeat that last bit again, Wooster."

Jophrey sighed. He hadn't been back a day, yet he felt as though he'd never been away.

'Welcome home,' came Mandrake's amused thought.

Home? Jophrey scowled and made his way to his own apartments. All of a sudden home was one place Mandragle Castle didn't feel like.

Chapter Five

Before Cronan had a chance to scrutinise the map, Volgen leaned forward and snatched it from the niche. "Later. When we get to my study," he said, rolling up the parchment. "Then you can look at it all you like. Come on. We'll take the short route." With that he grabbed his torch from the sconce and strode out of the grotto, the map tucked under his arm.

"Short route?" Tobias cast Cronan a puzzled look as he crossed the room to pick up his own torch from the wall.

"Beats me," Cronan answered. "The only route I know is back the way we came."

Tobias scowled, remembering the mass of humanity that waited in the merchants' quarter. He didn't want to face that mob again. Not without a club in his hand.

"Will you two get a piggin' move on?"

The sound of Volgen's voice echoing down the tunnel spurred them into action. In a matter of moments they caught up with the Wing Commander, who stood by the entrance to the sandy arena. "About bloody time," he snapped. "Now, keep close. If you go the wrong way you'll never find your way out. And I ain't coming back down to look for you. Right! You two do the left and I'll do the right."

"Do what, precisely?" asked Cronan.

"Snuff the piggin' torches out," snapped Volgen, striding off. "Can't leave the damn things burning away or we'll have none left when we need them. The snuffers are hanging on a peg beside them."

This time the heat from the sand came as no surprise to Tobias. Even so, by the time he and Cronan reached the rocky floor close to where they had previously entered the amphitheatre, Tobias had to look at his feet to make sure his boots weren't on fire. Although the warren of caves, tunnels and caverns of Hope was always warm, the heat coming from the sand was something else entirely. He shook his head in mystification as he turned to follow Volgen down the tunnel. It was as if the sand were being heated from below by some gigantic furnace.

It took some time to reach the tunnel's end. When they did, Volgen made Tobias and Cronan turn their backs while he operated the mechanism to open the doorway. Curses, grunts and groans accompanied the sound of his banging and hammering. The narrow tunnel echoed with a cacophony of noise, but there seemed to be very little other progress.

Growing bored with waiting, Tobias looked across at Cronan and scowled.

The librarian shrugged and raised an eyebrow. "Need a hand?" he called over his shoulder.

"Almost there," Volgen replied. "I haven't used this route for so long the damn lever's gone and seized up." A strained edge entered his voice as he exerted more pressure. "Any minute now," he grunted. "Bollocks!" The loud expletive followed the sound of something snapping. A short time later there was a rumbling noise and the floor of the tunnel shook.

When Tobias and Cronan spun round they saw the Wing Commander clutching a hand to his chest, his stocky torso framed by the light that spilled in from the partially open doorway.

"What happened?" asked Cronan.

Volgen looked up, tears of pain in his eyes. "The damn lever snapped," he ground between gritted teeth. "Near tore me piggin' fingers off, it did." He raised his hand and stared at his grazed digits. Droplets of blood welled from the deeper scratches. "That'll bugger up my mandolin playing for a while," he muttered, turning his hand to better view the damage.

"I never knew you could play the mandolin," said Cronan.

"I can't," snapped Volgen. "Now get in there and let's see if we can close the damn door."

The 'we' turned out to be Cronan and Tobias. While they heaved and tugged at the slab of rock, Volgen disappeared to find a bandage for his injured fingers.

After what seemed like an age struggling to get it back into place, Cronan leaned against the slab to rest. Sweat poured down his face. Reaching inside his jacket pocket he removed a grubby cloth and began to dab at his forehead. "Any more of this and I'll be ready for the funeral pyre, never mind looking for dragons."

"Me, too." Tobias rested beside him, breathing heavily. As he leaned against the rock he took stock of his surroundings. The door had brought them into Volgen's tiny dressing room. A tall, plain wardrobe virtually covered the right wall, while a dresser stood propped against the wall opposite it, a drunken back leg sporting a crudely bound bandage. A small mirror stood on the dresser's top, mounted in a wooden frame. An assortment of brushes and combs lay beside it. Tobias surmised that they must be for Volgen's bushy beard, the man's head being smoother than a skittle ball. Footsteps approached the room.

"Haven't you got that piggin' thing closed yet?" Volgen demanded as he strode in through the doorway opposite Tobias and Cronan. The fingers of his right hand were suitably swathed in a white cloth.

"It's jammed tight," grumbled Cronan, levering himself away from the rock slab. "It will take more than us two to shift it." He looked pointedly at Volgen.

Volgen pursed his lips, the meaning completely lost on him, and breathed heavily through his nose. "We'll have to hide it then." He turned his gaze to the wardrobe. "That'll do it. Shift yourselves. Then we can take a gander at this here map." He tapped at the rolled up parchment under his left arm. "I'll be through here when you've finished." So saying, he turned on his heel and strode from the room.

Tobias grimaced and moved forward to join Cronan. "So much for great leadership," he murmured.

"Aye," grumbled Cronan, staring at the empty doorway. "There is a fine line between delegation and abdication, and he has just crossed it." He turned and gave Tobias a tight-lipped smile. "But the sooner we get the job done the sooner we can take a good look at that map. If we are to be cast outside I at least want to know where we are going."

Tobias's face fell, his thoughts turning sombre. The great outside! Wind, rain, the sun and moon, strange people and, of course, the Blackabbots. Like all Ogmus he had dreamed of living outside, freely roaming the land, enjoying the seasons as his ancestors once had. But he had hoped to do it without the threat of being eaten alive by a big, black, winged reptile.

Tobias and Cronan took hold of the wardrobe and inched it

across the floor to hide the opening. When it was in place they trooped through into the room beyond, dishevelled and dripping with sweat. Cronan dabbed at his forehead with his cloth.

Tobias glanced at Cronan's mottled features with concern. The man looked as though he needed to sit down and rest. If he suffered a fatal seizure all would be lost before they'd even started. "Here," he said, grabbing Cronan's arm and guiding him to one of the two cushioned seats in front of Volgen's desk, "sit down for a while."

As Cronan sank into the chair he gave Tobias a grateful smile and patted his arm. "You're a good lad, Tobias," he murmured.

Volgen looked up from his desk, the map spread out in front of him, nestled amongst scattered papers and quills. "Who said you could sit there?" he demanded. His beard bristled in outrage as he thrust out his chin. "Get yourself stood until I tell you otherwise."

"He's not well. Can't you see? If he doesn't sit down he'll fall down!" Tobias shouted, before he realised what he was saying and to whom he was saying it. Realisation kicked in and he reddened. "Wing Commander," he quietly added.

Although his mouth opened to say something, Volgen sat in mute shock. After a moment he recovered his power of speech. "What did you just say?" he asked.

Tobias avoided eye contact and looked at the floor.

"He said that I was not well and needed to rest," Cronan answered, locking eyes with Volgen.

"Why didn't you say so?" Volgen spluttered, rising from his seat. He moved across the room to a cabinet set against the wall beside his desk. "Can't have you passing out with all that you have yet to do." He opened the cabinet and reached inside, removing two glasses and a decanter containing a grey-white liquid. Placing the glasses on top of the cabinet, he removed the stopper from the decanter and poured two small measures. He handed one to Cronan. "Drink this," he said. "It'll soon have you perked up."

"What is it?" Tobias asked, eyeing the liquid with distaste. He'd seen used dishwater that had more appeal than the slop Cronan was swirling in the glass.

"Fermented mushroom extract," Cronan answered, a contented smile on his face. "More commonly known as Funguy." He looked up and gave Tobias a grin. "It's powerful stuff. One shot of this will cure most ills, two will elevate you to a state of mild euphoria, three will bring on hallucinations, four will do irreparable damage to your innards, and five will probably see you off."

"Not for minors," Volgen rumbled, sitting back down behind his desk. "Especially lippy ones." His smile took the sting out of his words. He switched his attention to Cronan and raised his glass. "Well, drink up, then pull your chair closer. You too," he added, nodding at Tobias and indicating the other seat. "We have plans to make."

"What do you think?" Volgen asked, when Cronan and Tobias had pulled up their chairs.

Cronan took a small sip of his drink and looked at the ceiling as he swilled it round in his mouth. After a moment he swallowed and gave a contented sigh "A bit bitter, but not a bad brew."

"Not the Funguy, you nincompoop. The piggin' map."

"Oh!" Cronan leaned forward to peer at the map again. "Perfect," he murmured, studying it intently. "I have never seen its like before. It must have been drawn from dragon back. You could never get such detail from wandering the lands."

Volgen sighed. "Not the map. About where this Snor'kel and his horde will appear."

Cronan looked up, a scowl of irritation on his face. "Give me a chance to study the damn thing first," he snapped.

Tobias's jaw dropped in amazement. He had never heard Cronan cuss before, or even sound the least bit irritated. It must be the effects of the Funguy he decided. To his further amazement Volgen merely grunted a response to Cronan's outburst and resumed staring at the carefully drawn chart. Tobias shook his head. That Funguy must be powerful stuff indeed.

In the middle of the large paper sheet was drawn a land mass. Various shades of blue, brown, green and grey marked sections of it. When Tobias looked more closely he could see that some of the green areas had trees drawn in them, while the darker ridge that split the larger left section from the smaller right had jagged peaks in it. 'Fangtooth Mountains,' he read.

"What are those blue and brown squiggly lines?" Tobias asked. He had been studying them for a while and was still none the wiser. The brown lines connected one name with another, while most of the blue ones seemed to run from the Fangtooth Mountains to the blue edge surrounding the land mass, or to the small blue area in the middle of the map called The Inland Sea.

"Blues are rivers, browns are roads," Volgen answered. He stabbed a finger at a point on the map. "See here? This is Dragletown. Follow the brown line and it leads you to Viztown in the North."

Tobias nodded.

"Here," said Volgen, pointing a stubby digit at a blue line, "is the River Nazel. It runs from the mountains to The Inland Sea, then out again to the ocean in the west."

"Dragletown," murmured Cronan. "That's where our ancestors first crossed over to this world."

Volgen nodded. "Aye. Just over one thousand cycles ago."

Cronan shifted his attention to a point slightly east of Dragletown. "Mandragle Castle. Isn't that where the first dragons made their home?"

"Correct," answered Volgen. His eyes misted over. "A castle carved into the rock of a mountain, protecting a huge, natural warren of tunnels and caves. Ideal for dragons to nest in, apart from a natural supply of heat, that is."

Cronan straightened and looked at Volgen. "I don't understand."

"Heat!" Volgen frowned. "Birthing?"

Cronan shook his head. "Sorry. I don't know what you mean."

"Dragons need heat to hatch their eggs. Being cold-blooded, the queen would struggle to keep them warm and hatch them on her own. Plus sitting on the eggs for two cycles would seriously deaden her backside. Okay, maybe she could get some of the others to sit on them for a while, but it would still get to be a pain in the arse."

Tobias giggled. Volgen reddened. "If you see what I mean."

"So why choose there, then?" asked Cronan.

Volgen shrugged. "It provided a good base while they explored their new world. Until they found somewhere more suitable."

Tobias thought back to the warm sand in the cavern they had just come from. His eyes widened. "Hope!"

"Exactly," said Volgen, a wide smile on his face. He looked down at the map and pointed to a spot south of Dragletown, deep in the Fangtooth Mountains, not far from the blue that denoted the sea. "Hope! The future home of the dragons. A system of underground tunnels and caverns heated by the very fires of the earth. The sand was imported, of course. From the beaches bordering the sea."

"Does that mean the black dragons were birthed here?" asked Tobias.

Volgen shook his head. "The place wasn't ready by the time the old queen was found to be carrying. She would have lost the lot if she had tried to fly here to lay the eggs."

"In hindsight, maybe that wouldn't have been such a bad thing," Cronan said. A frown crossed his face as he looked up from the map. "How come you know so much about the dragons?" he asked. "Especially since you weren't even born when all of this happened."

With a heavy sigh Volgen sat back in his chair and gave Cronan a piercing look. "I was wondering when you would ask me that," he said.

"Well?"

"Being the Wing Commander, I have certain skills that are not common amongst the Ogmus. Not now, anyway."

Cronan nodded. "And they are?"

"Magic!"

Tobias sniggered. Volgen? Magical powers? Now he had heard everything.

"Sort of," Volgen amended. "In our previous world, all Ogmus were born with magical powers. They had far more ability than I, and were ideal partners for the dragons, who had powers of their own. However, in the spell to bring the dragons from that world to this, the magic was destroyed, lost forever. Aside, that is, from the original Wing Commander; the leader of the flight and its peoples. Seeing as I am a direct descendant of his, some of those powers have been passed down the line."

"And which powers would they be?" Cronan asked.

Volgen gave a wry smile. "To know the history of the dragons from crossover," he answered. "And that's it. Apparently I am able to communicate with the beasts, but I have yet to put that to the test. I couldn't communicate with the blacks, even if I wanted to. The knowledge, however, has been passed down through generation after generation. But it will die with me," he murmured. "As we no longer have good dragons, there is no need for the knowledge. I have vowed to abstain from coupling until they return. I don't want to pass my torment down the line for any future offspring to bear."

Abstain from coupling? Tobias shuddered at the thought. No wonder Volgen was a testy old bugger. Not that Tobias had ever coupled, but he'd dreamed about it and it certainly seemed like a pleasurable experience. He and Jophrey had often talked about coupling, and which comely lass they would most like to do it with. Tobias's thoughts turned maudlin at the memory of Jophrey. He had been the only true friend of his own age he'd had. And now it seemed he had been no friend at all.

Tobias flinched as Cronan sprang from his seat, placing his hands on Volgen's desk as he stared down at him. "Well, you had better go find yourself a partner," he said. "And ready some rocksmiths to finish the birthing chambers."

Volgen looked up and met Cronan's gaze.

"Because the dragons *will* be coming back, once Snor'kel has rid us of the blacks. And I know just where he will appear!"

"You do?" queried Volgen, hope shining from his eyes.

"You do?" asked Tobias, rising from his seat, his heart sinking.

"Right here!" said Cronan, placing a finger on the map over Dragletown. "Exactly where the original dragons appeared all those years ago. If that is where the dragons came into this world, that is where our saviour will also appear. On that I will stake my life."

With dread in his heart, Tobias realised that in all probability Cronan just had.

Chapter Six

By the time Volgen, Cronan and Tobias reached the large cavern that housed the merchants' quarter, the buzz of angry discontent from the gathered throng was palpable. The very air thrummed with disgruntled murmuring. If Tobias had held a tuning fork in his hand, it would be vibrating to match the current mood and emitting a harsh, discordant note. He was relieved when he saw that the masses were facing towards the library tunnel at the other end of the cavern, unaware of their entrance.

As soon as Volgen saw the gathering his stride faltered and his face turned ashen. "The whole piggin' lot of 'em must be here," he groaned.

"Best foot forward," Cronan advised, giving him a gentle shove in the back. "You have to face them sooner or later."

Volgen grimaced. "Later sounds good to me," he grumbled, walking forward.

Tobias peered out from behind Cronan, scanning the crowd for any sign of the old woman with the cane. He'd had quite enough of her for one day and did not fancy bumping into her again. Unable to see her, he felt less fearful for his own safety. Volgen's however, when the crowd spotted him, he wasn't so sure about.

Twenty paces into the cavern Volgen halted and turned to study a tatty stall, standing on its own away from the main thoroughfare. The owner was sound asleep. His head rested on the counter and loud grunts and snores issued from his heavily bearded mouth. The counter around his wild, woolly tangle of hair was covered with broken toys, used cutlery, cracked plates and other useless items. The red-lettered, hand-painted sign above the stall read, 'Wild Bill Halfcock, purveyor of fine quality used goods.' And underneath in smaller letters, 'Cash paid for all your crap. No item refused unless totally knackered.'

Volgen grunted and pointed to a small, battered table in front of the stall. One of its wooden legs had been replaced with a mountain goat's stuffed leg. "Go and get that table. I'll need something to stand on so that this lot can see me."

Cronan raised his eyebrows to the lofty cavern roof and sighed, then moved across to do as Volgen had bid. Tobias dutifully followed. Cronan went to one side of the table and Tobias to the other. As they stooped to grasp the tabletop, Tobias glanced at the price scrawled on a tatty piece of paper stuck to its scarred surface. "Ten coppers? Who'd pay that much for this junk?"

A huge, hairy arm shot out from behind the counter and grabbed Tobias's arm. "That, my son," a deep voice growled, "is a prize antique. Highly sought after." The hand tightened its grip. "And it seems to me that you be trying to nick it from Wild Bill."

Tobias turned and gave a nervous smile as he peered into the darkest eyes he had ever seen, set deep above a squat nose.

"Highly prized antique?"

The sound of Cronan's incredulous voice diverted Wild Bill's attention from Tobias, who sighed in relief. The hold on his arm was released as Wild Bill stood and glared at Cronan. Tobias gulped. The man was enormous. He stood at least a head taller than Cronan, who was not a short man himself, and was twice as broad. Somehow Tobias didn't think that the extra width was fat, not judging by the strength with which Wild Bill had gripped his arm.

"Damn right it's a prize antique." Wild Bill thrust out his bearded chin in outrage and folded his arms across his brawny chest.

"One of its legs is off a goat," said Cronan. "It's been nailed on to replace the wooden one that is missing. If it didn't have a six-inch peg hammered into it, it would fall off and the table would keel over. It is just a useless piece of junk like the rest of your ... your crap."

The man gave a knowing smile and tapped the side of his nose with a massive finger. "That's where you're wrong," he said. "That single goat's leg is typical of this particular style of furniture. It's an impressionist." He thrust out a huge hand. "That'll be ten coppers, sir." He drawled the 'sir' in mock deference.

"Ten coppers? That's outrageous. Who in their right mind would pay such a sum for ..."

"Are you two bringing that piggin' table, or what?"

Cronan looked across at Volgen and gave a small smile. "Just coming."

Seeing who it was that had called, Wild Bill's eyes widened. "Isn't that the ..."

"Yes it is," snapped Cronan, raising his end of the table. He gave Tobias a nod. "And he needs this." Tobias lifted and together they carried the table towards Volgen.

"Oy! Where's me money, yer bleedin' thieves?"

Tobias looked up, startled by the loudness of Wild Bill's shout. The nearest of the Ogmus also turned, and instantly Volgen was recognised. Within moments the cry had gone out and a veritable stampede of sweaty, disgruntled, stressed-out ogmanity approached him.

Wild Bill vaulted over his counter and charged after Cronan and Tobias, waving his fist in the air. "Where's me money, yer bloody table-nickers?"

Tobias and Cronan skidded to a halt beside Volgen and placed the table on the floor. Volgen immediately scrambled onto it and glared at the heaving crowd, with his arms outstretched. His voice thundered through the cavern.

"HALT!"

The front line came to a stop five paces away, sliding forward as the people behind pressed on. Wild Bill's head towered over them, his dark eyes wild and angry. He glared at Cronan. "Ten coppers!" he mouthed.

The buzz of angry voices continued as the mob stared up at the Wing Commander.

"SILENCE!" roared Volgen.

The voices gradually quieted.

Volgen nodded his approval and folded his arms across his chest. "I guess you are all wondering why I called you here," he said, his voice loud and powerful.

The people in the crowd looked at each other, puzzled frowns on their faces. One lone, aged, raspy voice called out. "When did you call us? We've been waiting for the past two candle marks for you to tell us about *the book*, and I don't recall you *calling* us."

The crowd turned to stare at Volgen and nodded their agreement.

"That'll be then, then." Volgen nodded.

"That'll be then, then, what?" the voice asked.

"When I piggin' called you, of course," snapped Volgen.

Low mutterings swept through the crowd.

"Anyway, you're all here now, so I can tell you about our news."

Tobias blanched and stared up at Volgen. Where had this *'our* news' come from? This little charade was all his idea.

"Where's the book?" the voice shouted.

Volgen scowled and stared into the crowd. "Who said that?"

"Me!" A walking cane appeared over the sea of heads, thirty paces away. A walking cane that seemed oddly familiar to Tobias.

"Me, who?"

"That's right."

"Who?"

The hand and cane disappeared. "Me!"

Volgen gritted his teeth. "Me, who?"

"Aye, that's right," the voice answered.

"FOR THE LAST PIGGIN' TIME," roared Volgen, his face turning purple with rage, "ME, WHO?"

"There's no need to shout, young man," called the voice. "I may be old, but I ain't deaf." The press of bodies began to part as someone pushed through, the speaker's voice drawing closer. "Missus Mehooda Velda. Mehoo for short, and Ms since my better half passed on. May the gods bless his soul, the cranky old bastard."

Volgen sighed and shook his head. "The book is safe," he shouted, placing his hands behind his back and crossing his fingers.

"Where?" Mihoo shouted, from closer than before.

"Where, what?" Volgen replied.

"Where is it safe? We heard it was stolen."

A low rumble of 'ayes' drifted through the cavern.

"Well you heard wrong," Volgen growled, his knuckles whitening. As Mehoo began to voice yet another question he uncrossed his fingers and held up his hands. "And if you care to listen to me, you might just find out what Cronan —" he pointed to the librarian, who reddened and looked at the floor, "— has gleaned from it."

Low murmuring again swept the room, but quietened as Mehoo pushed her way to the front. "Well tell us, then. We've been waiting hours for this and I need a pee. So it better be good," she said.

Tobias paled as he caught sight of the ugly old crone with the big mouth and gnarled walking cane. It was her! The one who had propositioned him earlier in the day. The one who had whacked him with her cane when he sprinted past on his way back to the library. He stepped behind Cronan, trying to hide himself from her line of sight.

Volgen puffed out his chest as he answered. "We know where our saviour, Snor'kel, will arrive."

Excited voices drowned out what he was going to say next. He held up his hands for silence. When the crowd had quieted enough so that all could hear, he shouted, "And when!"

A chorus of cheers echoed through the cavern. People laughed, hugged each other, and kissed their neighbours, nearly causing a fight in one quarter as an overzealous young man gripped Wild Bill and tried to kiss him. Fortunately for the young man's health, no tongues were involved. Eventually the merriment subsided and all looked to Volgen again.

The Wing Commander sighed as Mehoo's voice rang out. "So when's this here Snookle comin', then?"

"Snor'kel," Volgen corrected, emphasising the 'kel'. "In twenty days he will arrive. In twenty days Cronan and Tobias will meet him and battle lines will be drawn. The end of the Blackabbots is nigh. Our deliverance back into the world of natural light is assured. The good dragons will return."

Silence filled the room; an awe-struck and excited silence. A silence that was waiting for something to spark it into tumultuous, riotous noise. And who was Mehoo to keep it waiting? "Does that mean red-head wants a shag before he goes, then?" she asked.

The roar of laughter that greeted the comment was the catalyst for the mayhem that followed. It was also the moment that the goat's leg decided to make a break for it and snapped in half under Volgen's weight. With his arms windmilling, he toppled off the collapsing table and fell to the floor with a thud.

Tobias whitened as the crowd surged forward, Mehoo at the forefront, her cane tapping the floor furiously as she shuffled along. Wild Bill was not far behind her. Tobias fled from the cavern in panic. All of a sudden the great outdoors seemed mighty appealing.

* * * * *

After a fitful night's sleep, Tobias felt nowhere near rested enough to undertake their journey. Judging by Cronan's pallid demeanour as they met outside Volgen's study, neither did he. Volgen, on the other hand, was bright and cheerful as he opened his door, in spite of the bruising around his cheek and the shallow cut over his eye. "Welcome, welcome," he enthused, fixing them with a beaming smile. "I trust you both had a good night's sleep?"

"I've had better," grumbled Cronan, stepping into the room, his large pack still strapped to his back.

Tobias followed him in, his own small pack in his hand. The few items he owned didn't take up much space.

"Come in, boy," said Volgen, gripping his arm and dragging him further in to the room. "It's not a funeral, you know. This is adventure!"

Tobias grimaced. If this were the prequel to adventure, he'd settle for a life of boredom. His stomach felt as though a pack of cave-rats were trying to burrow out. He'd never felt so apprehensive.

"Take a seat. I have a few things for you before you go." Volgen gestured to the two chairs in front of his desk. "Things that will make your trek that bit easier."

Cronan eased the pack from his shoulders and placed it on the floor, then sat in one of the chairs. Tobias slipped onto the seat next to him.

Volgen had moved to the other side of his desk and was stooped over, rummaging on the floor beneath. After a moment he pulled up two sheathed blades and placed them on the table. "Long-knives," he advised, patting them. "You never know what you might meet out there, so best be prepared. And they come with a special feature." He picked up one of the knives and pressed a stud on its handle. The round knob on the end popped up, revealing a small glass bubble beneath. A tiny arrow swivelled around inside.

Both Cronan and Tobias leaned forward to get a better view.

"What is it?" asked Cronan.

Volgen snapped the knob closed and placed the knife back on the table. "It's called a Complete Ordnance Map Pointer And Section Sorter," he replied. "Compass for short. And always points to Hope, no matter where you are."

Somewhat sceptical, Cronan frowned.

Volgen rolled his eyes. "It's a magical device so you don't get piggin' lost. Wherever you are, the little arrow will always point back to here. That way you can always find your way home."

Cronan looked at Tobias and grimaced as Volgen bent down to pick up something else from the floor

"And here," he said, straightening and placing two leather belts on the table, "we have utilities belts."

"What?" asked Tobias, staring at the strange items clipped to the wide, brown strips of leather.

In answer Volgen pulled a long bone handle from a pouch and held it out. It was as thick as Tobias's thumb and as long as his forefinger.

"A multi-purpose knife," said Volgen. Using his right hand he levered out a section from the middle of the handle with his thumb nail. "See? Scissors." He waggled the blades at them. "And here, he continued, pushing the small scissors back in and levering out something else, "a fork. Here we have a saw and here we have a spoon. Whatever you want, this little baby will have it."

Tobias was amazed. Whoever would have thought you could pack so many items into such a small handle? In all there were twenty-two things jammed in there. It was the type of knife a soldier could use. A sort of top-notch, swish army knife. He shook his head, eyeing the other pouches on the belts with interest, wondering what mysteries they contained.

"In here," Volgen said, patting a different pouch after slipping the multi-purpose knife back in place, "is a length of extra-strong twine. Here we have a ..."

And so he went on. Tobias's eyes glazed over at the number of items the belt held. The whole ensemble looked weighty and he hoped he would be able to carry it. One thing was for sure, they would certainly be prepared for most eventualities.

Once Volgen had pointed out all fifteen items, he reached down and lifted two neatly wrapped parcels from the floor. "Food for the journey. Enough to keep you going. For a while, anyway."

"What happens when it runs out?" Cronan asked.

Volgen gave him a wink, opened one of the drawers of the desk and removed two weighty pouches. He hefted them then tossed them onto the desk. They landed with a heavy clatter. "More than enough gold coin in there to see you through," he said. "When you run out of eatables, buy some more. The map will show you where the towns and villages are."

"Us? Purchase food?" Tobias was aghast at the thought. "B-b-but how?"

Volgen shook his head. "Use your piggin' brains," he snapped. "I can't think of everything. It'll be just the same as in here, only different."

"But the map is more than three hundred years old," said Cronan. "Surely it will all be changed out there now. More people, for starters. Which means more towns. And the gods only know if they will be friendly to strangers."

"Do you want to go on this piggin' journey or what?"

"No!" Tobias and Cronan said in unison.

Volgen scowled. "Too late. It's decided. If you don't go, you'll be lynched. Or something even more horrible." He gave Tobias a knowing look. "Now come on, we'll go the secret way."

The secret way turned out to be back through the tunnels — once Cronan and Tobias had removed the wardrobe from the entrance — across the heated sand, and on through another tunnel that took them further underground. After a candle mark of walking, the tunnel started to grow cooler. A breeze sprang up, coming from the direction they were heading.

"Where does this tunnel take us to?" Cronan asked.

"The great outdoors," answered Volgen, turning to give him a wink. "There is a quicker route, but that one is sealed against unwanted visitors. This is the back door, so to speak."

Tobias needed no hints to guess who those unwanted visitors might be. The Blackabbots.

"This one will take us lower down the mountain, to a safe point for you to start your journey. Memorise the route, because you will have to come back this way."

"Now he tells us," Cronan grumbled under his breath.

Tobias smiled. At least Volgen was confident they would make it back.

After numerous twists and turns the tunnel started to brighten. The breeze had grown stronger, bringing with it the scent of rain. Tobias's heart skipped a beat. They were nearly there. Soon the real journey would start. His stride faltered. How would he cope? How would he survive? How could he be so stupid as to be doing this in the first place?

They rounded a bend in the tunnel and stopped dead. Straight ahead of them, not a hundred paces away, was a blob of bright light. Dust motes sparkled and shimmered in the air, drifting in the breeze. Tobias's jaw dropped and his eyes widened. Although he had spent brief moments outside on the high ledges, like most of the Ogmus he had never been outside for any great length of time, nor seen anything other than mountains, mist, rain and the occasional glimpse of sunshine. And now he was about to step out into a different world, an alien world, exploring strange new places, new civilisations, going where no Ogmus had gone before. A world in which he had no control. He was frightened. Or, to put it more bluntly, he was crapping himself.

"Come on," urged Volgen, striding forward. "Time is of the essence."

Cronan gripped Tobias's arm and gave it a gentle squeeze. "Don't worry," he said, "I am sure it won't be that bad."

Tobias gave a tight-lipped smile, but said nothing and let Cronan lead on. A few moments later they were standing at the edge of a narrow ledge. The cool breeze ruffled their hair and tugged at their clothes. Although the ledge glistened with water, the rain had stopped falling. High above broken grey clouds drifted across the sky and wrapped around the dark bulk of the mountain stronghold of Hope, its peak lost in the mist. Across from where they stood, separated by a huge chasm, another slab of mountain rose into the heavens, sister to the one they called home.

"Wow!" Tobias murmured in awe.

Volgen turned and gave him a smile. "Wait till you see what's below." He stepped closer to the edge and peered down, then turned and beckoned Cronan and Tobias forward.

Hesitantly they joined him. Far, far below Tobias could see a vast swathe of green. A narrow blue ribbon flowed through, neatly bisecting it.

"The Fangtooth River," Volgen murmured. "You'll spot it on your map." He raised a hand and pointed along the river to his left. "It runs through the valley until it merges with the main tributary.

This trail will take you down to it. Once you're at the bottom, just follow the river and you are on your way." He straightened and moved back from the edge.

Cronan and Tobias also stepped back. Tobias could see that Volgen had a tear in his eye as he gazed solemnly at them.

The Wing Commander smiled. "Off you go, then. Don't you have a saviour to meet? Can't keep him waiting, can we?"

Cronan seemed to be on the point of saying something, but didn't. Instead he gave a curt nod and turned to follow the trail down. After a brief moment Tobias followed.

Before they had travelled twenty paces Volgen's loud shout called them to a halt. They both stopped and turned to see his rotund, light-blue clad form running towards them.

Volgen skidded to a halt in front of them and wrapped his arms around Cronan, pulling him into a rough embrace. He then moved to Tobias and hugged him.

Stepping back, he raised his arm and wiped his eyes with his sleeve. "I've taken the liberty of supplying you both with something for the journey; something a little bit potent." He gave Tobias a pointed look. "So don't be drinking it all at once." Then, overcome by emotion, his voice broke as he said, "And don't be gone for too piggin' long." He turned and strode back up the trail.

Tobias and Cronan watched until his portly figure disappeared into the cave, whereupon Cronan gave a heavy sigh. "There goes the last of our great leaders." He shook his head and smiled. "Until the next one. Come on, lad. Let's go make names for ourselves. Who knows, we may even end up being heroes." He wrapped an arm around Tobias's shoulders.

Tobias gave a wry smile. Heroes? Weren't they usually the guys with STUPID stamped across their foreheads?

Chapter Seven

The narrow mountain trail meandered steadily downward, clinging tightly to the cliff face. So did Cronan and Tobias. To their right was the comfort of solid, grey rock; to their left, the horror of a sheer drop. Although the view of the lush vegetation below was spectacular, to hit it at a rate of knots from a few thousand feet? Not an option either of them fancied. All it would take was a careless footfall near the edge to send one of them plummeting to a bone-smashing death. Settling for safety, they walked in single file as close to the rock as possible, casting the occasional awed glance at the surrounding scenery.

New sounds and smells assailed their senses as they descended. Sweet, high-pitched birdsong never heard in the higher reaches of the mountain drifted up, strange grunts and calls of wild animals echoed in their ears, and the fusty smell of dampness changed to one of wet vegetation. The further they travelled the warmer it became, the constant cold mist that permanently enveloped the mountain home of the Ogmus thinning to allow the heat of the day to touch them.

After about three candle marks of travelling the sun broke through the cloud cover, bathing the lower reaches of the mountain and the valley below with bright light.

"My word," murmured Cronan, shielding his eyes with his hand. "I would never have believed it could get so hot out here."

"And bright," responded Tobias, squinting against the glare. Bright spots danced in his vision. He pulled up the hood of his cloak and ducked down so that it shaded his eyes.

"Good idea," said Cronan, doing the same. He peered over the edge of the trail from beneath his hood. "We should make the ground fairly soon. Fancy a spot of lunch?"

Tobias's stomach gave a loud grumble. He patted it and grinned. "Sounds good to me."

"Right you are, then. Here is as good a place as any." Cronan loosened the pack from his shoulders and dropped it to the ground, then stooped to unfasten the bindings. He removed the package that Volgen had given them and unwrapped it. "Hmmm. Let's see what our illustrious leader has given us, shall we?"

Tobias lowered his own pack and sank to the ground, leaning against the rock face.

"Damn and blast it," Cronan muttered, removing a round of goats' cheese. "I forgot to bring a knife." His eyes lit up. "No I didn't," he said, "we've got the ones Volgen gave us."

Tobias unclipped the multi-purpose knife from his utilities belt, eager to see how it performed. After levering out scissors, a toothpick, a nail file and something totally unfamiliar that would probably come in useful for castrating bats, he finally found the small knife and offered it to Cronan. "Try this."

Cronan took it and chuckled. "Let's see if something of Volgen's can come in useful." He held the blade in front of his face. "It looks sharp enough." He pressed the knife into the outer wax coating and sighed as it snapped under the pressure. "Typical Volgen," he muttered, pushing closed the snapped stump of blade. He tossed the multi-purpose knife back to Tobias and, removing his long-knife from its sheath, began to saw slices of cheese from the round. Cutting four slices, he handed two to Tobias and re-sheathed the knife.

After a brief repast, eaten in companionable silence, Cronan tied the fastenings of his pack and rose to his feet. "Right then, Tobias. Let's go and see what the big wide world has in store for us." He peered over the edge of the trail to the ground far below and smiled. "Look at those colours, Tobias. The greens are so green, and have so many shades." He shook his head, his smile fading. "We Ogmus have been inside too long, far too long. We belong out here, not cooped up inside some dim and dismal mountain." He turned and met Tobias's gaze. "For all our sakes, I hope that Nostra's prophecy is correct. I would like to think that sometime soon all our people could be out here feeling the sun's warmth on their flesh, enjoying such views …"

"Paying honest folk the bleedin' money they owe them!"

At the sound of the deep, gruff voice, Cronan and Tobias turned and looked down the trail. They saw Wild Bill Halfcock striding towards them, a pack slung over his shoulders, his hob-nailed boots crunching on the track as he walked, the tails of his black long-coat flapping in the breeze. His woolly tangle of beard parted as he gave a crooked smile. "Thought you'd seen the last of me, did yer? Yer bleedin' table-nickers."

Tobias wilted. He felt faint. Was their journey about to end before they'd even started? Wild Bill looked exceptionally, well — wild. Who knew what the man would do to them?

Cronan folded his arms across his chest. "You do not scare me, young man. If it's the ten coppers you are after, you can have them, with interest. And then you can go and crawl back under the stone you slithered out from."

By the time Cronan had finished speaking, Wild Bill was only six feet away and he had to crane his neck to meet his gaze. At Cronan's intended insult the smile on Wild Bill's face grew into a wide grin. He stopped and threw back his head as deep, throaty laughter erupted from within the wild tangle of beard. When it subsided he raised his arm, wiping the tears from his eyes with a tatty, moth-eaten sleeve. "I decided I don't want yer money," he growled.

Cronan frowned. "What do you want, then?" he asked.

Wild Bill dropped his pack to the ground and sat on it. "To go with yer, of course." He picked up a pebble and flicked it over the edge. After watching it disappear from sight, he turned and fixed Cronan with a steely gaze. "It's a big, bad world out there, for those that don't know it, and yer won't survive a single day without someone to guide yer."

Cronan studied him for a moment. "What's in it for you? Why would you want to go with us?" he asked.

A big, black cloud seemed to settle over Wild Bill. His face darkened and a hard edge entered his voice. "I have my reasons."

Cronan pursed his lips. "Which are?"

"None of yer business!"

Taken aback by the vehemence of Wild Bill's tone, Tobias stepped sideways to put himself behind Cronan. It was a bit too close to the edge for comfort, but it felt safer than being directly in the firing line. At the movement Wild Bill's expression softened. He looked down and picked up another pebble, which he began to jiggle in a large, tanned hand.

"Let's just say that I have my own score to settle with the Blackabbots." He sighed and looked up. "And believe me when I tell yer, yer ain't gonna survive without my help. There are some dangerous folk out there who will recognise yer for what yer are straight away. There's a good bounty for bringing in the likes of yer. And most of the folks —" he nodded in the direction of the valley "— are so badly off they would turn you in to Blackbishop as soon as piss on yer, dead or alive."

Tobias felt faint and thrust out a hand to grab hold of Cronan's arm before he collapsed over the edge. The librarian looked round and gave him a small smile of encouragement before turning back to Wild Bill. "Why should we believe you?" he asked.

"How tall am I?" Wild Bill responded.

Cronan shrugged.

"Tall for an Ogmus, hey?"

Cronan and Tobias both nodded.

"But short for a Tiernian. What about my eyes?"

Before Tobias could stop himself he blurted, "Deep-set and piggy."

Wild Bill gave a low chuckle. "Unlike big and round with large pupils, hey?" He shook his head and rose to his feet. "Those, my little friends, are the differences that will mark yer for what yer are. Ogmus. Cave dwellers. I am no different than the other folks out there, so yer will be singled out on sight, and dealt with accordingly. And another thing. Those knives." He nodded at the long-knives clipped to the utilities belts.

"What about them?" asked Cronan.

"Banned!"

"Banned?"

"No one, other than the Blackabbots, can bear weapons of any sort. On pain of death." His eyes briefly misted over. "Unless yer hide them, that is." He opened his long-coat to reveal an even longer knife strapped to his side.

Cronan's eyes narrowed. "How is it you know so much about the outside world and, more so, us?"

Wild Bill gave a humourless smile. "Let's just say that word of your prophesy and this Snor'kel abound in Tiernan Og, which is why there be a bounty on yer heads; and that there are certain of us that wish to see the prophesy come true. Well, me, to be precise. There were others …" He stumbled to a halt. After a moment's pause, he continued. "Which is why I made a point of seeking yer out." He gave a small smile. "Why else did yer think I carted all that useless crap around? The location of yer mountain home is an open secret out there," he nodded to the great outside, "so it was easy enough to find the high entrance. Took a while to find this trail, though." He folded his arms across his broad chest.

"If where we are is an open secret, why haven't we been attacked?"

Wild Bill shrugged. "I dare say the Blackabbots have their reasons. They sure as hell don't worry about attacking anyone else." He met Cronan's gaze. "So what's it to be?"

"Do we have a choice?" asked Cronan.

"Not if yer want to live long enough to greet this 'ere Snor'kel."

Cronan looked at Tobias and grimaced.

With frightened eyes Tobias met his gaze, then turned and spewed the contents of his stomach over the ledge. Cronan patted his back before fixing his attention on Wild Bill. He gave a resigned smile. "It looks like we are now a party of three, for better or worse."

"I knew you'd see sense," said Wild Bill, rising to his feet. "Now, if matey-boy has finished feeding the worms, we'd best be on our way. I know of this old shack in the valley. It's a bit on the battered side but will ..."

As Wild Bill strode off down the trail, chattering away, Cronan grasped one of Tobias's arms and helped him to straighten. "Best get going," he said. "Before anyone else decides to join us."

Tobias managed a weak smile and allowed Cronan to lead on. At that moment he longed for the comfort and safety of his own rooms, not some old shack stuck out in the middle of a strange new world.

* * * * *

At about the same time that Cronan and Tobias were making their reluctant way down the mountain trail, Jophrey was making an equally reluctant ascent of the ninety-two steps that spiralled up the circular Watch Tower of Mandragle Castle. He knew there were ninety-two because he had counted them, many years ago, when climbing to the highest point of the castle to watch the black dragons fly in.

At the thought of the magnificent beasts his mood lifted. That was why his father had summoned him to the tower! The meeting of the Blackabbots was to take place that evening, and as the only way they could reach the castle in time was on dragon-back ...

Setting aside his annoyance at his father's manservant for waking him when he had only just gone to sleep, he climbed the remaining forty-seven steps with renewed vigour. The leather soles of his boots slapped the stone steps in his excitement. By the time he reached the top he was gasping for breath and had to lean against the stone wall for a moment before daring to step outside. His head was spinning and he was wary of falling over the battlements if he went straight out.

He waited until the dizzy sensation faded before thumbing the latch to open the door. He stepped through and was nearly blown off his feet. His hair whipped across his eyes and he staggered back. He'd forgotten how gusty the wind could be this high up and had emerged unprepared for the onslaught. The door slammed shut behind him.

"Well met, my boy. Isn't this marvellous? Makes you feel glad to be alive, doesn't it?"

Lord Blackbishop stood with his back to Jophrey. The ends of his handlebar moustache were clearly visible either side of his close-cropped head, performing strange feats of gymnastics in the wind. One moment they were horizontal and quivering, the next carrying out a gyratory motion before standing upright. Jophrey was mesmerised. He half expected them to begin whirling around, to pull his father skyward.

"That is you, isn't it ..."

"Jophrey," Jophrey answered.

"I knew that." Lord Blackbishop turned and gave Jophrey a beaming smile. His moustache stood to attention in the wind, as though in salute. "What kept you? They'll soon be here." He turned his back on Jophrey and flung his arms wide. "The flight of the Blackabbots! My Blackabbots!"

Jophrey grimaced and shook his head. Somehow he had the distinct impression that the black dragons bore their riders more under sufferance than out of any sense of loyalty, if Mandrake's thoughts were anything to go by. He stepped forward to stand beside his father and leaned against the wall to scan the distant horizon.

With the sun beginning its leisurely descent behind the Fangtooth Mountains, the shadow of Mount Fang stretched across the land, inching its way toward the distant metropolis of Dragletown, barely visible on the horizon. It had been many cycles since Jophrey had last visited the town and he wondered if it were still the same semi-dilapidated cluster of wooden dwellings it had been back then. With his father demanding ever-increasing levies, it would be a wonder if the people of the township still survived, never mind eked out a living.

"Look, my boy. Over there!"

Jophrey squinted along the line of his father's pointing finger and saw a black speck in the distance, then another, and another, and another. Four black specks moved across the sky towards them, the dying rays of the setting sun bathing them in crimson light. They looked like demons. Jophrey ginned. He liked the analogy.

In his excitement Lord Blackbishop made to grip Jophrey's shoulder, but stopped short, then turned to look at the approaching specks again. They were closer now, and bigger. "Aren't they magnificent? The five Lords of Tiernan Og. Plus me, of course, even though I am here and not out there with them, which makes ..."

"Six," Jophrey prompted.

"That's right. The six Lords of Tiernan Og. What a sight, hey?"

Jophrey had to agree; it was amazing. He looked more closely. "Father?"

"Hmmm? What is it, my boy?"

"There only appear to be four."

"Of course, my boy. I'm here with you." Lord Blackbishop turned and gave Jophrey a condescending smile. "I've already told you that." He shook his head and turned back to view the rapidly approaching dragons.

"But that makes five. Where's the sixth?"

Lord Blackbishop gave him a puzzled look, then turned to stare at the dragons. They were close enough to make out the riders. He raised a hand and began to count them off. "Right, there's Lord Blackdeacon on Snaggletooth, Lord Blackcanon on Vizigoth, Lord Blackfriar on Nazier, Lord Blackcleric on Peladin and ..." He paused, squinting into the distance. "Where the devil is Lord Blackhead?"

Jophrey raised a hand and smoothed a wayward lock of hair from his eyes. It always amazed him how his father could remember the names of the dragons and their riders, but never that of his own son. "Isn't he the dimwit?" he asked.

Lord Blackbishop puffed out his chest and glared down at Jophrey. "He is not a dimwit," he answered. "He's a dragonlord and, as such, should be treated with respect. He is just a little slow on the uptake, that's all."

"Except where firesticks are concerned," Jophrey muttered.

Lord Blackbishop smiled happily. "No problems on that score, young fellow-me-lad. Lord Blackhead's over his little problem now. Well, ever since we set him up on that island in the middle of the Inland Sea and took all his combustibles away. He can't do much harm living on a rock surrounded by water now, can he?"

Jophrey nodded and forced a smile, sceptical of anything that would stop Lord Blackhead from lighting fires. The man was a walking fire-starter. His diminutive black dragon was equally bad. What was its name again? Spot! That was it. Spot, the dwarf black dragon. He stifled a snigger. "So where is he then?"

His father peered into the distance, hands clasped behind his back, rocking on the balls of his feet. "Don't worry. He'll be here."

'He's coming,' Mandrake's thought drifted into Jophrey's head. *'They were, ah, side-tracked.'*

'Oh?' queried Jophrey.

'Something to do with a flame-grilled fast food store in a small hamlet called Whimpee.'

'Does it have one?'

'It does now,' came Mandrake's amused reply.

Jophrey shook his head, a smile forming on his face. So much for Lord Blackhead's reformation.

"Here he comes." Lord Blackbishop shielded his eyes with his hand and squinted into the distance, where a small black speck had materialised. "Right then." He clapped his gloved hands together in satisfaction. "It would seem that all will soon be in place."

Dark shadows covered them. Jophrey looked up to witness the four black dragons commencing their fly-past. It was a ritual as old as the dragons themselves. Whenever a meeting of the Lords took place at Mandragle Castle, the Lords organised an aerial routine to impress their leader. The routines had become increasingly complex and difficult as the Lords tried to outdo their previous efforts. Jophrey waited in awe to see what they had dreamed up this time.

Arranged in a flying diamond formation, the four dragons swooped low over the battlements of the tower, nearly blowing Jophrey and Lord Blackbishop off their feet with the force of their passage. Blackbishop's moustache swung rigidly horizontal, its ends pointing forward in the wind.

As soon as the dragons had swept past they arced high into the air, whereupon the lead dragon — Snaggletooth — flew clear of the others. Peladin broke left and Vizigoth broke right, while Nazier performed a lower arc to fly immediately beneath Snaggletooth. Together, the two dragons went into a horizontal twist, each spiralling over the other as they flew along. From below Vizigoth and Peladin came shooting skyward, straight at Snaggletooth and Nazier, performing the same dizzying aerobatics.

Jophrey felt a cold sweat slick his skin. They were going to collide! He raised an arm to cover his eyes as the dragons neared impact. But at the last minute Vizigoth and Peladin took evasive action and looped over the other dragons before continuing in formation until they disappeared from sight.

Of their own accord, Jophrey's hands began to clap furiously. Lord Blackbishop joined in. It was the most amazing piece of skynastics Jophrey had ever witnessed. Moments later the dragons returned in their famous Black Arrows formation, flying slowly past the tower. Each rider held his clenched right fist, with the thumb side flat on his head, to the top of his flying helm in salute. Their faces beamed with pride as they acknowledged their leader. Even the dragons wore happy smiles, their long fangs protruding from curled-back lips.

A small black shape appeared at the rear. It came in so fast it nearly collided with the tail of Vizigoth. More by luck than good judgement Spot pulled up in time and joined the end of the parade, Lord Blackhead's face frozen in solemnity as he clenched his fist and pounded it on to the top of his head.

Lord Blackbishop shook his head as the five dragons dipped from view to enter the landing bays. "Show time is over and we have work to do. Come on, the Lords await."

"We, Father?" Jophrey was impressed. He'd never been invited to a meeting of the Lords before. Things must be looking up for his father to include him.

Lord Blackbishop paused on his way to the door. "Of course we have. I have a meeting to attend and you have some well-earned sleep to catch up on. I am sure you can't wait to get back to that bed of yours." So saying he opened the door and stepped inside, leaving Jophrey alone and despondent on the tower.

Jophrey glared at the door for a moment before opening it and beginning the long descent to the lower levels. Why should he have to miss out on this meeting when it was he who had brought the Book of Prophesies? It was he who had taken all the risks; shown all the cunning and guile to succeed; lost two cycles of his life living inside a mountain, and he was damn sure he wasn't going to miss out on what was to come, even if he had to use subterfuge to gain entrance. If his father thought he could toss him aside like one of his used paper slippers, he was sadly mistaken.

'That's my boy,' Mandrake's voice whispered inside his head. *'And then you can tell us poor, ignorant dragons all about it.'*

'No problem,' Jophrey sent back. As he made his way down, a frown tugged at his brow. There was something about Mandrake's tone that unsettled him, and he could not quite work out what it was. He shook his head and gave a wry smile. It was probably nothing. He had been in his father's company for too long, that was all. His father always managed to unsettle him, one way or another.

With a spring in his step he scampered down the remaining sixty-five steps. As soon as he found out what the Lords had planned for this Snor'kel he would go and join the dragons, to renew acquaintances and tell them what he knew. A smile crossed his face. He couldn't wait to meet them all again. Well, aside from Spot. That little bugger was totally unstable and was as likely to have a nip at him as greet him. Or flame him. Hopefully Mandrake would have him under control by the time he got down to the caverns. He reached the bottom of the stairwell and turned left along the narrow corridor. This evening's work called for cunning, guile and subterfuge if he were to find out what was going on, and he intended to bring all those skills into play.

Chapter Eight

Instead of taking a left turn at the end of the corridor and returning to his rooms in the North Wing, Jophrey took a right and headed towards the section of the castle that his father occupied. With any luck he could manage to secrete himself in the meeting chamber before his father and the Lords arrived.

Keeping close to the wall, he made his way along the stone-flagged hallway, tiptoeing past the numerous doorways that lined his route. The flames from the torches jerked and flickered as he made his way along, dancing to a beat only they could hear as they lit the windowless area with a dim glow.

At the next intersection Jophrey halted. He pressed his back against the wall and held his breath as he listened for any sign of activity. All was quiet. It was supper time and most of the castle's occupants would be below having their evening meal. Smiling confidently, he padded out into the corridor and took a right turn. After a short walk he arrived at the stairs leading up to the meeting chamber. He slowly climbed them, taking care to avoid the squeaky tread of the sixth step. From memory, the meeting chamber was a small, three-windowed, stone-walled room festooned with decorative wall hangings. It had very little in the way of furniture aside from a teak topped desk, a chair and some scatter cushions. Jophrey was sure he could find somewhere to hide. He was determined to, even if he had to stand behind one of the wall hangings.

The room squatted on the top floor of the square turret at the opposite corner of Mandragle Castle to the taller, circular watchtower. Lord Blackbishop's sleeping chamber was immediately beneath. With his father's rooms being in such close proximity, Jophrey had to be doubly careful mounting the stairs. The last thing he needed was for his father to discover him. As dim as Lord Blackbishop could be, even he would suspect something was afoot.

Jophrey arrived at the small, wood-panelled landing at the top of the stairs. Straight ahead was a single door: the door leading to the meeting chamber. Set either side of it were two pot plants, their clay containers supported on tripod stands. Jophrey was sure that the correct terminology for such things was potted plants, but after noticing how often the leaves seemed to be plucked, perhaps pot plants was what they were. The bushy shrubs certainly gave off a distinctive, pungent aroma.

Jophrey reached for the door handle, intending to slip inside, but voices from within made him pause. He pressed his ear to the wooden panel and listened.

It was his father; he was already in there. Jophrey silently cursed. All his plotting appeared to be for nothing. He frowned. Who was in there with him? It was too soon for any of the Lords to have made it to the room. He listened more intently.

"Now then, Wooster," he heard his father say. "Remind me of this prophecy thingy again. I wouldn't want to get it wrong in front of my underlings now, would I? I would look a right ..."

"Pratt, my Lord?"

"Exactly, Wooster. So, if you wouldn't mind?"

"As you wish, my Lord." There was a certain resignation in Wooster's tone.

Jophrey moved away from the door, his lips drawn tight. He might have known it would be Wooster. It was then that he heard footsteps approaching. Lots of footsteps, and laughter, and talking. The Lords had arrived. Where could he hide? They sounded pretty close; too close for him to make a break for it. Panic set in. His heart beat faster and his eyes darted frantically around the landing. The door behind him opened.

"Yes, my Lord. I shall go and see what is keeping them. A leaf, my Lord? Are you sure that is wise for such a momentous occasion?" A pause, then, "As you command, my Lord."

By the time Wooster emerged from the chamber, Jophrey had dived behind one of the plants for cover. He crouched down, the clay pot holding the leafy shrub level with his middle, the aromatic fronds with his face. He hoped his hiding place would prove to be effective, but had his doubts. At least if he managed to avoid detection he might be able to listen at the door. Although he doubted he would be able to hear everything, it should be enough to gather what they planned.

He held his breath as Wooster came into view, and nearly fainted as his father's manservant strode towards the plant he was hiding behind. He cringed, fearing discovery, trying to work out a suitable lie that his father would believe. To his immense relief Wooster plucked six leaves, then turned his back on him. He hadn't been seen. The laughter and jocularity reached the foot of the stairs. Soon the thump of riding boots on the wooden treads accompanied the sound of the voices.

"Ah, Woofter!" Jophrey heard one of the Lords exclaim over the prattle of the others. "Sent to keep guard, hey?"

Although he could hear the Blackabbots, Jophrey couldn't see them. Wooster's broad back blocked his view.

"It's Wooster, my Lord Blackfriar," Wooster responded with an air of boredom, handing over a leaf. "With my Lord's compliments, my Lord. He awaits within."

"Cheers, Woofter. Damn decent of you."

The other Lords chuckled.

One by one they filed past, each taking a leaf and offering some sort of facetious remark to the manservant before entering the room. In a few moments only two leaves remained in Wooster's outstretched hand. One leaf would be for his father, the other for ...

Jophrey frowned, wondering who the missing Lord was, and willing him to appear so that he could escape his confinement. The stench from the plant was playing havoc with his nasal passages and he was starting to feel distinctly light-headed. Sweat sprang out on his brow. He felt sure he would sneeze at any moment and blow his cover.

From out of nowhere a bright yellow blast illuminated the landing, the loud accompanying roar making Jophrey flinch. Wooster's figure appeared as a dark silhouette in the brilliance. Soon after, another blast shook the landing.

Jophrey cowered and shielded his eyes against the unaccustomed glare, wondering what on earth was going on. Were they under attack? It sounded as though flame had been thrown. Had the good dragons returned?

The brightness faded and the landing was returned to its customary gloom. Jophrey fearfully peered from beneath his raised arm, willing the small, black images of Wooster to fade from his sight so that he could see properly. If he were about to die he at least wanted a clear view of who was attacking them.

He frowned as he saw Wooster shake his head in bemusement.

"Lord Blackhead!" the manservant called out. "Will you stop messing around with those torches this instant, before you set fire to the whole damn place? My Lord," he added as an afterthought.

Lord Blackhead! Jophrey pursed his lips. Who else could it be? Good dragons? Pah! They were merely a myth. Lord Blackhead, however …

By the set of Wooster's shoulders and his clipped tones, Jophrey could tell he was less than impressed by the Lord's antics.

"It's my new trick," Jophrey heard Lord Blackhead enthuse in a high-pitched, nasal whine as he began to climb the steps.

"New trick, my Lord?"

"Yeah! Neat, huh?"

"Neat, my Lord? Not quite the expression that springs to mind. And I am sure the cleaning staff will have a rather different expression for it when they see the result of your, aherm, trick. It will take them a week to clean those scorch marks off the walls."

"Yeah, well. It'll give them something to do." Lord Blackhead's voice took on an excited note as he continued. "You should see me do it when I'm wearing my full dragon outfit; wooden wings, the lot. You can't tell the difference between me and the real thing. Dead ringer for one, I am. Er, dragon, that is. Only I haven't quite got the hang of this flying lark yet. But I will."

"Really, my Lord." There was a distinct tone in Wooster's voice that implied, 'I am dealing with an imbecile.'

Jophrey peered through the leaves of the plant and watched as Lord Blackhead arrived beside Wooster. He held a flaming torch in one hand and a small green bottle in the other. The short, podgy Lord had to look up to meet Wooster's inquisitive gaze. With his shaved head, big round eyes and full lips, Lord Blackhead was a dead ringer for a sucker fish, although the pastiness of his complexion and the darkness of his eyes suggested it would have to be a dead one, or, at the very least, one that was terminally ill. Unfortunately, however, Lord Blackhead was definitely in the land of the living; the only ill thing about him being his brain. What little he had was firmly gripped by pyromania.

"You've never heard of neat, Wooster? It's the new 'in' expression, don't ya know?"

"No. I didn't know, my Lord."

"It means ..."

"Yes, my Lord?"

Lord Blackhead's face screwed up in concentration. "I forget now." His eyes lit up. "Want to see my trick again?"

Before Wooster could answer, Lord Blackhead raised the green bottle to his lips and took a swig, raised the torch so it was level with his mouth, and choked. Globules of liquid sprayed from his mouth, igniting as they made contact with the flames. A fiery stream of liquid shot towards the other pot plant, reducing it to ashes. Its once delicate green leaves glowed amber as they drifted, lifeless, to the floor. Soon all that remained of the plant was three charred stalks. The heavy scent of smoke and burnt hemp hung in the air.

"Was that it, my Lord?"

Wiping tears from his eyes, Lord Blackhead straightened and met Wooster's gaze. He gave an embarrassed smile. "I must have taken too much in," he croaked. "I sort of swallowed some."

"I can see that, My Lord. Would you care to tell me what is in that concoction?"

Lord Blackhead reddened. "Er, Naphtha, mixed with some Brandy to sweeten the flavour."

"Ahhhh!"

The door of the meeting chamber opened and Lord Blackbishop's head popped out. Spotting the smoking plant, his eyes narrowed. He cast Lord Blackhead a look of sufferance and pursed his lips. "We're waiting," he said, disappearing from view.

As Lord Blackhead made to walk through, Wooster held out his hand. "The torch, if you don't mind, my Lord. And the bottle."

Reluctantly Lord Blackhead handed them over. As he passed the remaining plant, Jophrey was sure he heard the clink of glass knocking against glass from within the Lord's black flying tunic. He could see the secretive smile on Lord Blackhead's face.

When the door had closed Jophrey heard Wooster clear his throat, and looked to where his father's manservant was standing. His eyes widened in horror. Wooster was looking straight at him! Jophrey recoiled, trying to bury himself in the wall behind.

"Do come out, young master. You'll hear nothing from there.

Although what you hope to achieve by listening to their drug-induced rambling is beyond me." He held out a gloved hand and beckoned Jophrey forward.

Jophrey complied and stood, head bowed, inspecting the floor at Wooster's feet. Now he was in for it.

"If the young master would like to listen to their scintillating conversation, may I offer the benefit of my experience?"

Jophrey looked up, his brow creased in puzzlement.

"Second panel to your left. Push the centre of the flower carved in the top right corner and the panel will open, revealing a small niche. Inside the niche is a stool. You will also find a cup and a flagon of water on the shelf." He gave an amused smile. "You may have a long night ahead of you. Now, if you don't mind," he waggled two leaves in the air, "I have some goods to deliver."

Without waiting for a response, Wooster shooed Jophrey away and strode to the door. Knocking twice, he entered.

Jophrey stared at the space Wooster had occupied, wondering why he would want to help him. Wooster had never shown much liking for him and was always on his back about something or other: Tidy your room. Wash your face. Eat your food properly. Do your homework. In fact he acted more like a father than his father did. He cringed at the thought.

At the sound of booted feet approaching the door from the room beyond, Jophrey turned and moved swiftly to the panel. He pressed the centre of the carving as Wooster had instructed and it slid open. He slipped inside and pulled the panel closed behind him just as the door of the meeting chamber opened.

A moment later he heard Wooster's voice from outside. "Have a good night, young master. Try not to stay up too long. The meeting will finish way past your bedtime, and the Lords will be talking nonsense for most of the night, believe me."

Jophrey waited for the sound of Wooster's footsteps to fade before he dared move and take stock of his surroundings. The manservant's sudden co-operative manner was puzzling. Extremely puzzling.

Jophrey settled himself on the stool. Surprisingly, the niche was fairly bright and he could hear the Lords' voices quite clearly. When he turned to examine the inner wall he discovered why. The top section was covered with fine gauze, letting in enough light to make things less claustrophobic, and allowing the occupier to hear what was being said. Jophrey wondered how often Wooster had used the niche to listen to the Lords' plans, and why.

He pursed his lips, vowing to ask Wooster the very same questions the next time he saw him. For the moment he had other matters to attend to. Pouring himself a cup of water, he took a sip and settled himself for the long night ahead.

* * * * *

Echoes — the scrape of clawed feet on hard ground, the brush of scales against rock — bounced off craggy walls, their hollow reverberation indicating the hugeness of the cavern. And it was cold; cold and damp. Although not cold enough to cause Mandrake problems, it slowed his movements. He hated the cold. Dampness he could put up with, but being cold made him slower. One of the drawbacks of being poikilothermic, he supposed. The longing for a warmer habitat welled up in him. He gave a secretive smile as he lumbered around the cavern lighting more torches. It would not be much longer before that particular goal was achieved.

He stopped and breathed a narrow, controlled shaft of flame to ignite a torch. The pitch-soaked brand burst into life, joining the ten others that had already been lit. Mandrake smiled with satisfaction as he moved on to the next one. He hadn't lost his touch. It was still there when he wanted it. Fire and control, that was the key. Fire and control.

Without warning a savage blast of flame shot over his shoulder, blasting the torch he was about to light. Incinerating the bundle of dried reeds it hammered in to the rock behind, making a glowing spot appear.

Glowing spot? Spot!

Mandrake growled deep in his throat and turned his dark head toward the entrance behind him. His eyes swirled red with anger as he saw the diminutive dragon, wings held out for balance, head thrust forward, fixing his attention on another torch.

"SPOT!" Mandrake's angry voice hammered out.

The little dragon looked at Mandrake. The fire issuing from his mouth flickered, then died. He folded his wings, dipped his head and lowered his eyes.

"IF YOU HAVE QUITE FINISHED," Mandrake roared, "GET TO THE CENTRE OF THE CAVERN, SIT STILL, AND DON'T UTTER A WORD. Or a flame," he added.

Spot's mouth moved.

"Not a word, you understand? And if I catch you using flame in my presence again without permission —" Spot cringed "— it will be the last thing you ever do. Now get over there and sit!"

His head held low, Spot waddled to the centre of the cavern and sat down, sullenly staring at the ground in front of him.

Mandrake watched him. "Now observe how I do it," he said. He moved on to the next torch. "It is all about control." He breathed in, then exhaled a steady flow of flame, extinguishing it as soon as the brand was lit. He turned to look at Spot. "See? Nothing to it. Now, let us se e if you can master the art."

Spot jumped eagerly to his feet, a happy smile on his face. He thundered towards the next unlit torch, skidded to a halt, spread his wings and pulled back his head.

"CONTROL!" Mandrake roared, his deep voice echoing around the cavern.

Unseen, the remaining four dragons halted at the entrance, their long necks stretched forward as they strained to see how Spot's lesson was going. Having witnessed his lack of control in the past, they didn't want to get too close.

"That's better," said Mandrake, as Spot relaxed his stance. "Now ease out the flame, and when the torch is lit shut it off."

As if it were a bow being drawn and fired, Spot's neck swept back, then powered forward. A short, sharp, violent blast of flame discharged from his mouth. In seconds the torch was no more, and a blackened patch stained the rock wall.

Mandrake rolled his eyes and shook his head. "Go and sit down," he ordered with a sigh. With head bowed, Spot slowly returned to the centre of the cavern.

"And you four," Mandrake called over his shoulder, "come and help me show him how it should be done."

Quickly masking their surprise at being discovered, the four dragons lumbered in and set about lighting the remaining torches.

When they had completed their task they moved to the centre of the cavern to join Spot, casting him smug looks that the little dragon tried his best to ignore.

Mandrake looked on, surveying the group with a critical eye. Four magnificent beasts, and Spot. He shook his head. Five dragons who were ageing, nearing the end of their prime, like himself. From here on it was all downhill. And when they were gone, what would be left to show the passing of their time? Nothing! There would be tales, of course, of their majesty, their might, the fear they instilled. But tales get forgotten, or become myth. Just like the myth of the *supposed* good dragons. He snorted in contempt. The multicoloured weaklings! No one would get them back from where they had gone. He had made sure of that. The trusting fools!

His mood lightened and a cunning smile crossed his face. Soon they, the black dragons, would be in a position to leave this world a legacy to remember. And not only this world. There were other worlds out there; worlds that needed their guidance, their control, their domination. Worlds that would cower beneath their might. As the first hatched he had inherited the queen's knowledge and knew of these worlds. Until now he'd never had the necessary capabilities, or dragon-power, to realise his dreams. But that was about to change. The smile remained on his face as he waddled across to join his companions. It was time they were informed of his little secret.

Snaggletooth bowed his head in greeting as Mandrake drew close. "My Lord Dragon," he intoned, meeting Mandrake's gaze. "It has been a while since last we all met."

Mandrake dipped his head in acknowledgement and sat on his haunches. Snaggletooth looked well. There was a glossy sheen to his black scales; his yellow eyes glowed bright and healthy. "There has not been the need before now," Mandrake responded. His lips curled in a grin, drawn back over protruding fangs.

Nazier's stomach grumbled, loud in the silence. He peered around the gloomy cavern as if looking for something.

"Fresh goat carcasses have been prepared for our consumption, Nazier," Mandrake said, casting the overweight dragon a frown. "For after our meeting."

"What meeting?" Nazier rumbled, his forelegs rubbing his belly.

"The one we are about to have," snapped Mandrake.

"No chance of an appetiser, I suppose," said Nazier. It was a statement rather than a request.

Mandrake shook his head. Nazier sighed.

"What's the meeting about?" asked Vizigoth. "I thought it was just those cretins who were having one."

Short, deep barks erupted from Mandrake's mouth as he laughed. Cretins! How aptly put. He fixed Vizigoth with a penetrating look. "You will not be sorry to see the last of them, I take it?" he asked.

Vizigoth's eyes widened. He glanced at his companions before returning his gaze to Mandrake. "We're getting rid of them at last?" he asked, his voice low, as if fearful of being overheard.

"Soon," Mandrake answered. "Very soon."

There was a moment of stunned silence before deep, barking laughs — and a high-pitched squealing — filled the cavern.

To the uninitiated, their laughter sounded like a group of sex-starved bull-seals shouting their frustration to the skies. To Wooster, however, secreted in a dark corner of the cavern, safely hidden from prying eyes behind an outcrop of rock, it was instantly recognisable for what it was. Tears sprang to his eyes as memories of happier times came unbidden to his mind. He raised a hand and brushed the wetness away. If he wanted to learn something useful, something that would help him, he had to push thoughts of the past to the back of his mind and concentrate on listening to what the dragons were planning. He had waited three centuries for the chance to rectify a wrong, and he wasn't going to miss his opportunity through lack of attention.

He eased himself into a more comfortable position and peered through the gloom to where the six dark shapes squatted, conversing loudly, unaware they were being overheard.

"When?" demanded Snaggletooth, his eyes bright at the thought. "Blackdeacon makes my back ache, the fat fool."

"When we capture the new queen, of course." Mandrake replied.

"Capture the queen?" A frown formed on Snaggletooth's face. "It is the Lords' plan to kill her and her horde, along with this Snor'kel."

Mandrake gave a sly grin and shook his head. "They need us for that. And we won't oblige them. Not with the queen anyway. We need her and Snor'kel for our own purposes."

"And just what might those *purposes* be?" asked Snaggletooth.

The dragons waited with bated breath for Mandrake to answer. He gave each a knowing look before obliging. "Why, to hatch our young of course. If you hadn't noticed, we are all male."

As the realisation of what Mandrake had said sank in, smiles appeared on their scaled faces. Apart from Spot's. He cocked his head to one side as he tried to figure it out. When enlightenment finally struck, he became as excited as the others. Jumping up and down and flapping his wings, he shot a long flame into the air.

"Spot!" Mandrake scolded, casting him a sour look. The little dragon looked at the ground sheepishly.

Mandrake nodded his approval and continued. "There are more worlds than this one. More worlds to be discovered. More worlds that need our domination."

"What worlds?" asked Snaggletooth.

"Worlds like the one where the Ogmus came from," Mandrake answered. "Worlds that have an abundance of life. Worlds that are ripe for the taking. There are hundreds of them out there. What if we could each have a world of our own, instead of a small patch of land? Ours to do with as we pleased? No one to spoil our fun, spouting forth about stripping the natural habitat and ruining the pretty countryside?"

"But how is capturing the queen going to achieve that?" Snaggletooth responded. "If there are such worlds, how do we get to them?"

"Snor'kel!" Mandrake grinned. "He is the key. He has the power. He knows the means by which we can travel to these worlds. He is true Ogmus. Not like the retarded cave-rats that inhabit this world, but a descendant of pure Ogmus. A magic-user who knows the ways of the wyverholes."

A stunned silence descended. The dragons shifted their bulk uneasily.

"Wyverholes?" queried Peladin.

"The tunnels through space and time that link the worlds. In days of old, when dragons had strong magic of their own, they used them to travel between worlds, enrich their lives, seek adventure. With the passing of time, however, dragonkind lost the ability to use these pathways between worlds. They became sedentary and lazy." He scowled. "In short, they became content with their lot, ultimately leading to their demise as the peolpes of these worlds rose up, denying dragons the right to raid for food as they saw fit, to live as they wanted. It was the Ogmus who resurrected the old routes when the last of the dragons became threatened. They opened up the pathway to this world, and now one of their kind is coming back. And I intend to use his abilities to put dragonkind back where it belongs." He rose on his haunches, his voice gaining power. "I want to kick ass!"

The air in the cavern thrummed with excitement as the six dragons gave vent to their feelings. A wind whipped up as they flapped their wings, making the torches splutter and dance in their sconces. They quietened when Mandrake hissed a warning. His yellow eyes swirled and he turned his head and looked towards the entrance. "Someone comes," he said.

"Who is it?" Snaggletooth asked, his lips curled back in a snarl.

"At ease," murmured Mandrake. "It is only Jophrey."

Snaggletooth snorted. "I don't know why you keep him around. The whelp is a nuisance."

"He has his uses," Mandrake responded. "And there is something about him. Who else do we know that can communicate with us by mind-speak? Certainly not the Lords, that's for sure. I want him unharmed —" he cast Spot a meaningful look "— until I figure it out. And if I decide that he is of no further use to us, he will become dispensable. Like the others."

An evil smile formed on Spot's face.

"Until then he is to be welcomed as a friend. Understand?"

Spot nodded his agreement, but the twisted leer remained.

"Good." He turned back to the other dragons. "We will further discuss the matter of Snor'kel nearer to the time of the queen's arrival." He smiled. "But first we will hear from Jophrey about what the Lords have been discussing."

Wooster decided he had heard enough of the dragons' plans and slipped away from the outcrop of rock behind which he had been hiding. Although his eavesdropping had answered some questions, it had raised many more. The biggest surprise was young Jophrey. In all his years of knowing the boy he'd never suspected he could communicate with the dragons. And it would appear that the blacks were playing him along. Jophrey couldn't know what cunning, underhand creatures he was in league with. The situation would need watching carefully.

However the puzzle remained. Jophrey! The only way he could have inherited the ability to mind-speak would be if his father were a descendant of a true Ogmus — a Wing Commander. But since the last one with the power had vanished with the good dragons, that possibility appeared non-existent. Wooster knew that Blackbishop was not the boy's true father, and had no idea who the real one was. Perhaps he should have questioned Jophrey's mother before she decided to leave Mandragle castle. But it was too late now; she was long gone and could be anywhere on Tiernan Og. If she still lived.

With his mind in a whirl Wooster shuffled, on his hands and knees, to the secret cleft that led back up to the castle. He would have liked to stay and hear what Jophrey had to say, but if he did not get back to the Lords soon he would be missed, and that could lead to all sorts of questions being asked. The important thing was that he had acquired vital information this night. Information that could help him to realise his dream, if Jophrey didn't manage to get himself killed in the meantime.

Chapter Nine

Deep in thought, Jophrey made his slow, methodical way down the rough-hewn steps leading to the dragons' cavern. The slap of his feet on the hard rock echoed hollowly around him. His torch flickered in the barely noticeable breeze, and a cold tingle ran up his spine. He shivered and cast his mind back to the debacle he had been unfortunate enough to witness. He pursed his lips and shook his head. Perhaps he should have listened to Wooster and gone to bed. It would have saved him from terminal boredom and a numb backside. He stifled a yawn. His father's manservant had been right. The Lords had blathered incoherently for almost an hour before events took a more fiery turn. He raised his hand and rubbed at a soot-blackened eye. Lord bloody Blackhead! What a complete and utter nerk.

Jophrey had realised the meeting was likely to descend into a farce when the Lords spent the first ten minutes listening to Lord Blackbishop try to read Nostra's translated prophecy. His father was never a skilled reader and struggled over the most basic of words, so having to read ones with more letters than he had brain cells made for a somewhat mind-numbing experience.

Not understanding what Lord Blackbishop was talking about and becoming bored, the Lords giggled and hurled comments, gauntlets and any other available items at each other. This only served to enrage Jophrey's father, who stopped the meeting and demanded that the Lords clear up their mess before he continued. That took ten minutes. Ten minutes of frustration for Jophrey, who wished they would just get on with it. He had been getting desperate for a pee and was eyeing the pitcher as he sat with crossed legs.

When the room had been tidied to Lord Blackbishop's satisfaction, he had tried to read the verse again. And again, and again … Eventually, in exasperation, the Lords had asked if they could read it for themselves.

Jophrey sighed as he slowly descended the stairway. They had proved even worse than his father had been. At least he'd had the benefit of Wooster's intelligence beforehand. Not one of the other nincompoops had managed to get past the first line.

Then it all got worse as the effect of the leaves kicked in. Soon conversation was replaced by giggling and general hilarity from all the Lords apart from Lord Blackdeacon, who had fallen asleep in a corner. Jophrey had peered through the mesh and seen him slumped against the wall, his flying helmet awry and his goggles hanging loose to one side. Unaware of the other Lords' antics, he snored loudly as they took turns to try and land screwed up bits of paper in his open mouth from ten paces. To Jophrey's amazement even his father had joined in.

Jophrey knew there was going to be trouble when Lord Blackhead had snatched a torch from the wall and jumped onto Blackbishop's desk. "Wanna see my new trick?" he had shouted, trying to keep his balance as he fished inside his tunic pocket. By the time Jophrey had realised what the Lord meant to do it was too late. Lord Blackhead had torched the meeting chamber.

Jophrey had barely escaped the niche with his life. Smoke had billowed in, setting him to choking as he frantically fumbled for the latch that would let him out. When he eventually escaped the hallway was awash with servants crying the alarm as they scurried about with buckets of water. It was bedlam.

As Jophrey neared the bottom of the steps to the cavern, he cursed his father and the Lords for the idiots they were. Why the dragons put up with them he would never know.

'Not for much longer,' a welcome voice whispered in his head.

Jophrey smiled. Intelligence at last.

'Hurry! We are waiting for you.'

'Spot?' queried Jophrey, pausing in his stride.

He felt Mandrake's feathery laugh. *'He is as eager to see you as I.'*

Somehow Jophrey doubted that, but when he stepped into the cavern he was pleased to see all the dragons looking at him with friendly smiles on their faces. Although, on closer inspection, Spot's appeared to be more of a grimace.

"Well met, Jophrey," Mandrake's deep voice boomed. "Put your torch down and join us. We would hear what our mighty Lords have planned for the invaders."

Jophrey gave a wry smile and walked forward, admiring the sheer bulk of the beautiful, black creatures before him, their scales shimmering in the light from the torches. He felt dwarfed both in size and presence as he approached, but did not feel fearful. A warm, welcoming sensation bathed his mind. He felt as though he were truly home. A prodigal son returning to the embrace of a loving family. He noticed Spot's lip curl and the feeling fled, only returning when Mandrake swatted the little dragon on the back of his head with a leathery wing.

"What do you have to tell us?" Mandrake asked, beckoning Jophrey to him with a flick of his huge foreleg.

With a shrug and a resigned slump of his shoulders, Jophrey nestled himself into the crook of Mandrake's leg and let them know exactly what he thought of their riders. By the time he had finished regaling them with their Lords' antics, the smiles had left the dragons' faces and the air was filled with angry grumbles.

Mandrake silenced them with a wave of his wing and a sharp hiss. His head arched down to stare at Jophrey. "So what do you suggest?" he asked.

Jophrey shrank back under the dragon's hypnotic gaze, suddenly fearful. There was a manic gleam in Mandrake's eyes that he had never seen before and it made him nervous. "S-s-suggest?"

Mandrake nodded. "You have seen for yourself what fools we have been cursed with." His head withdrew as his voice increased in power. "In return for long life, a gift from their dragons, they have given us nothing. NOTHING!"

The air trembled with Mandrake's roar and Jophrey flinched.

"Apart from backache," grumbled Snaggletooth.

Mandrake cast him a warning look before continuing. "When first we were hatched, we chose the younglings best suited to our needs; those that we felt would help us grow into the fine dragons we wished to be, to help us rule this world in a fair and equal manner after the others had deserted us."

"Others?" queried Jophrey. "There really were others?"

Mandrake looked surprised. His eyes widened as he gazed down at Jophrey. "Of course," he answered. "Surely you did not think of them as myth?"

Jophrey swallowed nervously. "I-I-I never realised," he blurted. His mind raced with the tales of the good dragons he'd been told by Tobias.

Mandrake smiled, revealing his large incisors. "When first they came into this world, the other dragons ruled fairly and were loved by all. But the spells that were cast by the Ogmus to transport them warped their very being. Over the cycles the damage to their souls became evident. They became more and more deranged and rule by terror became the norm. From being in awe of the magnificent beasts, the people of the lands came to fear them. Fire and death held sway. Until we were birthed." He paused and glanced around at his companions. "The six saviours of Tiernan Og."

"Saviours?" whispered Jophrey. This was one tale he had never heard before.

"Upon our birthing, seeing how pure and unblemished we were, the queen realised the error of their ways. Once we had chosen our riders she bestowed guardianship of Tiernan Og upon us and disappeared from this world, taking her demonic horde with her."

"And now they are coming back," Jophrey murmured fearfully.

Mandrake nodded solemnly. "And now they are coming back," he whispered. "And what do you think will happen when they return?"

"Murder and mayhem?" Jophrey suggested.

Mandrake nodded. "And what have our once-fine riders become? Those magnificent young men who helped guide us to become the fine specimens of dragonkind we now are?"

"Idiots?"

"Exactly!"

"So what can we do?" Jophrey launched himself to his feet. "We have to save the world from those, those ... demons!"

Barks of approval greeted Jophrey's call to arms.

"Firstly, we have to deal with the demons when they arrive. Then, secondly, we have to capture the queen and their leader, this Snor'kel."

"Why?" asked Jophrey, puzzled. "Surely it would be best to kill them all."

"To see if she can be turned to the good," Mandrake answered, his voice grim. "There are other worlds out there besides our own. Worlds that have been blighted by their evil. We are too few to save those worlds. If the queen can be turned, then there may be a chance."

"How?"

"Hatchlings! More black dragons!" His dinner-plate eyes fixed on Jophrey. "You do see, don't you? What must be done?"

Jophrey nodded hesitantly. "But what about the Lords?"

Mandrake shrugged. "They have become fat, indolent and happy with their lot. The fire that once burned bright within them has diminished."

At the mention of fire Spot bugled loudly. Mandrake scowled at him before continuing. "If they cannot be returned to the fine young men they once were, we will remove our gift of longevity and they will die of old age. When their time is right!" An odd glint appeared in Mandrake's eyes, then quickly disappeared. "That means we will need new riders, new blood, new leaders; someone to find these younglings and train them. Are you such a one, Jophrey?"

Jophrey was dumbstruck. It only seemed like hours ago that he was wishing he had a dragon of his own to ride. Now he was being offered not one but all of them, until he found recruits to replace the idiotic Lords. "And who would I ride? If, of course, I accept your invitation?" he asked in a quiet voice.

A wide smile split Mandrake's face. "Why me, of course." He turned his head away, the smile drooping as though he was humble at the thought. Hearing Jophrey's loud whoop he turned back, the smile firmly in place. He raised his foreleg and placed it gently on Jophrey's right shoulder, then dipped his head. "Welcome, Jophrey. To the new brotherhood of dragons."

* * * * *

The acrid smell of smoke reached Wooster's nostrils long before he neared the end of the secret passage. His brow furrowed in concern and he increased his pace. At the top of the steps he pulled open the panel that led to the hallway and stepped out. He quickly pulled the timber panel closed behind him, relieved that nobody in the mass of water-carrying bodies had seen him emerge. He swiftly joined the press and moved with the flow towards the square tower.

"You there!" Wooster grabbed the arm of a man who was rushing past. "What has happened?"

"Fire!" the man replied, trying to pull away from Wooster's grasp. "In the meeting chamber. The Lords ..."

Wooster tightened his grip. "Yes?"

"Survived!" With that he pulled free and scuttled quickly away, water sloshing over the lip of his bucket.

Wooster grimaced. So the fools were still alive? More was the pity. Wondering what had caused the fire he moved forward with the throng.

The smoke became thicker as he neared the short flight of stairs leading to the chamber. Reaching inside his long housecoat he removed a pristine white handkerchief and covered his nose. He began to cough. What on earth had happened once he had left? He had not travelled much further when he received his answer.

The six Lords sat in the corridor at the foot of the stairs, silly smiles fixed on their faces as they gazed abstractedly at the people milling around them. Buckets of water were being handed along a chain of workers, to be thrown through the open doorway onto the flames that raged within.

"What happened, my Lord?" gasped Wooster, kneeling beside Lord Blackbishop and frowning as his master tried to focus on his singed moustache.

"Wooster!" Lord Blackbishop enthused, when he eventually recognised him. "You missed all the fun!"

"Fun, my Lord?" Wooster gazed around with a jaundiced eye. "I'd hardly class putting out fires as fun, my Lord."

"You should have seen him, Wooster! He was magnificent."

"Seen him, my Lord?"

"Lord Blackhead! He flew like a dragon and then he ..."

Wooster rolled his eyes and sighed, knowing full well what had happened next. "Breathed fire?"

Lord Blackbishop's eyes widened in surprise. "How the devil did you know that, Wooster?"

"A lucky guess, my Lord."

Lord Blackbishop shook his head. "You never cease to amaze me, Wooster."

"The feeling is mutual, my Lord. The feeling is mutual."

* * * * *

Mandrake waited until Jophrey had left the cavern before turning to the others. "It would seem that we have a recruit to our cause." He smiled.

"Why do you want him with us?" Snaggletooth asked. "It's not as if we need the manchild."

"That is where you are wrong," Mandrake answered, with a knowing look. "There is something special about young Jophrey."

Peladin snorted. "Because he is not an idiot like his father?"

It was Mandrake's turn to snort. "Lord Blackbishop is not his father, you fool. How could anyone so obsessed with avoiding bodily contact ever hope to produce a manchild?"

The collective gasps of surprise made Mandrake smile.

"Then who is the father?" Peladin asked.

Mandrake shrugged. "I have no idea, but I have always sensed that Jophrey is not of Blackbishop's line." He lowered his head. "He carries within him the seed of the Ogmus, that is why he can mind-speak. And that is why Blackbishop cannot be his father. When we chose our riders, we made sure that none carried the seed, little knowing that one day we might have a use for such a gift."

"I still don't see why we have to put up with him," Snaggletooth grumbled.

"Because," said Mandrake, "if Snor'kel will not help us, we will have to look to others to open the wyverholes."

"Others?" queried Vizigoth, his brow drawn into a frown. "What others?"

"There is another with the spark of the seed, I sensed it earlier today. I believe it must be one of the cave-dwellers as I have not sensed it before." He gazed into space. "Hmmm. Perhaps I have, long ago, when I was out hunting on the mountain." He snapped back to the present. "Well that is of no importance at the moment. What is of concern is that another with the power is heading towards us. Towards Mandragle Town, to be precise. And I intend to capture him alive. If Snor'kel will not help, we will have two options to work with."

"What about the queen?" asked Vizigoth. "What if she will not help?"

"She, my brother, will have no choice in the matter. Even if we have to hold her down and clip her wings, she will be impregnated. She *will* produce our heirs," Mandrake barked.

The loud laughs of the other dragons joined Mandrake's. Soon the whole cavern echoed with the guttural sound.

* * * * *

In the higher levels of the castle Jophrey was opening the door to his rooms when a cold shiver ran down his spine. He tensed, feeling uneasy but not knowing the reason why. He glanced over his shoulder. Seeing nothing he laughed nervously and strode into his room. It must be tiredness playing tricks with his mind. That coupled with the excitement of the events of the evening. He still couldn't believe the dragons wanted him to be their Lord, to help them beat off the demons that were about to invade his homeland. He grinned and began to undress. Not only was he going to be a dragon rider, he was going to be their leader. A *real* Wing Commander, not some jumped up nerk like Volgen.

As he lay in his bed, the covers pulled up around his neck, doubts wormed their way into his head. He couldn't help thinking back to his long conversations with Tobias about the supposed good dragons. He shrugged the doubts aside and nestled deeper into the covers, a smile forming on his face. Tobias would get a nasty surprise when he learned that his precious dragons weren't quite so good after all. In spite of the pleasing thought, he couldn't help but wonder. Tobias's dragons did seem so unlike the ones Mandrake spoke of. But then Mandrake had been there when it was all happening. He had memory on his side, and didn't have to rely on the drug-induced scribblings of a paranoid nut-job. Jophrey trusted Mandrake. The big black dragon wouldn't lie to him, would he?

Chapter Ten

Dusk had fallen by the time Wild Bill led Cronan and Tobias off the mountain. Black shadows encroached on the land, stealing the day's resplendent colours. In the sky stars started to twinkle and a pale moon appeared, spending a brief moment or two in the company of its brother the sun.

Tobias felt more and more tense as the daylight faded. He could hear strange snuffling noises and calls in the night, and cast nervous glances at the surrounding undergrowth. All the while he was careful to keep their self-appointed guide in sight, as he led them deeper into the tangle of bushes and shrubs.

The snuffling noises grew louder. Sweat beaded on Tobias's forehead, and the palms of his hands went slick. After a quick glance at the bushes on his left, where he was sure the noises were coming from, he increased his pace to get nearer to Wild Bill, who was using his body as a battering ram to force his way through the branches and shrubbery. In his haste Tobias got too close, and the branches that Wild Bill had pushed aside sprang back to batter him about the head. He shielded his face with his hands to avoid injury. Following close behind him, Cronan did the same.

After ten minutes Wild Bill turned on to an even narrower trail; a thin ribbon of bare earth where animals had left their spoor. Cronan and Tobias followed, trying to avoid the low-flying, leafy whips. By the time a tumbledown hut came into view, Tobias was feeling decidedly groggy. He felt as though he had done ten rounds with Tyke Myson, the pugilistic champion back at Hope.

With a grunt of satisfaction Wild Bill tore aside the ivy that grew over the door and strode inside. Not feeling quite so brave, Tobias stood in front of the collection of precariously balanced stones, eyeing the ramshackle hut with distaste. The goats' pen back home looked more appealing.

The door and the windows either side of it had long since rotted away, leaving gaping holes. Ivy clung to the stonework, its thick matt of strands growing up the walls and through the open jointing. It looked as though it was only the ivy that held the place together. Tobias peered up at the roof. Somehow defying the laws of gravity, the sagging, decayed tangle of thatch hung suspended over the three and a half walls that remained. It was beyond him how the whole lot still stood. By rights it should have collapsed ages ago.

Equally reluctant to enter, Cronan stood beside him eyeing the dark maw of the opening with narrowed eyes.

"You comin' in, or what?" Wild Bill called.

An oil lamp flickered to life within, illuminating the debris-strewn interior with an orange glow. Wild Bill's bearded face looked fierce in its light, the dark shadows accentuating his wrinkles and creases, his eyes deep-set and dark. He looked like a devil rising from the flames as he held the lamp in front of him.

A shiver ran down Tobias's spine and he took a step back. A loud rustling sounded from the undergrowth beside him, followed by strange snuffling noises. Tobias shrieked and ran inside, quickly followed by Cronan.

"W-w-what was that?" Tobias asked, his eyes wide as he stared fearfully into the bushes beyond the doorway, half expecting a monster to come charging through at any moment.

Wild Bill laughed. "Probably a wild pig. There's plenty of them running around here."

Tobias gave a nervous laugh and eased the pack from his back. Judging by the racket coming from the undergrowth, it was bigger than any pig he'd ever seen. It sounded large enough to fit with a saddle and ride. His nose wrinkled as a damp, fusty smell reached his nostrils. He glanced around the derelict interior trying to locate its source, but gave up. The whole place stank of it. He sighed. Some start to their great adventure this was. The first night out of Hope and they were about to spend it in a wild pig's latrine.

Wild Bill moved across the single-roomed dwelling and placed the lamp on the stone mantel above the soot-blackened fire-pit in the rear wall. Walking back towards Tobias and Cronan he rubbed his hands together. "Now we got here safe and sound, what we got to eat? I'm starving."

Cronan scowled as he examined the interior. After a moment he tutted, then met Wild Bill's gaze. "Nothing until we have a fire lit." He eyed the doorway warily. "At least that will keep whatever is out there at bay."

Wild Bill laughed. "Or it will encourage it to come in and get warm." When he saw the look of horror on Cronan's face his laughter subsided. "Right you are then. I'll sort out the fire while you two get supper ready."

Using the rotten timber that lay strewn around, Wild Bill soon had the fire blazing. Heat radiated out and the three companions huddled around the hearth. After a cold meal of bread and meat washed down with water Tobias felt his eyelids begin to droop, tired after the unaccustomed exertion. Despite the dilapidated condition of the hut he was relieved to be sleeping indoors. After spending all his life inside a mountain, he wasn't quite ready to try sleeping outdoors just yet, especially with enormous pigs on the prowl. He wrapped his cloak more tightly around himself and was asleep in moments.

It was not often that Tobias dreamed, but this night he did. He dreamed of dragons: reds, yellows, blues and greens. They had returned to Tiernan Og to cavort beneath clear blue skies, whistling and calling to each other in their own language. Tobias was sitting on a hillside that was covered with flowers, watching the aerial display in wonder as the dragons ducked and weaved, enjoying the freedom of the skies. A warm feeling built inside Tobias's chest as he watched. It was a magical moment.

To his amazement a radiant golden glow appeared in the middle of the flight, calling to him, trying to draw him in. Small at first, the glow grew until its brilliance dazzled him. He had to shield his eyes against the glare. The other dragons drew back from it and hovered, awaiting the arrival of whatever was within.

The glow grew bigger and bigger, getting brighter and brighter until it filled Tobias's whole vision. His head pounded with pain. He felt as if he was going blind. The other dragons had disappeared from view, engulfed by the golden light. He couldn't see. Terror gripped him. He started to sweat: something wasn't right. He wanted to scream, but was paralysed by fear.

Suddenly a huge black head shot out from the glow. It lunged straight at him, saliva dripping from long fangs. A forked tongue flicked out and its mouth formed words. "Come to me," it said.

Terrified, Tobias cowered back. "NOOO!"

The dragon's face creased into a scowl, then its head drew back and a split second later shot forward, spewing a stream of fire.

Tobias shrieked as he felt heat burning his flesh, incinerating him. He woke in a blind panic, levering himself up on one elbow before he realised it had all been a dream. He was pouring with sweat and was having difficulty breathing, such was his fright. The dream had seemed so real; he had felt the heat prickle his skin.

His nose twitched as something acrid tickled it. It smelled like burning straw, and the heat he had felt in his dream was still there. He glanced down at his legs and shrieked again. He was on fire. His scream woke Cronan and Wild Bill.

"What's up with yer, young 'un?" Wild Bill muttered, knuckling sleep from his eyes. "That pig come lookin' for yer? Randy little buggers they can be, I can tell yer."

"What's the matter?" asked Cronan.

"I'm on fire," Tobias shrieked, swatting at the smouldering spot on his leg. "I'm on fire!"

Strands of glowing thatch drifted down from above.

Wild Bill glanced up. "Bloody hell!" he shouted. "I must've used too much bleedin' wood. The damn roof's ablaze. Get yer sorry arses out of here before the whole place goes up, and us with it."

They grabbed their belongings and fled from the hut, stopping thirty paces away to look back. The fire had taken hold and the thatch was well and truly ablaze. The heat became intense as the conflagration grew and they had to shield their faces with their hands. With a mighty crash the roof collapsed into the building. Flames shot upwards and sparks flew into the nearby trees. To Tobias's alarm they started to burn along with the hut. The copse lit up as if dawn were about to break.

"Bugger me," murmured Wild Bill. "Looks like we'd better get out of here." He glanced at Tobias. "Good job you woke when you did, young 'un, otherwise we'd be toast by now."

"What snapped you awake like that?" Cronan asked.

Tobias shrugged. "The smell of smoke, and being on fire I suppose." He forced a smile and moved away, not wanting to tell Cronan of the dream. Not just yet. It was all too *real* in his mind. As they walked to the trail a shudder went through him. He couldn't shake off the feeling that the dragon in the dream wasn't a figment of his nightmare. It had seemed very, very real.

Whether it was his imagination, or the breeze whispering

through the trees, he wasn't sure, but he was convinced he heard rumbling laughter. He increased his pace until he caught up with Wild Bill, feeling safer with the big man beside him.

Dawn broke an hour later. The sun's first rays bathed the land with pale light, gradually brightening the trail that stretched before them. The grassy track snaked ahead like a well-worn carpet, green and undulating, with tufts of coarse grass sprouting in haphazard clumps. Pockets of mist hung in the hollows. Gorse, bracken and small bushes lined the route, and clusters of tall, imposing trees dotted the grassland that stretched to the mountains on either side. Colourfully plumed birds welcomed the new day noisily, twisting and diving through blue skies. Beyond the bushes the gurgling of a river could be heard as it chattered and chuckled on its way.

The horror of his dream pushed firmly to the back of his mind, Tobias marvelled at the birds' display, completely mesmerised by the wonders of the great outdoors. This is what it was all about: Nature at its best. It was everything he had imagined it to be, and more.

A large, long-tailed bird suddenly shot out from a bush, giving a startled screech as it launched itself skyward, its wings thumping the air. Tobias gave a screech of his own and stopped in his tracks, his heart racing. This was the second time in as many hours that he had been scared out of his wits.

Wild Bill's deep laugh boomed back down the trail. "It's only a pheasant, me lad. Nothing to be scared of." He shook his head and continued setting the pace.

"That's easy for you to say," Tobias muttered, resettling his pack on his shoulders before continuing. His heart thumped angrily against his rib cage.

Behind him Cronan chuckled. "It surprised me as well," he admitted. "And I knew what it was, having read about them somewhere. Game birds, I think they are. People out here catch them for food."

Tobias turned and gave his master a thoughtful look. "Are you sorry we left Hope?" he asked.

Cronan clapped him on the back. "No, lad, it had to be done." He watched the pheasant glide down and disappear in the long grass, his eyes hooded. "Although reading about things and actually experiencing them are very different." He shook his head and smiled. "Different things entirely, as I am sure we will find out." He squeezed Tobias's shoulder affectionately. "Come on. We had better increase our pace or we will lose our recently acquired guide."

Guide? Tobias grimaced. It was amazing how quickly, and readily, they had accepted a stranger to be their escort. Looking up the trail to where Wild Bill strode on, Tobias wasn't sure whether losing him might not be a blessing in disguise. They could use it as an excuse to return to Hope, if they could find their way back. His hand felt for the hilt of the knife beneath his cloak. At least they had Volgen's compass to guide them. Then again they would have the Wing Commander's anger to contend with if they did return, and traipsing around the great outside with its unknown dangers was preferable to the known danger of Volgen in a murderous mood.

Tobias still couldn't understand why Volgen hadn't come with them. Surely if the good dragons were coming back he would want to be there to welcome them himself. Deciding that it was pointless trying to work Volgen out, he concentrated on catching up with Wild Bill and Cronan, who had walked ahead, chatting, while Tobias dawdled.

The sun had reached its zenith when Wild Bill called a halt. By then Tobias was seriously flagging, and beneath his cloak his tunic was plastered to his skin with sweat. He sagged to the ground and leaned his back against a tree, gratefully accepting the water flask from Cronan and drinking his fill before handing it back.

"So how far is it to this village?" Cronan asked, passing the flask to Wild Bill.

Village? Tobias felt a nervous tingle run through his body. A village meant people: real people. People who were ... different, according to Wild Bill. He glanced across at the big man. And if they all looked like him, he wasn't looking forward to it at all.

"Should be there well before sundown," Wild Bill replied. He raised the flask to his lips and swallowed the water in noisy gulps. Little rivulets ran into his beard, disappearing in the wiry tangle. After quenching his thirst he belched and wiped his mouth with a tatty sleeve, before handing the flask back.

Cronan wiped the flask with his cloak before drinking his share.

"Although village may be a bit of a grand name to call it," Wild Bill added.

"Oh?" said Cronan.

Wild Bill shrugged. "You'll see soon enough." He grinned, revealing teeth stained green and yellow. "Now, what we got to eat?"

As Tobias nibbled on a rind of cheese, his thoughts drifted back to his dream. He hoped that this village had somewhere safe for them to sleep. Somewhere dragon-proof.

The sun hung low in the sky and the shadows had lengthened by the time they came upon a sign beside the trail. A wooden post had been hammered into the ground, next to a timber bridge spanning a narrow river. Scrawled in red paint on a scrap of planking nailed near the top of the post was the name of the village:

Hilltown
Populachun 75 - ish

They stopped beside the sign and stared up the trail. Ahead, nestled amongst gently rolling hills, they could make out buildings. Apart from one they were all single storey dwellings. With the onset of dusk the heat of the day had dissipated and tendrils of smoke were rising from some of the chimneys.

"What's that big place?" Cronan asked, pointing at the taller building sited on top of a small hill.

"That's where we be staying the night," answered Wild Bill. "The Hilltown Hotel. It's the only place around here that'll take in strangers. It's a bit posh, but after Hilltown there be nothing for three days travel, aside from some farms scattered here and there." He hefted his pack to his shoulder. "So make the most of it."

"Three days?" whispered Tobias. "Does that mean we have to sleep outside?"

Wild Bill grinned. "Yep. We can get some supplies in town."

As Wild Bill strode on Tobias looked at Cronan, fear gnawing at his belly. "I'm not ready for this," he said.

"Ready for what?" Cronan paused in his stride.

"Ready for ..." Should he tell him about the dream? He decided not and gave a weak smile. "Ready for ..." he shrugged. "You know."

Cronan raised his hand to ruffle Tobias's hair. "Neither am I," he admitted. "But it has to be done. Now come on. I'd sooner enter this town with Wild Bill than thirty paces behind him. And pull your hood up, just in case."

Cronan didn't need to elaborate for Tobias to know what he meant. After Wild Bill's warning about what the people from outside thought of the Ogmus he didn't have to.

The main thoroughfare was deserted when they entered the village. The few shops lining the dusty street were closed and dark. They passed Gran's Granary, with Dale's Deli next to it and, on the opposite side, Harry's Hardware Store and Col's Caff. A little further on a small cottage was set back from the road. Two horses were tied to a hitching rail beside the white picket fence that bordered its neatly tended garden. The horses eyed them and snorted as they passed. A sign above the door of the cottage read 'Pussy's Place'.

Tobias stopped and squinted at a narrow, full-length window beside the doorway. An old woman with grey hair scraped into a bun was sitting in a rocking chair, her knitting on her lap. The small lamp that sat on the floor beside her illuminated her saggy features with a red glow. Tobias's eyes widened. She was completely and utterly stark, bollock naked. He suddenly felt ill.

Seeing Tobias staring at her the old woman gave a lecherous grin and ran her tongue across her lips. She lifted her knitting from her lap and beckoned for Tobias to step forward for a closer look.

Tobias gave a terrified squeak and hid behind Cronan.

Beside them Wild Bill chuckled. "Probably the oldest saleable commodity in the world," he said.

"She's for sale?" queried Tobias, peering around Cronan for another look, his voice rising an octave in disbelief.

"Yep. If you fancy that sort of thing."

"What does she do?" Tobias asked, peering into Wild Bill's twinkling eyes.

"Anything yer want her to." Wild Bill laughed. "Within reason!"

Cronan turned his head and gave Tobias a stern look. "She's not for young lads such as you," he said, grabbing Tobias's arm and dragging him up the street.

As Tobias was hauled away he looked back. The old woman

gave a shrug, blew him a kiss and returned to her knitting as if nothing had happened. Tobias couldn't believe it. Who would have thought that you could hire naked old ladies to knit you woolly jumpers? The outside world was definitely a strange place.

Before long they arrived at the gravel drive leading to the Hilltown Hotel. Wild Bill took the lead as they strode towards the imposing front entrance. As they approached the short flight of steps leading to the oak doors he whispered out of the side of his mouth, "Leave all the talkin' to me. I knows about these kind of places."

A doorman stood between two fluted columns supporting the pitched canvas canopy. The light from the oil lamps either side of the entrance reflected off his highly polished, knee-high boots. He looked resplendent in his green jacket and trousers with green, peaked cap perched on his head, but as they approached his eyes grew hard and flinty and he widened his stance, lightly clasping his hands in front of him. He peered down at them with disdain. "Are *Sirs* lost?"

"Yer what?" asked Wild Bill, stopping on the second step and scratching his head.

The doorman sighed. "Are *Sirs* lost?"

Wild Bill gave a shrug. "Nope!"

"Then what are *Sirs* doing here?" The doorman's face creased in a puzzled frown.

"Lookin' fer a room."

The doorman gave a short, humourless laugh. "I think not."

"I bloody well think *so*," growled Wild Bill, his face reddening. He placed his hands on his hips and glared up at the doorman.

The doorman gave a low whistle and his right hand delved inside his jacket, reappearing holding a stout cudgel. Within seconds four muscle-bound giants emerged from the doors and stood beside him, huge clubs in their hands.

"As I was saying," said the doorman, "before I was so rudely interrupted. I think not."

Wild Bill's breath hissed out through clenched teeth. He turned to Cronan. "Give me yer money pouch," he demanded.

"Why?" snapped Cronan, hugging his side where the pouch was concealed.

"Because there are more ways to kill a ferret than one," Wild Bill retorted. "Unless yer fancy sleeping out of doors fer the night."

Encouraged by Tobias's sharp intake of breath at the mention of 'out of doors', Cronan relented and handed over the pouch. Wild Bill snatched it and fumbled with the drawstrings. Brawn overcame patience and he snapped the string and pulled out a gold coin, giving it a lingering look as he offered it to the doorman. "Will this help us find a room?"

The doorman nodded to one of the thugs beside him, who reached out and took the coin out of Wild Bill's hand. He handed it to the doorman, who inspected it for a moment before nodding. "I do hope *Sirs* enjoy their stay." He smiled and stepped aside, gesturing for them to enter.

With a gruff nod Wild Bill mounted the steps. With their hoods drawn tightly around their heads, Cronan and Tobias followed him through the large doors.

As soon as they crossed the threshold the two Ogmus stopped dead in their tracks. The sight that met their eyes was unlike anything they had seen before. The foyer was ablaze with light. A huge chandelier hung from the ceiling, the light from its twenty or thirty candles sparkling around the area through the crystal pendants that adorned it. The white marble floor and walls reflected the light with dazzling brilliance. Potted plants were dotted around the foyer, their varied shades of green helping to create a tranquil atmosphere. The heavy clump of Wild Bill's boots spoiled the mood as he strode purposefully towards the polished, mahogany reception desk that stood directly ahead.

Behind the desk stood a black-suited gentleman. He looked up from the ledger he had been studying, and a scowl furrowed his cultured brow as he saw Wild Bill approaching. He straightened and began to fiddle with his bow tie, then smoothed his oiled, dark hair. His eyes flicked nervously towards the doors behind them.

"We need a room," Wild Bill exclaimed, slapping a gold coin on the counter.

The man behind the desk flinched at the sound. Seeing the coin, however, his features transformed. A smile appeared on his face as he pulled the ledger towards him. "Of course, sir. And how many nights are we requiring the room for?"

Wild Bill turned to Cronan. "Two?"

Much to Tobias's relief, Cronan nodded. He wasn't looking forward to the three days spent sleeping in the wild.

"That'll be two nights then," said Wild Bill.

The man hummed and hawed as he ran his thumb down the page. "Two nights," he murmured. "Two nights. Now let me see. Ah, yes!" He looked up from the book and clasped his hands in front of his chest obsequiously. "The only room that we have available to accommodate a party of your —" he looked down at the two Ogmus, "— er, size, is the Penthouse suite."

"Sounds good enough to me," Wild Bill growled. "What's one of them?"

"The top floor," the man replied.

Wild Bill grunted.

"Which is," the man smoothly continued, eyeing the weighty pouch in Wild Bill's hand, "two golds per night."

There was a moment of stunned silence before Wild Bill reacted. "How much?" he thundered.

"In advance."

"Yer cheatin' ..."

The man took a pace back, his right hand shooting forward to hover over the desk-bell beside him.

Wild Bill saw the motion and sighed. Shaking his head he delved into the pouch and pulled out a further three gold coins. He tossed them onto the counter with a clatter. "I hope this includes breakfast," he grumbled.

"Of course, sir. Now I will get someone to show you and your children to your room." He snapped his fingers.

Tobias was still puzzling over the man's reference to children when a young girl appeared from a doorway behind the counter. At the sight of her all thoughts about Wild Bill being mistaken for his father fled. She was the prettiest girl he had ever seen. Not that he had seen that many, and all the ones he had come into contact with at Hope treated him as some sort of mutant because of his red hair.

The girl, her long, blonde ringlets bouncing around her head, stopped beside the man at the desk to observe the *guests*. Her deep blue eyes sparkled as she quickly scanned them. Tobias had difficulty breathing as he stared at her. He was relieved that the cowl of his cloak hid his face, otherwise she would have seen how closely she was being studied.

"Show these guests to the Wyvern Suite, Nina."

The raising of an eyebrow was the only reaction Nina gave to the choice of room. "Yes, Sir," she answered, and turned to snatch a key from the full rack behind her. She skipped round to the front of the desk. "If you would care to follow me."

Care to follow her? Tobias would have crawled over sharpened stakes, wrestled wild warthogs, fought a drag— Well, perhaps not the last one. But he needed no second urging. He was two steps behind her as she led them towards a staircase to the left of the entrance, and remained two steps behind as they climbed the stairs all the way to the attic. At the top of the stairs was an oak door inlaid with a carving of two dragons in flight. She thrust the key into the keyhole and turned it. The lock opened with an audible click.

The carvings on the door finally registered with Tobias. Dragons in flight! He stared at them. He could tell they were good dragons: they had kind faces and seemed to be playing a game of tag as they looped across the top of the arched door. Before he had the chance to stop it, a gasp escaped his lips.

Nina started at the noise. Seeing the direction of his gaze, she smiled. It was as if the sun had risen. Her smile was like no other smile Tobias had ever seen. It was the smile of ...

"What yer standin' out here fer, young 'un. Get yerself in." Wild Bill pushed Tobias in the back and sent him stumbling through the door.

Nina giggled. Tobias felt his face redden beneath the cowl.

As Wild Bill walked past, Nina handed him the key to the room. "Breakfast will be served a candle mark after dawn," she said. Giving Tobias a curious glance she left, closing the door behind her.

"Well, this is more like it," Wild Bill enthused, striding further into the room. He held his arms wide and did a pirouette on the deep-pile carpet. "Luxury."

"And so it damn well should be," Cronan grumbled, sliding his hood off his head. "It cost enough."

"Stop wittering, old 'un. It'll be hard on the road fer a while when we leave here. So we might as well make the most of it."

Tobias slowly lowered his hood so that he could see the room better. It was about twenty paces square, with a dormer window at the front and rear, set in the slopes of the roof. A red carpet covered the floor and a settee and two armchairs were arrayed around an open fire. A pile of logs was stacked neatly beside the hearth. Two doors led off to the right and one to the left.

The carvings of the dragons sprang to the forefront of Tobias's mind. "Did you see the carvings?" he asked Cronan, his voice shrill with excitement.

"What carvings?"

"The ones on the door."

Cronan frowned and shook his head. "I didn't see any carvings."

"You must have," Tobias exclaimed. "They were as plain as the nose on your face."

"The lad's gone mad," snorted Wild Bill. "All this travelling's gone to his head." He jabbed his index finger at his temple to emphasise the point.

"They *are* there," Tobias snapped as he strode to the door. "Come and see for yourselves if you don't believe me." He lifted the latch and hauled it open. "There you are," he said, pointing to the top of the arch as he glared at his companions. "Two dragons playing tag."

Wild Bill threw back his head and laughed. Cronan frowned. "Tobias," he said, "what are you talking about?"

Tobias turned and peered up at the top of the door. He gasped. The carvings were gone. The door was plain and unadorned. "B-b-but I saw them," he said, not understanding how they could have disappeared.

Wild Bill shook his head and walked over to a cabinet in the corner of the room. "Close that door, young 'un. Yer lettin' a draught in." He opened the cabinet and pulled out a bottle of spirit from within. Uncapping it, he took a sniff. "Bloody hell! It's ouiskey. Single malt, if I'm not mistaken. And I'm rarely mistaken with this stuff." He raised the bottle to his lips and took a drink. "Ahhh! It bleedin well is, an' all." He took another swig.

Tobias was oblivious, staring at the door and willing the carvings to reappear so that he could show Cronan and Wild Bill that he wasn't mad. But the door remained maddeningly plain.

"Come in, Tobias," Cronan said gently. "I think we could all do with some sleep."

As Cronan turned away Tobias started to close the door. He stared at the spot where the carvings had been, still convinced he had seen them. When the door was half closed he grunted with surprise. Cronan turned and stared at him. "What's the matter, Tobias?" he asked.

Tobias closed the door and stood facing it for a moment to compose himself. He didn't want his master to see the look of shock on his face. How could he explain that a dragon's head had just materialised out of the woodwork, winked at him, then disappeared as quickly as it had appeared?

"Nothing, Cronan. Nothing at all," he answered eventually. He turned to face into the room, holding his hand to his chest. "I got pricked by a splinter, that's all."

Cronan harrumphed, then switched his attention to Wild Bill. "If you have quite finished," he snapped, "will you put that bottle back where it belongs, before you end up completely pissed."

Tobias giggled at Cronan's use of the vernacular. That was twice in as many days he had heard his master cuss. It was getting to be quite a habit.

Chapter Eleven

Nina stared at the closed door in disbelief. The boy had seen them! He had seen the dragons! A smile crept over her face. He was the one. The one her grandmother had said would come. And he was staying in the very same room her grandmother had said he would; the room on which she had placed a glamour, to be triggered by *his* arrival. Nina clapped her hands in delight. Ever since she was a small child she had listened to her gran's outrageous tales of the good dragons, never quite believing them but hoping they were true. She'd passed them off as the ramblings of a senile old woman for the most part, but loved to listen to them anyway. She brushed a stray ringlet of hair from her eyes. She would have to tell her gran straight away; tell her that she had been right. That *he* was here. The Terminator!

The latch lifted and the door opened. Nina caught a glimpse of fiery red hair before she darted out of sight. Fortunately the boy was looking back into the room as he pointed to the top of the door, so he didn't see her hovering on the stairs.

Nina tiptoed down, barely holding her excitement in check. She frowned as she stepped out onto the first floor landing. She would have to think of a reason that Herrol, the owner, would believe for finishing early, so she could go and tell her gran. That might prove easier said than done. She pursed her lips. Perhaps it would be best to rely on the tried and tested story that her gran was ill: she hadn't used that excuse for a while.

Nina found Herrol exactly where she had left him, standing behind the reception counter studying the ledger. He looked up as she approached. "Our guests are suitably settled?" he asked, his voice the usual mix of boredom and cultured tones.

"Yes, Mister Herrol."

"Good!" Herrol bent down to the ledger again, his index finger moving down a set of figures beside the room numbers. He breathed heavily through his nose and shook his head. "This is not good," he murmured. "Not good at all."

"What isn't?" Nina asked, peering at the neatly written figures. Some of them were written in black ink, but most were in red.

Herrol looked up, his blue eyes sharp and piercing. "Haven't you got work to do?" he snapped.

Nina stepped back under his hostile gaze. She stared at her feet and fiddled with the hem of her apron. "I was wondering ..."

"Out with it, girl."

"I was wondering if I could have the night off." She heard the sharp intake of breath and looked up, a glimmer of tears in her eyes. "It's my Nanna ..."

"That witch?" Herrol virtually spat the word, making it sound like a euphemism for something he'd just trodden in. "What is the matter with her now? Has her broomstick struck back and refused to carry her, or has that cat of hers given her fleas?"

Nina was used to the unkind way people talked about her gran. Although their comments hurt, she had become inured to them and for the most part ignored them. She would like to see their faces if they knew that she really could do magic, and not the potion and powder kind either. With practised ease Nina forced tears to spill down her cheeks, an art she had perfected years ago. "She really is ill," she whimpered.

Herrol glared at her for a moment, then pursed his lips. "Go! Go and see what is wrong with the old harridan, then you had better get back here to bed." His eyes narrowed and a sneer formed on his face. "Because you will work a double shift tomorrow to make up for it. We have guests to attend to, and we cannot afford to upset them. Understand? Guests mean money!"

Nina nodded and raised her hand to wipe away the tears. "Thank you, Mister Herrol."

He shooed her away. "Vamoose, before I change my mind."

Nina turned and fled. Pulling the doors open she rushed out, clattering into Grolff the doorman.

"Steady on there, young lady." Grolff chuckled and caught her by the shoulders as she stumbled past. "What's the rush?" Noticing the tears in her eyes he gave the entrance a hard glare. "Has *he* been giving you trouble again?" he asked.

Nina shook her head and smiled. "No. I needed some time off, and ..."

Grolff laughed. "Off to see your gran, hey? What has she been up to this time?"

"Nothing," said Nina, with a grin. "I just want to ask her something, that's all."

"Well take care, young lady, and make sure that Herrol doesn't make you work doubly hard for the privilege."

"He already is," she retorted with a scowl. "Double shift tomorrow, because we actually have guests for a change."

Grolff sighed. "Times are hard for everyone, Nina, with the Blackabbots demanding ever higher levies." He shook his head. "Not so long ago this place would have been full to bursting, and we would not have admitted the likes of *those* guests, no matter how much gold they carried."

"They don't seem too bad." Nina smiled and skipped down the steps leading to the drive. She stopped at the bottom and gave Grolff a wave. "See you later."

Grolff doffed his cap in farewell and smiled.

The full moon cast its luminescence on the village of Hilltown. Everything appeared silvery under its light, with scattered orange glowing from windows not curtained against the night. The scent of wood smoke drifted on the early spring breeze, a reminder of how chill the night air still was. Nina shivered, wishing she had stopped to collect a coat from her room before leaving. It wasn't far to her gran's, so she wouldn't have to suffer the goosebumps for too long.

In a few minutes she neared the white picket fence that bordered her gran's garden, and frowned as she saw her gran's horses, Snowdrop and Buttercup, hitched outside. The sight was unusual. Her gran never left the horses out unless she was going to use them to pull her cart. And it was too late for her to be going on a visit.

Then she noticed the pale, pink light filtering onto the neatly tended lawn. A leaden feeling settled in the pit of her stomach and she quickened her pace. When she reached the gate and looked at the cottage her fears were confirmed. Her gran was sitting in the window, stark naked, doing her knitting. Nina groaned, hoping that no one had seen her. It was no wonder the villagers gave her such a hard time.

Nina pulled the gate open, stepped through, and slammed it shut with a crash before striding up the path.

Her gran heard the commotion. She looked up and squinted

into the night to see who approached. When Nina stepped into the light her jaw dropped and her knitting fell to the floor, forgotten. She bounded to her feet and disappeared from view. Moments later the door opened and Nina's gran stood framed in the light that spilled out, a long woollen night-gown draped over her thin body.

"Nanna Pussy!" Nina scolded, folding her arms across her chest. "After all we have said about ... about ..."

"Yes, dear?" her gran said, with an encouraging smile.

"Ohhh!" Nina barged past her into the cottage. She strode to the window niche and drew the curtains.

Lying beside the rocking chair, Baggles the cat raised his head and gave a wide yawn. He stretched his forelegs, dug his claws into the carpet and arched his back before giving Nina a meow of welcome. Nina stooped to tickle him under the jaw.

"Was there something you wanted, dear?" Nanna Pussy asked as she shuffled across the room to Nina, her arms wrapped around her middle.

Nina straightened and gave her best glare.

Nanna Pussy smiled and shrugged. "I was too warm."

"How many?"

"Ey?"

"How many?"

"How many what, dear?"

"How many callers?"

Nanna Pussy looked at the floor, a sad smile on her face. "No callers tonight." She shook her head, then looked up. "No callers tonight, or any night for that matter. There was a time when ..."

Nina sighed and stepped forward to embrace her. She crushed her close and patted her back. "I know, Nanna. I know."

"I can't help it, you know," her gran whispered. "It's the dragons' blood that does it. The dragons' blood that flows through these narrow veins."

There was a plaintive tone in her gran's voice that Nina knew only too well. She was always the same when her 'time', as she called it, came upon her. Like the dragons of her tales she claimed she had mating seasons and couldn't resist the urge when her hormones were charged. The craving to find a mate was strong in her, so she said. Fortunately the season only came every two years and lasted for two days. Two long days of Nina attempting to keep her indoors and fully clothed. The last time her 'time' had occurred she was in the village bakeshop. By the time Nina was called her gran had stripped naked, covered herself in icing and was asking the petrified baker to 'lick me clean, big boy'. Nina shuddered at the thought. Soon after the baker left town and they hadn't seen him since.

"Although there was this young lad."

Nina froze, then held her gran at arms' length. "What?"

Her gran smiled, her eyes gazing into space. "He reminded me of someone I once knew."

"Who?"

Her gran jolted back to the present. "Hmm?"

"Who did he remind you of?"

"Who, dear?"

"That's what I asked," said Nina.

"Did you?"

Nina sighed. She wrapped an arm around her gran's shoulders and guided her back into the main room. "How about I make us a nice hot tisane?"

"That would be nice, dear."

Sitting her in the armchair in front of the fire, Nina moved across the room and fetched the kettle from the dresser. Her gran lived with the minimum of comforts. Aside from the armchair, the rocker and the dresser, the room contained little. But it was always kept immaculate, the carpet clean and the dresser dusted. And there was always a fire blazing in the hearth, no matter how warm the day.

Nina filled the kettle and hung it on the boiling-hook over the fire. Before long it was steaming, and wrapping a cloth around the handle she lifted it and poured hot water into two clay mugs. The smell of herbs rose from within. Nina breathed deeply of the aromatic fragrance before handing one of the mugs to Nanna Pussy. She wasn't surprised to see that Baggles had moved to lie on her gran's lap. The big black cat gazed at Nina with half-closed eyes, a self-satisfied smirk on his face.

"Thank you, my dear. Now what were you saying about whoever it was?"

"I wasn't. You were," replied Nina, sitting on the arm of the chair and taking a sip of her drink.

"Was I?" Nanna Pussy shook her head. "This memory of mine, it gets worse as I get older." She raised the mug to her lips and took a noisy slurp.

"But I was going to ask *you* about something. Well someone really."

Nanna Pussy looked up, her eyes questioning.

"The Terminator."

Nanna Pussy nodded. "You want to hear about him? He was always one of your favourites." She patted Nina's leg and smiled.

"Who is he?" Nina asked.

"I've no idea," Nanna Pussy answered. "But I do know that only he can release the good dragons from whence they were banished, terminating the tyrannical, soul-crushing reign of those ba—"

"Nanna Pussy!"

Her gran looked up, her eyes wide and innocent. "Yes, dear?"

Nina sighed. "Nothing, Nanna. So tell me, how is this Terminator to do this?"

Nanna Pussy shrugged. "If I knew that I would do it myself, dear." She patted Nina's leg again. "I don't even know where they are, let alone how to get them back."

"So you have no idea who this Terminator is?"

Nanna Pussy shook her head. "But the door will," she said, raising her mug.

A companionable silence settled between them while Nina pondered the best way to approach telling her gran about the door. Baggles, seeming to sense that Nina was wrestling with some internal dilemma, raised his head and began to rub it against her leg. She reached down absent-mindedly and scratched him behind the ears. Baggles purred.

"Nanna?"

"Yes, dear?"

"How is it you know so much about the dragons? About them being tricked by the blacks and needing this Terminator to release them?"

"Because I am a witch, dear. Surely you know that?" Her golden eyes twinkled with amusement.

Nina pursed her lips. She had expected that answer. It was the one her gran always gave. "Oh. And what would you do if this Terminator appeared?"

The mug stopped half way to Nanna Pussy's lips, and the eyes that stared at Nina were suddenly bright with interest. "What was that, my dear?"

Nina fidgeted on the arm of the chair, staring into her mug as she swirled the tisane. After a moment, in hushed tones, she said, "The dragons appeared on the door."

The mug dropped from Nanna Pussy's hands. Its contents spilled on to Baggles, who leapt to the floor with a yowl of displeasure. He glared at Nanna Pussy reproachfully before sitting down in front of the fire and cleaning himself.

"Are you all right, Nanna?" asked Nina, rising to her feet.

Oblivious of the hot wetness that soaked into her night-gown, Nanna Pussy stared at the fire, her eyes wide and bright. "He's here!" she whispered.

Nina shrugged. "The dragons appeared on the door when he went into the room, like you said they would," she said. "So it must be him, mustn't it?"

Nanna Pussy rose quickly to her feet, almost knocking Nina off the arm of the chair. "Then we must go and meet him," she said. "And tell him of his obligations."

"Now?"

Nanna Pussy nodded and strode towards her sleeping area, a curtained alcove at the other side of the entrance. She stopped and scratched her head. "Now where are my clothes? I had them somewhere, but for the life of me I can't remember where I took them off."

Nina shook her head and placed her mug on the mantle. "This Terminator is asleep," she said. "And I daren't wake him or Herrol will have a fit. You know what he's been like lately."

Nanna Pussy harrumphed. "He's nothing but a jumped up little nerk, just like his father was." She placed her hands on her hips and did another scan of the room. "Now help me find my clothes will you, dear?"

"Tomorrow!" said Nina. "Once he has awoken I will come and get you and then we can both see him together. It will be less daunting for him than being woken in the middle of the night and interrogated. He only seems young, about the same age as I am. Anyway, I heard them say they were staying for two days, so ..."

"They?" Nanna Pussy turned to face Nina, her eyes narrowing.

Nina nodded. "He has two companions. One of them is that rogue Wild Bill Halfcock, the other I didn't see because a cowl covered his face. But there are definitely three of them." She took her arm and steered her back to the armchair. Nina was taken aback by how frail her gran felt. Although she was never a well-built woman, she never used to be this thin. "And another thing, he may not even know who he is. About being this Terminator, I mean. So you barging in firing questions at him might upset him."

Nanna Pussy sighed as she allowed herself to be led to the chair. "Yes, dear. You are right, as always." She gave Nina a friendly smile as she sat down. "We must plan this properly, so as not to scare the young man off. As you say, he may not even know he is the Terminator."

Nina stooped and gave her a hug. As she straightened she said, "I have to go now. I have to work a double shift tomorrow, so I am on early. I will come and get you as soon as I have served breakfast, then we can go and meet this Terminator together."

"As you say, dear." Nanna Pussy raised her hand to stifle a yawn. "I'm tired, and these things are best sorted when fully alert." Her eyelids fluttered as she fought to keep them open. "All that knitting has fair tired me out."

Nina smiled. "What about the horses?"

"Horses, dear?"

"Snowdrop and Buttercup. They're still outside tethered to the hitching rail."

"Don't you be worrying about them, dear. They'll be fine until morning."

"If you're sure," said Nina, walking to the door.

Nanna Pussy stifled another yawn. "I am sure, dear. You get yourself to bed. We have a busy day ahead of us tomorrow." Her head nodded forward and her eyelids closed.

Not wanting to disturb her, Nina quietly eased the door open, and after one last glance at the sleeping figure, slipped outside and closed it softly behind her. Her gran was right, she did have a busy day on the morrow. Folding her arms across her chest for warmth, Nina headed back to the hotel at a brisk pace.

Soon after Nina had left Nanna Pussy cracked open an eye. After a quick scan of the room she opened the other and rose to her feet, a cunning smile forming on her face. He was here! The Terminator! Why put off till tomorrow what you could do today? With a spring in her step she hurried across to the sleeping area, surprising Baggles, who was fast asleep in front of the fire. He gave a startled screech and darted out of the way as Nanna Pussy strode past.

"Don't you be getting in Nanna Pussy's way, Mister Baggles. There's a good cat. Nanna has something very important to do. Something very important indeed."

Baggles blinked at the retreating figure and resettled himself in front of the fire. He wrapped his tail around his body and closed his eyes, oblivious to the noise and cussing that was coming from the sleeping area.

Chapter Twelve

Like a polecat in a hen house, a liar amongst politicians or a fart in a crowded room, the shadow felt perfectly at home as it sidled along the front wall of the Hilltown Hotel: a black-clad figure skulking between dark shadows. With stealth born from need it disappeared around the right hand gable and padded towards the rear of the building, where the tradesmen's entrance was located. The shadow stopped at the end of the wall to check that no one was in sight. To its satisfaction nothing moved in the pale light of the moon. The manicured, silver-caressed gardens behind the hotel were silent. With a grim smile of determination the shadow stepped out and round, controlling the eagerness that made it want to run. Too much haste would attract attention; attention it did not want.

The length of time it took to reach the door felt like a full candle-mark but was, in fact, considerably less. When the shadow finally reached it, its nerves were all aflutter and it leaned back against the wall to still its racing heart, short, sharp breaths vaporising in front of its face.

A loud clatter broke the silence as a bottle skittered along the ground. The shadow shrieked. It was only a short one, high-pitched and girly, but it was definitely a shriek. The shadow jumped, stifling another scream as something rubbed against its leg. Something that was small, warm, furry, and purring with satisfaction.

Nanna Pussy pulled the black balaclava from her head and glowered at Baggles. "Mister Baggles," she snapped in hushed tones, "if you've quite finished scaring the pants off me, will you kindly take yourself off home this minute!"

At the sound of her voice Baggles looked up, blinked, and resumed his rubbing.

Nanna Pussy pursed her lips and put her hands on her hips. This wouldn't do, wouldn't do at all: she was on a dangerous and vital mission, and couldn't have Mister Baggles spoiling everything. Deciding that there was nothing else for it, she stooped and scratched the cat behind the ear, all the while mumbling to herself. Baggles continued purring, enjoying the attention, and peered up at Nanna Pussy with eyes half-closed. Suddenly they widened, before snapping shut. Even before the cat flopped to the ground he was snoring.

With a grunt of satisfaction Nanna Pussy straightened and pulled down her balaclava. It was time to resume her mission, but first she had to make sure that Mister Baggles wouldn't come to any harm while he took his enforced nap. Lifting the comatose body, she padded across the lawn and laid him under a bush, then returned to the tradesmen's entrance.

Giving the handle a twist, she cursed under her breath as the door remained firmly closed. Four quietly mumbled words later it unlocked with a soft click and she eased it open and slipped inside. Closing the door softly behind her she waited a few moments to let her fast-beating heart settle, before slowly moving forward. The hallway was pitch black, but she could see where she was going thanks to the legacy of her past life. She carefully placed one foot in front of the other, as she made her way along the narrow corridor. When she passed the door leading to the kitchen her nose detected the smell of the day's cooking in the blackness beyond. She grimaced. The aroma of stale food was not one of her favourites; she much preferred her food fresh.

The next door after the kitchen led to the dinning room, which she knew was just off the reception foyer. With the lateness of the hour no one should be around except, perhaps, for the night porter. She chuckled to herself. Old Bart was so deaf he wouldn't hear her, and, to cap it all, he was as blind as a bat. Some watchman he made! She doubted whether he would notice her if she did cartwheels across the floor and sang 'Ten Full Barrels' at the top of her voice. Still, there was no harm in being cautious. There might be others around.

When she reached the dining room she leaned against the door and pressed her ear to its surface. All was quiet. She smiled and stepped back, her black-gloved hand reaching for the latch.

Suddenly her left eye started twitching and her nose began to tickle; she was going to sneeze. It must be the fibres from the balaclava; she'd always had a mild allergy to wool. She snatched the balaclava from her head and began to frantically rub at her nose. To her relief, it seemed to work. She leaned forward and pressed her ear to the door once again. And sneezed.

It wasn't an everyday, run of the mill type of sneeze, either. It was a door-rattling, nose-blasting, eye-watering nasal explosion. Nanna's head shot forward and hit the door with a dull thud. Knocked half senseless by the impact and seeing stars in front of her eyes, she didn't hear the footsteps approaching until they were nearly at the door, but as it slowly opened she managed to step behind it.

"W-w-who's there?" Herrol's quavering voice called into the darkness. "I w-w-warn you, I have f-four ... no, ten b-b-big men with me."

Nanna Pussy saw Herrol's oiled-back hair as his head poked into view. A thin smile formed on her face, her dizziness suddenly disappearing. With a strength that belied her slight frame she slammed into the door, sending it hammering into Herrol's head. The hotel owner gave a grunt of pain before he fell unconscious to the floor.

Pleased with the outcome of her resourcefulness, Nanna Pussy stepped from behind the door and gazed dispassionately down at Herrol. How she despised the man. He was weak, grasping and ineffectual. Were it not for the fact that he was the only person in the village who would employ the granddaughter of a 'witch', she would have cursed him with the pox years ago. Not that it would have done her any good, other than giving her immense satisfaction, as the villagers would have run her out of town at the first whiff of 'magic' in the air. She knew they only suffered her living there because they thought she *might* be a witch. If they actually had proof she could do magic it would be another matter entirely.

Now she had a different problem to contend with: what she should do with Herrol. She had no idea how long he would be out cold. If he regained consciousness before she had completed her mission the alarm would be raised and she *would* be run out of town. She flicked a glance towards the kitchen as an idea formed in her mind. Stooping to grasp Herrol by the arms she dragged him along the corridor. If she couldn't use magic, there were other options at hand that would teach him a lesson.

She manoeuvred him into the kitchen and laid him face down on the floor. A quick search of the area armed her with a piece of cloth used for drying dishes and some twine used for tying rolls of meat. She made her way back to Herrol and bound his arms and legs, then tied his hands to his feet, effectively manacling him.

Lifting Herrol's head up by his hair, she squawked in surprise as his wig came off in her hand. She stared at the hairpiece in amazement, then turned her gaze on Herrol's head and began to chuckle. It was as smooth as an eggshell, apart from the small dabs of paste dotting the skin where the hairpiece had been stuck on. Whoever would have thought she could add vanity to the list of things she despised about him. She tucked the hairpiece under her arm before gagging the insensible figure. Taking the oily mop with her, she padded down the corridor and in to the dining room.

Across the room she could see the door leading through to the reception area. It was partially open. A narrow shaft of light cut through the darkness, slicing across the floor and up the wall, neatly bisecting a painting of Herrol's father. Nanna snorted. She remembered the old fool well, may the gods stomp on his foul-tempered soul. Whoever it was that had laced his brandy with belladonna had done the village a huge favour. To this day Nanna suspected Herrol of doing away with the old man, as did half the village. But in most ways Herrol was more of a rogue than the one who went before him, so the matter had been quickly forgotten.

After one last glance at the painting, Nanna tiptoed forward and peered around the door leading to the foyer. The sound of Bart's gentle snoring drew her gaze to where the night-watchman sat sleeping in a chair beside the reception desk. His head, fringed by short-cropped grey hair, lolled back, his mouth open, revealing teeth discoloured by decay.

With a wry smile Nanna scanned the rest of the area before stepping out, her black-slippered feet barely making a sound on the marble floor. It would appear that she would be safe from discovery by Bart, at any rate.

When she was half way to the stairs she remembered the hairpiece tucked under her arm and grinned as a mischievous plan hatched. She quietly returned to the reception desk.

When next she walked to the stairs it was to leave a snoring night-watchman sprawled in his chair, blissfully unaware that he was sporting a new hairstyle. Nanna glanced back as she stepped on the first tread. Bart looked rather fetching with a full head of slicked back, black hair. She could almost fancy him. Almost. Fortunately for her, her 'time' was fast fading, taking any thoughts of carnal desire with it. Then again it was probably more fortunate for Bart. She doubted whether the man's heart would cope with Nanna Pussy looking for sexual gratification. After all, he must be all of sixty-five. A mere one thousand, four hundred and fifty cycles younger than she was. Her soft, throaty chuckles filtered through the balaclava as she mounted the stairs.

When she reached the arched door leading to the attic room two dragons materialised out of the woodwork. They played and cavorted in excitement as Nanna placed a hand upon the latch. She raised the forefinger of her free hand and gestured for calm as the dragons smiled their welcome. Once they had settled Nanna tried the latch. It lifted and the door opened a fraction. Thankful that she did not have to use her magic and further tire herself, she pushed it open and stepped through. The room was in darkness, but loud snores emanated from behind a closed door on her left. They sounded too old and nasal for a young man, so she discounted the room from being the one the Terminator would be sleeping in.

Seeing the two doors on the right, she tiptoed across the room. When she reached the first she leaned forward to listen. She heard soft snores, but didn't get the right 'feeling' for the person within to be the one she was looking for.

She moved to the second door. Her heart started to beat faster and her mouth went dry. Tears sprang to her eyes. She could *feel* that this was the room, that beyond the wooden door slept the man who was to set her beloved dragons free. The Terminator!

A voice cried out from within. "Leave me be!"

Nanna Pussy froze, her eyes wide. Was the Terminator in trouble? Had one of Herrol's thugs sneaked in to rob him? Without pausing for thought she opened the door and sprang into the room, dropping into a crouch as she prepared to do battle. To her surprise the room was devoid of anything resembling assailants. She slowly straightened, the adrenaline still pumping through her body. She felt like a coiled spring, ready to lash out at whoever or whatever came her way. But to her further puzzlement nothing did. Apart from the young boy sleeping in the bed, no one else was in the room. Except for her. She began to relax.

"Leave me alone!" the boy shouted. He began to thrash around in the bed, his arms flailing.

Recovering from her initial shock at the outburst, Nanna rushed forward to kneel beside him, fumbling with one of her gloves as she tried to pull it off. Finally, in exasperation, she ripped it free and threw it to the floor. She placed her palm on the boy's forehead. Her hand flew up as if it had been scalded. He was burning up. He felt as though he was on fire. Something wasn't right, of that she was sure.

Not pausing to think about the wisdom of such an approach, she placed her palm on his forehead and sent her spirit forward. It flowed down her arm and out through her splayed fingers into the mind of the troubled soul who lay before her.

In his delirium the boy lashed out, his fist catching Nanna on the cheek, but she didn't flinch. Her concentration remained firmly fixed on calming him. Having just found the one who was to release the good dragons she wasn't going to let a bruised cheek stop her from helping him to battle his personal demons.

Her spirit flew into the boy's mind; flew into his world of fantasy, the world that was trying to take him away from her. It took her a moment to realise what world it was, and when she did she almost fled back the way she had come. Almost.

* * * * *

As dreams go, Tobias's was turning out to be a classic; one that he didn't want to wake from in case he forgot it. And he certainly didn't want to forget this one. He was in heaven, but it seemed so *real*. He *was* dreaming, wasn't he? He had to be. He'd only clapped eyes on Nina for the first time a few hours ago, and he certainly didn't remember inviting her for a walk in the country. And to have her lying on the grass beside him, relaxing in the warm rays of the sun and enjoying his company? He must be dreaming. The only woman who'd ever cast him anything that resembled sexual flirtation was the old crone back at Hope, if you counted offering a shag as flirtation.

With the realisation that it was a dream came a tinge of sadness. It looked like he'd better make the most of it, because when he woke she was likely to pay him as much attention as all the other girls did. None!

He rolled onto his side and propped his head on his hand so he could gaze down at her. She was perfect in every detail. He loved the splash of freckles across her nose and the mass of blonde ringlets surrounding her elfin features. And she was perfectly formed. He felt his face redden as his gaze strayed to the two bumps on her chest. His face positively glowed when she opened her eyes and saw where he was looking.

To Tobias's amazement Nina's pale, delicate hands rose to the buttons on her dress and began to tease them open one by one, revealing the porcelain flesh beneath. When the valley between the two mounds began to appear, Tobias felt stirrings in an area where he wasn't accustomed to such things. His breath began to quicken. His whole body grew hot and he began to sweat. His mouth went dry. He was mesmerised by those delicate fingers as they worked their way down the dress. They were at the belly button now. Only a couple more and they would be at ...

Nina's flirtatious giggle broke the spell. His eyes snapped to hers. She was staring at him, warm and welcoming. "Come to me," she breathed, teasing the last button open. Her eyes held his as she opened her dress to reveal the splendour of the body beneath. "Come to me."

Eyes? Since when had Nina had deep, bottomless, black eyes? He was sure they were blue. And why had her incisors become long, sharp and pointy? The hot flush disappeared, replaced by cold dread. All of a sudden he wanted the dream to end. He scrambled to his hands and knees and began to back away.

"Come to me."

The voice! That wasn't the voice of a young girl. It was the voice of the ...

Black, scaled claws shot forward and gripped his arms. They felt like vices as they dug into his flesh. He screamed in terror as Nina's features dissolved, transforming into those of a dragon. A black dragon. Her body changed, growing bigger, more bulbous, more grotesque by the second.

"I said come to me!" the dragon rumbled.

Tobias began to thrash. "Leave me be!"

The dragon laughed. Saliva dripped from long fangs as it drew its huge head close to Tobias's. "You will come to me, you know. Whether you like it or not."

"Leave me alone!" Tobias shrieked, thrashing ever more wildly. But it was useless, he was trapped. The dragon laughed again, its hot, foetid breath making Tobias gag.

Suddenly a dark shadow loomed over them. "Leave the boy alone, Mandrake," a soft, rumbling voice said.

The black dragon's brow furrowed in puzzlement at the intrusion. He looked up and the grip on Tobias's arms eased.

With a mighty wrench Tobias pulled free. He went sprawling to the ground, but immediately scrambled out of the black dragon's reach. When he felt he was far enough away to be safe he rose to his feet and looked back. His eyes widened. There were two of them!

Directly in front of the black dragon was another of the beasts, only this one was different. It was golden, and bigger. From the tip of its snout to the slender tip of its ridged tail it was the colour of burnished gold. It was a magnificent creature; a creature of myth and legend. Even in Tobias's dreams he had not imagined such splendour. It had to be one of the good dragons, didn't it?

As if sensing his confusion, the golden dragon's head turned and it fixed eyes the size of dinner plates on him. Golden eyes! Then, to Tobias's amazement, it winked.

A voice whispered on the breeze, so faint that it took Tobias a moment to realise the word that had been spoken. What was it the voice had said? 'Mummy,' that was it. The voice had definitely said, 'Mummy.' He looked at the black dragon. It hadn't moved and its face was frozen in a look of bewilderment. Then it spoke.

"Mummy?"

The golden dragon grimaced. "More's the pity, you traitorous scumbag."

"But you're, you're ..."

"Here!" The golden dragon stretched her neck until her face was inches from the black's. "So, unless you want to feel *mummy's* wrath, you'd better crawl back to the hole you slithered out from, you ..."

The speed of the strike nearly took the golden dragon by surprise. The talons of Mandrake's foreleg raked across her shoulder as she swayed to avoid the blow. Small droplets of red blood welled in the scratches, scarlet against gold.

The black dragon saw them and sneered. "You're too old and too slow," he snarled. "And you can't harm me — us — in the *real* world. You're not really here, you're ... SOMEWHERE ELSE!" The last was said in a roar that made Tobias flinch. "I know where you are, and who put you there. And you aren't never coming back."

"Ever, dear," said the gold, cradling her injured shoulder.

The black dragon frowned, taken aback. "What was that, Mummy *dear?*"

"The word you're looking for is 'ever', not 'never'."

The black's face clouded with rage. He reared and bellowed his anger to the skies, before turning to face the gold. "Always the clever one, weren't we? Well not clever enough, as you found out." With a final roar of defiance the black winked out of existence. One second he was there, all bulging muscle and slathering muzzle, the next gone.

For a brief moment the golden dragon stared at the spot he had occupied, then she swung her head to face Tobias. She gave a heavy sigh and waddled towards him. "He wasn't always like that," she said with a smile. "Once he was quite a likeable little bastard."

That was more than enough for Tobias. This dream had turned into a nightmare. Progressing from a naked girl to a black dragon and then to a golden dragon, who knew what would happen next? A herd of prancing wildebeest pirouetting to the latest offering by Hope's Bullshoy Ballet? It was way past time he was awake. Surely the state of wakefulness could be no worse than the state of his dreams?

When he awakened and saw the black-clad figure sprawled on the bed beside him, he realised that in all probability it could.

Chapter Thirteen

The sound of Mandrake's mind-speak roused Jophrey from a dreamless sleep. *'Jophrey, wake up. We need to talk. Jophrey? Jophrey!'*

Jophrey lurched upright in bed with a start, his eyes flicking around the room looking for the speaker. But it was as black as the inside of a coal-miner's sock and he couldn't see a thing. The sun was still hours from rising, and no hint of pre-dawn light lifted the darkness.

"Wh-who's there?" Jophrey called, knuckling the sleep from his eyes.

'It is I, Mandrake,' came the dragon's reply. *'I need to speak with you. Now!'*

'Can't it wait?' Jophrey asked, a little peeved at being woken so rudely. *'Wooster had me cleaning soot out of my father's chambers all day yesterday, and I'm worn out.'* He sensed more than heard the dragon's sharp intake of breath, and realised that the beast would not take 'later' for an answer. *'I'm on my way,'* he said, with a sigh.

'Good boy,' the dragon purred. *'I knew I could rely on you. Do not keep me waiting too long.'*

Jophrey had a quick wash with cold water and threw on his clothes, before making his way down the rough-hewn steps to the dragon's lair. He wondered why Mandrake had to wake him in the middle of the night to discuss whatever was bothering him. It must be important for the dragon to make such a fuss about seeing him at such an ungodly hour.

He paused at the threshold of the huge, vaulted cavern. Mandrake was pacing the torch-lit room, his long tail flicking from side to side. He didn't look like he was in the best of moods.

"What's the matter?" Jophrey asked, walking forward, doing his best to hide his unease.

Mandrake stopped his pacing and swung his head to look at him. His lips curled back in a smile. "Jophrey! Well met!" His head dipped lower until it was level with Jophrey's. "We have matters to discuss."

"What matters?" Jophrey asked, stopping in front of Mandrake, his brows drawn into a frown.

The dragon sat on his haunches. "It would appear that a rogue element has entered our plans. One that could disrupt everything we are working towards."

The frown on Jophrey's face deepened. "A rogue element?"

Mandrake nodded. "It would appear that there is another with the power. One who has the spark of Ogmus within him."

Jophrey gaped. He thought he was unique; one of a kind. "Another?"

"And it would seem he is working for the others. The demon queen and her horde."

Jophrey felt the colour drain from his face, wondering how the demon dragons had managed to gain an ally on this world. "Does this person have a name?"

Mandrake growled deep in his throat. "Tobias, I believe he is called." The words came out low and menacing.

Jophrey gasped as though he had been punched in the stomach. "T-Tobias?"

It was the dragon's turn to frown. "Why? Do you know of him?"

"Know of him?" Jophrey gave a humourless laugh. "You could say that. He was the one I conned into giving me the information about the Book of Prophesies. He's working with Cronan and the Wing Commander to try to bring back the *supposed* good dragons."

"Well it would seem they have the advantage, as they know where this Snor'kel will appear." His eyes hardened as he dipped his head to peer at Jophrey. "We must find out that information."

"How?" Try as he might, Jophrey couldn't keep the tremor from his voice. He had a bad feeling about where this was leading.

The dragon smiled. "I have a plan; here is what you must do ..."

Two marks of the candle later, Jophrey stood at the door leading to the guest rooms where his father had been domiciled while his own quarters were reconstructed. He had been standing there for a while and hadn't yet mustered the courage to knock on the door. The sun had only just risen and it was unlikely that his father would be awake.

Deciding that if he was going to be ready and away from Mandragle Castle before lunch he'd better get on with it, Jophrey raised his hand and knocked twice on the door.

There was no response. As he raised his hand to knock again the door opened to reveal Wooster, immaculately dressed in black leggings, black long-coat, white shirt, black bow tie and white gloves. He peered down his nose at Jophrey and raised an eyebrow in query.

Jophrey felt his face redden and dropped his gaze to the floor.

"Yes?" asked Wooster.

Jophrey looked up and gave a weak smile. "Is my father awake?"

Wooster inclined his head. "But he is not receiving visitors. He is not feeling too well. After the other night, you understand."

Jophrey grimaced.

"Maybe later," said Wooster, stepping back and starting to close the door.

Jophrey lunged forward and pushed against it. "But I have to see him, now!"

Wooster pushed him back. "I said 'later'," he ground between gritted teeth.

"Now!" snapped Jophrey.

"Later!"

"Now!"

Lord Blackbishop's voice called out from within the room. "Who is making that infernal racket?"

"No one," shouted Wooster.

"Jophrey!" yelled Jophrey at the same time.

"No one Jophrey?" queried Blackbishop. "Who's he?"

"It's me, father," shouted Jophrey, exerting more pressure on the door, which Wooster had nearly managed to close. "I need to speak with you now! It's urgent."

"Jophrey?"

"He's not well," growled Wooster, locking eyes with Jophrey. "Go away!"

"No!" Jophrey's arms ached with the strain of trying to force the door open.

"Why didn't you say so?" Blackbishop's voice said, from closer than before. "Wooster? What *are* you doing?"

Without warning Wooster stepped away from the door and it

flew open. Jophrey managed a squawk of surprise before he went sprawling to the floor.

Blackbishop laughed. "Ah, I see. Well done Wooster. Entertaining the lad, hey? That's the spirit. Got to keep the boy happy. You know what these youngsters are like. All energy and laddish behaviour."

Jophrey scrambled to his feet and gave Wooster an icy glare before facing his father. He frowned. Something was different about him, but at first glance he couldn't put his finger on it. He squinted in the dim light and looked closer. The clothes were the same. He was wearing his usual garb of black leggings and tunic. What was it that had changed? Then it struck him. It was his father's face that looked strange. Naked. The moustache had gone.

"Father?" said Jophrey. "You're — different."

A puzzled frown crossed Lord Blackbishop's face. He patted his sides, glanced down at his black boots, then peered at Jophrey. "No, it's still me, young fellow-me-lad."

"Your moustache?"

A pale hand rose to rub at the bare area above Blackbishop's lip. "Ahhhh, yes. There's a story behind that." He reddened.

Sensing his unease and not wanting to upset him before he'd got him to agree to his plan, Jophrey tried some flattery. "It makes you look, er, younger," he said.

"Really?" Blackbishop's face lit with a smile.

Jophrey nodded. "Definitely younger," he enthused.

"Hmmm." Blackbishop fingered his face again. "I think I may keep it this way. What do you think, Wooster?"

"Whatever you wish, my Lord," the manservant responded, dipping his head. He turned to Jophrey. "You wanted to ask my Lord something?" he prompted, his eyes boring into Jophrey's.

"Come in, my boy," Blackbishop said, gesturing for Jophrey to move further into the room. "Come, sit by the fire. Wooster will serve us breakfast while we relax, won't you Wooster?"

The manservant bowed, but his eyes never left Jophrey. "As you wish, my Lord." Giving Jophrey a lingering, thoughtful look, he turned and left the room, closing the door behind him.

Jophrey walked across the polished boards and sat in one of the armchairs beside the freshly banked fire. The logs crackled and popped as flames licked hungrily at them. It had been years since Jophrey had last entered these quarters; about ten, he thought. He'd used them when he'd played 'Hide and Hiding' with the servants' children: a game similar to 'Hide and Seek', except that when found, the hider got a hiding with the cudgel that the seeker carried.

Jophrey smiled to himself. Those were the days. Carefree and innocent. How he'd enjoyed those games. Not that he ever got found; he'd been something of an expert at hiding. Then again, it might have been because his father was Blackbishop.

"Make yourself comfortable. I'll be back soon," said Blackbishop, intruding on Jophrey's thoughts. He strode to the door leading to the sleeping chamber, giving Jophrey a grin as he passed. "I just want to check something out." Still rubbing at his bare lip, Blackbishop sauntered away, mumbling. "Younger, hey?"

When his father had left Jophrey looked around the small room, memories of those happy days drifting through his mind. His glance rested briefly on the painting of Mandrake that hung on the wall by the door. The dragon looked even more magnificent on canvas than in the flesh. That famous artist, whatshisname, Leon Ardo, had captured his majesty to perfection. The dragon's scales seemed to glow with an inner light as his dark eyes stared moodily out from the painting, seeming to follow every movement in the room, an enigmatic smile caressing his lips.

Although the rooms were seldom used now, Jophrey's nose detected the smell of fresh wax mingled with the woodsmoke. He guessed that they must have been aired and prepared for Blackbishop when his own quarters were incinerated.

His thoughts turned to the plan that he and Mandrake had hatched. For it to succeed Jophrey had to convince his father to let him leave Mandragle Castle — on his own. Somehow he didn't think it would be as easy as Mandrake said it would. On top of that, there was the matter of Wooster's strange behaviour to puzzle out. Thinking back, it had started yesterday when they were cleaning his father's rooms. Jophrey had seen him giving him the odd, calculating look when he thought Jophrey wasn't paying attention. Something was obviously bothering the man. What it was, Jophrey had no idea.

"There, that's better," said Blackbishop, emerging from the

bedroom. The skin above his upper lip was red and tender, as though it had just been scraped with a knife. He patted at it with a soft cloth as he sat down in the chair opposite Jophrey. "Now, what was it you wanted to see me about?"

This was the moment. The moment his father would probably burst out laughing and forbid him to leave the castle. "I have a request," he said.

Lord Blackbishop leaned back in the padded chair and steepled his fingers. "Hmmm?"

"When I was with the cave-dwellers, I met someone."

"Hmmm?"

"Someone special."

"Hmmm?"

"Someone I miss."

"Hmmm?"

"Someone I want to go back for."

"Hmmm — what?" Blackbishop's eyes widened and he stared at Jophrey. "You want to go back? What on earth for?"

"To fetch someone."

"Someone who?"

"Someone special."

"Hmmm?"

"Someone I miss."

"Hmmm?"

"Someone ..."

"Breakfast is served, my Lords."

Jophrey had never been so relieved to see Wooster. The conversation with his father was becoming tedious and he was fast losing his nerve.

Wooster backed into the room, a serving tray in his hands, then turned and walked across to where they sat. "Two tisanes, two slices of hot, buttered bread, two small pots of honey, and a dollop of strawberry jam for you, my Lord."

"Ah, excellent Wooster," said Blackbishop, eyeing the jam. "Put down the tray, then you may serve us. We were just having the most marvellous chat, weren't we ..."

"Jophrey," said Jophrey.

"I knew that," said Lord Blackbishop, rolling his eyes.

"Really, my Lord?" said Wooster, with an air of indifference.

The look in Wooster's eyes as he glanced at Jophrey showed he was anything but indifferent. For the life of him, Jophrey couldn't figure out why Wooster was behaving so strangely towards him.

"And what was the topic of this scintillating discourse, if I may be so bold as to ask?" said Wooster.

A puzzled frown creased Lord Blackbishop's brow. "Sintating what?"

"What were you talking about, my Lord?"

"Ahhh!" Lord Blackbishop smiled in understanding. The smile faded as he turned to Jophrey. "What were you saying?" he asked.

Wooster stared at Jophrey expectantly.

"I have to leave Mandragle Castle. Today." The words came out in a rush, before they had the chance to dig in their heels and get stuck in his throat. "I left someone behind. Someone I want to bring back here."

"Who?" asked Wooster.

"Who, what?" Jophrey replied.

"Whom are you intent on bringing back?" Wooster asked.

"My old room-mate. I believe he is on his way here, so I thought I would go and meet him to save him getting lost." The last sounded lame, even to Jophrey's ears.

Wooster's face became contemplative. "But why would he be coming here?"

"Questions, questions, questions," snapped Lord Blackbishop, rising to his feet and placing his tisane on the mantel. "If the boy wants to have a friend round for a sleep-over, let him. It's not as if the lad is queer, is it?" He looked down at Jophrey. "Is it?" he asked.

"Of course not," snapped Jophrey. "How could you think such a thing?"

Lord Blackbishop sighed in relief. "You had me worried for a moment." He shivered. "Women are bad enough, but men?"

"He can't go alone."

Lord Blackbishop spun to face Wooster. "Why ever not?" he asked. "When I was his age I used to roam all over the place. Got into all sorts of bother, I did."

"With due respect, my Lord, when you were his age you were accompanied everywhere by a big, black dragon, so no one would have bothered you. Quite the reverse, I would have thought. Jophrey, on the other hand, will be on his own. Alone and unprotected. Anything could happen to him."

"Hmmm. You do have a point, Wooster." He tapped at his reddened upper lip and paced the floor between the chairs.

A distinct feeling that all was not going according to plan descended on Jophrey. He rose to his feet, placed his cup next to his father's and in his most confident voice said, "I'll be fine, father. I'll borrow one of your stallions. Tobias is already at Hilltown. We'll be back inside of two seven-days." He reddened, realising his error.

Lord Blackbishop paused in his pacing.

"How do you know all this?" Wooster asked.

That was the question Jophrey was dreading. It was one that could have been easily brushed aside if he were only dealing with his father. In fact it was probably the one question his father wouldn't have thought to ask. Wooster, however, was another matter; he possessed intelligence. "Mandrake told me," he blurted, avoiding Wooster's gaze and concentrating on Blackbishop.

"Mandrake?" queried Lord Blackbishop.

"He met with him when he was out hunting last night," answered Jophrey, his brain going into overdrive as he strove to maintain the lie. "Tobias must have seen him and hailed him. When Mandrake landed, Tobias asked him about me and said he was coming to visit. Mandrake offered to bring him here, but Tobias declined. He has his elderly father with him as an escort, and the old man wouldn't be able to cope with the strain of travelling on dragonback."

Lord Blackbishop sighed. "So we are to have two house guests?" He shook his head. "As if the place wasn't full enough already." He smiled. "But who am I to spoil a young lad's fun? Take Dancer, he's the fastest horse we have. He'll have you there and back in no time."

Jophrey gave a whoop of delight and made to embrace his father, but stopped short as he saw him flinch in alarm.

"Might I suggest a cart?"

Inwardly Jophrey groaned. Intelligence had buggered his plans yet again.

"A cart, Wooster?" A frown formed on Blackbishop's face.

"Yes, my Lord." The manservant gave Jophrey a triumphant smile. "Even Dancer couldn't carry two young lads and an old man. A cart would be much more comfortable. And I could drive it. That way young Jophrey would have company."

"What a splendid idea, Wooster. Why didn't I think of that?"

'Exactly,' thought Jophrey. 'Good old Wooster, the interfering old b—'

"Hang on," said Blackbishop, his brows drawn in concern. "What about me?"

"You, my Lord?" queried Wooster.

"Who will look after me? What with you traipsing around the countryside ferrying these young fellow-me-lads around, I shall be unat— unten— all alone," Blackbishop spluttered.

Jophrey felt his hopes rise. If his father thought he would be left to fend for himself, he might reject Wooster's suggestion.

A smirk appeared on Wooster's face, but he quickly masked it. "I shall have Jeeves look after you, my Lord. My boy in training."

Jophrey's hopes were dashed as he saw his father nod his head in approval.

"Jeeves, hey? Rather an odd name for a manservant, isn't it?"

"Trainee," muttered Jophrey.

"What was that?" asked Blackbishop, peering at Jophrey.

"I said it sounds good to me." Jophrey gave a weak smile even though, inside, he felt deflated. Wooster! Of all the people who could accompany him, he was the one most likely to see through what he was up to. His thoughts turned dark and sinister. There could always be an accident. One with terminal consequences.

'Snatched by the demon dragons in the dead of night?' Mandrake's suggestion whispered in Jophrey's mind. He smiled.

"Right, then. That appears to be settled," said Lord Blackbishop. "Have this Grieves attend me right away."

"Jeeves, my Lord."

"Hmmm?"

Wooster sighed. "I shall go and fetch him, my Lord." He turned to Jophrey and gave him a small, victorious smile. "Then I will make the arrangements for our little journey." He dipped his head. "Enjoy your breakfast, my Lords."

Chapter Fourteen

When he jerked awake and saw the black-clad figure draped across the bed, instinct overrode caution and Tobias screamed. Much to his embarrassment it was short, sharp, and exceedingly high-pitched. Although no one was in the room to witness his lapse, he felt his face redden.

The figure on the bed groaned.

Tobias stifled another shriek and shuffled back, pulling the covers up to his chin as he stared fearfully at the dark form that was clearly discernible in the hazy light filtering through the thin curtains. Questions peppered his brain, but although they hit home no one was in to take notice.

Who was it? How had it got there? What did it want? Why pick on him to jump into bed with? And why was it bleeding from a row of gashes on its upper arm?

A picture of the big black dragon flashed into his mind, the talons of its forelegs slashing across the pure, unblemished shoulder of the magnificent gold. His mouth dropped open as he peered at the gashes. They were in exactly the same place.

What did it mean? Yet another question that his brain struggled to cope with.

The figure groaned again, low and feeble.

Tobias peered at the gashes more closely. Blood was dripping from them and forming small, red splotches on the white, woollen cover. Whoever was underneath the black garb must be in pain. Although fearful, curiosity got the better of him and he let go of the sheet and reached tremulously for the balaclava. He had to know who was beneath.

As his hands inched toward the black headgear he began to have second thoughts. What if it disguised some form of demon sent to kill him? Or hid a face so hideously disfigured that it had to be kept covered? He shrugged such fancies from his mind and gently worked his fingers under the edges until he had a grip. What was he? A man or a small furry creature that ate cheese and went 'Eek!'?

The figure remained still as the balaclava eased up, and never uttered a word or groan of disapproval when it caught under its nose. Tobias paused in his endeavours, holding his breath as he worked his fingers to lift the edge of the woollen bonnet clear. When he was sure it was free, he began to pull again.

As more of the wrinkled visage was revealed, Tobias frowned. There was something about the aged, female features that was familiar, but for the life of him he couldn't remember where he had seen the old woman before. Surely it couldn't be the crone from Hope, could it? The face had a similar lived-in look about it, that was for sure.

With a final tug the balaclava came off. Tobias tossed it to the floor and leaned further forward to better see the features of the old woman. His eyes widened in recognition. It was the naked jumper knitter! The one sitting in the window of the cottage when they'd first walked into town. Had Wild Bill put her up to this?

The old woman's eyes snapped open.

Tobias lurched back with a start, his hands scrabbling to pull the covers up to his chin again. What they would do to protect him, he never stopped to think; somehow he felt safer with the flimsy shield between himself and the woman.

A slow smile formed on the woman's face as her golden eyes locked with his. "I knew you were the one," she whispered.

Tobias slowly lowered the sheets. "The one?" he heard himself ask, held in thrall by her hypnotic gaze.

Crinkles formed around her perfect golden eyes. "The Terminator."

"Right then, lad." The door burst open with a crash and Wild Bill strode in, all hob-nailed boots and dirt-encrusted vest. Seeing the old woman on the bed with Tobias, his face split into a lecherous grin. "Bloody hell, young 'un. When'd you sneak her in?" He began to tug at his vest. "Any chance of a share?"

"Get out!" Tobias yelled. "It's not what you think. Go away and leave us alone." For some strange reason he felt protective of the old woman.

Wild Bill paused, his vest half way up his chest, his hirsute belly revealed in all its glory. Slowly he lowered the vest and gave Tobias an injured glower. "Share and share alike we do. When we're on the road, like. Know what I mean?"

Tobias didn't, but did not want to further any discussion with Wild Bill. Neither, it seemed, did the old woman. She levered herself up on her uninjured arm and cast him a withering look. Wild Bill stared back at her, a half smile on his face. Gradually it faded, replaced by a slack-jawed, vacant expression.

"The boy and I were having a nice little chat, that is all," the old woman said, her voice low and melodic. "Now if you would be so kind!" Wild Bill stood and stared. He started to dribble, small rivulets running into his matted beard.

"Leave us," the old woman said in a firm voice.

To Tobias's surprise Wild Bill did just that, the vacant look still in place as he turned and went out of the door.

"Oh!" said the old woman. Wild Bill turned to face her. "Find Nina and ask her to bring breakfast to the suite. Tell her that there will be one extra, that Nanna Pussy has arrived."

Nanna Pussy? What kind of name was that? Tobias was none the wiser as the door closed behind Wild Bill. "How did you do that?" he murmured.

"Do what, dear?" Nanna Pussy asked.

"That!" Tobias nodded towards the door.

Nanna Pussy sat up, grimacing as she put pressure on her injured arm. "An old woman's trick, Tobias. An old woman's trick."

Tobias? How did she know his name? *He* certainly hadn't told her. He shook his head. Things were getting stranger by the moment. All he needed was for Cronan to enter the room and his morning would be complete.

As if on cue the door opened and the man himself entered. "Now then, young man. What is all the fu—" His hand still on the latch, Cronan stopped and stood immobile, his eyes bulging as he stared at the bed.

"Well come in if you're coming," said Nanna Pussy. "You're letting in a draught and it'll play havoc with my arthritis."

Tobias giggled, more from nerves than out of any sense of amusement. He couldn't think of anything less funny than the predicament he now found himself in. Caught in bed with a woman old enough to be his great-grandmother, Wild Bill wandering around the hotel in his underclothes, and now Cronan looking as though he had just seen a dragon.

A dragon? Tobias's gaze switched to Nanna Pussy. A golden dragon? His thoughts must have been obvious, because Nanna Pussy turned to face him, her eyes narrowed in warning. Had he voiced his concerns out loud?

"What is going on in here?" Cronan demanded.

"Nothing, master," said Tobias, easing himself out of bed. Clad only in his shorts, he stood with his hands clasped in front of his crotch. "Honestly."

Cronan crossed his arms and gave Tobias and Nanna Pussy a stern look. "Out here, now. The pair of you. I want an explanation immediately."

Nanna Pussy sighed and rose to her feet. "If you must," she muttered, and began to shuffle past Cronan to the main room.

Cronan noticed the red stain on the bedcover and he turned questioning eyes on Tobias. "Immediately," he repeated. "And put some ruddy clothes on."

As he quickly dressed, Tobias could feel Cronan's gaze boring into him. So the librarian wanted answers. Well, he would not be getting any from him. All he had was questions. And lots of them.

* * * * *

Nina rose from her pallet and crossed to the small window. She drew aside the moth-eaten curtain, its once-bright lilac flowers now naught but faded splotches on the greyed linen. She sighed as she pulled the shabby material to one side. Why she bothered to do it she didn't know. Her *cupboard* was situated in the basement; the only view through the grime-streaked glass being the stone-lined gully that went around the building, and the metal grill that covered the top. To stop idiots from falling down she supposed. What little light came through the window was diffused by the mesh, its criss-cross shadows spreading across the room.

She turned and looked around what passed for her quarters. Nearly two cycles she had lived here, in a room big enough to hold a bed and a small dresser, but little else. At least she had managed to squirrel away some savings from the pittance that Herrol paid her. Not much, but enough so that she had some money when she told him what he could do with his poxy room and left his employ for good. A wry smile formed on her face. At the rate she was saving, it would be many cycles before she could do that.

Her thoughts turned to the hotel's guests. If she didn't get to serving them soon Herrol would be hopping mad and would dock her money. She snorted in contempt and shook her head, her ringlets bouncing. It was definitely time for her to be moving on and making her own way in the world, money or no money. The only problem was her gran; what would she do if Nina left? She had no one else.

As she sluiced her face with cold water she thought about the boy with the red hair. In some weird sense she felt drawn to him, but not in a sensual, flirtatious way. There was something about him that she found comforting. It was as if she knew him somehow, although she had only seen him once. But he had spotted the dragons.

She smiled. Yes. He *had* spotted the dragons. And the sooner she served breakfast, the sooner she and Nanna Pussy could speak with him. She dressed quickly and made her way up to the foyer with a spring in her step.

As soon as she got there she knew something was wrong, because Herrol wasn't in his customary place behind the desk. She walked across the foyer towards the kitchens. As she was going through the dining area she heard groans, and the excited chatter of the kitchen staff coming through the partially-open door leading to the hallway.

She frowned and increased her pace, a feeling of unease creeping over her. There was something about the babble that troubled her. It wasn't the normal kitchen banter that she could hear, it carried an air of surprise. No — fear.

Nina was running by the time she entered the kitchen. She skidded to a halt and stared in disbelief at the scene before her. Sitting on the floor, groaning in pain as he rubbed at chafed wrists, was a bald man. The cook and her two assistants flustered about, offering him damp rags and cooing words of comfort.

Nina stared at the man, wondering who he could be. She gasped in astonishment as she recognised Herrol's cultured features. But where was his hair? She noticed the paste dabs on his head and giggled.

Herrol looked up at the sound, his blue eyes boring into hers. Ducking her head, Nina tried to compose herself before she looked up again. It took a few moments, but eventually she managed it.

Herrol struggled to his feet. "Fetch Grolff!" he commanded. "I want the perpetrator of this ... of this ... of this act of violence apprehended. Understand? Now if you will excuse me I am going to have a lie down." He raised a pale hand and rubbed at his forehead. "I feel quite unwell." He swatted away a proffered rag. "The feeding and wellbeing of our guests is in your hands. Have Grolff attend me in my rooms." Without another word Herrol swept out of the kitchen.

As soon as he had left the cook and her helpers began to chatter excitedly amongst themselves. Nina clapped her hands to get their attention. "We have guests to serve," she said, in her most commanding voice. "Breakfast for three, if you please, at your earliest convenience."

The cook looked at her assistants, shrugged and, raising a shaggy eyebrow, nodded towards the cooking range.

"I'll be back shortly," Nina called over her shoulder as she turned and walked out of the kitchen. "After I have woken Grolff."

She was crossing the foyer, heading for his shack in the hotel grounds, when Grolff barged through the entrance doors, dragging Bart in by the scruff of his neck. Clasped in Grolff's other hand was a dead black cat.

Surprised by Grolff's appearance, Nina stopped. "Wh-what's going on?" she spluttered.

Grolff pulled Bart upright by his collar. "This!" he growled, waving the cat in the air.

Bart sobbed with terror and flinched away from the bedraggled swatch of hair that Grolff thrust at him.

"It weren't me," Bart wailed. "It weren't me! It appeared on me 'ead! I don't know now't about it!"

"That's what *you* say," Grolff snapped. "But we'll wait and see what Mister Herrol thinks about it, shall we?"

Bart whimpered.

Nina looked more closely at the object being dangled in front of the night porter's face. Her eyes widened in surprise; it wasn't a dead cat. "It's a wig!" she murmured.

"Too bloody right it is," Grolff snapped, then reddened and mumbled an apology for his language.

"Herrol's?" Nina asked, knowing that it was.

"Aye, Herrol's!" Grolff stooped, bringing his face closer to Bart's. "And we would like to know how a certain night porter managed to come by it." He gave Bart a shake. "Wouldn't we?"

"It weren't me," Bart repeated. "Honest! I never knew it were on me 'ead until you spotted it. Someone must 'ave planted it when I was sleepin'."

Grolff straightened, his lips drawn tight in disapproval. "Sleeping on duty, were you? Yet another nail in your coffin." He turned to Nina. "Where's Herrol?"

"In his rooms," Nina replied. "He sent me to fetch you. He's …" She glanced at Bart, doing her best to smother a grin, "not quite himself today."

"Right, you," said Grolff, dragging the protesting night porter towards the stairs leading up to Herrol's rooms, "time for you to explain how you came by this." He waved the wig in front of Bart's face again, prompting another bout of protestation from the quaking man.

Nina could still hear Bart whining as she turned and made her way back to the kitchens. It would seem that the case of the phantom wig-napper had been solved. But who would have thought it of Bart? Usually the man was as timid as a mouse.

As she entered the dining room she heard the heavy clump of booted feet coming down the stairs from the guest rooms and turned to see who it was. Her eyes nearly popped out of her head as Wild Bill came into view, with his hairy legs and dirt encrusted underwear on display. "Wild Bill Halfcock!" she snapped, hands on hips, glaring at the slovenly excuse for humanity that stepped onto the marble floor of the foyer. "What on earth do you think you are doing?"

Wild Bill stopped at the sound of her voice, his eyes glazed and vacant as they slowly swept the room. They fastened on Nina and he started to dribble. A salacious smile formed on his face and something stirred in his stained shorts.

"And you can stop that this instant," Nina scolded. "If you do not go back to your room and get dressed right now, I'll have my gran put a curse on you. She's a witch, you know." She folded her arms across her chest and glared at Wild Bill. Even someone as dumb as Wild Bill would have heard about her Gran, and would understand the threat.

"Nina?"

The dull, flat tone of Wild Bill's voice made Nina frown. "Yeees."

"There will be one more for breakfast. She said —" The frown on Nina's face deepened at the mention of 'she', and a leaden feeling settled in the pit of her stomach, "— to tell you that Nanna Pussy has arrived."

Nina gasped.

So did Wild Bill. As soon as he had delivered his message the vacant expression left his face. He stared at Nina in astonishment, his mouth forming an 'O' of surprise. Then he glanced down, and seeing his lack of attire and the lump in his shorts he swore. He looked up again, his face reddening as he covered his crotch and gave Nina a weak smile. "Someone's nicked me bleedin' clothes," he murmured.

"And I know who," snapped Nina, striding forward. "Come," she ordered, sweeping past him. "You need to get dressed and I need to have words with a certain person. Strong words."

She didn't bother to look and see if Wild Bill followed. At that moment she really couldn't have cared. Thoughts of what she would do to the old lady when she saw her banished all other notions from her head.

Chapter Fifteen

Tobias flinched as the door smashed back against the wall. Before the dust had a chance to settle Nina stormed in. She stopped inside the threshold and stood with her hands on her hips as she glared at Nanna Pussy.

"Well? What have you got to say for yourself?"

Nanna Pussy, sitting beside Tobias on the divan, visibly shrank. Cronan turned and stared at the intruder.

Beating an impatient tattoo on the floor with her foot, Nina waited for an answer. Behind her Wild Bill sidled into the room and inched along the wall, his back pressed against it as he made for the safety of his own room. Nina ignored him, her eyes fixed on Nanna Pussy.

Tobias's gaze flicked from Nina to Nanna Pussy and back again as he wondered what was going on. It was bad enough having Cronan interrogate them about what had been happening without Nina getting in on the act as well. On a more positive note, Nina was a darn site more pleasing on the eye than the old librarian. She looked stunning when she was angry; all bouncing ringlets and flashing blue eyes.

He frowned. Why was she so angry? What had Wild Bill said to her? With eyes narrowing, he glared after him as he disappeared into his room.

"I'm waiting!"

Nanna Pussy sighed, her lips compressed into a smile of resignation. But before she could answer, Cronan butted in.

"Can I help you, young lady?"

A scowl formed on Nina's face as she turned her gaze on Cronan. "Pardon?"

Cronan gave her a hard stare. "Can I help you?" His voice became cold. "If it hadn't escaped your notice, I was in the middle of a conversation with these two." He gave Tobias a withering look before turning back to face Nina.

She met him stare for stare, two strong-willed characters vying for control. "And if it hadn't escaped *your* notice, I have words of my own to say to my gran."

Cronan's jaw dropped. "Your gran?"

Nina folded her arms across her chest and thrust out her chin, as though daring him to pass comment.

Tobias groaned. Standing before him was the girl of his dreams, and he had been caught in bed with her grandmother. Just what he needed! He squealed as Nanna Pussy squeezed his leg.

"And you can stop that this instant!" Nina scolded.

The door of Wild Bill's room opened. Dressed in tatty leggings, stained tunic and his customary hob-nailed boots, he clumped out to take a seat beside the window.

"Stop what, dear?" Nanna Pussy asked, wide-eyed.

"That!" Nina nodded at the hand resting on Tobias's thigh.

Cronan turned his head to see what it was that Nina objected to. A glower darkened his features as he spotted Nanna Pussy's hand rising from Tobias's leg. "It would seem that they owe us both an explanation," he said, his gaze resting briefly on each of them.

Nanna Pussy sighed and rose to her feet. She winced.

"You're hurt!" Nina ran forward to inspect her gran's arm. Her eyes narrowed when she saw the four tears on the shoulder of her tunic. "How did you do this?" she asked.

Nanna Pussy shrugged. "I really don't know, dear. I must have caught my arm on a bramble in the dark." She gave a small smile. "They're only scratches, and I heal quickly. They'll be as right as rain in no time. Now be a good girl and sit next to Tobias. It looks like I have some explaining to do."

Tobias wilted under Nina's accusatory look as she sat down beside him, ensuring there was as much distance between them as the divan would allow.

"Take a seat, will you?" Nanna Pussy requested, her attention fixing on Cronan. "And you!" she turned to Wild Bill, "bring your seat over here, and one for your companion. This may take a while." She strode to the door and closed it. "Can't have anyone eavesdropping, can we? Now before I answer your questions I have a few of my own."

"Now see here," Cronan spluttered, half rising from the chair Wild Bill had provided him with. "I don't think you are ..."

"Enough!" The power of Nanna's voice instantly quieted Cronan and made Nina gasp.

"As I was saying, I have a few questions of my own." Her eyes met Cronan's. "And I expect to hear honest answers. I will be able to tell if you are being economical with the truth."

"Nanna?" Nina's voice came out as a whisper, her earlier anger gone.

"Yes, dear?"

The smile on Nanna Pussy's face took years off her. To Tobias she didn't look a day over one hundred and fifty.

"A-a-are you, er, well?"

Nanna Pussy winked. "Never better, my dear."

Tobias looked on, bemused. In the past few hours he'd dreamed a nightmare, woken to a nightmare and seemed to have entered a living nightmare. When was it all going to end?

"Why have you left Hope?"

Cronan choked as Nanna Pussy fired the question at him. Composing himself for a moment, he spluttered, "I have no idea what you are talking about."

Nanna's eyes narrowed. "Oh dear. And here I was thinking you were intelligent. I will ask you again. Why have you left Hope? Ogmus are not welcome in the outside world, since those damned Blackabbots took control. So it must be something of importance for the likes of you to risk being caught. Or worse, be eaten by a big black dragon."

Tobias gasped, recalling his nightmare. He also remembered his rescue by the beautiful golden dragon. Before he could stop himself he blurted, "To bring back the good dragons!"

Cronan choked again, his face going the colour of an over-ripe plum. He tugged at the collar of his tunic and turned to glare at Tobias.

Tobias glared back defiantly. If Cronan knew what he knew, he would not be so reticent about telling the truth. Straightening himself on the divan, he switched his attention to Nanna Pussy. "We are here to help bring back the good dragons."

Nanna Pussy smiled and nodded. "Right. Your question?"

Cronan, still suffering from apoplexy, couldn't speak. Instead Wild Bill broke in. "Why'd yer shack up wi' him?" He nodded at Tobias.

"Shack up?" A furrow formed on Nanna Pussy's brow.

"Why were yer in bed wi' him?"

A strange choking sound emerged from Nina's mouth and she inched further away from Tobias. Nanna Pussy laughed. "I wasn't in bed with him, you fool. He was in the bed while I was on top of it."

Wild Bill shrugged. "All the same to me."

"He was having a nightmare, so I took it upon myself to soothe his fevered brow."

"But why were you in our rooms in the first place?" Cronan asked, recovering the power of speech.

Nanna Pussy shook her head. "My turn. How are you intending to bring back the good dragons? Assuming there are such things."

Tobias had never seen so many expressions vying for control of the librarian's face; Cronan appeared to be having a major internal debate. Eventually he sighed, his decision made. Giving Tobias a tight-lipped smile he told Nanna Pussy about Nostra Ogmus and the prophecies, the book's theft, their suspicions concerning the Blackabbots, and their need to reach Snor'kel before the black dragons.

Nanna Pussy listened intently. When Cronan had finished, she said, "Well, that is a tale and a half." She nodded her approval. "Strangely, I believe every word you have said."

"Well, 'ows about a few ..."

The raising of her hand silenced Wild Bill. "No questions," Nanna Pussy said. "It's my turn to speak." So saying, she told them what she knew of the good dragons. Tobias listened in awe as she explained how it had been her lifelong ambition to see them return to Tiernan Og. When she spoke of the one foretold to bring back the dragons, he gasped in amazement and murmured, "Snor'kel."

Nanna Pussy smiled at the interruption and shook her head. "No. Not Snor'kel. The one who brings back the good dragons is called the Terminator. Snor'kel may be the catalyst for their return, but the Terminator will bring them back."

"You mean our quest is for nought?" Cronan asked, his face ashen. "That Nostra's prophecies are wrong? That *we* are wrong?"

"Not at all. Just that one vital element was not included in his verses."

Cronan sagged in his seat, deflated. "But how will we find this

Terminator? We will have enough problems meeting Snor'kel without having to look for someone else as well. Someone we don't even know."

Nanna Pussy laughed. "But we've already found him. Why else do you think I was in Tobias's room?"

Cronan jerked upright, as if he'd sat on a rather prickly thistle while not wearing any underwear. "Tobias's room?" He turned to stare in amazement at Tobias. "Him?"

Completely mystified, Tobias peered at the faces that were turned towards him. "Wh-what's the matter? What have I done?"

"Bloody hell, young 'un. It seems like you's important."

"Me?" Tobias squeaked, as understanding dawned. "The Terminator? There must be some mistake. I am only a librarian's apprentice, not some magic-wielding, dragon-rescuing hero from legend." His gaze flicked from face to face, hoping for some sign that they didn't mean him, that it was a joke. That he wasn't this ... this Terminator guy. But the looks of respect on their faces dashed his hopes. "H-h-how do you know?" he whispered.

"The dragons," Nina answered.

To Tobias's amazement Nina shuffled closer and grasped one of his hands in her own. She looked him in the eye and said, "You saw the dragons on the door. They welcomed you. They knew you. That is how we know you are the one." A smile lit her face as she glanced to her gran before continuing. "The spell is one of my Nanna's, placed over the door to tell us when the one who was foretold arrived. And it did." Her bright blue eyes fixed on Tobias. "And the one is you, Tobias. You are the one."

Nina's smile was radiant. A smile created just for him. And this time razor sharp fangs didn't accompany it.

* * * * *

The bell above the entrance to Mingel's Mart tinkled and the door opened to admit a rotund, balding man of middle years. The elbows of his woollen tunic were worn through and his trousers had seen better days. Even the patches on the knees had patches sewn over them. He wore knee-high, muck-smeared green boots that were strapped to his legs with coarse bits of rope, and another length had been looped around his waist to hold his trousers up. Strands of straw poked out of his woolly thatch of hair.

Mingel immediately recognised the wart-speckled features of the farmer. He rested his elbows on the counter and cupped his chin. "Mornin', Stampff," he grunted. "What brings you into town?"

"Supplies," Stampff growled, stomping to the counter. Dollops of muck fell from his boots onto the bare boards as he made his way between precariously leaning shelves stacked high with tools and outdoor equipment. He swerved round the numerous boxes, stuffed to overflowing with sheets of canvas, coats and woollen hats, that littered his passage.

"Ey?"

"Supplies," Stampff repeated more loudly. "Run outta stuff." He fished in his pocket and pulled out a heavy purse, which he slapped onto the timeworn, wooden counter. "An' I got coin ta pay fer it."

"Well why didn't yer say so?" Mingel eyed the pouch and straightened, rubbing his hands together as he tried to work out how much coin Stampff had with him, and how he could get him to part with a goodly proportion of it. Coin was one commodity that the farmer rarely had, so he had to make the most of it. "What can I be gettin' fer yer?"

Stampff rubbed a calloused hand across his unshaven jaw and scanned the well-stocked shelves. He pointed. "I'll be 'avin four of those, three of them, five of ..."

Mingel held up his hands. "Whoa there, feller. Don't be goin' so fast. I ain't as quick as I used to be, yer know."

Stampf grunted.

"Now then, what yer wantin'?"

"Fork 'andles."

"Ey?"

"Fork 'andles!"

Mingel bent down under the counter and rummaged on the shelf. Moments later, he placed four candles in front of Stampff. "Next."

Stampff stared at them for a moment, then met Mingel's gaze. "Fork 'andles!"

Mingel frowned. "That's what I give yer. Four candles."

Stampff growled low in his throat. "Fork 'andles. Fer diggin'." He mimed the act of turning turf.

"Fer diggin'?" Mingel scratched his head and watched Stampff's strange performance. After a few moments he grinned. "Ah. Fork 'andles!"

"That's what I said, didn't I?"

"Er, well, sorry 'bout that. It's me ears, yer know." He tapped the side of his head. "A bit Mutt and Jeff."

"Ey?"

"Deaf!"

Stampff rolled his eyes and waited while Mingel replaced the candles below the counter and moved to the other side of the shop to collect a fork handle. "Two!" he called, just as Mingel stepped off the wooden trestle that served as a hop-up for reaching the higher levels of shelving. Mingel grunted and stepped back up. With the fork handles cradled in his arms he made his way back to the counter and placed them on top. "Next!"

"Four candles."

Mingel scowled. Was Stampff taking the ... "Four candles?"

Stampff nodded, a half smile on his face.

Mingel sighed and reached beneath the counter to retrieve the four candles. He placed them beside the fork handles. "Next!"

The bell above the door tinkled. Mingel grinned. Two customers in one day? He hadn't been this busy in years. When he looked up to see who had entered the grin faded. It was the witch, and, if he was not mistaken, that layabout Wild Bill Halfcock. Mingel's face fell. This was all he needed. The man never had any money and tried to barter for everything with the crap he hauled around in his cart. And as for the witch ...

"We're closed," Mingel muttered, folding his arms across his ample girth.

"You seems open to me," Wild Bill responded, a wide smile splitting his matted beard. "And me and my friend would like to make a few purchases."

"We're closed," Mingel repeated.

"We can pay," said Wild Bill.

Mingel snorted. "That'd be a first."

When he had finished rearranging the fork handles and candles on the counter, Stampff turned to look at the new customers. Seeing Wild Bill his face became hard. "You!" he growled.

The colour drained from Wild Bill's face. "Er, nice to see you again Stampff."

"Not half as nice as it be fer me," Stampff growled, pushing his tunic sleeves up over forearms rippling with muscle. "You owes me money fer the table and chairs yer took."

Nanna Pussy eyed Stampff warily and took a step back.

Wild Bill fumbled inside his long-coat and removed a large, weighty pouch. He delved inside and pulled out a gold coin, which he quickly flipped toward Stampff.

Stampff plucked it from the air and raised it to eye-level. He peered at it, then locked eyes with Wild Bill. "Yours?" he asked.

Wild Bill nodded. "That should more than cover it."

Stampff gave a malicious grin and slowly shook his head.

"More? But it was a crappy old table with a goat's leg nailed to it, and the chairs were half eaten by woodworm."

Stampff shrugged and held out a hand. "Interest!"

Two coins later Stampff was happy. He turned his back on Wild Bill and leaned against the counter, spinning the coins on the wooden top, a contented smile on his face.

Mingel watched the coins, the sight of the gold seemingly casting a hypnotic spell on him. Wild Bill cleared his throat. "You still closed?" he asked.

A wide smile cracked Mingel's face. He spread his arms. "Fer you? Fer you we always be open. Now what was it yer be wantin'?"

Nanna Pussy stepped forward. "We require five water—"

"I be speakin' to the *gentleman*," Mingel interrupted, studiously avoiding Nanna's gaze.

Nanna Pussy folded her arms across her chest and glared at the storekeeper. "Now listen here, Mingel Mangle ..."

"It's fine," Wild Bill interjected. "Really. We knows each other." Winking at Mingel he turned and looked down at Nanna Pussy. "I can sort out the stuff. You go bring your horses and cart round. By the time yer get back, I'll have everything we need."

With one last glare at Mingel, Nanna Pussy turned on her heel and stalked out of the shop.

Mingel eyed Wild Bill with a new respect. He'd never heard anyone deal with the witch like that before. "What yer be wantin'?" he asked.

"Good prices," Wild Bill retorted, with a smile. He hefted his recently depleted money pouch. "Because I be wantin' a lot."

Mingel rubbed his hands together, his eyes following every rise and fall of the pouch. "Just name yer goods, an' I'll see what I can do."

By the time Nanna Pussy returned with the cart, the porch outside the shop was piled high. Bedrolls, canvas, rope, pots, pans and everything else they would need on the journey lay waiting to be loaded. Mingel looked at the small cart, then at the pile of goods. He scratched his head. "You fittin' that lot in that there cart?" He pursed his lips and shook his head. "There be no room left fer the two of you when yer done."

"Five," Wild Bill corrected.

"Five?" Mingel shook his head again. "Hopes they's small ones." Still chuckling, he helped Wild Bill with the loading.

A short while later the cart trundled up the road towards the Hilltown Hotel, with Wild Bill and Nanna Pussy on the driver's bench and their purchases stowed in the well between the bench seats behind.

"Where'd he get the money fer that little lot?" grunted Stampff, emerging from the store and peering after the cart.

Mingel shrugged. "Buggered if I know. I ain't never seen so much gold, specially in his 'ands. He must've robbed it, or offloaded all his crap on some poor, unsuspecting sod."

Stampff snorted. "Probably sold his rubbish. Robbery's too much like 'ard work for the likes of 'im. He'd sell his own father if the price were right."

Mingel chuckled and turned to enter the store. "If he knew who his father was."

Stampff pulled one of the coins from his pocket and examined it closely before following Mingel inside. "The coins be gold all right. But I ain't seen the likes o' them afore. Still, at least we got our money outta 'im, which is more than most folks. Now then, what be next on me list? I know. Ave yer got any of them ..."

153

Chapter Sixteen

Plumes of red-brown dust billowed up from the cart's passage, the rapidly shrinking outline of the Hilltown Hotel barely visible through the cloud. Sitting on a bench in the back of the cart, Tobias stared down the trail, deep in thought. He hugged his cloak tighter to his body and settled the hood lower over his eyes to shield them from the brightness of the midday sun. Although sweltering inside his protective cocoon, his eyes and skin could not cope with the brightness of the great outdoors, and he had severe doubts that they ever would. But in the grand scheme of things, that was the least of his problems.

"Are you feeling all right?"

Tobias looked up at the sound of Nina's voice and smiled. "As well as can be expected, considering."

Nina grinned, her blue eyes twinkling with amusement. She reached over the provisions piled between them and gently grasped Tobias's knee.

Tobias flinched, then blushed as Nina laughed her bright cheery laugh. As if reading his thoughts she said, "You'll be fine. My gran will protect you."

Somehow that did little to settle his nerves. Who would protect him from her? He gave a crooked smile and settled back on his bench.

As the cart jarred and bounced along the pot-holed road, Tobias absently surveyed the cultivated fields and hedgerows. The news that he was supposed to be this Terminator guy had really unsettled him. What did it mean? What was his role? Was he capable of doing whatever it was that he was supposed to do? How could Nostra have been so wrong? Just what was Nanna Pussy? So many questions without answers, and so little time in which to find them. In seventeen days Snor'kel would appear. But where? And what would happen if Nostra was wrong? If Cronan was wrong? If Volgen was wrong? What if ...

"A copper for them?"

"Hmmm?" Tobias jumped at the question.

"Your thoughts. You seem a little preoccupied."

Tobias met Nina's gaze and smiled. Why was it that her smile could make him feel so much better? "Questions," he answered. "So many questions and so few answers."

"All in good time, Tobias," Nanna Pussy called back from the driver's bench, flicking the reins to guide the horses and surprisingly showing no sign of her earlier injuries. "No point in fussing your head with problems before they've arisen. Just settle back and enjoy the ride."

Tobias grimaced.

"How long until we reach the next village?" Cronan asked. He was squashed between Wild Bill and Nanna Pussy on the driver's bench, his hood drawn up over his head like Tobias.

"Be about three days, if we're lucky," Wild Bill answered. "More like four, though. The cart's well loaded and those nags 'ave seen better days."

"I will not have you speak badly of Snowdrop and Buttercup, Mister Halfcock!" Nanna Pussy scolded. "Especially in their hearing. They may be old, but they've got feelings, and you will not find better carthorses this side of Hilltown. Will he, girls?"

Snowdrop, the bay mare, snorted her agreement.

Wild Bill laughed. "Not wantin' to cast doubts on yer horses, ma'am, but it be a long way to where we be goin', and they ain't the youngest of beasts."

"They will be fine, Mister Halfcock. Just you worry about yourself. The horses will take care of themselves." Worryingly, the strength of her conviction did not manifest itself in the tone of her voice.

Aside from the clop of horses' hooves, the rumble of iron-shod wheels on hard ground, bird calls and the occasional greeting from animals in the fields, the rest of the afternoon passed in relative silence. Even Wild Bill seemed subdued, his constant babbling strangely absent. As they travelled the well-tended fields gave way to open grassland pockmarked with small copses of trees. In the distance a misty-grey smudge materialised on the horizon, growing taller as they approached.

"The Forest," murmured Wild Bill, nodding towards it.

"What's it called?" asked Cronan.

Wild Bill shrugged. "The Forest. Probably because it's full of trees. And wild pigs." He turned his head to peer over the back of the driver's bench at Tobias.

"Ignore him," said Nina, giving Wild Bill a glare. "He's only trying to frighten you."

Tobias snorted. Frighten him? It would take a lot more than stories of wild pigs to do that after what Nanna Pussy had revealed.

To the relief of all Wild Bill called a halt, indicating for Nanna Pussy to pull off the track at an area of flattened ground. The sun hung low in the sky and it would not be long before dusk fell.

"Travellers camp site," said Wild Bill, jumping to the ground. "Most travellers use it fer an overnight stop before entering the forest."

"Why's that?" asked Tobias, leaning over the back of the driver's bench and looking around.

Wild Bill gave a sly grin. "Folks don't like trampin' through the trees in the dark, young 'un. Because of the wee beasties. Evil little bastards they are. Bite yer bum as soon as look at yer."

"Wee beasties?" There was a nervous tremor in Tobias's voice.

"Ignore him," Nina snapped, jumping lightly over the side of the cart. "The only wee beastie around here is him."

Wild Bill laughed and walked round to the rear. "Yer may be right there, miss. But don't say as I didn't warn yer."

Cronan groaned as he shuffled along the bench and dropped to the ground. "My poor back." He pressed his hands against the base of his spine and leaned backwards. "It feels like it has been kicked."

"You'll get used to it," said Wild Bill, pulling a tarpaulin from the back of the cart. "Before yer know it, yer arse will be tougher than old boots." He grunted as he hefted the tarp onto his shoulder. "Young 'un, grab those poles, will yer? Then Wild Bill will show yer how we make a shelter round these parts. And while we makes our camp the old 'un can start a fire and the ladies can carve up some grub. I'm starved. Me poor stomach thinks me throat's been cut." The look on Nanna Pussy's face as she watched Wild Bill toss the tarpaulin to the ground suggested that throat-cutting was at the forefront of her mind.

Tobias lifted the willow poles from the back of the cart and took them to where Wild Bill was rolling out the canvas. "Aren't we a bit near to the road?" he asked.

Wild Bill shrugged.

"But what if someone comes along and sees us? Or drives over us in the dark?"

With his knee joints clicking, Wild Bill rose from his crouched position and grinned. "You worry too much, young 'un. Now hand me them poles; that's if yer want to sleep under cover tonight."

While Cronan scraped a hole in the ground for the fire, and Nina unloaded a pot, water and a ration of dried meat and herbs, Wild Bill and Tobias set about forming a frame to support the tarpaulin. In no time the fire was blazing and the pot was coming to the boil. The night shelter, however, was nowhere near completion. A tangled mass of willow poles, lashed together with rope, lay on the ground looking like it had been run over by a cart. Wild Bill was getting madder by the minute as he pulled on the poles and tied them randomly together. Tobias watched, at a loss to know how he could help.

The evening wore on and the light began to fade. The stars came out, but the shelter still appeared to be hours away from completion. Having given up jumping up and down on the poles and throwing rope around, Wild Bill sat amongst the carnage and glowered as if it were the poles' fault.

Nanna Pussy strolled over from the fire, leaving Cronan and Nina to finish cooking the broth. "Nearly there?" she asked, regarding the mess.

Wild Bill looked up, his eyes narrowed and lips taut. "No we're bloody well not," he growled. "That crook Mingel conned us."

"Really?"

"These bloody poles!" he shouted, rising to his feet. His arm swept out to encompass the mess with a gesture. "Wrong bloody size! And as for the tarp."

"Yes?"

"Too heavy!"

Nanna Pussy nodded sagely and tapped at pursed lips with her forefinger. "Hmmm! I see your problem. But we have to have the shelter, because it will be dark soon and we won't be able to see a thing."

"Tell me somethin' I don't know," snapped Wild Bill, taking a kick at an unfortunate pole that was within striking distance.

"Mind if I make a suggestion?" She gave Tobias a sly wink.

"Feel free. 'Coz it's got me beat. Bloody shopkeepers. They haven't got a clue when it comes to living outdoors. They sit on their big, fat ar—"

"Shut up and give me a hand," Nanna Pussy ordered, stepping forward and untying the ropes that bound the mangled mess together. "And you, Tobias."

Once the poles were unbound, they sorted them into three piles; long, not-so-long and short. Selecting two tall poles, she told Wild Bill and Tobias to hold them upright, six paces apart, with one end pushed into the ground. Bending them over until they met, she lashed the ends together with a length of rope. Two more tall poles and a dome-shaped framework was beginning to take shape. When it had been braced with short poles it was ready for the canvas to be thrown over.

"What about them other poles?" Wild Bill asked as he stood back to admire their handiwork, nodding at the stack of not-so-long poles.

"Not needed," Nanna Pussy answered, wiping her perspiring brow with the back of her hand.

Wild Bill swore and shook his head. "I told you that shopkeeper conned us. No wonder I couldn't get the bloody thing up." So saying he turned and walked over to the fire. "Now where's this broth. I've worked up a right appetite doing that lot."

"The ungrateful …"

"Now, now, Tobias," interrupted Nanna Pussy. "It's up, so let's just be thankful that tonight we will have a roof over our heads. Come, we'd better get some broth before he eats it all."

Apart from the crackle and pop of burning wood the meal was eaten in silence, the travellers too tired to do more than enjoy their food and think their own thoughts. Unconcerned by their presence moths fluttered and dived around the fire, drawn to the light.

The silence was broken by a loud belch. Rising to his feet Wild Bill dragged his sleeve across his mouth to wipe his broth encrusted beard. "Right. That's me fer bed. Girls to the right, boys to the left and men in the middle. That's me, by the way. Pots can wait till the morning. They'll only need washing again after breakfast." He tossed his bowl to the ground. "Don't be too long, we 'ave an early start tomorrow." His beard parted in a grin, his face looking demented in the orange glow of the fire. "It gets cold here at night, so the sooner we get snuggled in together the better." Chuckling at Nanna Pussy's snort of disgust he strolled to the shelter.

"If he thinks I am cuddling up to him, he's got another think coming," she murmured. "But he's right; it does get cold at night, so we'd best get to bed. And we do have a long day ahead of us tomorrow."

As Tobias made to rise Nanna Pussy gripped his arm. "You can help me rinse the pots and check the horses, while the others prepare the sleeping furs, dear." When Cronan and Nina had nodded their agreement and walked away, she added in a whisper, "And we have things to discuss."

A leaden feeling settled in the pit of Tobias's stomach. Things to discuss? What things? Terminator things? A horrible thought entered his mind and he shuddered. What if it was thigh clutching things? His good mood retreated; went into hiding at the thought. Why couldn't he enchant young girls? What was it about him that attracted older women? A vision of the crone back at Hope sprang into his mind and he felt his gorge rise.

He squealed as Nanna Pussy squeezed his arm. "Don't fear me, Tobias," she said with a laugh. "Now come on. Let's get these pots washed and the horses checked so we can have our little chat."

The chores were finished too soon for Tobias's liking; it seemed like no time at all before they were ready for their 'little chat'. He was at the back of the cart when Nanna Pussy stopped him with a softly spoken word. "Dragons."

Tobias paused in the process of stowing the pots in the cart. The hairs on the back of his neck rose and a hot flush ran through his body. He felt faint. Dragons! The word conjured all sorts of emotions in him. Fear of the black dragons, joy at the prospect of the good ones and love of the gold; the dragon that had saved him in his nightmare. "Dragons?" he whispered, his hand still resting on the pots.

He felt the presence of another beside him. Close beside him. Too close. He felt strangely uncomfortable.

'Can you hear me, Tobias?'

The voice whispered in his head, light and feathery. "Of course

I can," he answered, puzzled by the question. "You are standing right beside me."

Nanna Pussy giggled.

'Can you speak to me?'

Tobias turned to face her. "Huh?"

'Can you speak to me?'

"What?" He frowned and looked more closely at Nanna Pussy's face. Although it was almost pitch black, the light from the half moon and stars was sufficient for him to make out her wrinkled features, and he was sure that her mouth hadn't moved when she asked the question.

She smiled. *'Can you speak to me?'*

Her mouth definitely hadn't moved! He gasped in shock and took a pace back, tripping over his own legs and falling to the ground. He scrambled to his feet. "Wh-wh-what are you?" His voice was high and tremulous.

'I am what you saw in your dream, Tobias, which is why we must talk. I cannot tell you all just yet, but you need to know what I am. What you are. Now, talk to me'

"B-b-but I am!"

A loud voice echoed through the night. "Oy! You two comin' to bed, or are you at it again? Ouch! There's no need for that, young lady. I didn't mean now't by it."

Nanna Pussy sighed. "We'll be there soon. After we have tidied the pots away. Now shut up and go to sleep," she shouted.

"What are you?" Tobias whispered, knowing all along what she really was. Deep inside, locked within denial, he knew she was the dragon from his dream. But how? She was an old woman. How could she and the dragon be one and the same?

'Use your mind, Tobias. Think your questions, don't speak them. I have to be sure before I tell you more.'

"Sure?"

'Use your mind, Tobias. Use thought.'

Thought? What was the crazy old crone on about?

'I heard that!' The thought was filled with excitement.

Tobias swallowed hard. She'd heard him?

A broad smile formed on Nanna Pussy's face. Tobias was sure he saw tears in her eyes; the watery droplets gleaming in the moonlight.

'I heard you loud and clear, Tobias.' She launched herself forward and threw her arms around him. *'I knew you were the one.'*

"I bloody knew it!" They both started at the sound of the voice and broke their embrace, their eyes drawn to the figure of Wild Bill standing beside the cart, arms folded across his chest, dark eyes glaring down at them. "What is it with you? Yer can't keep yer bloody hands off 'im, and he's young enough to be yer grandson. Why not try someone nearer yer own age?" He puffed out his chest. "Like me, fer instance."

His wide face had a hopeful look about it, like a puppy waiting for a treat. If Nanna Pussy had told him to roll over, sit and beg, he probably would have. Instead she laughed.

"You wouldn't get near me with a tent pole, never mind anything else young man. And if you must know, I am old enough to be his great-great-great-great-great-grandmother." With that she strode past him and made her way to the tent.

As she walked her voice whispered in Tobias's head. *'We will talk tomorrow, now that we can do so without the others hearing us. Sleep well, Terminator.'*

Sleep well? He very much doubted whether he would sleep at all this night.

"Right then," said Wild Bill, rubbing his hands together and staring after Nanna Pussy. "Now I knows she likes to play hard to get, I'll have to rethink me approach. What say you, young 'un?"

Tobias shook his head. Things were getting stranger by the minute. "Give up on it, Wild Bill," he muttered, stepping past him. "She's way out of your reach."

Wild Bill's laughter followed him to the tent. "No need to get jealous, young 'un. If yer lucky, I may even teach yer a trick or two. About how to please the ladies, like."

A flush of embarrassment at such coarse words heated Tobias's face. But they were only words.

'You are learning, Tobias,' came the now familiar tickle in his head. *'You are learning. Sleep well.'*

Surprisingly he did. No sooner had he snuggled into his sleeping fur than he was sound asleep, and this time without dreams.

Chapter Seventeen

The enticing aroma of sizzling bacon tickled Tobias's nostrils, stirring him from a deep and untroubled sleep. Memories of happier, carefree times surfaced as he stifled a yawn with the back of his hand; of waking warm and cosy in his room at Hope to the smell of breakfast and the sound of Jophrey whistling merrily as he cooked in their small galley kitchen. Jophrey sure was a whiz in the cooking department.

Jophrey!

The carefree feeling fled at the thought of the one person he'd considered a true friend, and who had turned out to be anything but. Visions of what Tobias would do to him should they ever meet forced their way into his head. And they were not pretty!

A heavy appendage thumped down across his chest, accompanied by the sound of guttural snoring. Tobias gasped in horror as the arm wrapped itself round him and began to pull him into a fierce embrace, dragging him towards a hideous, gaping maw. A gaping, saliva dribbling maw whose rancid breath would curdle milk at ten paces. A gaping maw fringed by a filthy, matted black beard and belonging to Wild Bill.

Tobias shrieked.

Wild Bill snorted at the sound. With a roar he lurched upright, eyes darting frantically around the tent as his hand scrabbled for his long-knife.

Freed from the restraining arm, Tobias scuttled away on his backside; his eyes flicking between Wild Bill's manic expression and the huge, wickedly sharp knife he held ready for action. One thing was for sure: Tobias didn't want to be on the receiving end of that blade.

Realising that there was no immediate danger, Wild Bill turned to Tobias. "What's the matter, young 'un?" His voice was gravelly and sleep laden. "I heard a right scream." He lowered his knife. "What were that racket that woke me?"

Tobias clutched his sleeping fur to his chin and shook his head.

Wild Bill gave a sly grin. "It was you that shrieked, weren't it? What's the matter? Havin' nightmares again?"

"Y-y-you put your arm around me. Then tried to kiss me," Tobias stammered defensively.

Crows-feet splayed out from Wild Bill's eyes as he smiled. "Is that all?" Tossing aside his sleeping fur, he rose to his feet and sniffed the air appreciatively. "Smells like the womenfolk have been busy."

"But you tried to kiss me!" Tobias yelled. "And I'm a man!"

Wild Bill winked and clicked his tongue. "Don't knock it 'til you've tried it, petal," he said. "Now come on, or that lot will 'ave eaten the grub before we gets a look in."

It was some moments before Tobias found the will to move. He couldn't shake the image of Wild Bill's beard-fringed mouth puckered for a wet one from his mind. The man had to have been dreaming of someone more ... well, feminine, didn't he?

'Are you coming out for breakfast, Tobias?'

Tobias flinched as the voice whispered in his head. "W-w-what?" This was the second time this morning he had been scared out of his wits, and he'd only been awake for a moment or two.

'Use your mind, Tobias. Speak to me.'

"How?" he whispered.

Although he had barely spoken the word, Nanna Pussy heard him. *'Instead of saying the words, think them at me. And do not worry, I cannot read your thoughts. Only if you do not control their direction.'*

Thoughts? Direction? What was she on about?

'Think the words at me, Tobias. And do hurry, otherwise your paramour will have eaten your share of the breakfast.' The words contained a hint of mirth.

Wondering what on earth a paramour was, but thinking it must be along the lines of a dirty, smelly, odious pig, Tobias thought his next words at Nanna Pussy. *'I'm coming.'*

'Good boy. With a bit more practice you'll be perfect.'

Although the sun had barely risen, Tobias had to shade his eyes for fear of being blinded by the unaccustomed light as he made his way to the fire and breakfast. Outside the ring of the camp site mist hugged the ground, rippling and undulating as the light breeze disturbed it. The chill air reminded him of how cold he had been during the night; the same coldness that filled the warrens of Hope when summer waned and winter was about to descend on the outside world.

Nina handed him a plate containing three rashers of bacon and a slice of coarse, brown bread. "Sleep well?" she asked. Wild Bill looked up from where he crouched on the other side of the fire and blew Tobias a kiss.

"Y-y-yes, thank you," Tobias stammered, feeling the heat of embarrassment on his face as he reached for the plate.

Nina giggled and moved away. She joined Nanna Pussy beside the cart and began to rinse the dirty bowls under the tap of one of the water barrels strapped to its side.

Cronan was sitting near the fire staring into its amber glow with unfocussed eyes. He looked up as Tobias joined him.

"What's the matter?" Tobias asked. "Aren't you feeling well?" He bit a chunk off the bread and began to chew.

Cronan smiled and shook his head. "I'm fine. Just worried." He pursed his lips and resumed staring at the fire.

"What about?" Tobias asked, placing a comforting hand on the old man's arm.

"Nothing, and everything," Cronan answered with a wan smile. He turned his head to peer into Tobias's eyes and held his gaze. "Aren't you?"

Suddenly Tobias didn't feel hungry. He put his plate on the ground and swallowed his mouthful of bread. "A little," he admitted, not daring to give voice to the terror he felt at being some sort of dragon saviour, for fear of feeding Cronan's dark mood.

"But what if Nostra is wrong, if there is no such person as this Snor'kel? What if we are travelling on a fool's errand?" Cronan's eyes misted over as he murmured, "What if we fail?"

Realising that his hand was still on Cronan's arm, Tobias squeezed it affectionately before picking up his plate again. "Nostra is not wrong," he said firmly, shoving a piece of bacon into his mouth. Although he'd lost his appetite, he felt he must appear normal, calm and confident for Cronan's sake.

"He was wrong about *you*, Tobias."

A nervous shiver rippled through Tobias, making his hand shake. He hoped Cronan didn't notice. "My role was probably in the next verse," he answered, between chews. Now that he was eating, the bacon tasted good and he realised he was famished. "The one you were getting to before Jophrey stole the book."

Cronan didn't look convinced.

"Anyway," Tobias glanced towards the cart where Nanna Pussy and Nina were attaching Snowdrop and Buttercup in the traces, "we have *her* to back up what Nostra told us. And she seems to know more about it than Nostra ever did, judging by his ramblings." Tobias wished he could tell Cronan what little he knew of Nanna Pussy, but he suspected that she would be less than pleased if he did.

A snort of amusement escaped Cronan's lips. "So we have one old man, an even older woman, a young girl, a boy and a purveyor of dubious second hand goods to save the world." He shook his head. "That doesn't exactly fill me with confidence, Tobias, even if Nostra is proved to be correct."

"I heard that," said Wild Bill, placing his plate on the ground and rising to his feet. He stomped round the fire and hauled Cronan upright by the scruff of his neck. The old man's toes scraped the ground as Wild Bill dangled him aloft. Tobias looked on, agape.

"And we'll be havin' no doubts. Understand? Wild Bill doesn't fail in what he sets out to do, and he won't be havin' no talk of defeat before we even be tryin'. If we think we be failin' before we even start, we got no chance. So buck yer ideas up, and don't be fillin' the lad's head with rubbish." He lowered the dumbstruck Cronan to the ground and smoothed down the librarian's crumpled robes. "Now that there is today's lesson, courtesy of Wild Bill." Turning on his heel, he strode past Cronan and began to remove the canvas cover from the tent.

From beside the cart Nina and Nanna Pussy looked on. Nina appeared as shocked as Tobias, while Nanna stared after Wild Bill, her face unreadable. *'Now I wasn't expecting that,'* she murmured into Tobias's head.

It was not long before they were underway again. In what appeared to be the established order, Nanna Pussy, Cronan and Wild Bill sat on the driver's bench, with Tobias and Nina in the back. Wild Bill whistled a tune, out of key, as he attempted to break the apparent gloom that had settled over them. He didn't know that while he whistled Nanna Pussy and Tobias were having an intimate chat.

Tobias was the first to mind-speak. Although nervous and not understanding how or why he could communicate with Nanna Pussy in that way, he sensed that she was waiting for him to make the first contact. It was her way of making him find the ability. By the time he plucked up the courage to try The Forest loomed, dark and threatening. Wild Bill's claim about wee beasties 'biting yer bum' still unsettled him, despite Nina's assurance that no such things existed.

'A-a-are there such things as wee beasties in the forest?' he thought at Nanna Pussy.

A ripple of pleasure caressed his mind in reply, and he smiled.

"What are you smiling about?" Nina asked, a half smile playing on her own lips as she looked across at him.

Tobias peered at her from beneath his hood. "Nothing. Nothing at all." His mind frantically whirled, trying to come up with an excuse that Nina would believe, so she would not think him some sort of grinning imbecile. "Just enjoying the company." He felt his face redden as Nina looked away, rosy patches appearing on her cheeks.

'Nicely said, Tobias,' whispered Nanna Pussy's voice.

By the gods, had he just flirted?

"Yer smooth-talkin' feckler," leered Wild Bill, leaning over from the driver's bench and punching Tobias on the arm. "You've been listening to me too much, young 'un. Got fed up with the old 'un, have we?" He rubbed his hands together. "Just as well I'm around to pick up the pieces, hey?"

"Leave him alone," snapped Cronan. "The boy's got enough on his mind without you adding to his problems."

"Ooooo, get you, mister. If I didn't know better I would say yer were jealous of the lad."

Cronan folded his arms across his chest and stared ahead, not rising to the bait.

"Hit a nerve, have I?" Wild Bill laughed. Settling himself back on the bench he peered over Cronan's head at Nanna Pussy.

"In your dreams," she said, snapping the reins.

"Always!" Wild Bill gave a sly wink and recommenced his tuneless whistle.

'That man has a mind like a sewer,' said Nanna Pussy.

'On a good day,' retorted Tobias, lying back and closing his eyes to feign sleep.

'What did you ask before we were so rudely interrupted?'

'Wee beasties,' Tobias answered. *'Are there such things?'*

'Of course not, dear. The only wee beasties around here are figments of that man's imagination.'

'Nanna Pussy?'

'Yes, dear?'

'What are you?' Although fearful of being so forthright, Tobias needed to hear her confirm what he already knew. Judging by the pregnant pause that followed it was one question she wasn't too keen to answer.

Eventually, just when Tobias was beginning to regret the question, Nanna Pussy's voice whispered in his head. *'I am what you saw in your dream, Tobias.'*

'A-a-a golden dragon?'

'Yes. Or at least, I was.'

'Was?'

'It's a long, long story, my dear. One that deserves telling, but not just yet. There is time enough for me to tell you of my history, of the history of the dragons, both the good and the blacks. And of how I came to be how you now see me.'

Realising that was all the answer he was going to get for the time being, Tobias asked another question that had been plaguing him. *'How come we can talk to each other with our minds when most people struggle to talk with their mouths?'*

'It's in your blood, Tobias. Like the dragon's blood that runs through my veins, Ogmus blood runs through yours'.

'But I am Ogmus,' said Tobias, confused by her reasoning. *'And no Ogmus I know can speak with their minds. Even Cronan, and he is the brainiest Ogmus in Hope.'*

'True Ogmus, Tobias. There is a difference.'

'True Ogmus?' he asked, wondering what she meant.

'Time enough, my dear. Time enough.'

This was starting to get very frustrating. The answers he had received so far were not answers at all, merely precursors to yet more questions. He decided to ask one more question, one that had been concerning him ever since he'd learned he was the Terminator. *'What am I supposed to do? What is my role in bringing back the good dragons?'*

A wave of anguish washed over him.

'Sadly, Tobias, that is the one question to which I do not know the answer. I wish that I did. I am rather hoping that this Snor'kel can tell us, when he arrives. Now get some rest; we have several hard days travelling ahead of us and mind-speaking can be very tiring at first. We don't want to overdo it and have you incapacitated at the vital moment, do we? Don't worry. All your questions will be answered in due course.'

As if confirming Nanna Pussy's warning, Tobias yawned. He did feel rather sleepy. Settling himself into the corner, he cushioned his head from the side of the cart with his hands and closed his eyes.

Lying flat on his stomach at the fringe of the forest, Grimble parted the foliage of a small bush and scrutinised the approaching cart. He smiled as he spotted the amount of cargo stashed in the back. It had been ages since anything worth stealing had come their way, so it would pay for him to study the travellers well before he reported back and boarding plans were made.

A heavy sigh escaped his lips when he counted the number of big-folk that accompanied it. Five big-folk would be a lot to take on, especially if they were skilled fighters. Would the load be worth the risk? As his gaze fixed on the two oldsters sitting on the driver's bench his mood lifted. That made the odds better. They should be no problem, but the big, bearded fellow was a different matter. He looked like he could handle himself. That left the two in the back. Guards? After closer inspection it didn't seem likely. The hooded one looked sound asleep and the other was ... A girly? Feeling ever more confident, he grinned a gap-toothed grin and began to slither back into the forest.

When he was sure he was safe from detection, he rose to his feet and hurried back to the camp. Brimble would want to hear all about this. He would know what to do; how to relieve the travellers of their belongings. After all, he was the best leader the Beastie Boys had ever had. Come to think of it, Brimble was the only leader they'd ever had. Shrugging, he increased his pace, eager to impart his news.

The cart jumped in the air. Tobias woke with a start as his head bounced off his arm and hit the timber side. "W-w-what was that?" he cried, sitting upright and grasping his head, squeezing his eyes closed against the pain.

"We must have hit something," Nina answered, extracting herself from the pile of provisions. She brushed her ringlets from her eyes as she sat back on the bench.

"Too bloody right we did," Wild Bill grumbled. "A bleedin' great big log stuck in the middle of the trail. Even a blind man could 'ave seen it. But her? Bloody women drivers."

"We'll have less of that, thank you. Unless you wish to walk the rest of the way," Nanna Pussy scolded.

"It'd be a damn site safer."

"Can we just get on with it?" snapped Cronan. "This forest is giving me the creeps. The sooner we are out of here the better, and I could do without you two sniping at each other and further fraying my nerves."

"Forest?" From beneath the hood of his cloak, Tobias looked up at the trees towering over their heads, the leafy branches forming a lofty arch over the trail. Green-tinged sunlight filtered down from above. "When did we enter The Forest?" he asked.

"About a candle mark ago," answered Nanna Pussy.

"Only another two days and we'll be out of here," said Wild Bill.

"Two days?" Cronan's voice sounded shrill.

"One and a half, if we're lucky."

"Don't worry, Cronan. They're only trees. There's nothing to fear," said Nanna Pussy.

"Only yer drivin', woman," muttered Wild Bill.

"I heard that, mister. Any more of that sort of talk and you walk! Understand?"

Wild Bill stifled a chuckle. Nanna Pussy growled under her breath and urged the horses on.

From the depths of the closely packed trees bird calls sounded, short, sharp and eerie; the rustle of the upper branches in the breeze adding a haunting counterpart. Muffled by accumulated layers of leaf-mulch, the horses' hooves whumped softy on the ground. Looking back down the trail, all Tobias could see was trees, trees and more trees; of the grassland there was no sign. Reassured by the absence of direct sunlight, he slowly slipped off the hood of his cloak. His eyes widened, all his earlier fears about beasties forgotten as he took in the splendour that was the forest. "I've never seen so many trees," he murmured. "They look like giants; tall, strong and imposing." He reddened at Nina's giggle.

"I keep forgetting this is all new to you," said Nina. "What's it like living in Hope, not knowing what the outside world looks like?"

"We do have books," retorted Tobias, more stiffly than he had intended. "And we do get out on the mountainside occasionally."

Nina lowered her eyes and looked into her lap. "I'm sorry, Tobias. I didn't mean to be insulting."

Tobias groaned to himself. Yet again he had said the wrong thing. He leaned across and grasped Nina's arm lightly, feeling clumsy in his efforts to make amends for his rudeness. He felt clumsier still when the cart lurched, propelling him across the pile of provisions to land head first in Nina's lap.

"Bloody hell, woman. You've gone and done it again! Pull the bloody cart up and let me drive, it'll be safer all round," snapped Wild Bill.

The cart continued on its way.

"Did you hear me? I said pull the bloody ..."

Tobias levered himself up from Nina's lap, shocked at where his head nestled and surprised that she hadn't uttered a word of reproach. His shock turned to fear as he noticed the glazed, vacant expression on her face. Although her eyes were open, they were not seeing. "By the gods" he whispered, "I've killed her. Nina! Nina! Wake up!"

Panic-stricken, he scrambled to the back of the driver's bench and thumped Wild Bill on the shoulder. Wild Bill keeled over and slumped against Cronan, who in turn slumped against Nanna Pussy. As she sagged from their weight she was prevented from falling out of the cart by the timber brace that served as an armrest.

"By the gods," Tobias whispered again. "They're all dead!"

Before hysteria could take hold he felt a sharp pain in his right cheek and slapped his hand at the offending area. A splinter-like object stuck into his palm. Before he had the chance to pull it out the world turned black. Very black.

Chapter Eighteen

The fuzziness inside Tobias's head started to clear and awareness that he still lived penetrated his sluggish mind. He groaned. Something was trying to tunnel out of his skull with a pickaxe, and his mouth felt as though he had been chewing on a sweaty sock for a week. Allied with the dull pain running the length of his left side where the hard ground had numbed his body, he was feeling decidedly uncomfortable. Wondering how long he had been lying there, he attempted to move his hands from behind his back, but couldn't. For some reason they refused to budge. He tried again. With rising dread he realised they'd been lashed together. He tried his feet. They'd been tied too!

Panic-stricken, his eyes flew open. Bright speckles and wavy lines danced in his vision, the green of the leaf-tinged sunlight creating a pulsating background. He screwed his eyes shut as nausea gripped him, but it was too late. He vomited. When he had finished he rolled onto his back, wincing as his weight crushed his already bruised wrists. Arching his body off his hands, he dragged in great lungfuls of air, attempting to clear his head and make sense of his predicament.

Where were they? What had happened? The last thing he could remember before darkness had claimed him was the sight of Nina, Cronan, Nanna Pussy and Wild Bill all slumped in apparent death. But they were not dead. They were out cold, like him. But how?

He remembered the pain in his cheek, and something sticking out of the flesh. He frowned at the memory. A splinter? Then realisation struck him. They'd been knocked unconscious by tiny darts. Poisoned darts! Back at Hope he'd read of such things in one of the few books, beside Nostra's, in the library; of how aboriginal tribes used them to bring down game or enemies. But who would want to capture them? A horrifying picture of a big black dragon filled his mind. The Blackabbots! His concern for the whereabouts and safety of his companions grew. In desperation he probed with his mind, searching for the one person he knew he could communicate with.

'Nanna Pussy! Can you hear me?'

No response.

'Nanna Pussy! Answer me, please!'

Silence shrieked back.

Tobias groaned. Where was she? He daren't risk opening his eyes to take a look around, as he still felt nauseous and did not know whether his throat could stand another bout of vomiting. A rustling in the grass caught his attention. He felt a presence beside him. "Wh-wh-who's there?" he whispered, rolling onto his side. The heady stench of vomit made him gag.

"Oy, Brimble! He's awake!" a voice, high-pitched and shrill with excitement called out. "Want me to knock him out again? Please? May I? Go on, let me."

"No! Leave him be Trimble." Although still high-pitched, Brimble's voice was slightly deeper than Trimble's.

Brimble? Trimble? Who were these guys? The rhyming brothers? Fighting his nausea, Tobias cracked open an eye and tried to focus. A diminutive shape, standing two or three paces away, began to materialise. Tobias's mouth formed an 'O' of surprise and he eased open his other eye to confirm his first impression. He gulped. Now he could see two of them! Four rapid blinks later he stared in amazement as the two figures merged into one. It must be a wee beastie! Involuntarily the muscles in Tobias's backside clenched.

Standing no higher than his knees — had he been standing and not lying trussed on the ground — was a little man. A little green-skinned man, with a neatly trimmed dark green goatee beard. Dressed in forest green leggings and tunic, and with a cap perched on his head at a jaunty angle, a feather sticking out of the hat band, he blended perfectly into the woodland background. The only things about him that weren't green were the brown belt strapped around his narrow waist and the piercing brown eyes staring down at Tobias.

Without warning, Tobias vomited again.

Trimble jumped back in alarm. "Oy, that's not very nice mister. You don't go puking on strangers without any warning or by-your-leave. Hey, Brimble, see what he nearly did to me? Nearly covered me in puke, he did. And me being so friendly to him, and all."

The physical act of being sick cleared Tobias's head. The headache receded to a dull throb and his vision stayed in focus instead of wavering around. Another similarly clad figure came into view and stood beside Trimble. The newcomer cupped an elbow with one hand and tugged at his goatee as he stared down. With a blowpipe tucked into his belt and a leather bandolier looped over his shoulder, different coloured fluffy-tailed darts thrust through its retaining loops, he looked like a big game hunter. Or a little man who hunts big game.

"Be quiet," said Brimble.

"Be quiet? You saw what he did." Trimble began hopping from foot to foot. "He deserves punishment for that, he does. Let me stick him. Go on. Just a little one?" he wheedled. "I'll give you the pipe back as soon as I've used it." He held out a hand expectantly.

Brimble rolled his eyes and shook his head.

"But he nearly covered me in foul-smelling sticky stuff. Let me stick him. Go on. I can handle it. Just let me ..."

Lightning fast, Brimble reached to his bandolier, snatched free a yellow-tailed dart, whipped out his blowpipe, loaded, swivelled and blew. The dart struck Trimble in the cheek, whereupon he flopped to the ground in mid-sentence and immediately began to snore. Tobias was amazed by the speed and efficiency with which Brimble had struck, and by the rapid action of the drug.

Staring at the comatose form for a moment, Brimble sheathed his blowpipe and stooped to remove the dart from the little man's cheek. He placed it in a pouch fixed to his belt and turned to face Tobias. "When he gets too excited he always talks too much. Sometimes it's the quickest way to shut him up," he said. He paused briefly. "In fact it's the only way to shut him up. Don't worry, he'll come round shortly."

Worry? As far as Tobias was concerned, Trimble was one *less* to worry about. "Who are you?" he asked, his voice croaky from retching.

Standing taller Brimble said, "The Beastie Boys, at your service." His hand swept the ground with a flourish as he bowed. "Masters of this here forest. And you," he leaned forward to fix Tobias with an unamused stare, "have trespassed."

"Trespassed? But the road runs right through the trees. Surely it's open to all who wish to travel it."

Brimble put his hands on his hips, leaned back and laughed. "That's what everyone thinks." His demeanour turned serious and he gave Tobias a sly wink. "But we know different."

"Where are my friends? What have you done with them?"

"They're around, somewhere." Brimble gazed into the trees and shrugged. "Probably with the rest of the boys. When you fell off the cart we decided to truss you where you lay, you being too heavy to carry, and all. The others should be back at the camp with the cart by now. That's if they managed to catch the damn thing and stop it."

"Catch it?" Tobias was horror-struck. "You let a fully laden cart go careering into the trees with four drugged people on board?"

"And the stash," grumbled Brimble, staring morosely at the ground and scuffing a pointy-toed boot in the grass.

"Stash? What stash?"

Brimble grinned and shook his head. "You'll not be fooling me with the 'what stash' trick, mister." He wagged a finger in admonishment. "We saw it. Piled on the back of the cart and covered with a sheet. Pupff. Do you think we're stupid or something?"

High, warbling shrieks interrupted them before Tobias could reply. From out of the trees beside the trail, three little green men swung into view, each clutching a vine. As they noisily announced their arrival, two of the men let go and landed lightly on the trail beside Brimble. The third, however, with eyes screwed tightly shut, continued to cling to his vine as though his life depended on it.

"Let go, you idiot!" yelled one of the new arrivals, "before you hit a ..." Thunk! "... tree," he finished lamely.

Brimble shook his head, his lips a taut line of displeasure. "For goodness sake, Thatch. How many times have I told you not to let Grommet use the vines? Hey? How many times? You know he has no head for them."

"He said he'd been practising. Didn't he, Boo?" Thatch turned to his companion for confirmation.

Boo nodded and gave a wry smile. "Guess he needs to practice a bit more, hey?"

"Go get him out," snapped Brimble. "Now!" When they had departed Brimble turned to Tobias. "See what nincompoops I have to put up with?"

Tobias grimaced.

"We've found him boss!"

"Well, bring him out then."

"Will do, once we get him out of the tree. He seems all right; no harm done, aside from a couple of cuts and bruises."

"More's the pity," Brimble muttered, staring into the trees, his hands on his hips.

Recovering from the shock of witnessing more little green men arriving on the scene, Tobias put his mind to trying to figure out a way to escape. He had to find his friends, and Wild Bill, otherwise their cause would be lost and the Blackabbots would never be defeated. One way or another he had to find a way out. A plan began to form in his mind.

"That stash you're after; you wouldn't be thinking of stealing it, would you?"

Brimble laughed. "Now whatever put that thought into your head? Of course we mean to steal it. Why else would we be taking the cart?"

Tobias tutted and shook his head.

"What's up with you?" Brimble asked, a half smile forming on his face. "Ahhhh, I see. Doesn't quite meet with your approval, hey? What's the matter? Don't like to see honest folk make a living?"

"Honest folk? You stole our cart. After knocking us all out with drugs, I hasten to add!"

"Well how else were we supposed to take it?"

"You could have asked, for starters. We would have been more than willing to pay a toll to get through."

Brimble frowned. "What's one of them?"

"What?"

"A toll."

Tobias sighed. This was turning out to be more difficult than he had anticipated. "Payment for safe passage."

"You mean you would be willing to pay *us* for letting you through *our* forest?"

Tobias smiled. At last! "Yes."

Brimble shrugged. "What's the point? We've got the cart anyway."

Boo and Thatch trudged out of the trees, a bedraggled looking

Grommet suspended between them. Twigs and bits of greenery stuck out of his tunic, his face was cut and grazed and his hat had been squashed flat on his head, the feather in the hat band now a sad looking stalk.

"The point is," said Tobias, attempting to get his plan back on track, "that the Blackabbots will be less than pleased if their taxes don't arrive."

Brimble's face paled. "Blackabbots?" he murmured.

"Blackabbots?" yelled Boo and Thatch in unison, releasing their hold on Grommet who collapsed to the ground. "Big black dragon-riding Blackabbots?"

Tobias nodded. "The very same. And I fear they are rather expecting this delivery. And when it doesn't arrive ..." He shrugged. "I would hate to be in the shoes of the person, or persons, that had waylaid their shipment."

"What are we to do?" shouted Thatch, running to Brimble and tugging at his sleeve. "It's thanks to those black dragons that we now number less than te—"

The rest of his words were lost in a 'whump' as Brimble clapped a hand over his mouth.

"Be quiet, moron," he ground through gritted teeth, motioning towards Tobias with a flick of his head.

Thatch's eyes widened in understanding and Brimble removed his hand. Beside them Grommet groaned and struggled to his feet. He stood swaying on the spot. "Wh-what happened?" he croaked.

Boo grabbed his arm to steady him. "Trouble, with a capital T," he said.

"We don't know that," snapped Brimble. "All we have is his word for it."

Tobias grinned. "Your funeral."

"Funeral? I hate funerals," wailed Boo. "Especially if it's my own."

"How would you know?" snapped Thatch. "You've never been dead before."

"And I don't intend being dead now either!"

"Dead? Who's dead?" Trimble yawned and scratched his head as he rose to join his companions. "What have I missed?" He stopped scratching and rubbed at the reddened spot on his cheek.

"It would appear that the cart we acquired is *supposed* to belong to the Blackabbots." Brimble gave Tobias a pointed look.

"Blackabbots? Big black dragon-riding Blackabbots?"

"We've been through that already. If you hadn't been sleeping you would have heard."

Trimble threw his hands up and cried, "We're dead! We're dead. By the gods of the moon, the sun, the stars and, er, everything, we're dead!"

"Do shut up. You're as bad as Boo. We don't know the stash is for the Blackabbots, we only have his —" he jerked a thumb at Tobias "— word for it."

"That is good enough for me," said Trimble, looking over Brimble's shoulder at Tobias. "Sorry about wanting to stick you and all that. I was only joking. Friends?"

Tobias scowled, making Trimble duck behind Brimble for protection.

"Well, it's not good enough for me!" snapped Brimble.

The statement began the most heated debate Tobias had ever had the misfortune to witness. All five of the Beastie Boys immediately began to jabber and shout, finger wag and gesticulate. Within moments the verbal sparring turned more physical. In a flurry of tiny bodies they began pushing and shoving, each striving to make his point known. A mass brawl ensued as they went for it with gusto, all thoughts of saying their piece forgotten in the adrenaline rush of a good, old-fashioned scrap.

As the Beastie Boys fought, Tobias began to work the bindings on his wrists. With teeth gritted, stomach tensed and arm muscles bulging he forced his hands apart, exerting pressure on the thin cords that bound him. He felt them give a little and redoubled his efforts. Suddenly they snapped. Tobias groaned aloud and cradled his hands to his chest, certain he'd sawn through the skin to the bone. On closer inspection he was relieved to see that he hadn't, although the skin around his wrists was puckered and angry. His fingers tingled as previously constrained blood began to flow, their tips throbbing in time with his heartbeat. But that didn't matter; he was free! Or he would be as soon as he had untied his legs.

Untying the bindings round his ankles proved tricky. His fingers wouldn't work properly and felt like unwieldy sausages as he tried to pick at the minuscule knots, but somehow he managed it. Fortunately the Beastie Boys were too busy fighting to notice his struggle. They were still fighting when a huge dark shadow settled overhead.

Fear rippled through Tobias's very being as he looked up. His knees began to shake and shivers wracked his body. He was overcome by abject terror.

Out on the trail the five tiny figures ceased their fighting and cursing to stare fearfully up at the black shape that was visible through the leafy canopy. The heavy whump of wings carried down to the forest floor, the uppermost branches of the trees swaying and clashing in the down-draft.

"A black dragon!" Tobias muttered. His heart beat hard against his chest.

The Beastie Boys clung to each other in fear; whimpering and mumbling prayers to the gods as the shadow dropped lower and the down-draft grew to gale force proportions. The trees thrashed and bent under its immense force. The Beastie Boys screamed. Tobias could see it all, yet was powerless to move, his muscles frozen in terror.

The dragon dropped lower still, ripping at the tree tops with its mighty talons. Realising that it was after the Beastie Boys, Tobias clambered to his feet and sprinted across to the five little men, sweeping them up in his arms. Without pausing for breath he charged off into the trees, neither knowing nor caring where he ran to, the five struggling figures clamped to his chest.

Chapter Nineteen

Mandrake tore at the branches in fury, snapping limbs and tearing out whole trees with his clawed feet. He knew that Tobias was down there and that he needed help; he'd seen those little pests the Beastie Boys surrounding him. If he didn't scare them off, or better still kill them, Tobias would not be able to meet with this Snor'kel when the time came, and that would ruin Mandrake's plans. Things had gone too far for anything to thwart him now. Roaring his anger, he redoubled his efforts to reach the forest floor.

Strapped in the saddle at the base of Mandrake's neck, Lord Blackbishop screamed in terror as chunks of tree flew through the air. "Stop pruning the shrubbery this instant, you hear me? We have foresters to do that sort of thing. What's got in to you? I command you to stop!"

The words were accompanied by savage tugs on the reins that were attached to Mandrake's nose strap; but the dragon ignored them, eager to feel Beastie Boy flesh on his tongue. Although tiny, they were sweet tasting and made smashing hors d'oeuvres.

"Didn't you hear me? I said stop! Cease! Desist!"

The tugging on the reins grew more frantic, further infuriating Mandrake. When the jagged end of a snapped tree trunk gouged his belly, pain lanced through him and his rage exploded. He bugled loudly and shot skywards, hovering above the trees and glaring at the empty spot where the Beastie Boys had been. Of Tobias there was no sign.

"That's more like it," shouted Lord Blackbishop. "What got in to you? One minute we were flying nice and steady, enjoying the pretty countryside; the next, tearing at the forest as if your tail was on fire. Are you ill or something?"

Mandrake ignored the Lord and circled, wanting to make sure that Tobias was free and able to continue his journey. The mass of trees stopped him getting a clear view, but he was sure he spotted a figure crashing through the undergrowth, away from where the Beastie Boys had been.

Grunting with satisfaction Mandrake turned and made his way back to Mandragle Castle. Maybe he would visit Jophrey on the way, to see how he was getting along with Wooster. He grumbled low in his throat. There was something about the manservant that Mandrake didn't like. He had only met him a couple of times, but sensed something about him that didn't ring true. What it was he couldn't tell, but he didn't trust him.

The tugging on the reins started again. Mandrake growled in annoyance. The sooner the Lords could be disposed of the better. Hopefully it would not be long.

"Now where are you going? I never told you to go this way. Stop this instant or I'll ... Or I'll ... Blast it! Just stop, will you? Mandrake! Mandrake! Are you even listening to me?"

As he flew Mandrake's thoughts turned to his mother. Ever since she had appeared in the dreamscape he had been plagued by nightmares, usually culminating in her banishing him to a dark and gloomy world for being 'a naughty boy'. He shuddered at the thought. Just how had she got there? She and her blasted horde had been sent to limbo, to a world of eternal gold and riches; a world he had tricked them into going to. He had seen them disappear himself, so he knew she couldn't be on this world. So how had she come back to save the boy? Alarmingly, since then he'd been unable to penetrate the boy's dreams. It was as if a protective veil had been thrown over him. That was until earlier today, when the veil had suddenly lifted and he'd sensed Tobias and flown straight to him.

"Damn Dragon! Will you tell me where we're going? Because I haven't a clue, and I'm the blasted driver!"

Mandrake's wings paused in their beating as a chilling thought struck him. What if his mother was no longer in dragon form? What if, somehow, she had used her dragon-magic to achieve the ultimate and transform herself into a mortal, never even entering the other world? What if she was now in the party that accompanied Tobias? What if she was seeking revenge on him and his brothers? What if she had engineered the arrival of this Snor'kel?

Shivers ran down his spine. It all fitted. She had to be with Tobias. She was the instigator of all of this. He had no idea how she intended to use Snor'kel to defeat him and his brothers, or which mortal she might be disguised as. But one thing was for sure; she couldn't do anything if she were dead. With powerful thrusts of his leathery wings he raced over the forest, heading toward Mandragle. This was a job for Jophrey.

"Whooaahhhh!" Lord Blackbishop screamed in terror as he was pushed back into the saddle. Wind pummeled his face; the skin of his cheeks flapped and his lips were pushed back in a demented grin. From between clamped teeth, he ground out, "Glasted dragon!"

* * * * *

The warm breeze and gently rolling motion of the wagon worked its soporific magic and Jophrey began to doze, leaving Wooster to drive the team as he had done since they had left Mandragle Castle. Two days they had been travelling now; two days of complete boredom with nothing to do but stare at the passing countryside, wave at farmers and worry about his reunion with Tobias; a meeting that he was not looking forward to. And not just because of the expected backlash for stealing Nostra's book. Somehow he must overcome Tobias's antipathy towards the black dragons and convince him that they were the good guys, and persuade him to join their cause. He grimaced at the thought. There was nothing like the impossible to focus the mind.

The hard wood of the driver's bench numbed his flesh and he shifted to ease the pain. The past couple of days had played havoc with his backside, so much so that he was convinced he now had a flat arse instead of a rounded one. This journey was proving to be a pain in more ways than one. To complement his physical discomfort, Wooster was proving to be as much fun as a poke in the eye with a sharp stick. The manservant's mood had been sullen ever since Jophrey had refused to answer his questions about Tobias and his probable motives for visiting Mandragle Castle. Now Wooster only spoke if he had to, which was not often.

The wagon lurched to one side as an iron-shod wheel hit a rock. Mumbling a curse, Jophrey righted himself and sat up straighter on the seat, his eyes opening to observe their surroundings. All he saw was grassland, grassland and yet more grassland, stretching as far as the eye could see, the narrow ribbon of the dirt track meandering through. "How much longer till we reach Wellstown?" he asked.

From beneath the wide brim of his black hat Wooster stared up the trail and did not seem the least bit interested in replying. Just when Jophrey thought he would have to ask again, Wooster said, "Tomorrow afternoon, at the earliest."

Jophrey sighed. Yet another night spent sleeping in the back of the wagon with only Wooster's snorting for company.

In the distance a black speck appeared in the clear blue sky. It couldn't be, could it? His heart skipped a beat as the shape of a black dragon powered closer.

'Mandrake!' he thought, enthusiastically.

'Yes. It is I,' Mandrake's deep voice boomed in his head. *'Order the man to stop the cart, otherwise the horses will panic when I land. I would hate to have to chase around the countryside trying to catch them. Especially after the morning I have had.'*

'Is there a problem?'

'Not now there isn't. Stop the cart, then we can talk.'

Mandrake's bulk was now clearly visible and the beating of his huge wings could be heard on the breeze. The horses snorted, their ears flattening, the whites of their eyes showing as fear gripped them. Wooster cursed and hauled on the reins to stop them before Jophrey could tell him to. Slamming home the wooden brake, Wooster grabbed two lengths of cloth from behind the bench and leaped to the ground. Murmuring words of comfort to the skittish animals he wrapped the cloths around the horses' heads to prevent them from observing the approaching dragon.

Jophrey jumped down, excitement at meeting the dragon banishing all other thoughts from his mind. Shielding his eyes with his hand, he ran to the back of the wagon and watched in awe as the mighty black circled above, turning in the air so that he was down wind of the horses when he came in to land. The animals neighed nervously and pawed at the ground as Mandrake spread his wings and slowed for his landing. In a cloud of dust his bulk settled on the ground and Jophrey rushed forward, eager to meet his friend. Soothing the frightened horses, Wooster checked the wagon's brake once more before following at a more dignified pace.

The dust had begun to settle by the time Jophrey reached the dragon and the dark glossy sheen of his scaled hide glistened in the afternoon sun. Strapped into the saddle at the base of Mandrake's long neck, Lord Blackbishop looked nowhere near as magnificent. His hands gripped the pommel as if he were trying to throttle it. Dust and grime coated his clothing, goggles and cap. His face was streaked with dirt and his lips were curled back in a feral grin, frozen in place, his muck encrusted teeth clamped together.

"What's the matter with him?" Jophrey asked, peering up at the dishevelled figure of his father.

Mandrake chuckled; a deep, rolling vibration that thrummed through Jophrey's being. Jophrey waved his arms in the air, but his father remained unseeing and unmoving.

"Velocity sickness," snapped Wooster, barging past and making his way to Lord Blackbishop.

"Velocity sickness?" said Jophrey.

Mandrake's large, wedge-shaped head swung round on his sinuous neck and eyes the size of dinner plates scrutinised Wooster as the manservant reached up and prised Lord Blackbishop's fingers from the pommel. *'How on earth does a manservant know about such things as velocity sickness?'* he mused.

Jophrey shrugged and looked at Wooster. Yet another puzzle to add to the list of questions surrounding the man.

'Beware of that one,' said Mandrake. *'I have the feeling he is more than he seems. Perhaps our little accident will have to occur sooner than we thought.'*

With a grunt Wooster heaved Lord Blackbishop sideways out of the saddle. Although hard to get moving, once started he was impossible to stop. Wooster cried out in surprise as Lord Blackbishop slid to the side and fell to the ground, flattening him in the process. The sudden jolt broke through Lord Blackbishop's paralysis. He launched himself to his feet and yanked the goggles from his head, flinging them to the ground in fury. He glared down at his manservant, hands on hips, then ran forward and aimed a kick at his ribs. "Let that be a lesson to you, Wooster. And this!" Another kick stopped just short of connecting with Wooster's head. "And this!" A stamp struck the ground a finger's width from Wooster's groin. "And this!"

"Father!"

Lord Blackbishop looked up, his eyes wide and wild, his foot raised. "Huh?"

"Will you behave?"

Lord Blackbishop lowered his foot. "But he touched me." He glared down at Wooster. "And he knows not to do that unless it is specifically requested."

"He was trying to revive you!" Jophrey shook his head. His father could be a complete and utter prat sometimes. Most of the time in fact. "You had, er —" he glanced at Mandrake, who was watching Lord Blackbishop with an amused curl on his lips "— velocity sickness."

Lord Blackbishop frowned. "Felicty who?"

"Velocity sickness, my Lord," said Wooster, rising to his feet and dusting himself down. "You blacked out, if you'll pardon the expression, due to the g-forces created by supersonic flight, which caused a differential between the blood pressure on the aortic and ventricle alignment of …" He stopped speaking when he noticed the glazed look in Lord Blackbishop's eyes. "You blacked out, my Lord."

Lord Blackbishop tutted and rolled his eyes. "Well why didn't you say so, instead of all that mumbo jumbo about Felicity and her g-spot? I don't even know the lass."

"Quite, my Lord," said Wooster, dipping his head.

Lord Blackbishop clapped his gloved hands together and turned his attention to Jophrey. "Right then, young fellow-me-lad, where's this friend of yours? I can't wait to meet him." He looked over Jophrey's shoulder at the wagon. "Hiding in the cart like a scaredy cat, is he?" He chuckled. "Tell him to come out. Mandrake won't bite, will you …"

A sullen pout formed on Lord Blackbishop's face and he rounded on the dragon, placing his hands on his hips and glaring up at him. "You mutinous beast! Now I remember. You refused to obey orders, flying willy-nilly all over the place when I specifically asked you to obey me. Well? What have you got to say for yourself?" He folded his arms across his chest and tapped his foot on the ground, waiting for the dragon to answer.

Outwardly Mandrake was a picture of subservience; his head lowered to the ground and tears in his eyes as he avoided his Lord's gaze. Inwardly, however, he seethed, wanting nothing more than to grind Lord Blackbishop to a bloody pulp. But that pleasure would have to wait. "Forgive me, mighty Lord. I know not what came over me." Lord Blackbishop harrumphed, but his stern demeanour softened. Tears trickled down Mandrake's cheeks. "It has been an age since last we flew together, and I was caught up in the excitement and forgot myself. Can you forgive your humble servant for causing his master such distress?"

"Well, I ..." Lord Blackbishop visibly relaxed as he mulled it over. He straightened and wagged a finger in Mandrake's direction. "Don't let it happen again. Understood?"

Mandrake nodded solemnly. *'Until the next time,'* he silently informed Jophrey.

Jophrey giggled. Lord Blackbishop glared at him before striding towards the wagon. "Wooster, attend me!" he barked over his shoulder. "That fool Jives ..."

"Jeeves, my Lord," Wooster corrected, picking up the discarded goggles and following his master.

With a wave of his hand, Lord Blackbishop dismissed Wooster's comment and continued to the wagon. "Jeans, that's him. Anyway, he's damn near useless. Why you ever insisted on ..."

Jophrey shook his head in bemusement as they wandered away. "Just like old times," he muttered.

Mandrake snorted and turned to Jophrey, a sly smile on his face. "While I am feeling rebellious, should we take to the skies?"

"Y-you mean ..." Lost for words, Jophrey stared at the dragon.

"Well don't just stand there, get on board before his Lordship comes back and spoils the fun."

Needing no further prompting, Jophrey hurried to the dragon's side and hauled himself up. Settling himself into the moulded leather saddle, he buckled himself in with the restraining strap and prepared for takeoff. His stomach sank to his knees as the dragon launched himself skywards, but the uncomfortable feeling fled with the exhilaration of flight. Wind rushed past his face as Mandrake soared through the air with powerful strokes of his wings, making Jophrey shriek with delight.

Down below Lord Blackbishop looked to the sky and stared after the rapidly dwindling black shape. For the second time that morning he threw his goggles to the ground in fury.

'What will my father say when we get back?' Jophrey asked, his

concern about the reception they would get on their return attempting to push the excitement from his mind.

Mandrake shrugged. *'Who cares? Anyway, up here we can talk in peace.'*

'So there is a problem,' said Jophrey.

'One that can be easily solved.' The dragon twisted his head round to peer up at Jophrey with huge, unblinking eyes. *'It would appear that there will be two accidents to arrange.'*

Chapter Twenty

Chunks of tree rained down, thundering through the branches, bushes and whatever else got in the way to crash to the ground in clouds of dust and leaves. The crack of timber against timber, the thud of wood on earth and the screeching of startled birds resounded through the forest. Bright shafts of sunlight appeared through the leafy canopy where branches had been torn away by the dragon and the falling debris.

Dodging and weaving, Tobias ran for his life, the five shrieking Beastie Boys clamped to his chest. Mind-numbing terror fuelled him as he hurdled fallen logs and careered through the trees like an athlete, oblivious to the branches and vines that whipped into him. Battered and bruised from his trial by flagellation, he dared not pause in his flight; not while the black dragon rained terror from above. Eventually his strength gave out. He could hardly run and his breath came in ragged gasps. His legs felt like lead weights and the figures in his arms were growing heavy. The aerial bombardment had ceased, but fear drove him on. Without warning he tripped, crying out as he fell to his knees. The Beastie Boys flew from his arms and tumbled to the leaf-strewn ground.

Brimble landed softly and rolled to his feet in one fluid motion. He brushed the leaves and twigs from his tunic and gazed at Tobias, who was on his hands and knees, gasping for breath, trying his best not to heave.

Not landing so softly, Trimble scrambled upright and glared at Tobias. His tunic was ripped and both knees had gone through his leggings. "Did you see that?" he asked, of no one in particular. "He threw us away, the inconsiderate sod. After all we did for him he treats us like a sack of potatoes and tosses us around without a care in the world. Stick him, Brimble. Go on. Give him what for. Teach him a lesson. Show him that you don't mess with the …"

Brimble's hand shot out and covered Trimble's mouth, but muffled words still spewed forth indignantly. Heaving a sigh, Brimble removed a yellow plumed dart from his bandolier and jabbed Trimble in the neck. Trimble's eyes rolled and he collapsed to the ground.

With a shrug Brimble pouched the used dart and said, "As I previously mentioned, sometimes it's the only way to shut him up." He walked across to Tobias and placed a tiny hand on his shoulder. Behind him Thatch, Grommet and Boo disentangled themselves and rose shakily to their feet. They gazed at Tobias with undisguised admiration.

"Why?" asked Brimble.

Now that he could breathe more easily and the nausea had passed, Tobias raised his head and met Brimble's inquisitive stare. "Would you have left me at the mercy of the black dragon?" he countered.

Without pausing to consider the question, Brimble said, "Yes. Which makes it all the more remarkable that you risked your life to save us." He removed his hand from Tobias's shoulder and stepped back. Thatch, Grommet and Boo shuffled forward and stood beside him. "Thank you," they murmured in unison, their eyes downcast.

Tobias grunted an acknowledgement and settled back on his haunches to examine the dragon free canopy above. His legs felt like jelly and he doubted whether he would be able to stand for a while yet. "It looks like our attacker has given up."

The Beastie Boys followed Tobias's gaze, smiles of relief on their faces.

"It would appear that we owe you," said Brimble, the tight-lipped look on his face indicative of his thoughts on the matter.

Tobias nodded, his mouth curling into a smile. "It would seem that you do. My companions?"

Brimble looked at Thatch. "Back at the steading, safely trussed. Grimble is looking after them," he said.

"Well then, what are we waiting for?" Tobias rose to his feet, grimacing as his muscles complained about the movement. Tucking the snoring Trimble under his arm, he gestured for Brimble to lead the way and followed the Beastie Boys through the trees. The trek was slow, and by the time they arrived at a small clearing surrounded by tall trees that formed a lofty arch overhead, the light had faded and Tobias was completely lost. He was amazed that the little men knew their way; every tree had looked the same to him: tall, made of wood and covered in greenery.

In the centre of the clearing stood the cart, with three slumped figures visible on the driver's bench. Tobias's eyes lit up. Still in their traces, the horses turned their heads to wicker a greeting when he and the Beastie Boys emerged from the trees.

"Who the bloody hell's out there?" a voice called out. "If yer don't let me free this instant I'll jump out and rip yer bloody heads off."

The Beastie Boys immediately reached for their blowpipes, loading them with red-tailed darts.

Tobias shook his head. "Leave this to me." He frowned. "On second thoughts, keep them handy." So saying, he placed the sleeping form of Trimble on the ground and walked over to the cart.

"Bloody hell, young 'un. Where'd you appear from?" Wild Bill asked. His neck craned as he tried to look over Tobias's shoulder. "None of them little green buggers about, is there?"

"Who's he calling a little green bugger?" Thatch's reed-like voice piped up.

"What's a bugger?" asked Boo.

Wild Bill's eyes narrowed. "Who said that?" he growled.

"Are they all right?" Tobias asked, examining Cronan and Nanna Pussy. They were leaning against each other, doing a good impression of a loving old couple who had taken an afternoon nap.

Wild Bill shrugged. "They's still breathing, so they must be. It was their bloody snoring that woke me. Now untie me, there's a good lad. Then I can go midget hunting."

Four high-pitched squeaks greeted his comment.

"They're bloody well here." Wild Bill wriggled round on the bench to expose his bound wrists. "Hurry up, young 'un, before they stick us again. Let me free so I can get at the little bastards!"

Tobias spotted Nina in the back of the cart. Ignoring Wild Bill's protestations he climbed over to her and broke her bindings, then sat beside her and placed her head on his lap. Relief washed through him when he saw that she still breathed.

"Bloody hell, young 'un. Forget the girl and set me free before we get stuck!"

"Do it yourself!" snapped Tobias. "The bonds aren't that strong. I managed to break mine."

With a roar of rage Wild Bill pulled his hands apart. Wrenching the bindings from his legs, he launched himself off the driver's bench, growling deep in his throat when he caught sight of the Beastie Boys.

Tobias realised that perhaps having Wild Bill free and rampant, before he'd had the chance to explain the situation, could prove fatal. "Brimble!" he yelled. "Watch out!" He needn't have worried; within three paces Wild Bill was once again comatose, four red-tailed darts protruding from his cheeks.

Brimble climbed onto the cart and peeked over the back of the driver's bench. "Who's she? Your woman?"

Tobias shook his head.

Excited shouts sounded from below and Brimble turned to look down. "It's Grimble," he explained. "Hey, boy! Where have you been?"

"Call of nature," came the reply. "What's happened to him?" Grimble asked, stopping beside the huge, shaggy form of Wild Bill."

"He got free so we stuck him," explained Thatch.

"Oh!" Grimble looked up. "How come *he's* free?" he asked, nodding at Tobias.

"Saved us from the dragon, he did," cried Boo, hopping from foot to foot in excitement. "You should have seen him, Grimble. He was like a hero of legend, racing to protect those in need. He snatched us from the jaws of death in the nick of time. Big, salivating jaws, filled with …"

"Enough!" shouted Brimble.

Boo reddened and spluttered to a halt. "I was only telling him what happened."

"Later, Boo. Now come up here and help us revive the oldies."

Nina stirred in Tobias's lap. A small smile tugged at the corners of her mouth as her eyes flickered open and she saw him. Then she noticed Brimble, who had scrambled into the back of the cart to check beneath the tarpaulin. She screamed.

So did Brimble.

"It's all right," soothed Tobias, stroking her cheek. "They're … er, friends. How are you feeling?"

Her eyes remained fixed on Brimble. "Thirsty," she answered, her voice dry and raspy.

Brimble grinned and scampered away. "I'll be right back," he called. Moments later he reappeared with Boo and Thatch, pulling a water canteen between them.

Nina shrank into Tobias as she warily eyed the little green men. "There's more of them," she whispered.

Tobias chuckled and took the canteen. "Thanks, guys," he said.

"Right," said Brimble. "Let's get these oldsters up and about."

As Nina returned the canteen to him, Tobias sensed that something was not quite right. The tone of the Beastie Boys' constant chatter had changed and an aura of apprehension hung in the air. "What's the matter?" he asked, leaning forward to see what they were up to. Cronan still lay slumped on the bench and was snoring again, but it was Nanna Pussy who seemed to be the object of their concern. Brimble, Grimble, Grommet, Thatch and Boo were grouped around her, eyes fearful.

"She won't wake properly," Brimble replied, looking at Tobias, his face ashen. "We've never had this happen before."

Tobias eased Nina off his lap and scrambled forward. "Had what happen before?"

"This," said Brimble, moving aside so that Tobias could see.

Tobias gasped. The skin of Nanna Pussy's face had turned gold and was stretched tight over her skull as if it had been shrunk. Through parchment flesh, every vein was visible. "By the gods," he whispered, leaning over the bench and pressing his fingers to her neck. A weak, erratic pulse met his touch.

Behind him Nina's hand flew to her mouth to stifle a sob. Tears spilled down her cheeks as she gazed at the still form of her gran. "She's dead," she whispered.

"Not yet she isn't," Tobias snapped. "Move aside, I'm coming through." The Beastie Boys scampered out of the way as Tobias vaulted the backrest and lifted Nanna Pussy in his arms. He only managed to raise her a finger span or two before laying her back on the bench. She weighed a darn site more than her size suggested. Although he was not very strong, Tobias knew he should have been able to lift her. There was nothing else for it; he would have to get Cronan out of the cart to make room for Nanna Pussy to lie down.

"Give me a hand," he said to Nina, moving across to grip Cronan's shoulders. "We need to get him out of the way."

They pulled Cronan out of the cart and laid him on the ground next to Wild Bill. When he was comfortable, Tobias ran back to the cart and eased Nanna Pussy flat onto the bench. "Get me water," he demanded.

Nina reached into the back of the cart and retrieved the canteen. "She's still alive?" she asked, her voice thick with emotion.

"Barely."

"It's not our fault," wailed Boo, wringing his hands as he looked on. "Is it Brimble?"

Brimble stared down at Nanna Pussy, silent and pensive.

"Brimble?" Boo whispered. "Is it?"

"Is there anything we can do?" Brimble asked.

Tobias looked into his troubled eyes. "Maybe you could get a fire going. I think we could all do with something to eat. There's plenty of supplies in the back of the cart." He gave a tight-lipped smile. "We'll be with you shortly."

Needing no second urging, the Beastie Boys clambered down to go and prepare the fire. Tobias watched them for a moment, thankful that they were out of the way, before turning his attention back to Nanna Pussy.

"What *are* we going to do?" Nina asked, clambering onto the bench beside Tobias.

Tobias didn't have a clue. The nearest he'd come to being a medic was when he had been nominated first-aider at kindergarten. That was fine for cut fingers and grazes, but this? He was completely lost. Looking at Nina's stricken features he realised he had to do something, anything, to ease her anguish.

With a smile of encouragement he unstoppered the canteen. "Hold this while I lift her head."

Nina took the bottle from him with shaking fingers.

"When I get her head at the right angle, trickle some water between her lips. She looks dehydrated." The diagnosis sounded plausible, and Nina must have been reassured because she nodded her understanding.

Seeing Nina so upset, Tobias realised that he had also become attached to Nanna Pussy. The old lady was special and he knew he would move heaven and earth to save her. Willing her to live, he eased his hands under her head and screamed. The green-tinged forest twilight disappeared in a kaleidoscope of flashing colours, his very being dragged into a landscape of pain and suffering.

* * * * *

High in the sky to the north of Wellstown, his enormous wings propelling him with ease, the huge dark shape swept majestically through the air. Enjoying the freedom of flight, Mandrake ducked and dived, twisted and turned, while Jophrey squealed and shrieked with delight. This was the best experience of his life. Although he knew his father would be furious when they returned, at that moment he didn't care. This was fun. This was life. This was what being a dragon rider was all about. The exhilaration was addictive and he didn't want the feeling to end.

A scream of surprise tore from his throat as Mandrake suddenly went into a dive. His fingers gripped the pommel more tightly as the ground rapidly rose to meet them. At the last possible moment, the dragon pulled out of free fall and soared back into the sky. Once his stomach had rearranged itself, Jophrey gave vent to his feelings with a loud cry. *'That was amazing,'* he mind-spoke, not at all confident that he could speak out loud after such a manoeuvre.

The dragon twisted his head round, his lips curled in a smile. *'Glad you approved. Care for another before we return?'*

'You bet!'

As if overcome by paralysis, Mandrake's smile suddenly froze and his huge wings stopped flapping. Losing momentum, he began to fall; this time without control he spiralled down.

Jophrey cried out in terror. "MANDRAKE! MANDRAKE!"

With a shake of his head the dragon broke free of his trance and spread his wings. The dizzying downward spiral slowed and Mandrake turned and headed back to where they had left Lord Blackbishop and Wooster.

'What was all that about?' Jophrey asked, feeling decidedly queasy. His eyes had lost focus and he swayed in the saddle, sure that his stomach had risen to greet his throat before settling down again.

'Magic,' Mandrake replied. *'Ogmus magic, but with a little something extra.'*

By the tone of his reply Jophrey could tell the dragon was both excited and a little concerned. *'What magic?'*

'Your friend. Tobias.' He twisted his head to look back at Jophrey. *'It would appear that he is a lot more than we thought he was. He will be an invaluable asset to our cause. This makes your quest even more important than I initially thought. A lot more important.'* Mandrake swung his head to face forward.

Sensing that the dragon did not want to discuss the matter any further, Jophrey settled back in the saddle, his mind whirling. Tobias! What had Tobias got that Mandrake was so fired up about? What had Tobias got that he didn't have? His mood turned sombre, the pleasure of flight lost as he focussed on the forthcoming meeting with his former friend. Whatever it was that he had, Jophrey vowed to get it off him one way or another. Even if he had to arrange a little mishap.

He groaned in dismay at the thought. All he had ever wanted was Mandrake to himself. Not a lot to ask, yet here he was considering murder to fulfil his ambition. Where would it all end? Doubts infiltrated his mind. Would it all be worth it? Could he live with himself afterwards if he had to resort to killing to achieve his aims? His mind was still awhirl when Mandrake slowed to land. For the second time in the past few days he wondered whether the dragon was telling him the whole truth. The thought left an uncomfortable itch in the back of his mind, one that would need scratching in the very near future.

Chapter Twenty One

Silent screams emanated from non-existent lips and incorporeal hands flailed against the void, but it did no good. The essence that was Tobias tumbled inexorably towards the dark abyss ahead. Around him bright, yellow-tinged lights streaked past at a dizzying speed, forming an undulating tube that twisted and turned its way into the darkness. Unknown forces attempted to rip him apart, but he fought them, holding his being together by sheer willpower. Part of him knew that his body lay waiting for his return and that if he fell here it would not only be Nanna Pussy that met an untimely end. That thought was the one he held on to; the one that gave him strength.

Imperceptibly his rapid descent slowed. The lights no longer streaked by quite so fast and his flow was more controlled. The darkness loomed closer, larger, but he approached it with something akin to calmness.

A bright, flickering golden fleck appeared ahead. Small at first, its presence grew in size as he neared it, its erratic movement in the dark leaving streamers of gold from its motion. The golden fleck called to him, begging for help. In answer he arrowed forward, only this time with control.

As he flew closer the golden glow blossomed into a recognisable shape. Tobias gasped. It was the dragon from his dream, and she was fighting for her life. Beset on all sides by darkly scaled reptiles the size of mountain goats, she snarled and snapped in an attempt to fight them off. Blood gushed from numerous wounds as she struggled to keep the attackers at bay. But for all her size and strength, she was losing the battle. Losing her life.

A deep, dark fury took hold of Tobias. With a strength born from need, his being plummeted into the darkness, intent on knocking a group of attackers away from the dragon's head. But instead of barging them aside his vaporous presence passed straight through them. The beasts vanished, leaving nothing to show they had ever been there. Aside from a tingling sensation that affected his whole being, Tobias was unharmed. Stunned by the creatures' reaction to his contact, he paused in his flight and stared back at the spot where they had been. Where had they gone? What had he done to them? Why had they vanished?

As he pondered the questions, two reptilian creatures appeared from the darkness and leapt onto the dragon's back. They tore and bit into her hide, talons and teeth shredding her scales in a frenzy, ripping through to the softer flesh beneath. Blood spurted, exciting the creatures even more. With a snarl of rage Tobias thundered through them. Again the attackers vanished.

Not stopping to wonder how he could manage such a feat, he turned and arrowed towards another group that had appeared out of the dark perimeter, sending them silently into the void with his touch. More appeared to replace the vanquished; more red-eyed, darkly scaled reptiles whose sole intent appeared to be the destruction of the golden dragon. They either ignored Tobias or were not aware that he was there, until it was too late. But as each reptile vanished, it seemed that some of his strength went with it and he could feel himself tiring.

The golden dragon, however, appeared to grow in strength now that she had some respite from the relentless attacks. She silently roared her defiance and crushed her assailants in huge jaws, swiping others away with her tail. Beside her Tobias fought on, vaporising the foe with noiseless but deadly attacks. But no matter how many he saw off, others appeared to take up the fight. His strength was almost gone and it became a struggle just to hold on to his being.

When he thought he could fight no more, the flow of creatures suddenly stopped. Not able to believe that it was finally over he darted around the dragon, looking for more of them to fight.

'They are gone.'

After the silent barbarity, the sound of the light, melodious voice startled him. Beneath the relieved tone he could sense a great weariness. *'What were they?'* he asked, floating around to hover beside the dragon's head.

The dragon sat on her haunches, her body ripped, torn and bleeding from wounds too numerous to count. Her eyes, when she gazed at Tobias's presence, were dulled by weariness and pain, but she managed a smile of gratitude. *'Cancers,'* she replied. *'Normally quite deadly for one of my kind.'*

'Cancers?'

The dragon smiled again. *'Without your assistance, I would now be dead.'*

'But how?' He glanced around. *'Where are we? How do we get back?'*

The dragon laughed. *'I am already back. In fact I never left. You could say that you came to me in my time of need. And as for you getting back —'* she gave him a wink *'— just will it.'*

Now this was confusing. She was in a place she had never left and he just had to want to get back to his body and he would be there? What did he have to will? Take me back to my body, I've had enough?

No sooner had the thought formed than his essence began to retract, back the way he had come, back to his body. But without the restraint he had used when defending the dragon.

'Control, Tobias,' the dragon's voice whispered urgently. *'You have to exercise control or you will ...'*

* * * * *

A scream of agony tore Nina from a troubled sleep. Her heart hammered a painful tattoo against her ribs as she sat bolt upright. When she saw the figure of Tobias sprawled across her gran, the blankets that had been wrapped around his shoulders tossed aside, her fist flew to her mouth in alarm.

Lying alongside her, Brimble also jerked awake. Seeing the collapsed form of Tobias, he immediately scrambled across the back of the cart and jumped onto the driver's bench. "He's alive! He's alive! The magic's gone! We can move them now!" he yelled, gazing down at Tobias and frantically waving Nina forward. Nina was beside him in a flash, reaching down and pressing her fingertips against Tobias's neck.

Tears flowed down her cheeks as she felt his pulse. "He lives," she whispered. Her frantic gaze moved to her gran. In the predawn light she could see that the golden sheen had left her skin and that she breathed more easily. Emotion choked her.

"What's all the bloody racket about?" Wild Bill's tone was kindly and filled with concern, belying his words.

The mop of matted hair and bushy beard came into view over the side of the cart and dark, beady eyes peered down at the two figures. His eyes filled with tears, but he turned away before they spilled down his cheeks. "Looks like they could do with some warming up. I'll get the fire stoked, then come back and carry them over. Come on yer wee laddies," he called to the rest of the Beastie Boys, who had gathered round the cart, "you can help me. No point in us all gettin' in the way."

Nina was sure she saw Wild Bill wipe his eyes with a moth-eaten sleeve as he walked off, but swore herself to silence. She'd let Wild Bill have his secrets; it was enough that she had the two people she loved back in the land of the living. The thought surprised her. *Two* people she loved? She gazed down at Tobias and smiled. She did love him, but not in a physical sense. Her love for him was similar to the love she felt for her gran. Kindred love. She frowned. Now whatever put that thought in her head? It might have been a trick of the light, but she was sure her gran's lips curled into a small, secretive smile.

"Do you think we'd better wake him?"

Nina looked up. "Hmmm?"

"Him." Brimble nodded to the back of the cart.

Nina turned her head and looked at Cronan lying on a makeshift bed on one of the side benches, his loud snores joining the dawn chorus in discordant harmony. She smiled. "I suppose we'd better," she answered. "He's not left their side these past two days either."

It took Brimble three finger pokes, four shakes and two face slaps to wake Cronan. His glower of displeasure soon disappeared when Brimble told him the news. Tossing the blanket aside Cronan swung his legs off the bench and made his way to the front. He peered down at Tobias. "He looks dead," he murmured.

"He lives," said Nina, placing a comforting hand on Cronan's arm. "His pulse is strong and the colour is returning to his cheeks."

"Right then, me laddies. And ladesses," Wild Bill amended, giving Nina a sheepish smile. "Let's get these two by the fire. The lads have got a couple of makeshift beds made up so's they can keep warm until they come to proper, like. So if yer don't mind, let the humper see the bodies." He reddened. "If you'll pardon the expression."

Cronan clambered down and followed Wild Bill as he carried Tobias to one of the cots beside the fire. While the big man went back for Nanna Pussy, Cronan stooped to wrap Tobias in blankets before sitting on the ground next to him and mopping his brow with a damp cloth.

"Bloody hell," muttered Wild Bill, struggling to lift Nanna Pussy off the bench. "She's heavier than a pig in heat. What's she been eating? Lead pellets?" Grumbling under his breath, he manoeuvred his load off the cart and made his way to the second cot, with Nina in tow. When Nanna Pussy had been made comfortable and covered with blankets Wild Bill slumped to the floor. "I'm bleedin' knackered," he mumbled.

Nina looked up from where she knelt on the ground, her hands clasping one of her gran's. "You have my thanks," she said.

Wild Bill grinned and gave a sly wink. "Can't have my woman curling up and dying on me, can I? Not before we've consummated our relationship, like."

Nina scowled and shook her head in exasperation before fixing her attention on her gran's pale face.

"I don't suppose there's any chance of some breakfast?" Wild Bill asked, of no one in particular. He patted his stomach. "I'm starved."

"I'll cook it," said Trimble, his voice high-pitched and excited. "Please?" He looked across the fire at Brimble. "You said I could cook today. Go on. I won't burn anything. Or set fire to myself like last time. I'll be careful. You'll see. I'll ..."

"Enough!" snapped Brimble, raising a hand.

Trimble looked at him expectantly.

After a moment Brimble sighed and said, "All right. But any mess and you clear it up."

"Woohoo!" Trimble scampered to the edge of the clearing where the supplies had been stored and began to ferret in the sacks and containers.

"Are you sure that was wise?" asked Grimble, stooping down to warm his hands by the fire.

Brimble shrugged. "We'll soon see."

"Have faith," said Wild Bill. "What can go wrong?" Brimble and Grimble looked at each other, brows raised knowingly.

"Anyways. What's with you three guys having similar names? It gets mighty confusing trying to remember who is who."

"It's because we're twins," said Grimble, nodding wisely.

Wild Bill frowned. "But there's three of you."

Grimble rolled his eyes. "That's why we're twins." Shaking his head he followed Trimble to the supplies, muttering under his breath about the stupidity of humans.

Wild Bill watched him go. "Twins, hey?" he muttered, snorting in amusement. "How long till they come to?" he asked, turning his head to look at Nina and nodding at the comatose forms in the cots.

Nina shrugged. "I've no idea. We'll just have to wait and see." Although her gran's face had a healthy sheen to it and she breathed more easily, she still showed no sign of coming round.

"It had better be soon," said Cronan, fixing Nina with a worried look. "We're but days away from Snor'kel's appearance and if we're not there to greet him," he shrugged, "then all this has been for nothing and the Blackabbots have won."

At the mention of the Blackabbots, Boo shrieked and hid behind Thatch.

"Who's this Snor'kel?" asked Brimble.

"Our saviour," whispered Nanna Pussy, her eyes flicking open. Her lips curled into a smile as Nina gaped in surprise. "Any chance of a drink? My throat feels like it's been rasped raw."

* * * * *

Sitting in Cronan's padded leather armchair with his elbows resting on the surface of the time-worn timber desk and his chin cupped in his hands, Tobias stared vacantly at the empty bookshelf in Hope's small library, his mind awhirl. He knew that he was not in the real library; that the small room was an illusion, a refuge he had created to house his shattered spirit while it recuperated from the sudden snap back into his body, but it still felt like home. It *was* home. It was the one place where he had felt safe. Now its chimera provided a haven for his essence to recover before it returned to his body and the tasks that lay ahead.

Shortly after his arrival Nanna Pussy shuffled into the library and stopped before the desk, her face pale. With a click of her fingers a chair materialised and she sat down. "Thank you," she said, her hand reaching across to stroke Tobias on the cheek.

Although her entrance should have surprised him, it didn't. Somehow he had known she would come. "What were those, those creatures?" he asked, meeting her gaze.

Nanna Pussy settled back in the chair. "Cancers, created by the toxins in the darts that were used to knock us out. To those of mortal stock, the toxins are mere soporifics; but to those with pure dragon blood they are lethal. Something within the drug reacts with our system and cancers are produced, resulting in a slow and painful death. If it were not for your intervention I would have died."

This was all so confusing, the explanation raising yet more questions. "But they looked like big lizards, with sharp teeth and claws. They were ripping you apart."

Nanna Pussy smiled. "To you they did. To me they were shapeless blobs attacking my immune system. The Ogmus magic within you created their image to give you something tangible to fight." She chuckled. "You have far more power than I ever thought possible for one of mixed blood."

"Mixed blood? What do you mean?"

Nanna Pussy sighed. She suddenly appeared older. The lines on her face deepened and her eyes lost their lustre. "It is time for answers, Tobias, some of which you may not like. But I hope you can understand the reasons behind what I did."

Tobias swallowed, not at all sure he wanted to hear what she had to say, but nodded his agreement. "I'm listening," he said.

After a moment's pause Nanna Pussy grunted and stared at a point above and behind him. "When we dragons first came to Tiernan Og our powers were still strong, as were those of the Ogmus. It was only with the passing years that those powers began to fade. Unlike other worlds that we had inhabited, Tiernan Og was not filled with earth magic that we could draw upon and, instead of us drawing from it, it began to draw from us, trying to regain what it had lost. Oh, it had minor pockets of natural magic dotted around, but in reality it was a world where magic had long since faded. Only one area held enough for us to thrive as we used to, but we discovered it too late."

"Hope?" Tobias ventured.

Nanna Pussy nodded. "By the time we discovered Hope and set to work preparing it for habitation, the blacks had been born and our fate was sealed."

"How?" asked Tobias.

"Throwbacks!" For the first time since he had known her, Tobias saw anger in her eyes.

"Young dragons warped by the lack of magic in the world while they were still in the shell. Dragons with a dark side. Dragons who should never have been allowed to survive." She smiled. "But what was a mother supposed to do? I nurtured them and loved them, then watched in ignorance as the little bastards turned on me!"

A crimson glow coloured her cheeks and, embarrassed, she cleared her throat before continuing. "Loveable little bastards, all the same." She smiled wryly. "Especially Spot. He was my favourite.

"Spot?"

Nanna Pussy giggled. "Spot, the all black dragon. He was the runt of the litter, but a right little battler." She shook her head at the memory. "His name was a bit of a joke, really, and I am sure he has never forgiven me for naming him so."

"But how did they get rid of you all? Surely you must have known something was wrong."

"Not until it was too late. By which time all the others had passed through the wyverhole to the other world. I lagged behind, sensing that something was not as it should be, but didn't know what it was. Then, through the portal, I saw what bothered me. The world was bewitched."

"Wyverhole? Bewitched? What world? You've lost me."

"Wyverholes are pathways through the void leading to other worlds, Tobias. Pathways that only those with the power can open. We dragons used them all the time until our numbers dwindled and the need to find new worlds was no longer there. As to which world we were travelling to, it was Midas, a world made of gold." Nanna Pussy leaned forward, her eyes boring into Tobias's. "All dragons love gold. But not for the colour or the apparent accumulation of wealth, but because it holds earth magic. Gold is the receptacle of all earth's magic. The more gold we gather, the closer we are to the magic. Now do you see?"

Tobias shook his head.

"To live in a world of gold would be to live in magic. It would be a living paradise to dragons, but also a trap. What dragon would want to leave such a place? The blacks knew this, which was why they were so keen for us to open the wyverhole to the legendary world of Midas before our powers grew too weak, even though it was a world that we dragons had sworn never to enter." Her eyes misted over. "We should never have let them persuade us."

Sensing her distress, Tobias leaned across the desk and grasped her arm. "How did you know it was a trap?" he asked, his voice soft and gentle.

"Because the scheming little bastards were nowhere in sight when the time came for them to go through!" Nanna Pussy snapped. "Like the toerags that they are, they waited until all but me had entered, then flew off before the lure of the magic dragged them in too. Realising they had gone, I knew it was a trap. But there was nothing I could do to bring the others back and I could feel the gold's tug on my being, so I did the only thing I could. I used every ounce of my power to change myself to human form. As a mortal I could resist the world's pull, thus saving myself from entrapment and ensuring that I survived to work for my kindred's return."

"But what about the Ogmus? Surely they and the Wing Commander could have done something to stop the blacks."

Nanna Pussy shook her head. "The Ogmus never knew what we were about. Like us, they knew of the world of Midas and the vow we had taken. Our planning was done in secrecy, gullible fools that we were. I was," she corrected. "If I had not been so trusting, none of this would have happened. But the enthusiasm of Mandrake and his brothers dragged us along with them. By the time the portal had been opened, we were as enthusiastic as they about the journey. No, the Ogmus could have done nothing. And when I was in mortal form I was too ashamed to go and seek their help. It was centuries before I plucked up the courage, by which time they had retreated to Hope and all the Ogmus of old had passed away. We, the good dragons, were but a legend."

Nanna Pussy became silent, lost in her own thoughts. Tobias sensed there was more to come but was reluctant to press her. "Which leads me to you, Tobias," she said eventually.

Tobias started. "Me?"

Nanna Pussy nodded solemnly. "I travelled the lands for countless years after my kin had disappeared from the face of Tiernan Og, searching for a way to bring them back. I knew that I did not have enough magic to open a portal, and that the magic of the Ogmus was fast diminishing. Even though they had moved to Hope, to the seat of this world's earth magic, their own powers faded. Soon all magic would disappear from the world and I would never be able to achieve my aim. That was when I ventured to Hope for the first time, and where I met Nostra Ogmus."

"You met the prophet?" Tobias was dumbstruck.

"Met him, befriended him and read his work. That is where I first learned of Snor'kel, and of you Tobias. Through Nostra, may the gods rest his soul. That was when I made my plan. Our plan, actually. If it were not for Nostra I doubt very much whether we would be where we are. It was he who envisioned the time scale and the guide, the cryptic tome you know as the Book of Prophesies."

Tobias snorted. Cryptic? That was an understatement.

Nanna Pussy ignored him and continued with her tale, her voice becoming low and serious. "In order for Snor'kel to succeed, he needed a helper from this world; someone with the power of the Ogmus and the dragons, yet someone who would not be held trapped by the magic of the golden world. Someone who is half Ogmus and half dragon."

A nervous laugh escaped Tobias's lips. Half Ogmus and half dragon? "How could you hope to achieve that?" he asked, completely bewildered by what he was hearing.

"I was not always an ugly old hag," Nanna Pussy said with a smile. Tobias's jaw dropped. "In fact I used to be rather a stunner, in a classical sort of way." Tobias's jaw dropped even further. "You could say I was drop dead gorgeous, with the help of a bit of magic."

The copper coin dropped. "M-m-mother?" he whispered.

Nanna Pussy nodded, the smile on her face showing the depth of her feelings for him. "You were the first, Tobias."

It took a moment for what she had said to penetrate his stunned mind; to push away the unbelievable thought that he was the son of a queen dragon. "First?" he murmured, as realisation kicked in.

"Of three. You popped out, then Nina and shortly after, Jophrey."

If Tobias had been in his body he would have fainted at the news; since he wasn't, he settled for open-mouthed gaping instead.

"Triplets!" You should have seen my face when three of you appeared."

Seen *her* face? Tobias would have liked to have seen his own face at that moment.

"Nostra hadn't predicted that, I can tell you. So that is when I amended my plan. I left you in Hope, safely swaddled in a basket outside the foundling's quarters; took Jophrey to the Blackabbots and ensorcelled Lord Blackbishop —" her face darkened at the mention of his name "— into thinking he was the father, and kept Nina with me. My hope was for you to grow into the man you have become, for Jophrey's true nature to shine through to thwart the Blackabbots and for Nina to work with me in my dotage."

This was almost too much. Not only had he discovered a mother he never knew he had, but he'd also found out he had a brother and sister; one of whom he wanted to kill, the other he wanted to …

"My father?" he whispered.

"Can you not guess?" Nanna Pussy responded, with a grimace. "Believe me, I had no choice in the matter. If I could have chosen anybody else I would have, but I needed pure Ogmus seed."

"By the gods," Tobias murmured, the image of the rotund, bearded nerk dressed in the powder-blue flying suit springing into his mind. "Tell me it isn't him."

Nanna Pussy shrugged. "Sorry. But beggars can't be choosers."

"Volgen?" he whimpered.

Hesitantly Nanna Pussy nodded, her lips compressed into a tight line.

"Does Nina know?"

Nanna Pussy shook her head. "And neither does Jophrey." She leaned forward and grasped his hands. "And I would appreciate it staying that way, for the time being."

Dumbly Tobias nodded. Although he already suspected the answer, he asked, "Volgen?"

"He doesn't know either. In fact I very much doubt whether he remembers the occasion of your conception at all." She shuddered. "I know I have tried to forget it these past twenty cycles."

"Twenty? But I am ... we are," he amended, "only fifteen."

"Long gestation," she responded. "And damned uncomfortable it was, too." She rose slowly to her feet. "So now you know it all." Her face fell and the watery glimmer of tears appeared in her eyes. "I hope you think no ill of me for what I did, Tobias. Believe me, if there had been any other way to bring back my kindred I would have used it. But there wasn't." She suddenly smiled. "Now are you going to return to your body so you can give your mum a hug, or what?"

With tears in his own eyes, Tobias looked up from the knothole he'd been staring at on the desktop. "Give me a moment," he replied quietly. "You understand?"

Nanna Pussy nodded, her smile fading. "Do not stay here too long," she advised. "Otherwise you may not get back at all." With that she winked out of existence, her essence returning to her body.

Not get back? After what he had just learned that might not be such a bad thing. He stared at the empty bookshelf on the far wall, where Nostra's book used to lie. Perhaps he should just stay here, safe in the only place he had ever known as home.

Chapter Twenty Two

Nanna Pussy's softly spoken words hung in the air. For a moment no one spoke, then Nina squealed with delight and leaned over and embraced her gran. Wild Bill launched himself to his feet and punched the air with a loud 'Yeah!' Brimble, Boo and Thatch jigged around the fire in delight and even Cronan managed a smile. In a world of his own and unaware of Nanna Pussy's return to the living, Trimble, arms laden with eggs, bread and bacon, a large pan balanced precariously on his head, shrieked at the sudden clamour. His arms flew wide as he jumped in surprise, his load dropping to the ground and the pan landing on his foot. He yelled again, this time in pain, hopping up and down clutching his injured toes and mashing the spilled food into a raw, muddy omelette.

Grimble, busy covering the remaining stores with the tarpaulin, looked up and shook his head in displeasure. He yanked the tarp off the store again and began to extract the second breakfast of the morning.

"I thought you were going to die," whispered Nina, her head resting on her gran's chest.

Nanna Pussy wrapped her arm around her. "I would have done if it weren't for Tobias. That boy is special."

"I know," said Nina, smiling as she eased herself back up onto her knees.

"Help me sit up, there's a dear."

"Here, let me." Wild Bill stooped to raise Nanna Pussy to a sitting position. "Can't have my girl getting uncomfortable, can I?"

Nanna Pussy grimaced, then noticed the Beastie Boys who had stopped their dancing and were now standing beside the fire, hands clasped in front of them as they stared coyly at her. She smiled. "My, my. Pixels!"

Brimble removed his hat and bowed low, the feather brushing the ground. Looking up from his stooped position he noticed that Boo and Thatch were still standing and whispered a command. They immediately removed their hats and bowed. Satisfied, Brimble straightened and, with hat clutched to his chest, stepped forward. "The Beastie Boys. At your service, ma'am."

Nanna Pussy laughed, but was overcome by a bout of harsh, rasping coughs. Ever thoughtful, Wild Bill handed her a flask of water. When the coughing had subsided and she had drunk her fill Nanna Pussy dipped her head to the Beastie Boys. "Cooil ferragh, Beastie Boys, nee Pixels."

The Beastie Boys gasped and dropped to the ground, prostrate. Trimble, his head bowed in dejection, limped over to where his friends lay and stared at them in puzzlement.

"Getten downsky!" snapped Brimble. He cast Nanna Pussy a look of wide-eyed wonder. "Gert draconan."

A shrill squeak escaped Trimble's lips. Flicking a quick, nervous glance at Nanna Pussy, he snatched off his hat and dropped to the ground.

"Getten upenzy," commanded Nanna Pussy, not unkindly.

Wild Bill scratched his head as the Beastie Boys rose to their feet. "What's all this about?"

Nina, surprised by the Beastie Boys reaction and by her gran speaking in a foreign-sounding language, said nothing. Her gaze flicked between the little green men, who were now standing awestruck, their hats clasped in front of them, and Nanna Pussy. This journey was getting stranger by the minute.

"Pixels!" said Nanna Pussy, as if that explained everything.

"Who?" said Wild Bill.

"Forest minders. The oldest inhabitants of Tiernan Og. They were invaluable friends to the good dragons." She smiled warmly at the Pixels. "And still are."

Smiles of pleasure formed on the faces of the Beastie Boys.

Nina shook her head. In all her time with Nanna Pussy she had never heard mention of them before. It would seem that her gran was full of surprises these days. And just what was that language she spoke?

"Where are the rest of your people?" Nanna Pussy asked.

Brimble nodded towards Grimble, returning from the stores, his arms laden with the makings of breakfast. "He's over there."

"He?" Nanna Pussy turned to look at Grimble and a sad smile formed on her face. "It would appear that your people have suffered," she said, turning back to face Brimble.

He nodded, his features hardening. "Black Dragons!" he said.

Boo shrieked and ducked behind Thatch.

"Not here, you moron!" shouted Brimble, rolling his eyes.

Boo eased himself from behind Thatch and gave a nervous smile.

His voice tight with emotion, Cronan said, "In case it had escaped your notice, there is still one of our party who is not quite with us yet!"

Nanna Pussy gave him a kindly smile. "Don't worry, he soon will be. He used great magic to save me from those ... cancers."

"I told you he used magic," said Brimble, excitement making his voice even shriller than usual. "I could feel it."

Cronan snorted. "Magic? ... Tobias?" He shook his head. "He wouldn't know magic if it jumped up and slapped him in the face. The lad is as normal as you or I. Well I, anyway."

Nanna Pussy sighed. "Normal he is not; he is very special. The dragons on the door were not wrong when they signalled his arrival. Tobias is a direct descendent of Ogmus stock. He *is* magic."

Cronan looked down at Tobias's face, peaceful in rest, his mop of red hair contrasting sharply with his pale features. "Well why doesn't the lad come back to us then?"

"He will, in his own good time. Saving my life has taken much out of him. After a good rest he will come round."

"I hope you're right," murmured Cronan, reaching down and clasping Tobias's hand. "The lad is like a son to me." He looked up and met Nanna Pussy's gaze. "You understand?"

Nanna Pussy nodded, her smile of encouragement not manifesting itself in her eyes. The old woman looked worried to Nina, but she decided that now was not the time to voice such concerns. "Anyone for breakfast?" she said, rising to her feet.

"Now yer talkin'," Wild Bill enthused, rubbing his hands together and moving across to the fire. "There's nowt like a good scran to start the day."

"Can I still cook?" asked Trimble, his eyes gleaming with excitement.

"No!" shouted Brimble and Thatch in unison.

Before long the enticing aroma of sizzling bacon wafted through the clearing. Shafts of bright light lanced through gaps in the canopy and a feathery breeze ruffled the leaves. Birdcalls echoed through the forest, along with the occasional grunt of a wild pig or cry of a fox. All was at peace, and the Beastie Boys and their guests sat round the fire in companionable silence, eating their fill, deep in their own thoughts.

A loud belch from Wild Bill disturbed the peace. He scanned the faces turned his way, then placed his platter on the ground and wiped his mouth with his sleeve. "Seems like we have a decision to make," he said. He looked around, as though he was expecting some comment. When none was forthcoming, he continued. "Either we wait for Tobias to come round, which could take days judging by how long it took Nanna Pussy to recover, and risk missing the meeting with this 'ere Snor'kel; or we load the lad onto the cart and continue on our way, hoping that he comes round before we need him."

"Now see here," cried Cronan, rising to his feet. "The lad is ill." He folded his arms across his chest and glowered down at Wild Bill. "I won't allow him to be moved until he has recovered."

Wild Bill shrugged and folded his arms. "It's your funeral." He looked up and met Cronan's gaze. "Or Snor'kel's."

"Funeral?" wailed Boo.

"Not again," groaned Brimble, clasping his hands to his head.

Raw emotion flickered across Cronan's face as he looked over to where Tobias lay.

"As much as I hate to admit it, Wild Bill does have a point," said Nanna Pussy, her voice filled with compassion. We have to continue with our journey or it will all have been for nothing. Tobias would not want that, would he?"

Cronan shook his head.

"You have my solemn word that Tobias is fine. His spirit is resting, that's all. His body is strong. He will be back with us long before we reach the meeting point."

Cronan bit his lip, indecision gnawing at him. After a moment he turned to Nanna Pussy. "You promise?"

Placing her right hand on her chest, Nanna Pussy gave a curt nod. "You have my word on it."

Once again Nina noticed a trace of concern on her gran's face. There was something going on; she was keeping something from her, she could tell. Although she was used to her having secrets, normally they involved scrapes or escapades that Nina would not have approved of. But this time was different. All of a sudden she saw her gran through different eyes. It was as though she didn't know her at all. Gone was the scatter-brained, frail, old lady; replaced by a woman with strength, who knew what she wanted and would ensure that she got it.

"Right then," said Wild Bill, rising to his feet. "That's that settled. Let's be gettin' the cart loaded so as we can be on our way."

"One moment of your time," said Brimble, standing.

Wild Bill looked down at him.

Brimble cleared his throat and glanced at his friends. Grimble nodded encouragement. As though wanting the words out before they lodged in his throat, Brimble spluttered, "We're coming with you."

The silence that greeted his words was broken by a guffaw from Wild Bill. "You? Coming with us? Whatever for?"

Nanna Pussy leaned forward and looked at Brimble expectantly.

"Because ..." Brimble lowered his eyes before he continued. "Because there is nothing here for us. The black dragons hunt us down and kill us. If we stay, we die." He shrugged and looked up. "If we go we may die, but at least we will go out fighting!" The word 'fighting' came out as a growl, his small hands clenching into fists for emphasis. The rest of the Beastie Boys nodded their solemn agreement.

Wild Bill stared at Brimble for a moment. "Well, that's good enough for me," he said. He glanced around at his companions. "What say you lot?"

"We would be pleased to have you with us, myne freunds," said Nanna Pussy, giving Brimble a warm smile.

"Right," Wild Bill rubbed his hands together, "let's get the show on the road. At the rate we're going, we'll soon have a bloody army." Chuckling to himself he wandered over to the cart, the happy cries of the Beastie Boys ringing in his ears.

* * * * *

Approaching noon on the second day's travel, Nina noticed that the trees were less densely packed and she could see a window of daylight in the distance, signalling the end of the forest. Overhead dark clouds were visible through treetops that swayed and clashed in a strengthening wind, and rain could be felt in the air. Sitting between Cronan and Wild Bill on the driver's bench, she pulled her cloak more tightly around her shoulders, a cold shiver running through her body.

Beside her Wild Bill sniffed the elements and eyed the ominous clouds. "Storm brewin'," he muttered. He shook his head. "Not sure I fancy being out in the open when she breaks. Wellstown's a good day's travel from the forest. We'd never make it before that lot drops on our heads. And I, for one, don't fancy getting piss-wet through."

From the back of the cart Nanna Pussy's voice sounded in concord. "For once, I agree with you."

Wild Bill winked and cocked his head in Nina's direction. "See? She's coming round," he said. A half smile formed on Nina's lips; the man never gave up.

"Up ahead is a path to the left leading to a small clearing," said Brimble. "That should do us for the night."

"Right you are," said Wild Bill.

By the time they reached the clearing and began putting up the tent the sky had turned as dark as night and the first drops of rain started to fall. Aided by the Beastie Boys, Wild Bill and Cronan struggled against the wind to erect the shelter while Nina and Nanna Pussy gathered wood for a fire. Safely settled on the ground beneath the flapping sheets, Tobias slept on.

The rain lashed down by the time the final peg was driven home, hammering against the tent's taut cover with a staccato beat. Under the awning, sheltered from the weather front by the cart, Nina and Nanna Pussy coaxed the fire to life. The small flames flickered as drops of rain sizzled in the heat, but soon the fire caught properly and heat billowed into the tent.

Outside the trees swayed, thunder crashed and lightning forked across the sky. After shrugging out of their wet clothes, they wrapped themselves in blankets and ate a quickly prepared meal before settling down for the night. Space was limited in the tent, but they were too tired to complain. Soon Wild Bill's loud snores joined the racket coming from outside.

Despite her fatigue, Nina could not sleep and tossed and turned in the confined space. She was no nearer to discovering the secrets that her gran had kept from her. Although she had tried to voice her concerns on numerous occasions over the past two days, the situation had never arisen where they could speak in private. She was starting to get frustrated. Tobias jerked, a low moan escaping his lips as his elbow flew out and dug into Nina's ribs. She groaned and rolled onto her side facing her gran.

"Are you all right, dear?" Nanna Pussy whispered.

Nina's eyes flickered open, but she could see nothing. The dull glow from the fire did little to illuminate the tent's interior. "I can't sleep," she replied, her voice pitched low.

"Worries?" Nanna Pussy asked.

This was her chance. With everyone else asleep, perhaps now she could get some answers. "Some."

"Tobias?"

"Yes," said Nina.

"He will be fine. Just give him time and he will come round."

Nina sighed. "I saw the doubt in your eyes, Granny, when you told Cronan that very same thing. What's wrong with him? Why hasn't he come round yet? He is young, strong and healthy; he should have recovered faster than you did."

"He is not ready yet."

Her gran's reply did nothing to clarify things. "Why isn't he ready? What happened to him?"

For a moment there was silence, apart from Wild Bill's snores and the loud rumble of thunder. Then Nanna Pussy spoke. "Tobias is more than he seems, Nina."

Nina felt more than saw her gran turn to face her.

"What he is I cannot disclose for the moment, for reasons of my own; but he is a special boy. A rare boy. A boy born for prophecy."

"You're confusing me now. Why can't you tell me who he is? What he is? Or even what happened to him? I think … I think I care for him. A lot." Tears formed in her eyes. "I need to know."

A hand fumbled for hers and Nina grasped it, the aged flesh feeling dry and parchment-like to her touch.

"As to what he is: he is a boy, soon to become a man. His mother and father were, are special people …"

"But he's an orphan," interrupted Nina.

"So he thought." Nanna Pussy sighed. "But there was a reason for him thinking that, for everyone thinking that. Otherwise he would not have become the boy ... the man he is now, and Nostra's prophecy could not come true, and there would be no return of the dragons. You understand?"

"No," admitted Nina. "Your answer doesn't explain a thing."

"He is true Ogmus, Nina, with a bit extra. That is what makes him special. He has the power, the magic, that the Wing Commanders of old possessed. That is why he hasn't recovered yet. Until he saved me from death, only I knew of his birthright. That is why he needs time to himself; to think things through. He's had a mighty shock."

Nina listened, dumbfounded, as her gran explained how Tobias had used his magic to project his inner being into her body and fight the cancers caused by the poison on the darts. Of how he had battled to save her life, and how his spirit had retreated to the one place he called home after the journey back to his body had gone wrong.

Although deep down Nina sensed that there was more to the story than was being told, shock at what she was hearing stilled her tongue. When her gran finished her tale Nina lay in silence, trying to comprehend the powers that Tobias obviously held. But it was beyond her. All of a sudden her gran's tales of the good dragons rang true. With a sinking heart she realised that she didn't know her at all. "What are you?" she whispered.

Nanna Pussy squeezed Nina's hand. "Someone who loves you very much," she answered.

That was no answer at all, but realising it was the only one she was likely to get, Nina let go of her hand and rolled over to face Tobias. "Goodnight Nanna Pussy," she said, before closing her eyes.

In the dark she could not see the tears that spilled down the old lady's cheeks.

The morning broke fine and clear. Around the clearing branches and clusters of leaves lay scattered on the ground, evidence of the ferocity of the wind. The air smelt of wet bracken, clean and fresh, and a steady stream of vapour rose from the tent as the sun's early warmth evaporated the dampness from its skin. Not wanting to travel in wet clothes, Wild Bill hung his leggings, jerkin and long-coat over a branch of a nearby tree to dry. Wandering around the camp in his hobnailed boots and grubby underwear, he whistled a tuneless song, unmindful of the looks of reproach he was receiving from Nanna Pussy.

With her mind on other matters, Nina sat by the embers of the fire stirring it to life and feeding it small twigs from their stock of dry wood. Inside the tent Cronan tended Tobias. He had propped him up and was spooning weak broth into his mouth. Tobias swallowed by reflex, but still showed no sign of waking. With nothing else to do, the Beastie Boys wandered into the clearing to gather the fallen branches and stockpile them under the trees.

"Ever the foresters," said Nanna Pussy, stooping to warm her hands by the fire. "The branches will eventually rot down to form a mulch, which in turn will feed the trees to create new growth."

Nina nodded, but said nothing as she looked across the clearing to where the Beastie Boys were working.

Nanna Pussy sighed. "If I could tell you more, I would. But the rest of the tale is partly Tobias's, and I'm afraid your view of me, and him, would change if I told you now." She placed her hand on Nina's shoulder.

Nina looked up. "What makes you think my view of you hasn't changed already?" As soon as the words were out she regretted them. But it was too late to take them back. She saw the hurt in the old lady's eyes.

"It would seem that it has." Nanna Pussy rose stiffly to her feet and walked into the tent, where she sat down beside Tobias.

Angry at what she had said, Nina stabbed at the fire with a stick, sending sparks flying into the air.

"A copper for yer thoughts?" said Wild Bill, squatting down beside her. "Yer look like yer got the problems of the world on yer shoulders, young 'un."

Nina smiled, but looked up as she heard a shriek of pain. "That's not fair," yelled Trimble, rubbing his head and stooping to pick up his hat. "You clobbered me when I wasn't ready."

Boo giggled. "Catch me if you can!" he bellowed and vanished into the trees.

Grumbling to himself, Trimble placed his hat back on his head and picked up a short, thick branch. He scampered towards the trees where Boo had disappeared. "Coming, ready or not," he shouted. Thatch tiptoed round from behind the tent. Seeing Nina and Wild Bill, he placed a finger on his lips and winked. Nina giggled, her mood lifting.

"That's better," said Wild Bill approvingly. "Yer a damn site prettier when yer smile. Feisty little buggers, aren't they?" he added, nodding towards Thatch.

At that moment Boo thundered out of the trees. "Riders!" he cried. "Riders!"

Wild Bill leapt to his feet. "Where?"

"Out there!" yelled Boo, waving an arm in the general direction of the trail as he stopped, breathless beside him. Cronan and Nanna Pussy emerged from the tent.

Confirming his warning, a covered cart pulled into the clearing. It was driven by a man dressed in dark clothing, a wide-brimmed black hat perched on his head. Beside him sat a young lad with dark hair. Seeing Nina his eyes lit up, and without waiting for the cart to stop he jumped down and strode to where the small group stood. Bowing low he said, "Allow me to introduce myself, I am ..."

"Jophrey!" growled Cronan, stepping forward. "The thieving little toerag that stole Nostra's book."

Jophrey swallowed nervously and his smile faded, then his face froze. Silently he collapsed to the ground, a fluffy red-tailed dart sticking out of his cheek. On the cart the driver lay on the bench, unconscious.

Out of the trees strode the Beastie Boys, spread out in a shallow 'V' formation with Brimble at its head. They stopped before the tent and holstered their weapons. "No one messes with the Beastie Boys," said Brimble, casting the comatose Jophrey a disparaging look.

Chapter Twenty Three

"What do we do with them now?" asked Wild Bill, scratching his head. "We can't take them with us."

"Leave them here to rot," snapped Cronan. "We wouldn't be in this mess if Jophrey hadn't stolen the book. Truss them and leave them, I say."

The old man's vehemence surprised Nina. It was an emotion she'd never expected to see coming from him. "Isn't that a bit barbaric?" she asked. Cronan didn't reply.

"I think we should take them with us," said Nanna Pussy. "Safely bound, of course."

"Whatever for?" demanded Cronan, glaring at her. "They're in league with the Blackabbots and I'll be damned if I'll share a cart with such as they."

"Hostages," snapped Nanna Pussy. "I'll feel safer knowing we have Lord Blackbishop's son with us as insurance against attack, and if he gets out of hand we have the Beastie Boys to protect us."

At the mention of their name the Beastie Boys stood taller, their tiny chests puffed out. Brimble slapped at his bandolier. "They won't mess with us!" A shrill chorus of 'Ayes' greeted his statement, followed by the smack of tiny hands on leather.

Nanna Pussy smiled. "Looks like it's settled then."

Grumbling under his breath, Cronan stomped into the tent and squatted beside Tobias, his brows drawn into a hard frown.

Nanna Pussy shrugged. "You can't please everyone," she murmured, walking towards the covered cart.

"Where are you going?" asked Nina, as she hurried to catch up. Guilt over her earlier words gnawed at her and she wished, more than anything, to make amends before further damage was done to their relationship.

"To see who drove the cart," her gran answered, mounting the step and peering down at the sleeping driver.

"Granny ..."

"Oh, my word." Ashen faced, Nanna Pussy turned to Nina. "You'll have to drive, I have work to do."

"What do you mean? What's the matter?"

Nanna Pussy stepped down. "Look for yourself."

Worried by her gran's reaction, Nina mounted the step and looked at the driver's face. She gasped in horror. His skin had shrunk onto his skull and turned yellow. "He-he looks just like you did when you were stuck by the dart." She looked down at her gran. "What does it mean?"

"He has dragon's blood," whispered Nanna Pussy. "He is one of my kin."

Before she could stop herself, Nina snorted. "Dragon's blood! That's just a story you made up to keep me amused."

Nanna Pussy shook her head. "Would that it were." She met Nina's incredulous gaze. "I am dragon, as is he."

Feeling faint, Nina stepped down from the cart. "What do you mean, exactly?"

"I mean he was once dragon, as was I. That is one of the secrets I was keeping for when Tobias woke. He knows, you see." She gave a wry smile. "The driver has been affected by the poison on the dart the same as I was. If I do not do for him what Tobias did for me, he will die. And I can't allow that."

"Can't allow?" Nina's head was buzzing. How could a dragon be a mortal? "I-I-I don't understand."

Nanna Pussy grasped Nina's arms. "I promise you that once I have dealt with the driver's illness I will tell you all, whether Tobias has come round or not."

"Supposing that what you say is true and that I believe you; how do you know the driver isn't a … a black dragon?" As much as her head told her that what her gran had said could not be true, her heart knew it to be so. If nothing else, this journey had proven her gran to be more than the witch the villagers thought her. So why not a dragon in disguise?

"I just know," she replied, tapping the side of her head. "In here I know."

Nina nodded hesitantly. "Is there anything I can do?"

"That's my girl." Nanna Pussy smiled and shook her head. "Driving the cart will be enough. Now let's get the others; it's time we were on our way."

* * * * *

The two comatose passengers rested in cots in the covered cart as it bounced along the trail in the wake of Nanna Pussy's, which was now driven by Wild Bill. Not wanting to arouse suspicion about what she was about to do, Nanna Pussy had made sure that all but Brimble and Trimble travelled with Wild Bill, while Nina drove the recently acquired addition to their fleet. Although loath to have even two witnesses, she knew she had to have protection in case Jophrey woke and started causing trouble.

Kneeling beside the yellow-faced man, Nanna Pussy rested her hands either side of his head and looked over her shoulder at the two Beastie Boys. The little men sat on upturned boxes near the back of the cart, blowpipes and darts at the ready. "Remember what I told you," she said. "Any sign of him coming round, stick him. Got it?"

Brimble and Trimble nodded. "Loud and clear."

"And whatever you do, don't worry about me. I will be fine. Just concentrate on him." She indicated the still form of Jophrey. "I may be away for some time."

Closing her eyes, Nanna Pussy took a deep breath and prepared herself for the journey. She felt as nervous as a young queen on her first mating flight. The fact that the man was formerly a dragon was in no doubt, but who was he? Despite her assurances to Nina, she could not be certain it wasn't one of the blacks sent with Jophrey to make sure he succeeded in the mission he had been charged with.

Deciding that prevaricating was getting her nowhere, she sent her essence flowing into the man, spreading through veins and arteries, clearing vital organs and fighting the cancers that threatened to kill the body. Fortunately it had only been a short time since the dart had injected its poison so the cancers were not strong. She reached the brain and felt her essence being drawn to a deep, dark area. Panic set in and she fought the pull, but it was too strong. She was old and still tired from her own fight with the cancers, but the being whose body she'd invaded was in its prime.

'Relax and go with the flow.'

The thought calmed her. *'Who are you?'*

'Your servant, who is most eager to meet you. Do not be afraid to reveal your form.'

She smiled to herself, half recognising the voice. If it was who she thought it was, it was a friend indeed. Swiftly her being coalesced into the bright, golden shape of a dragon and flew silently into the darkness. *'Where are you?'*

'Right ahead.'

A circle of pale light appeared, and at its centre sat a large, red dragon. It raised its head as the gold spread its wings and landed softly beside it. Dipping its head, the red spoke. *'My Queen.'*

'Winegrath?'

Winegrath looked up, his large eyes gleaming. *'Yes, it is I. It has been a long time, Nanapussy. Far too long.'*

Although she saw him, or rather his essence, she still could not believe it was Winegrath. She had seen him, as a young dragon, fly through the wyverhole with the others. *'How?'* she asked.

Winegrath shrugged. *'I was chosen to come back to seek a way of permanently opening the wyverhole; chosen because I was the youngest and most likely to survive the, ahhh, change, as well as the journey.'*

'Chosen by whom?'

Winegrath sighed. *'Without you there was dissent on Midas. The old ones revelled in the power, the lure of the gold; while we younger dragons quickly grew bored and longed for the sight of green fields, wind in our faces and the feel of our riders on our backs. We decided to seek a way home. But even with the magic of Midas our meagre skills could only open a small portal; one large enough for a mortal to pass through, but nothing larger. And that took an eternity to achieve. I was chosen to undertake the journey and, once back on Tiernan Og, find a way of bringing back the others.'* His long neck drooped and his head hung low. *'But I have failed. I thought that by travelling to the stronghold of the blacks I would find a way to open a wyverhole to Midas; of using them like they used us.'* His neck straightened and his eyes whirled in anger. *'But it seems that the blacks have a plan of their own, one that threatens not only Tiernan Og but a host of other worlds, too.'*

'Explain!'

'I learned that there is an Ogmus of power due on Tiernan Og, an Ogmus versed in the ways of the wyverholes. And he is bringing with him a flight of dragons, amongst them a queen.'

'I know this,' said Nanapussy. *'That is why we travel to meet them.'*

A tight-lipped smile formed on Winegrath's face. *'But what you may not know is what the blacks plan for this Snor'kel and the queen. They plan to capture them!'*

'Why?' That made no sense. An Ogmus with power would be a threat to the blacks, and a queen would not bow to their wishes. She had always thought that the blacks intended to kill them.

'They believe that Snor'kel will open wyverholes to new worlds for them and their demonic offspring to control.'

'What offspring? They have no offspring. They need a qu—' Suddenly it all became clear. They planned to capture the queen and force themselves upon her, creating a race of black dragons. *'By the gods!'*

'And they have Jophrey converted to their cause, too. After they have killed off the Lords he will be their new 'token' leader.'

'Jophrey? He is made of better stuff than that.' She shook her head. *'He would never fall for their lies.'*

'He already has, my Queen. But do not be too hard on the boy; all he ever wanted was some love and affection. The gods know he received little of that from his idiot of a father.'

'Lord Blackbishop is not his father, Winegrath.'

The red dragon smiled. *'I suspected as much. Blackbishop has no Ogmus magic in him and I know that Jophrey can communicate with the blacks, so either his father was a Wing Commander or his mother was a direct descendant of one.'*

The essence of Nanna Pussy sighed. It looked like there would have to be another who would know the truth — who needed to know the truth. Winegrath deserved it after all he had been through in his efforts to save his kin. Their kin.

She told him of her early suspicions regarding the young black dragons, of her change and subsequent travels in Tiernan Og, her journey to Hope and the plans that were made, culminating in the birth of her children and the journey they were now making to meet with Snor'kel and his horde. Her thoughts turned to her wayward son. *'Is Jophrey lost to us? Is he totally enthralled by the blacks? Can we convince him that we are the good dragons?'*

Winegrath shrugged. *'I do not know, Nanapussy. I have no idea what lies they have filled his head with. But he is a good lad.'* He smiled. *'He must take that from his mother's side, so there may be a chance.'*

'That is enough for me. Come. It is time we were back in the world of the living. Time has a strange way of running away with itself when we commune in spirit, and I can feel a pull on my being. Something is about to happen. I can feel it.'

A ripple swept through Winegrath's essence. *'I can feel it too.'*

'Then let us rouse ourselves before we are too late.' With that she winked out of existence.

* * * * *

The cart was stationary; Jophrey knew this because he wasn't getting bounced all over the place. But where they were he hadn't a clue. Thanks to those sadistic green gimps and their red-barbed darts he'd spent most of the past few candle-marks, maybe days, in a drug-induced sleep. For all he knew they could have transported him all the way back to Hope. He shuddered at the thought, an image of Volgen's angry face flashing into his mind. That would be all he needed; having the the powder-blue fruit-loop to deal with.

Careful not to arouse the suspicions of the little green men, who he could sense perched at the back of the cart, he cracked open his eyes, relieved when he glimpsed daylight through a chink in the curtain covering the window above Wooster's cot. They were still out in the open; they hadn't reached Hope yet. Now if he could only get a message to Mandrake.

Through slitted eyes he peered at the old woman who, hands pressed against Wooster's head, hovered over him like an old crow. What was she doing to Wooster? Every time he had previously woken, albeit briefly, he had been aware of her stooped over the manservant; but before he'd had the chance to tell Mandrake about it he'd been struck by a dart and sleep had claimed him. But not this time. This time he would be careful. He *had* to communicate with the dragon.

As he prepared himself a shiver ran through his body and he felt tingles all over his skin. It felt like a hundred small needles were being repeatedly pricked into his flesh.

"What's that?" one of the little green men asked, scratching at his arms, fear in his voice. "I feel like I've just been rolled in a bed of stinging nettles."

"Me, too," said the other. "Wait here while I go and check with Wild Bill. If *he* wakes, stick him. Got it?"

Jophrey gulped.

"Got it."

The creak of a door being opened and closed reached Jophrey's ears. The remaining green man began to whistle to himself; bright, cheery, high-pitched and hopelessly out of tune. The racket sounded like something sharp being dragged across glass. Jophrey cringed, and fought the urge to scratch at his own prickling skin.

Moments later the door opened and Jophrey closed his eyes.

"It's happening! The mighty Snor'kel's coming. You want to see the sky, Trimble. It's amazing." The little man's voice trilled with excitement.

"Let me see, let me see! The boy's still asleep. Can't I come out, just for a little while? What harm can it do? Pleease?" Trimble's words came out in a mad rush.

After a moment's hesitation the other voice reluctantly gave him permission. "But only for a bit. If he wakes and causes trouble we'll be for it."

"Woohoo!"

The cart rocked as the two little men jumped off. Fearful that it might be a trick so that they could 'stick' him again, Jophrey continued to feign sleep. Muffled by the planked walls of the cart, excited shrieks and yells sounded from outside. So they weren't going to Hope, he realised. They were at the meeting point, where ever that was. Wanting to seize the opportunity of the distraction to contact Mandrake, Jophrey focussed his mind.

'Mandrake! Mandrake! It is I, Jophrey!'

'Jophrey? Where are you? I have not been able to contact you for nearly two days. What happened?'

'We were attacked by agents of the others and drugged to keep us asleep. Poor Wooster is still out cold with some old crone stooped over him.'

'He is of no concern. Now tell me where you are.'

Although Mandrake's dismissal of Wooster made Jophrey pause

in his thoughts, he set aside the manservant's plight to continue. *'I've no idea, but I'm guessing we're at the meeting point as there's great excitement outside.'*

'Outside?'

Jophrey grimaced. *'I'm stuck in the back of Wooster's cart.'*

'That is of no importance as I, too, have felt a stirring in the ether. Snor'kel's arrival is imminent, and close to Mandragle. I can sense its focus. It is close, as are you. I have already called the others. They will be here shortly. It is time, Jophrey; soon all our plans will bear fruit. Stay where you are. Once we have captured Snor'kel and the queen I will come for you.'

'After? Why not now? There aren't many guarding me.'

'There is no time. We have to gather the flight. Tell me, have you seen this Tobias?'

Jophrey frowned. Come to think of it he hadn't. *'No. Why? Is there a problem?'*

'Not as yet. Now sit tight. I will be with you shortly.'

'Mandrake! Mandrake!'

The black dragon didn't answer and Jophrey lapsed into mental silence. Then curiosity about what was happening outside got the better of him and he levered himself up on his elbow. Opening his eyes the first thing he saw was the face of the old lady. She was staring straight at him, her golden eyes boring into his, evaluating him. Behind her Wooster sat on the cot, arms folded across his broad chest, lips compressed in disapproval.

Jophrey's eyes widened in surprise and, with a sinking heart, he slumped back. Like all best-laid plans, this one had also turned to crap.

Chapter Twenty Four

Overhead the sky roiled and darkened and ever-strengthening winds threatened to tear the heavens asunder. Standing on a small grassy hill overlooking Mandragle town, Nina and her companions watched in awe as clouds swirled and eddied towards a focal point over the town itself. Grass, tree branches, bushes and the occasional small rodent sped through the air, sucked up by the vortex.

Wild Bill ducked as a hedgehog went whizzing by. "Bloody hell!" he shouted over the roar of the wind. "The damn thing near made a colander of me head! Get behind the carts. Quick, before something else chucks itself at us!"

"We're already here!" squeaked Brimble, clutching the spokes of a wheel, his body horizontal in the wind. Beside him the other Beastie Boys were in a similar plight.

Wild Bill and Nina struggled to their side and threw their arms around the little men to clamp them securely to the wheels. On the back of Nanna Pussy's cart Cronan lay across the comatose Tobias, using his body as protection against flying debris.

From behind the covered cart, Nanna Pussy struggled into view. Beside her stumbled Jophrey, his hands bound, shepherded forward by the man who had previously been yellow.

"Nina, Wild Bill, Beastie Boys; meet Wooster!" Nanna Pussy yelled when they drew level.

Wooster dipped his head.

"He's one of us!" Nanna Pussy shouted.

"What about him?" growled Wild Bill, releasing his hold on the Beastie Boys and jabbing a finger into Jophrey's chest. Another gust of wind blew the unsecured Beastie Boys horizontal. Alerted by their shriek of alarm, Wild Bill quickly clamped them again.

Nanna Pussy shrugged, then turned to look at the manifestation in the sky, her long skirts billowing in the wind. "It's happening!" she cried. "I can feel it. Snor'kel is about to come through!" A rosy blush coloured her cheeks and her eyes were feverish with excitement.

As they watched the turmoil, the dark ovaloid at its epicentre grew and appeared to become a deep, dark hole. Or as Nostra had so succinctly put it, 'a black sun.' Whirlpool clouds spun around it, spiralling inwards, dragging everything unfortunate enough to be airborne into its embrace. Including small, furry animals and at least one low flying hedgehog.

In the distance Nina noticed a black speck, coming from the direction of the far distant mountain range. "What's that?" she shouted, raising her arm and pointing.

"Mandrake!" shouted Jophrey, his eyes gleaming as they fixed upon the speck, which was rapidly getting closer. "And there's the rest of the Lords."

Six dark shapes could now be seen, each heading with unerring accuracy towards the hole in the sky. Jophrey turned to face Nanna Pussy. "Now you'll witness your demons beaten at first hand."

Lightning fast Brimble whipped out his blowpipe, loaded a dart and fired. Jophrey flopped to the ground.

Wild Bill laughed. "Well done that man. I couldn't have put it better myself."

Like vultures circling their quarry, the black specks orbited the wyverhole, waiting for Snor'kel and his horde to appear.

"What can we do?" shouted Nina. "Snor'kel will be ripped apart as soon as he comes out. He'll have no idea they're there."

"Trust in the gods, my dear," Nanna Pussy yelled back, her eyes suddenly fearful, fixed on the sky.

"He is Ogmus," Wooster interjected. "Have no fear." Somehow that did little to alleviate Nina's concerns.

Suddenly a large red shape dropped from the hole and plummeted towards the ground. Like a pack of wolves, the blacks descended on it. In moments it was gone and the black hole winked out of existence. No sooner had the hole disappeared than the wind began to drop; the massed clouds ceased to spiral out of control and began to drift lazily across the clearing sky. For a moment the blacks circled around the area where the hole had been, then they flew off towards the distant Fangtooth Mountains and Mandragle Castle.

Stunned, the watchers gaped at the scene of their anticipated triumph. It had all been something of an anticlimax.

"Is that it?" murmured Wild Bill, the first to break the silence. He eased himself away from the wheel and stood, hands on hips, watching the black shapes flying away. "We travelled all this way to witness a bleedin' dragon feast?"

"Wh-wh-what happened?" Cronan called from the back of the cart, lifting his head above the side.

"I'll tell yer what happened," Wild Bill stormed. "Bugger all, that's what happened. We're back where we started; up shit creek without a bleedin' paddle, mate!"

"That wasn't Snor'kel." Although Nanna Pussy's words came out as a low whisper, they caught everyone's attention.

"Well who in hell was it, then?" Froth sprayed from Wild Bill's mouth as he turned on her, his eyes holding a manic gleam.

With his arms folded across his broad chest, Wooster stepped between them. "No one addresses Nanapussy in that manner."

Wild Bill strode forward menacingly, pushing the sleeves up his brawny arms. "Well ..."

Nina watched it all as though in a trance, words and images blurring into an incoherent montage. Tears had formed in her eyes at the demise of their hopes, but had refused to spill. It was her gran that she felt most sorry for. Everything she had worked for had come apart before her very eyes. What now for her aspirations?

'Where are my people?' Nina gasped as the voice echoed in her head. *'You told me my people would be waiting to acclaim me. Yet I see no one. Not a dragon, an Ogmus, nothing save for two dismal mountains and some scrawny trees. Have you taken me to the correct world?'* A pause, then, *'Are you sure you knew what you were doing?'*

"Nanna Pussy!" Nina's panic-stricken cry focussed everyone's attention on her.

"What is it, dear?" her gran asked, rushing to her side.

Staring at the spot where the red shape had met its doom, Nina answered. "A voice! A voice in my head!"

"What voice, dear?" Nanna Pussy demanded, her own tinged with excitement as she grasped Nina's arms. "What is it saying?"

Nina shivered. "It seems confused, wanting to know where its people are, what world this is."

Nanna Pussy's grip tightened. "Answer it, Nina! Answer it!"

"How?" Nina's vision cleared and she looked into her gran's eyes.

"Just think the words at the voice, Nina. Come on. If Tobias can do it, you surely can."

"Tobias?"

"Later, my dear. Now think the words!"

Not at all sure what her gran wanted her to do, Nina wrestled with her instructions, trying to make sense of what she'd said. Think the words like Tobias? What had Tobias to do with this?

"Think the words!" her gran repeated.

Nina winced at the tone of command in her gran's voice, then hesitantly thought her words. *'H-h-hello?'*

No answer.

'Is anybody out there?'

Still no answer. Nina slumped in dejection.

"Try again," Nanna Pussy urged. "Ask its name, but do it with feeling."

Nina nodded, then projected her thought. *'What is your name?'*

'Kraelin!' came the reply. *'And whom do you think you are speaking to, addressing me like I am some common peasant?'*

"Kraelin!" The name came out as a shriek. "It says its name is Kraelin!"

* * * * *

As soon as he had formed the detour to get rid of Chyrsothenalazm, Snorkel ran to catch up with Meelan and the others, his feet sinking into the strange flesh-like substance of the tunnel. He was pleased with himself. Not only had he managed to perform another feat of magic, he'd got rid of that blasted demon once and for all. With any luck there should be no more problems between here and the New World, other than Kraelin and her unpredictable mood swings. Typical woman!

It took longer than he thought to catch up. By the time they came into sight he was beginning to worry that the detour he'd set had affected his own route as well. Sweat poured from him in buckets and his red flying suit clung to his body in all the wrong places. Even his beard had droplets in it where it protruded from the sides of his flying helmet.

'It's Mum!' Draco's cry of excitement hammered into Snorkel's

head with the subtlety of a blacksmith pounding metal. It made his head spin, as did the cacophony of happy chirrups and squeaks from the hundreds of other dragonets flying down the tunnel to greet him. In their wake the she-wolf bounded along, yapping with glee.

The dragonets powered towards Snorkel in a seemingly solid mass. With a shriek of terror he stopped dead in his tracks and ducked, covering his head as they descended on him in a flurry of wings. A dead weight landed on his padded shoulder and he felt Draco nuzzle his neck.

'Stop cowering, you wimp. We're here to welcome you back, not to attack you.'

Snorkel peeked out from under his arms, eyeing the squawking dragonets warily. "Sometimes your welcomes could be taken as an attack," he grumbled, remembering the incident in the cannibals' village. He grunted as the she-wolf leapt up and, with her front paws on his chest, began to lick his face. "And you can stop that," he snapped, ruffling the wolf's fur. With a happy she sat and stared up at him, her tail wagging.

"Norkel!"

Snorkel felt rather than heard the heavy tread of feet pounding down the tunnel towards him, their passage creating ripples in the walls. "Meelan!" he cried, running forward to greet his intended and nearly tripping over the she-wolf, who quickly darted out of his way and cast him a reproachful look.

Huge hairy arms gripped Snorkel in a fierce embrace. "I thought you never come back," Meelan sobbed, burrowing her head into his chest.

Snorkel raised his hand and ruffled her wiry mop of hair. "Me? Leave you? Never!"

"Me never let you go again," Meelan wailed, her tears further dampening his already wet tunic.

'Sorry to break up the party, but her royal pain-in-the-assness does not seem too pleased by the delay.'

At Draco's words Snorkel peered over the top of Meelan's head to where Kraelin and Reizgoth waited. The queen dragon tapped a clawed foot impatiently as she glared in his direction, while Reizgoth merely waited.

"I see what you mean," Snorkel murmured. Prising Meelan off him he looped an arm through hers and walked on, the dragonets in tow.

"About time," snapped Kraelin, her large golden eyes flashing with annoyance.

"I'm pleased to see you, too," whispered Snorkel, bowing.

"What was that?"

"He said that he is sorry to have kept you waiting, my Queen," rumbled Reizgoth, flicking Snorkel a warning look.

"And so he should be," Kraelin sniffed. Turning abruptly round she waddled off down the tunnel. "I can't keep my people waiting any longer. Tell him to keep up."

Reizgoth rolled his eyes and shrugged. "Forgive her, she's ..."

"Yeah, I know. Young."

"I do wish you would try to be a little more circumspect around her, Galduran. It is me that has to pick up the pieces after your spats."

Snorkel giggled. "Why spoil the fun?" he said, striding past the huge red dragon. "Come on, or we'll be late."

"For what?" asked Reizgoth, frowning.

"The coronation."

They continued down the tunnel for what seemed an age before the end came in sight. Snorkel stared from the tunnel mouth at the turbulent mass of clouds. "What now?" he asked, staring fearfully at the spiralling, rain-spewing clouds before him, his beard tugging in the wind. "We can't go back the way we came, because I closed off the tunnel."

'I'll go take a looksee,' said Draco.

"A looksee?" Snorkel turned his head to observe the lime-green dragonet perched on his shoulder like a malformed parrot. "You could be swept to your death in that little lot. You can't go out there."

'What else do you suggest? We can't stand around here all day and I don't sense any danger. If it makes you feel any better we dragonets will all go, and when we've discovered where we are I will let you know.'

Before Snorkel could disagree Draco launched herself from his shoulder and out into the void, swiftly followed by her brothers and sisters.

"I wish she wouldn't do that," Snorkel grumbled, rubbing at his shoulder.

"Where are they going?" Kraelin demanded, craning her long neck to examine the clouds. "I, as their queen, should be the first to arrive on the New World."

"They have gone to announce your arrival, oh golden one," Snorkel replied.

Kraelin sniffed in approval.

'Good thinking,' Reizgoth's voice whispered in his head.

'It's all clear, Mum!' Draco's voice came through. *'You can come out. It's a bit tough flying at first, but you soon get through the clouds. Reizgoth will have to carry you though. It's a long drop.'*

"Draco says it's all clear," said Snorkel, relief flooding his body. The gods only knew what would have happened had the world proved to be the wrong one. "But we are high up and it's a long way down."

Reizgoth dipped his shoulder. "Then climb aboard, Galduran. Let us away to our New World."

"Queens first," snapped Kraelin, barging past and launching herself into the clouds.

Snorkel watched her disappear from sight before helping Meelan onto Reizgoth's shoulders. "I know, I know, she's young," he said, before the dragon could say it for him. He whistled to the she-wolf who, tail wagging and tongue lolling, jumped into his outstretched arms. Once they were aboard, Reizgoth launched himself into the clouds, heading for the New World and a new life.

Chapter Twenty Five

When Mandrake's teeth closed on the falling figure and crushed its life away he knew something was wrong. Apart from the fact that the flailing, lizard-like creature had no wings, the taste of its blood made him want to vomit. It was neither mortal nor dragon-kin. Suspecting the creature, whatever it was, to be the vanguard, he spat the carcass from his mouth and circled the wyverhole to await the arrival of Snor'kel and the queen.

The other blacks tore the body apart as it fell, their riders yelling encouragement and urging them on. Spot, attempting to flame-grill a leg, incinerated it and looked on, crestfallen, as its smoking ashes scattered in the wind.

Lord Blackbishop hollered in delight at the kill, but Mandrake ignored the outburst; the man was a fool and only along for the ride. With a knowing sneer, he continued to watch the wyverhole. The lords would be in for a mighty shock when they captured the queen and Snor'kel instead of killing them.

Wind-blown and rain-lashed, Mandrake continued to circle, impatient for the next phase of his plan to come to fruition. But nothing appeared. No dragons, no Snor'kel. His unease grew. What was keeping them? Where were they?

The hole started to shrink and Mandrake rumbled low in his throat, excitement vying with his growing anxiety. The hole was shrinking at an alarming rate, and if the queen did not emerge soon it would be too small for her to come through. With an audible snap the hole disappeared. The winds lost their ferocity and the clouds ceased to churn.

'Where are they?' Snaggletooth asked.

Mandrake swung his head to glare at the dragon. *'We've been tricked!'* he growled. *'The others set this as a decoy to disguise where Snor'kel would really appear.'*

'Tricked? What do we do now?'

The remaining dragons drew closer to wait for Mandrake's response, apart from Spot who was busy shooting flames at the place where the wyverhole had been.

Mandrake roared his frustration at the lack of a backup plan and clawed at the air with his forelegs as if trying to tear it apart. Lord Blackbishop gripped the pommel more tightly. "Steady on there, Mandrake. I know that you're rather excited at having vanquished this Snor'kel chappy and his horde, but ..." He paused. "Er, sorry to appear dense, but isn't a horde normally more than one?"

Mandrake inhaled rapidly and stopped clawing the air. His lips curled back in a feral snarl as he twisted his head round to glare at the lord. Without saying a word he powered away, heading for the dragon-caves at Mandragle Castle. It was time to regroup.

* * * * *

"Ask Kraelin where she is!" Nanna Pussy demanded. "We need to know where they are before the blacks find out."

Nina's excitement at conversing with the voice in her head had ebbed, and had been replaced by confusion. Only vaguely aware of her gran's request, she was slow to respond.

"Nina! Where are they?" The urgency in Nanna Pussy's voice caught her attention. With a sheepish smile Nina apologised and, remembering Kraelin's haughty manner, she phrased her question to the dragon politely. *'Excuse me, your ...'* Just what did you call a queen of the dragons? *'Magnificence.'*

No response was forthcoming and Nina began to fret. Had she imagined it all? And if not, had she managed to upset Kraelin? She tried again. *'Your magnificence?'*

'I am in the middle of berating my aides. Do you mind?' A moment later Kraelin's voice sounded in Nina's head again. *'What is it you want?'*

'Where are you?'

'Is that the correct way to address your queen? Where are you is more to the point. I expected to be greeted by my people upon my arrival, but instead I emerge — after a traumatic journey, I might add — to find myself unannounced. I am not amused!'

'We travelled far to greet you, my Queen. But it would appear that you have come to our world ...'

'Our world?'

'Oh. Sorry. Your world, at a point we were not expecting. Can

you describe where you are so we know where to come to greet you in the manner you deserve?'

As she talked Nina became aware that her companions had crowded round her, wanting to know what was being said. "I have asked Kraelin to describe where she is," she murmured.

Nanna Pussy nodded and the Beastie Boys nudged each other and winked.

'Who are you talking to?' Kraelin asked.

Nina flinched. The dragon had heard her speak out loud. That was something she had not expected. *'More of your people, my Queen. They are as eager to greet you as I.'*

Kraelin appeared satisfied with the answer, as no rebuke was forthcoming. *'We are in a valley and there are mountains either side.'*

Nina relayed the flimsy description.

"That could be anywhere," Wild Bill grumbled, frowning and folding his arms across his chest.

Nanna Pussy grasped Nina by the shoulders. "Get Krealin to show you. I shall link with your mind and, with any luck, be able to tell where she is. Don't be afraid. You will hardly feel me as I'll have to remain hidden in case Kraelin senses me."

Before she had a chance to question what her gran meant, Nina felt a feathery touch in her head, followed by a feeling of warmth and friendship.

'Did that help?' Kraelin asked.

'Not much, my Queen. Can you project a picture of where you are so I can see it?'

In a heartbeat, as if viewed from the air, an image of a lush green valley appeared, superimposed over the inquisitive staring faces of Wild Bill and the Beastie Boys. Nina saw thick woodland either side of a narrow river. She recognised spruce, larch, oak and ash amongst the many trees that covered the ground. When they reached the hills they grew more sparsely, disappearing altogether where the foothills rose to meet the mountains that, tall, snow-capped and imposing, stood watch over the land below, the fuzzy image of Wild Bill's face nestled between them. As she examined the scene more closely she spotted a dirt track that followed the path of the river, twisting and turning through the trees until it broke cover and traced a route up one of the mountains. Strangely, the last section of trees had been ravaged by fire.

The presence of Nanna Pussy left Nina. "Hope!" the old lady said, her voice tinged with relief. "They are at Hope!"

"Bloody hell!" said Wild Bill. "That were bleedin' lucky."

Wooster shook his head. "Not luck. Magic! Snor'kel is true Ogmus; he makes his own luck."

'You are at Hope,' Nina broadcast.

'I have no idea of what you are talking,' sniffed Kraelin. *'What is this place called Hope?'*

"She doesn't know of Hope," said Nina, in a panic. "What can I tell her?"

"Perhaps I can be of some assistance." Cronan broke through the crowd surrounding her. "Tell her that the people of Hope have long awaited her arrival, that they have prepared a home suitable for a queen and that they are awaiting her and her flight."

Nina smiled at the old man and relayed what he had said.

'That is all very well,' Krealin replied. *'But with our welcoming party having gone to the wrong meeting place, how do we find this ... this Hope?'*

When Nina voiced Kraelin's concern, Cronan removed his long-knife from his belt and cleared an area of ground. He drew a plan of the valley and the mountains, showing the entrance to Hope's dragon-caves. When he had finished the sketch he jabbed the knife at a point half way up the mountain. "That is where they can enter. With any luck Volgen will have prepared the caverns for their arrival." Nanna Pussy grasped his arm and smiled.

Wanting to show the image to Kraelin, Nina focussed on the plan and projected it to the waiting queen, telling her what Cronan had said.

'Well if there are others there to attend me I suppose we had better go. It is not as if we have any choice in the matter, is it?' Nina could sense the frosty tone in the queen's voice. *'But let it be known that we are most unamused. We shall expect you shortly.'*

"What did she say?" asked Nanna Pussy, eyes bright.

Now that the voice of Kraelin had gone, Nina felt light-headed, almost faint. She wiped her brow with the back of her hand and sagged against the cart. "It would appear that our new queen is *most unamused* by the situation." She gave a wry smile at her attempt to match the queen's lofty manner.

Nanna Pussy grimaced. "She's a young one then." She shook her head and turned away. "Kids, hey?"

"Where are you going?" Cronan demanded, chasing after her and grabbing her arm. Nanna Pussy glanced down at his restraining hand and, very slowly, peeled it off her arm. She looked him in the eye. "I think you will find we have another journey to make. One that will take you home."

Cronan's eyes hardened. "Not before we cure Tobias we don't," he said. "The lad has been unconscious for days now and I am not going anywhere until he's back with us. He's wasting away before my very eyes and I'll not move until *you* do something about it. After all, it was saving you that did for the lad."

"He's fine. He'll come round of his own accord," Nanna Pussy snapped. "The Terminator won't be needed until we meet with Snor'kel. Let him have his rest. The gods only know he needs it."

"He'll be no use at all unless he wakes up and eats proper food instead of the broth I've been forcing down his throat."

"I'm with him," said Wild Bill, stepping forward. Not wanting to be outdone, the Beastie Boys added their voices.

Still feeling frail, Nina watched the argument unfold from where she was slumped against the cart. Although she understood her gran's need to get away to greet Snor'kel and the queen, she also sympathised with Cronan as she, too, was worried about Tobias's condition.

Standing beside her Wooster pursed his lips and shook his head. Stepping over the comatose form of Jophrey, he walked over to where they were remonstrating. "Silence!" The loudness of his shout caused all discussion to cease. "If I may make a suggestion?"

"No yer can't, yer bleedin' great nerk," stormed Wild Bill, eyes blazing. "This has now't to do with yer, so bugger off."

Wooster sighed. "It has everything to do with me. If you will permit, I can bring Tobias back while we travel."

"Truly?" asked Cronan.

Wooster nodded. "I do have certain —" he glanced at Nanna Pussy "— skills in that department."

Wild Bill snorted.

"I suggest that Tobias be loaded into the back of the covered cart along with Jophrey, while you all ride on the other. That way I can work undisturbed."

"Why should we trust yer?" demanded Wild Bill, jabbing a dirt-encrusted finger into Wooster's chest. "We don't know now't about yer. And," he added pointedly, "yer arrived with *him*!" He nodded towards Jophrey.

"I trust him," said Nanna Pussy, walking to where Wooster stood.

With a heavy sigh Cronan nodded his agreement. "That's good enough for me," he said. Before Wild Bill could object Cronan gripped his arm and led him to the cart. "If you would be so good as to carry Tobias across?" With one last look of defiance, Wild Bill allowed himself to be guided away.

As they walked over to the other cart Nina could hear Wild Bill muttering. "The bleedin' great toerag's trying to muscle in on my girl. You saw him, didn't yer? Actin' all high and mighty? Well if he thinks he's gonna steal her away from me, he's got another think coming. No one steals Wild Bill's woman."

"Shut up," snapped Cronan, "and help me across with the lad, instead of whinging."

Cronan's rebuke surprised Nina, as did Wild Bill's reaction. Instead of continuing his tirade, he shrugged and climbed on to the back of the cart, muttering, "No need to get shirty, old 'un. I were just making a point, that's all."

"Point taken," Cronan responded, grunting as he clambered aboard. "Now keep quiet and give me a hand."

Shaking her head, Nina followed her gran. It was time for some answers.

* * * * *

The atmosphere in the dimly lit cavern was charged with anger. Anger and frustration. Now that the lords had retired to Lord Blackbishop's quarters to celebrate their *supposed* victory with some leaves from their favourite plant, Mandrake paced furiously while the other blacks sat on their haunches and watched. Despite repeated attempts to contact Jophrey he'd had no success, and his mood was not improved by the realisation that the boy had, in all probability, been drugged again. Snarling, he turned to his companions. "Well?"

After a moment's silence Vizigoth asked, "Well, what?"

"Suggestions, fool!"

"Supper?" Nazier interjected hopefully, rubbing at his rounded belly with his foreclaws. Spot bugled his agreement and sent a small flame spurting into the air.

Mandrake rounded on him, eyes blazing. "And you can cut that out or we will be one dragon less in the very near future." The flame died and Spot gave a nervous smile before sidling behind the huge bulk of Nazier.

"We could split up and each search our own lands for them," Peladin suggested.

Mandrake shook his head. "That would take too long, by which time Snor'kel may well have done his work and brought back the others. And that would ruin all of our plans. There must be a quicker way. No, we have to think about where they would hope to emerge on their arrival. It would have to be somewhere safe, somewhere …"

"Hope?"

Mandrake scowled at the interruption. "Who said that?"

Peladin waddled forward. "You said hope." Mandrake frowned. "Hope? You know, that last bastion of Ogmus supremacy?"

The frown disappeared and a smile crept onto Mandrake's face. "Hope," he whispered. "Of course." He fixed Peladin with a steady gaze. "You have done well. I will remember that when the new worlds are allocated."

Peladin dipped his head in acknowledgement and returned to take his place with the others.

"At least one amongst us is thinking," Mandrake boomed, briefly regarding each of the dragons, apart from Spot who still hid behind Nazier. "But before we go rushing off to capture the queen we have to know how many we face, so we need someone to scout the area. Do we have any volunteers?"

All the dragons looked away, unwilling to meet Mandrake's gaze. Nazier, a malicious smile playing on his lips, kicked out a hind leg.

Unprepared for physical assault, Spot somersaulted across the floor of the cavern as Nazier's foot connected with his chin. He rose groggily to his feet to find Mandrake towering over him. Spot gave a sickly grin and backed away, but was stopped by Snaggletooth's bulk.

Mandrake dipped his head and smiled, revealing his razor-sharp teeth. "What? Still here, volunteer?"

Chapter Twenty Six

With his hands on his hips Volgen stood on a ledge at the mouth of one of the higher tunnels leading out of the amphitheatre and admired his handiwork. Having managed to get the dragon-caves cleaned out and ready bang on time, he was more than pleased with progress. The numerous passageways and caves that led from the main cavern had been swept and cleared, and the debris had been piled in a heap at the centre of the sandy arena. The mound of muck was now being transported outside via the widest tunnel; the one the dragons would use when they returned. Almost all of the inhabitants of Hope had been dragged in to help with the task, which was being completed under Volgen's watchful eye.

Volgen smiled at his success and flicked a minute grain of dirt off his powder-blue tunic. A buzz of expectancy filled every tunnel, nook and cranny of Hope; the small colony was awash with high spirits, and everything was falling neatly into place. He scowled as he noticed one of the youngsters slouching on his shovel. "Rimbart!" he bellowed. "Shift your piggin' arse and get shovelling!"

Dirt-streaked and grubby, the youth looked up, reddening under Volgen's glare. "I'm waiting for the cart to come back," he called.

Volgen grunted and looked away, his gaze sweeping across the vast expanse of the brightly-lit amphitheatre, which was illuminated by the numerous torches that now dotted the craggy walls. Nearly all the debris had been removed. A couple more cartloads should do it, leaving the caverns pristine and ready for habitation. By dragons that is; he wouldn't much fancy living in the place himself. It stank and was far too hot for him. As if on cue, a bead of sweat ran down his forehead to hang on the end of his nose. He wiped it away and removed a cloth from his pocket to dab at his head.

Not for the first time he wondered how Cronan and Tobias were getting on with their quest. By his reckoning Snor'kel and the dragons were due any day now. He hoped that the intrepid duo had managed to get to the meeting place, otherwise his little enterprise would have been a complete waste of time and he would go down in history as the Wing Commander who totally bolloxed the return of the dragons. Not an epitaph he particularly relished.

But there was no point in worrying about it. He'd done his job and he'd be buggered if he would worry about others screwing up their side of the deal. At least that's what he told himself. Deep down he knew he'd be gutted if their venture failed, or the dragons' arrival proved to be a figment of Nostra's drug-induced illusions.

The rattle of a cart entering the amphitheatre distracted him. Pulled by two mules, whose hooves were wrapped in cloths to protect them from the heat of the sand, it trundled over to where Rimbart and his colleagues waited. Aware that the Wing Commander was watching, the young lad shovelled with gusto, the first load hitting the flatbed before the driver had chanced to stop.

"That's the spirit, Rimbart. We'll have the place finished in no time," Volgen enthused.

Rimbart grinned and continued to shovel, encouraging the men beside him to do likewise. Soon the cart was full and the driver called the mules to action. The stocky beasts plodded forward and circled the mound, making their way towards the tunnel that led outside. They entered it as a second cart emerged and made its way to the pile to be filled.

Volgen watched it stop and moved to the ladder. It was time for a break. It was hard work supervising this little lot. He gripped the two supports and began to descend. When he was half way down he became aware of a breeze ruffling his hair. It was as if a wind had risen within the amphitheatre. He frowned, confused. And what was that noise? Voices? No, not voices. It was more like chittering; high-pitched and excited. When he reached the bottom of the ladder he turned to face the breeze. It was coming from the wide tunnel, as were the noises. Work stopped as his fellow Ogmus became aware of the disturbance and exchanged worried looks.

The shrieks grew louder and the wind stronger. A nervous flutter developed within Volgen. It started as a sensation deep in his gut that grew to a weird feeling which set his whole body to trembling. The beads of perspiration on his head multiplied until a veritable lake had formed, running off his head in a constant stream.

A scream of terror joined the fast-approaching shrieks, accompanied by the braying of frightened mules. Suddenly out of the wide tunnel shot the cart that had left only moments before, its load scattering over the ground as it bounced and swayed on its frenzied run. The eyes of the two mules were wide, and froth coated their flanks; while the driver clung to the front rail, knuckles white, eyes screwed tightly closed.

Seeing the danger, Rimbart dropped his shovel and sprinted alongside the runaways, hauling the reins of the nearest mule and forcing its head to the side. With his heels dug into the sand he managed to drag the beasts to a stop.

Before Volgen could commend the lad on his speed of thought, bedlam emerged from the tunnel, in the form of hundreds of brightly-hued demons. They spewed from the dimly lit maw, their leathery wings flapping noisily as they shrieked and cavorted in the air. Panic-stricken, a tide of Ogmanity fled for the living area of Hope, shoving, fighting and dragging others out of their way as they sought sanctuary.

Paralysed by fear, Volgen stood open-mouthed with shock as his dreams came crashing down around him. Was it all to end like this?

"Silence! I will not have my entrance spoiled by such unseemly behaviour."

The booming shout had the desired effect and immediately there was quiet within the amphitheatre. The fleeing Ogmus stopped and turned to see who had spoken in such a commanding voice, and the flying demons scattered to perch silently on the rocky outcrops around the cavern.

Astonished by their reaction Volgen peered up into the gloom, his gaze fixing on one of the creatures that was perched on a ledge by the tunnel mouth where he had previously been standing. Its flesh was the colour of summer gold. Volgen's eyes widened. They weren't demons: they were mini-dragons. Perfect in every detail, except smaller.

The creature noticed him watching and gave him a mischievous wink before turning its attention on the main tunnel.

Volgen followed its gaze and his eyes locked on to a sight he had longed to see all his days. "It's a —" tears sprang to his eyes and he sagged to his knees "— piggin' dragon," he murmured.

A beautiful golden dragon swooped into the amphitheatre, closely followed by a huge red with two riders perched on its back, one of whom carried a large dog in his arms.

The sight was too much for Volgen and tears trickled down his cheeks. He sobbed unashamedly. "There's two of them."

The golden dragon glided in to land. Hot sand swirled in the draught caused by its descent, stinging Volgen's face, but he didn't feel any pain. He was enthralled.

The red landed beside the gold and a figure dressed in red flying gear, whom Volgen surmised to be Snor'kel, jumped off its back and released the dog. It yelped as its paws touched the hot sand and it raced for the cool of one of the tunnels, where it lay down and began to lick at its feet.

Snor'kel shook his head and turned to help his female companion down. At least Volgen thought it was female; she certainly had lumps on her chest, but there the similarity to womanhood ended. The muscles on her arms would make a miner green with envy and he was sure he spotted the beginnings of a wispy beard on her chin. His suspicions were in no way dispelled when Snor'kel stooped to kiss her, especially after the revelations about Charlie Vuntlewedge. Volgen cringed as muscular arms rose to encircle Snor'kel. Arms like hers could crush rocks.

"Well?"

At the sound of the voice Volgen's attention was drawn to the golden dragon. With back straight, neck extended and head tilted towards him, she peered down, her yellow eyes swirling in annoyance. He gulped and rose unsteadily to his feet. Now that his dream had come true, he did not have a clue what was expected of him.

"I'd bow if I were you. Then offer a welcome to the queen of the dragons," said Snor'kel, walking to Volgen's side, his arm wrapped round the chunky waist of his lady friend.

Volgen smiled nervously, then nodded his head to the dragon in greeting. He would have bowed as suggested, but his paunch got in the way. "Mmph urg ..." He tried again. "Mmph urg ..." He felt his face redden. Although the mind was working, the mouth was fully disengaged. Forcing aside his apprehension, he tried again. "Welcome to Hope, your Highn— Majes— My Queen."

Snor'kel chuckled.

The dragon sniffed disdainfully and swung her head to look at the group of Ogmus who were edging towards her, clinging to each other as they moved in a single unit. "Is this it?" she asked.

The question was confusing and Volgen looked at Snor'kel for help.

Snor'kel shrugged, his beard parting as he grinned. "I think she was expecting a more spectacular welcome, especially as the party sent to meet us went to the wrong place."

Volgen scowled. Wrong place? That piggin' librarian and his 'I know where they ...'

"She's waiting," said Snor'kel, nodding in the direction of the queen.

Volgen felt his face redden. Turning to the dragon he said, "Forgive us for the poor welcome, my Queen. Please allow me to call the rest of my people."

The dragon dipped her head. "*Your* people?" Her voice was pitched low and menacing.

"Krealin, be nice to him," urged the red dragon.

To Volgen's annoyance Snor'kel chuckled again. "Don't worry," he said, out of the corner of his mouth. "She's young, her ..."

"Galduran!" The red dragon's voice carried a hint of warning.

Unconcerned, Snor'kel chuckled and gripped his companion more tightly, and she responded with short, deep barks. It took a moment for Volgen to realise it was laughter.

"Fetch them!" demanded Kraelin. "I am eager to meet my brethren."

Nonplussed Volgen turned to where his people stood. He'd never thought to hear a dragon refer to Ogmus as brethren.

"I'll go, Wing Commander." It was Rimbart. Smiling in relief, Volgen nodded his permission. Sand sprayed from beneath Rimbart's feet as he ran from the amphitheatre into the tunnel leading to the upper levels. Once he had left, Volgen turned to face Kraelin. "Your people will be here shortly, my Queen."

"And not before time," Kraelin rumbled.

"Kraelin!" murmured the red.

"So how many are there?" asked Snor'kel.

Volgen frowned. "Sorry?"

"You know. Dragons."

"What dragons?"

"The ones that young lad's gone to fetch."

Volgen shook his head and frowned. "He's not gone to fetch

pig— er, dragons. He's gone to fetch the rest of the Ogmus so they can welcome *her*." He nodded towards Kraelin.

It was Snor'kel's turn to frown. "But what about the dragons?"

"What dragons?" asked Volgen, mystified by the question.

"The ones that live here, of course!" Snor'kel's voice had risen in exasperation and he flung his arms wide to indicate the cavern, nearly hitting his companion with a forearm smash. She quickly ducked and only received a glancing blow.

"There's no dragons here," snapped Volgen, his own patience wearing thin at Snor'kel's apparent incomprehension. "That's why you're here!"

"Who's here?"

"You!"

"I am here because I have brought her —" Snor'kel pointed at Kraelin "— to rejoin her kin."

"You're here because we need you to bring back the other dragons!" Volgen retorted. "You and your horde!" He pointed at the mini-dragons dotting the cavern roof, then lapsed into silence as his eyes followed his pointing finger. "Horde?" he murmured. "That's your piggin' horde?"

The summer-gold mini-dragon he had observed earlier smiled, and with a happy chirrup glided down and landed on his shoulder. Volgen stood rooted to the spot as its talons pressed gently into his flesh and it craned its neck round and gazed into his eyes.

'Hi. My name's Flame, what's yours?'

Volgen's mouth fell open as the voice sounded in his head. The mini-dragon cocked its head inquisitively, waiting for an answer.

'Well?'

"Volgen," Volgen heard himself say.

The mini-dragon bobbed its head, then cocked it to the side again. *'Volgen. Nice name. Pleased to meet you, Volgen.'*

"Er ... Likewise ... Flame," Volgen murmured.

"If you have quite finished!" Kraelin roared. Flame flapped quickly back to her ledge, making Volgen wince as her talons dug into his shoulder when she took off.

'Sorry,' Flame's voice sounded in his head.

Snor'kel chuckled. "You'll get used to that." He tapped knowingly at the padded quilt sewn onto the shoulder of his flying tunic.

"What was that you said about the other dragons?" Kraelin demanded. "I want to know where my people are!"

From the tunnel leading into the amphitheatre the growing buzz of excited voices could suddenly be heard. Kraelin looked across, her mouth drawn tight in displeasure. Moments later a mob surged into the cavern, an old lady with a walking stick leading the way. Reaching the sand she yelled, "So which one's Snookle then?"

* * * * *

The truth about who his parents were was not what Tobias was having most difficulty reconciling, nor the fact that he had a brother and sister. The problem was that for nearly sixteen cycles he had thought himself bereft, alone, parentless; and it now turned out that his father had been at Hope all along and his mother had left him there to be reared by strangers. That his birth was part of a master plan, engineered by his mother, further muddied the waters. The whole situation left a bitter taste in his mouth.

He did not know how long he had been away from his body mulling these feelings over, but he guessed it must have been some time as, for some strange reason, his spirit image was starting to fade. Tobias raised a hand to eye level and stretched it out in front of him. Faintly, he could see the outline of the bookshelf through it, appearing as a shadow through his flesh.

"It will get worse the longer you stay in here."

The sound of the voice made Tobias flinch, his chair toppling over as he sprang to his feet. He backed away as a figure materialised in the doorway. It was a man.

"W-w-who are you?" Tobias stammered.

The man smiled and dipped his head. "I am known as Wooster in the world of men," he answered. "However, amongst my kin I am called Winegrath. May I join you?" Without waiting for an answer he walked into the library and sat in the seat Nanna Pussy had left there. "Please do not be afraid. Sit." Wooster gestured to the chair Tobias had knocked over.

Instead of complying, Tobias studied the man. He could sense no danger from him, yet how had he appeared in the library that Tobias had created with his own mind?

As if reading his thoughts, Wooster smiled. "Nanapussy told me how to find you. Do not be afraid, Tobias. I know how you must be feeling. Exactly how I would if I were in your place."

Tobias still made no move towards the chair. "W-w-what do you mean?"

Wooster shrugged. "Dragons, parents, expectations. That sort of thing."

Tobias gulped. Did he know it all?

Wooster nodded. *'I am dragon, Tobias. The kin of your mother.'*

The sound of the deep, melodious voice in his head shook Tobias to the core. *'How come you can speak to me with your mind?'*

'I think the question should be how can you communicate with mine, Wing Commander?'

"W-W-Wing Commander?" Tobias said aloud.

Wooster smiled. "As a direct descendant of the current incumbent, what else could you be?"

Now that was one thought that had never crossed Tobias's mind. Shocked by its implications, he shuffled to the chair and righted it. Suddenly he needed to sit down. He leaned his elbows on the desk and dipped his head to cover his eyes with his hands.

"Shocking, I know," continued Wooster. "But rest assured, given your parentage you are more a Wing Commander now than your father has ever been. And he will realise that once he discovers the truth."

The truth? Volgen? The two did not sit comfortably together. More than likely Volgen would rant, rave and then flatten him if and when the truth came out. Tobias looked up. "If you are dragon, how come I see you as a man?"

The smile faded from Wooster's face. "I know you are aware of how we dragons were tricked into entering the world of Midas."

Tobias nodded.

"Well, it would seem that while Nanapussy worked on a way to bring us back, we were also working on a way to get back. A world made of magic is not true paradise, believe me. But I digress. I was chosen to make the change and return to Tiernan Og through the small wyverhole we managed to create, and once I got there I set about trying to discover a way of opening a bigger gateway for my brethren's return."

"B-but how?" Despite his worries, Tobias was intrigued and wanted to know how it tied in with Nanna Pussy.

"That, young Tobias, is a tale for another day." He leaned forward. "At this moment my main concern is to persuade you to go back to your body, before you fade away altogether."

Tobias pursed his lips and shook his head. "I don't want to go back just yet. I ... I still have things to think over."

"Look at your hands, Tobias. Look at your hands." Wooster grabbed one of Tobias's hands and held it up. "The flesh is almost translucent. Soon you will not have the strength to return." He lowered the hand to the table. "And if you do not, you will fade away entirely and your body will die."

Tobias shrugged.

"Well, think on this Tobias. If not for Nanapussy, what of the old man who has sat beside your sleeping body these past days? How will he feel if you die? He loves you like the son he never had. If you pass away, I would not give it long before he follows."

Cronan! An image of the old librarian's kindly face sprang into Tobias's mind and he realised that he loved the old man like a father. To all intents and purposes Cronan had been his father these past fifteen cycles. "Days, you said. But I have only been here for a few marks of the candle. Ten or twelve at the most."

"Time runs differently when you are in spirit form, Tobias. Believe me, you have been away from the world of Tiernan Og for over five days."

"Five days?" Tobias was gobsmacked.

"And Snor'kel and the dragons have arrived."

"The dragons?" A smile formed on Tobias's face. "Where? Are they with the others now? How many of them are there? What are they like?"

Wooster held up his hands and laughed. "Whoa there. So many questions. Why not come back and see for yourself? You know it makes sense. Come, take my hand. We can leave together."

Tobias stared at Wooster's outstretched hand for a moment in contemplation. While he struggled to come to terms with what Wooster had said, the image of Cronan's kindly face came to the fore and Tobias realised he could not bear it if he caused the old man pain. Rising, he gripped Wooster's hand. "Why not."

Chapter Twenty Seven

The first thing Tobias saw when he awoke was Wooster's smile. He returned it with one of his own; at least he hoped he did. The muscles of his face felt as though they had been starched and he feared it came out more like a grimace. "Any chance of a drink?" he asked, his voice weak and raspy.

"Is he awake? Was that him? Let me see! Let me see!"

The green-tinted face of a Beastie Boy came into view.

"Trimble," croaked Tobias. "Is that you?"

The little green man grinned, his brown eyes gleaming. "We thought you were a goner, we did. But Wooster said he'd save you and he did, which makes everything all right, and now that the dragons have arrived, even though we ..."

Wooster's hand clamped over Trimble's mouth. "Please allow young Tobias to draw breath before you send him back to sleep with your incessant prattle."

Trimble nodded, his eyes wide.

"Thank you," said Wooster, removing his hand. Tobias's laugh was overcome by a fit of coughing. "Fetch some water," Wooster commanded, leaning forward to lift Tobias and push pillows under his back to support him. Trimble returned, dragging a water flask across the floor. Tobias drank greedily.

"Easy now," Wooster warned. "Too much too soon will give you cramps."

Heeding his warning, Tobias drank sparingly and sagged back against the pillows. The cart lurched and for the first time he noticed the creak of harness and cart. "We're moving?" he asked.

Wooster nodded. "We are on our way to Hope."

Tobias frowned. "Why?"

"To meet the dragons," Trimble broke in, excitement making his voice even shriller than usual. "We went to the wrong place, you see. Where we went, the dragons didn't and where they went, we didn't, then Nina spoke with the queen and ..."

Wooster's hand clamped over Trimble's mouth again. This time the Beastie Boy continued to prattle on.

"Yellow-tailed dart," murmured Tobias, not having understood a word Trimble had said, but knowing that the little man was working himself into a vocal frenzy. He pointed to the bandolier looped over Trimble's shoulder. "Stick him."

Wooster hesitated.

"It's the only way to shut him up."

Trimble was so wrapped up in his ramblings, arm waving and gesticulating that he never suspected anything as Wooster removed a dart from the bandolier and stuck it into his cheek. Trimble's eyes rolled back and he slumped to the floor.

Tobias sighed and settled into the pillows. He felt so tired; so very tired. "It's the only way," he whispered.

"Tobias! Stay alert!"

Tobias came awake with a start. "I feel drained," he mumbled, shuffling back to sit more upright.

"Understandable, in the circumstances," said Wooster. "If you will allow, I will notify Nina and Nanapussy that you are back with us, and ask them to call a halt for the day so that we may eat." He smiled. "I don't know about you, but I feel hungry."

At the mention of Nina's name his mind turned to his sister. He wondered whether Nanna Pussy had told her yet. As Wooster stepped over Trimble to move to the front of the cart, however, all thoughts of his 'family' fled. His eyes fastened on the figure lying in the cot opposite. It was Jophrey. Contradictory emotions surged through him, although he predominantly felt revulsion: Jophrey's duplicity rankled and Tobias found it hard to believe that someone so rotten could be his brother.

His deliberations were disturbed by the cart sliding to a halt. It had barely stopped moving before the rear doors were flung wide and Nanna Pussy entered, closely followed by Nina. Both wore smiles of relief.

"It's about time," scolded Nanna Pussy. "You gave us a real fright, young man."

Tobias smiled meekly and peered over her shoulder to where Nina waited. By the sheepish look on her face, he could tell she knew the truth. For some reason that knowledge eased his mind. "Hi, sis," he said.

* * * * *

The sight of the goat carcass being torn to pieces and consumed turned Volgen's stomach, but in some perverse way he found the scene compulsive viewing and could not tear his eyes away from the carnage. Neither could the Ogmus who had remained in the amphitheatre to watch the dragons having dinner.

'Messy eater isn't she?' said Flame, from where she was perched on Volgen's shoulder, her tail wrapped lightly round his neck. *'Unlike Reizgoth. Now there's a real hunk.'* Her eyes fixed adoringly on the big red dragon, who had delicately torn his carcass apart before eating it. Volgen chuckled and tickled the dragonet's chin.

Sitting on the rocky ledge beside him with Draco perched on his shoulder, Snorkel — without the ' — tucked into a meal of roast chicken and sautéed mushrooms, washed down with a tot of Funguy. Meelan sat beside him, her eyes averted from the gorefest below.

"Does Kraelin always eat like that?" Volgen asked, staring at the blood splattered sand.

"Up to now," Snorkel answered, spraying bits of chicken as he spoke. "Some creatures just ain't got no couthness, know what I mean?" He chewed a chunk of leg, then sipped some Funguy to wash it down and belched. "Want some?" he asked, waving the leg in front of Draco's mouth.

The dragonet rolled her eyes and shook her head.

"Suit yourself."

"So what happens now?" asked Volgen.

"Hmmm?"

"About the others. How are you going to get them back?"

Snorkel shrugged. "Beats me. Best wait 'til Cronan and Tobias arrive, hey? Before I make any rash decisions." Unconcerned, he carried on eating.

"I don' feel ver' well," said Meelan, doubling over, her hands holding her stomach. "Need sleeps — and bucket. Big bucket."

Leaning forward Volgen peered around Snorkel. "She doesn't look too good," he said, noticing the sickly green cast of her face. "Want me to get some of the lads to take her to the guest rooms?"

"Might be an idea," agreed Snorkel. "I don't think flying agrees with her. She always comes over funny after a flight."

With some struggling and manhandling, Rimbart and his brother Josh managed to get Meelan down the short flight of steps. Taking an arm each they half dragged, half carried her to the tunnel leading to the upper levels.

"That's some, er, girl you've got there, Snorkel," said Volgen, watching them disappear from sight.

"Sure is." Snorkel wiped grease from his beard with the back of his hand. "Best thing I ever did was kidnap her from her people."

Volgen fixed him with an inquisitive stare. "Kidnap?"

"Cannibals they were, the lot of them. Nice people all the same." He tore into the chicken again and spat out a small sliver of bone. "Disgusting eating habits though."

Volgen grimaced as Snorkel chewed off another chunk. "But why kidnap her?"

Snorkel chuckled happily. "It was what she would expect from a god." Draco shook her head and launched herself from his shoulder. "So what if you have?" Snorkel yelled after her retreating form. "He hasn't!"

"Hasn't what?" asked Volgen

'Heard the story before,' said Flame. *'Somehow I think it would bore me too, so I'm off. Catch you later.'* She bunched her muscles and launched herself into the air.

Volgen squealed as her talons dug in to his shoulder, and he raised his hand and rubbed at the injured spot. Snorkel laughed and tapped at his shoulder pad. "Told you. You'll need one of these. Now where was I?"

It was at least a candle-mark later that he concluded his tale; the telling being lubricated by numerous sips of Funguy. By then Volgen had lost the will to live. His eyes had glazed over long ago and he hoped he had managed to nod and gasp in the right places. "Sho there you have it." The quantity of Funguy Snorkel had imbibed manifested itself in a slight slurring of his words. "The whole shtory of how I became a god to a tribe of cannibals and managed to convert them to Moremen … Moremenish … Moremenishisism. Wanna hear how I cheated death at the hands of the elves?" [*]

Before Volgen could plead for mercy Kraelin interrupted. "We have to leave!"

---

[*] As told in *Reluctant Heroes*. Available from all the best book shops.

Volgen lurched to his feet in horror. Struggling to make himself heard over the babble of worried voices he yelled, "Leave? Where? Why?"

Kraelin turned her large, golden eyes on him. "To fetch my future companion," she answered. "Do you dare to question me?"

A deathly silence settled on the amphitheatre and all eyes turned to Volgen. He stepped back under the dragon's baleful gaze, thinking fast on his feet — never one of his strong points: Feet, yes. Thinking, no. "Never, my Queen. I was worried that we had upset you, that is all."

Staring at him for a moment, Kraelin nodded. "I believe you." Turning to Reizgoth she said, "You will come too. There are others that need bringing and I cannot carry them all on my own."

Snorkel struggled upright and began to sway. After a couple of blinks to try to focus his gaze he raised the beaker. "Thatsh shtrong shtuff," he murmured, then toppled backwards, sending spirals of dust swirling into the air as he landed.

"I did warn you," said Volgen, a small smile playing about his lips.

Reizgoth's huge head appeared over the ledge. He looked down at the prone form of Snorkel and sighed. "It looks like it will have to be you," he said, turning to Volgen.

Volgen blanched. "M-m-me? Me what?"

"To come with us, of course."

The watching Ogmus cheered. At last they would see their Wing Commander riding a real dragon. It was what Wing Commanders were for, wasn't it?

Aware that he was the centre of attention, Volgen drew himself taller and puffed out his chest, trying to appear calm and confident. Outwardly at least; inside he was crapping himself. Masking his fear he dipped his head and said, "It would be my pleasure to accompany you."

'Do not worry. I will make it an easy flight.'

The sound of the dragon's voice in his head made him gasp. If Flame had not already introduced him to the phenomenon of mind-speak, he knew he would have fainted away in dead shock. "Th-thank you," he mumbled.

'Come down and join me, Wing Commander.'

With buttocks clenched firmly together, Volgen waddled to the steps and slowly made his descent. One wrong step could result in a very messy accident, and one that would be immediately obvious to the watching crowd. Powder-blue was not a good colour for disguising ugly stains.

When Volgen reached the floor of the cavern Reizgoth stooped and offered his foreleg as a step-up to his back. Very carefully, Volgen mounted. Once he'd settled in the crook between the wing pinions and neck Reizgoth rose, throwing him back.

'Press in with your knees,' the dragon advised. *'It will make the flight more comfortable.'*

Volgen did as he was instructed and instantly felt more stable. For how long, he didn't know, but at least for the moment he was secure.

"After you, my Queen," said the dragon.

The watching Ogmus ducked and covered their faces as, in a whirlwind of sand, Kraelin launched herself into the air and flew towards the tunnel.

Excited by the queen's departure, the dragonets swooped and dived, screeching and chirruping their encouragement. When she had disappeared into the tunnel they began to spiral towards the remains of her dinner, like vultures circling a kill.

With eyes screwed tightly shut, Volgen leaned forward and braced himself for take-off, his knees clamped and hands gripping a knobbly ridge on Reizgoth's neck. When the dragon rocketed into the air his stomach descended down his legs and through his boots to be deposited on the sand; or so it felt. The wind streaked past his face and the metallic odour of dragon filled his nostrils. His stomach returned with a vengeance, then slopped to left and right as Reizgoth manoeuvred the long, slow bends of the tunnel. Volgen understood why Meelan had looked so ill; any more of this and he, too, would be calling for the sick-bucket.

Suddenly cold air battered into him, carrying with it the scent of recently fallen rain. After the confines of Hope its freshness felt wonderful. The exposed skin of his face came alive as if it were glowing under the wind's assault. His travel sickness eased, helped by the fact that they were out of the tunnel and Reizgoth was not swerving all over the place. At least Volgen thought they were out of the tunnel; he had not yet plucked up the courage to open his eyes and take a look.

With his head bowed against the wind he cracked open an eyelid, but all he could see was cloud. Feeling somewhat braver he opened his other eye; at the exact moment that Reizgoth broke through the cloud cover. Far, far below, further down than he thought was possible, he could see the valley. The River Dragle appeared as a slender grey thread as it wound through the varied green shades of the miniature trees, and the setting sun cast long shadows on the ground.

Reizgoth swooped lower. The trees grew rapidly bigger and Volgen's stomach rose to his chest with the rush. He shrieked in terror then relief as Reizgoth levelled out.

'How are you enjoying the flight, Wing Commander?'

"P-p-piggin' marvellous!" yelled Volgen, realising that he was, in fact, thoroughly enjoying the thrill of it all. A huge smile formed on his face, turning into a grimace as a rather large insect splattered on his teeth. He removed a hand from the dragon's neck to wipe away the mess, immediately realising his mistake as he began to slip from his perch. Sensing his impending plummet, Reizgoth swung to the left, his rising right side throwing Volgen back into position.

"Thanks!" yelled Volgen, spitting bits of dead insect from his mouth.

'My pleasure! According to Kraelin it will be some time before we meet with your friends, so sit back and enjoy the ride.'

A thought struck Volgen. "Kraelin said she was going to pick up her future companion, but how does she know? Neither Cronan nor Tobias can speak with dragons. Only I can, being the Wing Commander."

'I do not know of whom you speak,' said Reizgoth. *'Kraelin's future companion is called Nina. But she is with others of your kind, so it may be that your friends are with her.'*

Nina? Volgen had never heard of anyone called Nina. "Can Kraelin ask this Nina if Cronan and Tobias are there?"

'Ask me yourself,' Kraelin's frosty voice broke in.

Volgen gulped. Could every piggin' dragon hear him?

'Yes!' said Kraelin. *'So kindly control your thoughts and your*

language. Otherwise someone of a more sensitive nature than I may take offence.'

"Yes, my Queen," Volgen murmured, trying to clear his mind of anything that could cause insult.

After a moment Kraelin spoke again. *'Nina says her companions are called Tobias, Cronan, Wooster, Nanna Pussy, Jophrey, Wild Bill Halfcock and the Beastie Boys.'*

The information startled Volgen. How in the gods' names had those two idiots managed to accumulate such a following? And how did that screwball Wild Bill get to join up with them?

'Volgen!' warned Reizgoth. *'You are broadcasting again.'*

Broadcasting? What the piggin' hell was that?

'Exactly what you are doing now,' scolded Kraelin. *'So mind your language.'*

"Yes my Queen," Volgen responded, cursing himself for a fool. Being a proper Wing Commander was scary stuff.

Suddenly the air around them exploded. Volgen shrieked as a wave of heat washed over him. Reizgoth roared in surprise, nearly unseating him as he reared in the air.

Unseen, a small black shape powered to the safety of the clouds, its reconnaissance complete.

Chapter Twenty Eight

A light breeze blew wood smoke into the awning, the acrid smell mingling with the more pleasing aroma of damp grass. Wrapped in a warm blanket and feeling relaxed, Tobias didn't mind. He wiped his watering eyes with the back of his hand and sniffed the air appreciatively. It felt good to be back in the world of man, back to real sensations. Outside the fine drizzle had ceased to fall and, through gaps in the retreating clouds, he saw that the setting sun had painted the sky with pink and orange blushes. How did that old verse go, the one written before the Ogmus were confined to living in a cave?

> *Red sky in the morning, Ogmus storm warning,*
> *Red sky at night, Ogmus delight.*

Tobias smiled. It would be a fine day tomorrow. He glanced down as Nina sighed. With her chin cupped in her hand, she leaned on her elbow and gazed into nothingness, wrapped in her own thoughts. They had spoken little since he regained consciousness, and he could sense that their relationship had changed now that his lustful thoughts were well and truly squashed. On reflection it was a change for the better; at least he no longer felt tongue-tied around her.

From inside the tent he could hear Cronan's soft snoring. The old man slept the sleep of the totally shattered; he had been overcome by emotion when he learned of Tobias's return and the shock of seeing him had proved too much. Almost as soon as they'd made camp he had made his apologies and retired. Cronan seemed to have aged dramatically in the last few days. Deep lines etched his face and grey bags showed beneath his eyes. Tobias felt slightly ashamed, knowing that worry over him was the cause.

"Will you two stop arguing?"

Tobias looked across to where the wagons had been left, some twenty paces from the fire. The horses were hobbled between them and were busily grazing on tufts of grass, but even they looked up and pricked their ears at the sound of Nanna Pussy's voice.

"He started it!" snapped Wild Bill, trying to wrest the cooking pot from Wooster's hands.

Wooster sighed and rolled his eyes, then shook his head and yanked the pot back. "It does not take two of us to carry this over to the fire."

"I had it first!"

"No you did not!"

"I bleedin' did!"

"Does it really matter?"

"Too bloody right it does!"

Nanna Pussy interjected. "Boys! If ..."

Tobias grimaced. This was the third spat between the two men since they'd stopped to make camp. The first was over who helped Nanna Pussy tend to the horses, and the second who held which pole to erect the tent. Tobias pursed his lips and shook his head. Their mutual dislike was becoming irritating. Trying to shut out the confrontation, he resumed staring at the sky. It was spectacular. The distant horizon was ablaze. His thoughts turned to Hope. Could he cope with living inside a mountain again after this?

"She comes," whispered Nina.

Dragged away from his thoughts, which were becoming too maudlin for his liking, Tobias looked at Nina. The orange of the sky reflected from the watery glimmer in her eyes. He smiled. "We'd better let them know —" he nodded towards Wild Bill and Wooster, who had now squared up to each other "— before there's a fight."

Nina giggled. "We could always get the Beastie Boys to stick them."

"After the last time I doubt whether Wild Bill would forgive them if they did. I still don't know how they managed to get round him. They're all the best of mates now." He shook his head. "I don't understand it. The last thing I remember, Wild Bill wanted to kill the 'little bastards'."

"That, Tobias, is a tale for another day." Nina raised her eyebrows knowingly. "Let's just say that it took a certain amount of womanly charm to bring him round."

Tobias laughed and turned to scan the camp site. "That's a point. Where are they?"

"Who?"

"The Beastie Boys. Since they got the fire going I haven't seen any of them."

"Hunting," said Nina. "They fancied fresh meat and have gone looking for rabbit."

Their discussion was interrupted by two cries of pain. Looking across towards the carts they saw Wild Bill and Wooster struggling to their feet. Both were rubbing their jaws.

"Let that be a lesson to you," said Nanna Pussy, slapping her hands together twice before resting them on her hips and glaring at the two men. "Any more shenanigans and there's more where that came from. Understand?"

The men nodded.

"Now shake hands."

Reluctantly they did.

"Time to tell them the news," said Nina, rising to her feet, "before war breaks out."

Less than a candle-mark later the smell of boiled rabbit wafted through the darkening camp. Shortly after Wooster and Wild Bill's altercation the Beastie Boys had returned with a brace, skinned and ready for the pot. After chopping the meat and adding oats and vegetables, they'd set the broth cooking.

Everyone sat silently around the fire, deep in their own thoughts, while their dinner cooked. The news that the dragons were coming had caused great excitement at first, but as they waited they grew more pensive. Nanna Pussy fretted about the forthcoming return of her brethren, Nina about meeting the queen for the first time, Wild Bill and Wooster about each other and Tobias about his upcoming role, whatever that might prove to be. The Beastie Boys, sensing the unease, were unusually quiet and sat in a huddle slightly apart from the others, whispering amongst themselves.

Woken by the smell of supper, Cronan sat beside Tobias under the awning and stared into the flames. "Had we better see if Jophrey has come round?" he asked, breaking the silence. "Although it goes against my instincts, I suppose we'd better feed him. We can't have the lad dying on us; that would make us as bad as the Blackabbots."

"I'd forgotten all about him," said Nanna Pussy, looking up.

"I'll go," said Brimble, jumping to his feet. "Want me to stick him if he's awake?"

Nanna Pussy shook her head and gave a wry smile. "Leave him be for the moment. He's been kept out cold for days now. Let the boy join us for something to eat if he's up to it."

Brimble nodded and walked towards the covered cart, waving his comrades forward. As one the Beastie Boys rose and joined him.

"But keep the darts ready, just in case," Nanna Pussy called.

Tobias watched them walk to the cart, his thoughts in turmoil. Knowing that Jophrey was his brother rankled, as did the fact that he was a con man and a thief. Beside him Cronan tensed. Tobias knew the old man felt much the same.

Suddenly cries of outrage rang out, as the Beastie Boys entered the covered cart. "What's all the screaming about?" asked Wild Bill, frowning.

"I can hazard a guess," said Cronan, rising to his feet.

"He's gone!" yelled Brimble, jumping from the back of the cart. "He's gone and scarpered!"

"That's not all that's gone," said Wild Bill, looking between the two wagons, where the vague shadows of three horses could be seen cropping the grass. "The thievin' toerag's nicked one of the damn nags."

* * * * *

Jophrey was a good half league from the camp before he paused in his flight to remove the muffling cloths from Dancer's hooves. He hadn't heard any commotion from his former captors, so he assumed that his escape had not yet been noticed. With a bit of luck he would make Wellstown before morning. Although he still felt groggy, having been out cold for the past few days, he did not feel the least bit sleepy. Once he had removed the cloths he scrambled onto Dancer's back, grabbed handfuls of the horse's mane and urged him forward.

After another half league his head felt clearer and he decided that he was ready and able to contact Mandrake. No doubt the dragon already knew that they had been tricked, although he would not know where Snor'kel and the others had actually appeared. But he soon would! A grim smile formed on Jophrey's face. Tobias and the others had pretty much ignored him once the cart had stopped and the camp had been made, and this had allowed him to listen in to their conversations.

'Mandrake! Mandrake! It's me, Jophrey!'

'Jophrey?' came the dragon's response. *'What happened? Where are you?'*

'I've escaped and I'm on my way to Hope.'

'Really? That is rather fortuitous.'

Jophrey frowned. Did the dragon already know?

'Of course,' Mandrake purred. *'You did not think we would be fooled by the tricks of those demons, did you?'* The news had a deflating effect. *'As we speak Spot, is on his way back from there, having carried out a supposedly covert reconnaissance.'*

Jophrey could sense the barely concealed anger in Mandrake's words. *'Supposedly covert?'*

'The little fool couldn't help himself,' Mandrake snapped. *'In his excitement he had to go and let loose a flame. He very nearly scorched one of the demons and barely escaped with his life. It was just as well that the clouds were thick, or he would never have got away. I've ordered him back here so that we can regroup, as we are still none the wiser how many dragons actually came through. He only saw two, but there may be more.'*

'Perhaps I can help you there,' said Jophrey, smiling. *'The two that Spot saw ...'*

'Yes?'

'That's it. That's all that came.'

'Two? Are you sure?'

'Positive. I heard them talking about it. Only two came through.'

'But two could hardly be classed as a horde. What happened to the others?'

Jophrey shrugged. *'There are no others. Just Snor'kel and the two dragons. Apparently one of the women can speak to the queen and she said that there were only the two of them. I think the queen was expecting more of her kind to be waiting for them on this world.'*

Mandrake laughed, deep and humourless. *'Indeed there are, Jophrey. Indeed there are. I'll tell Spot to go back and wait with you until we arrive. It looks like our plans are about to come to fruition.'*

No sooner had Mandrake's voice faded than a cold shiver ran through Jophrey's body. His skin came out in goosebumps, as if someone had stepped on his grave. Dancer whinnied nervously and stopped, his eyes wide and ears flat against his head, prancing on the spot as a breeze rose and ruffled his mane. Jophrey raised his hand to remove a wind-blown lock of hair from his eyes. He peered into the night skies, but could see nothing. Clouds obscured the moon and what few stars were out gave little illumination. The breeze died as quickly as it had risen. Shrugging aside his concerns Jophrey urged Dancer forward, whispering soothing words as the skittish horse reluctantly complied.

Had Jophrey spent a moment longer studying the heavens he would have seen that two of the clouds were moving rather more quickly than the rest, and in the opposite direction.

* * * * *

After Brimble broke the news of Jophrey's flight the camp decended into pandemonium. Wild Bill ran to the horses and snatched the severed hobble from the ground, waving it in the air and venting his fury to the sky. The Beastie Boys chased Trimble, threatening to pulverise him for not ensuring that Jophrey was properly 'sticked'. Somewhat calmer, Nanna Pussy, Nina and Wooster stood watching their antics, while Cronan sat staring moodily into the fire.

"What now?" asked Tobias, rising and standing beside Nanna Pussy.

She shrugged. "It changes nothing," she said, "except that speed is now of the essence. How long is it until the dragons arrive?"

There was a moment's pause. "Any time now. They are almost here," said Nina.

"We should have left him drugged," mumbled Cronan. He prodded at the fire with a stick. "That boy could be the end of all our dreams. He must have heard everything we've said. I wouldn't put it past him to find a way of getting in touch with the blacks and telling it all to them."

Nanna Pussy forced a smile. "He probably has already."

"What?" Cronan sprang to his feet. "How?"

"Mind-speak," she answered. "I'm afraid to say that young Jophrey can communicate with the blacks with his mind. That was the main reason we kept him drugged."

Cronan looked at each of their faces in turn, noting the lack of surprise they showed. "You already knew, didn't you?" he said. "You knew he could speak with the blacks."

Tobias felt his face redden. "It wasn't meant to be a secret," he said, looking at the ground.

"It might well have been," Cronan snapped. "Do they know?" He nodded towards Wild Bill, who was still busy stamping on the hobble, and the Beastie Boys who were chasing round the camp after Trimble.

"No," answered Nanna Pussy. "Only we four." She grasped him by the arms. Looking into his eyes she said, "When this is all over you will know the whole truth, and of the vital role you had to play in bringing all of our dreams to reality. And believe me, some of us have had those dreams a lot longer than others. If it were not for you, I very much doubt we would be where we are now. We have a lot to thank you for, Cronan."

"But why the secrets?" he asked, his shoulders slumped, his voice a whisper.

"There are no secrets, Cronan. Only truths yet to be told. And told they will be, trust me."

Cronan met her gaze, unconvinced. It was then that Tobias realised how much the journey had taken out of the librarian. He looked half the man who had left Hope some twenty days ago. It was he who had led the way and he who Tobias had looked to for guidance. Somehow in the past few days the roles had reversed. He deserved to know the truth.

Stepping forward, Tobias motioned for Nina to join him and wrapped his arm round Nanna Pussy's waist. The old man looked surprised at the familiarity.

"Cronan," said Tobias. "Meet my mother and —" he looked at Nina "— my sister."

Cronan's mouth fell open.

"There is another; one who shares our bloodline and who also has the power of mind-speak. And I think you know who that is."

"Jophrey?" Cronan murmured.

Tobias nodded.

"But how?"

Before Tobias could answer a wind started to rise and the sound of huge, leathery wings could soon be heard. The horses neighed fearfully and began to buck, and Wild Bill ceased his deranged dance and scrambled clear.

"She's here!" yelled Nina, running to the carts and staring into the sky as two immense dark shapes glided down to land.

"W-what are they?" cried Boo, hiding behind Thatch.

"Dragons," whispered Nanna Pussy.

"Dragons? I'm dead. Order the box, dig the hole and pop me in."

"Shut up, you fool," said Brimble. "It's the good ones, not the blacks." He looked nervously into the darkness. "I hope."

The wind dropped, and from out of the gloom strode a figure. A rather rotund figure sporting a powder-blue flying suit, his bushy beard sticking out from the sides of his flying helmet. He stepped into the circle of light thrown out by the fire and stood, bow-legged, with his hands on his hips, surveying the group.

"What the bleedin' hell is that?" asked Wild Bill.

"Volgen?" queried Tobias in disbelief.

The Wing Commander smiled. "You betcha piggin' ass it is." His face creased with pain and he rubbed at his backside with his hands. "Talking of which, mine feels like it's been pummelled with a paddle."

"Where's Snor'kel?" asked Tobias.

"Snorkel," corrected Volgen, still rubbing his tender behind. "He's, ahhhh, incapacitated right now. Nothing too serious, but I wouldn't like his head when he wakes." He chuckled.

"Cease the chatter and introduce me to my people, fool," a voice scolded from the darkness.

Volgen reddened, the orange glow from the fire accentuating his embarrassment. Clearing his throat, he said, "Fellow Ogmus! Allow me to introduce you to Kraelin, our queen."

Chapter Twenty Nine

Snorkel felt sure the top of his head was about to explode. The dull throbbing at his temples had grown to seismic proportions and it was only a matter of time before his cranium erupted. The last time he had felt this bad was when he and Ryzak had got bladdered on Joliff's brandy. After that he'd vowed never to drink spirits again, and at the moment he wished he'd stuck to his promise.

"Norkel? You wake?"

It was Meelan. She sounded worried. Unable to open his eyes for fear of aggravating his malaise, or to open his mouth to speak in case he hurled, he settled for grunting an acknowledgement. The bed dipped as Meelan's bulk settled on to it.

Bed? What was he doing in a bed? The last he remembered he was on a rocky ledge in the main cavern. Just where was he?

"Wh-wh—" He couldn't speak. His tongue was firmly glued to the roof of his mouth by a furry coating that tasted of sweaty socks.

"What you say?" asked Meelan, stroking his brow.

He tried again. "Wh-where am I?"

"In bed, silly Norkel. Where else you be?"

Snorkel licked his dry lips. "In bed where?"

"In room in mountain. Nice men carry you here ages ago. They say you not well."

That was for sure; he'd rarely felt less well. Preparing himself for the pain, he cracked open an eye to check out his surroundings. The pain didn't materialise. The grotto they were in was almost dark; what little light there was filtered in from the corridor beyond the open doorway. Feeling braver he risked the other eye. The room began to spin. He squeezed both eyes shut again and heaved.

"Me get bucket," said Meelan. She left the bed, returning moments later and clattering a bucket on the floor beside Snorkel's head. That was all the encouragement he needed. With amazing accuracy, he spewed the contents of his stomach into the wooden container — four times. After that dry heaves wracked his body; he could puke no more. What was inside him had all been emptied out, including his stomach, or so it felt. Eventually the convulsions subsided and he lay back, drained.

"You better now?" Meelan asked, sitting on the bed and wiping his face with a damp cloth.

Snorkel grunted. Surprisingly he did. Not much, but at least the pounding in his head had eased. "Water," he croaked.

"Me get some."

Snorkel heard her pad across to the dresser he had seen beside the far wall, followed by the glug of water being poured. He took the proffered vessel when she pressed it into his hands. "Help me sit up," he said, "so I don't end up drowning myself."

Sitting more upright, with pillows propped behind his back, he drained the beaker in one and held it out.

"Another."

Five beakers later he felt almost alive. At least his mouth no longer tasted like he'd been chewing on a badger's arse and the pounding in his head had receded to a dull throb. He sighed and leaned back into the pillows, easing his eyes open. To his relief the room stayed where it was and didn't start to spin.

Meelan took the empty beaker and returned it to the dresser, then came back and sat next to him. "You look better, Norkel. Face not green."

He peered myopically at her fleshy features and smiled. "What about you? Are you feeling better?"

Meelan frowned. "What you mean?"

"You were feeling ill. Earlier on, in the cavern."

"Ahhhh!" She nodded, her chins jiggling at the movement. "Me feel lot better now." She patted her tummy. "Must be something I swallow."

"Ate," Snorkel corrected. "Something you ate."

Meelan shook her head. "No Norkel. Swallow."

Snorkel sighed. Trying to teach her his language had proved harder than he had thought. Since he had kidnapped her, he had only managed to get her to grasp the basics. Enough to get by with, but that was about it. Trying again, he mimed putting food into his mouth and said, "Ate, see? Put food into mouth to eat, then swallow." He pretended to swallow. "Understand?"

Meelan smiled. "Meelan understand. But that not what Meelan mean."

Snorkel frowned. What on earth was she on about?

"Me show." Standing up, she leaned over and grabbed him by the crotch.

He squealed in surprise, then watched in amazement as she let go of his manhood and grabbed her own crotch.

"Now see?" she asked, removing her hand.

If anything Snorkel was more confused. What had his manhood and her ladybits got to do with eating?

Meelan folded her arms across her chest and sighed. "Me no explain good. Me try again." She grabbed his crotch. Although this time he was prepared, he still flinched.

"You feed —" she removed her hand and grabbed her own crotch "— me swallow. Now see?"

"By the gods," Snorkel murmured, gobsmacked by the thought that was worming its way sluggishly past the alcohol to enter his brain. "You don't mean …"

Eyes bright, Meelan nodded vigorously, setting her chins to wobbling again. "Yes, Norkel. We gonna have chickens."

* * * * *

The cavern erupted as the dragons glided in to land. The dragonets cavorted and shrieked with excitement and the waiting Ogmus cheered and yelled. The she-wolf, ever wary of venturing onto the hot sand, settled for barking from the cool of one of the tunnels, her tail wagging as she bounced up and down on her front legs.

Basking in the acclaim, Kraelin stretched out her neck and bugled an acknowledgement as soon as she landed. The dragonets immediately scattered, hiding amongst the rocky ledges and peering warily down at her. The Ogmus cowered and covered their ears.

One by one the dragons' passengers slid to the ground and stood bow-legged, rubbing the circulation back into their legs and backsides.

"Where is the dwarf?" demanded Kraelin, scanning the rocky ledges for any sign of the crimson-clad figure.

Reizgoth sighed. "Manners, Kraelin. Manners."

The queen dragon gave a crafty smile and dipped her head to wink at Nina before turning to face Reizgoth. "Well? Where is he?"

"I have called him," Reizgoth answered. "Apparently he was tired after the journey and went for a rest."

"Harrumph!" Kraelin rolled her eyes. "And how does he think we are feeling after our exertions?"

"If you don't mind," broke in Volgen, "could we go and have a sit down? My piggin' arse ... Sorry, my Queen." He bowed his head in apology. "We're all feeling a bit tender." He rubbed his backside for emphasis and gave a sheepish grin.

Tobias chuckled. His own backside felt like it was rubbed raw, but the discomfort paled into insignificance when compared to the exhilaration of flight. His first dragon-ride would never be forgotten, even though he could not see a thing because it was pitch black. Even Cronan seemed more like his old self after the flight. Tobias glanced over to where the librarian stood beside Reizgoth, still exactly where he had landed after sliding from the dragon's back, staring in amazement at the transformation of Hope. The smile on his face made him look years younger. Next to him the Beastie Boys hid behind Wooster and Wild Bill and peered out at the gathered crowd, their eyes wide with wonder.

"If you must," said Kraelin. "But do not go far. We have plans to make once that wretched dwarf shows his face."

Volgen nodded and walked to where the gathered Ogmus waited, gesturing for the others to follow him.

"Not you two," said Kraelin, placing a restraining foreleg in front of Nina and Nanna Pussy. She looked deeply into Nanna Pussy's eyes. "I need to speak with you — Nanapussy."

The old lady nodded.

Wondering what was going on, Tobias glanced over his shoulder as he followed Volgen across the sand. His musings were interrupted by a familiar voice from the throng.

"Oy, carrot-top! The offer's still there if you want it!"

Turning to see who had called, his suspicions were confirmed. Standing at the front of the milling Ogmus was Mihooda, walking stick waving in the air as she tried to attract his attention. Lowering his head he waited until Wild Bill and Wooster caught up with him and ducked behind them. Brimble gave him a nervous smile. The little man's eyes were wide and Tobias noticed that there was a sheen of perspiration on his forehead.

"Don't worry," he said. "You won't be harmed."

Brimble looked at the high, vaulted ceiling. "It's not the people," he murmured. "It's being stuck inside a mountain. We need trees, not rock."

Tobias gripped his shoulder. "Soon Brimble, and without fear of being eaten by the blacks."

The crowd parted as they approached, forming an avenue to the tunnel leading to the living areas. Instead of shouting out questions as they passed, the Ogmus remained silent and dipped their heads in respect.

"I've never seen them this piggin' quiet," Volgen muttered out of the side of his mouth, puffing out his chest and striding through. When they reached the mouth of the tunnel he called a halt. "Best wait here," he said.

Rimbart strode out of the crowd and stopped beside them with a bow. "Refreshments, Wing Commander?"

Volgen rubbed his hands together and grinned. "That's more like it. Good lad. What's on the menu?"

* * * * *

"I have no wish to return to my previous form," said Nanna Pussy firmly. "I made my choice many years ago, my dear." She smiled up at Kraelin. "You are the queen now, not me." She grasped Nina's hand. "I have my children to think about now. When the others return, they will respect you as their queen. To them I will merely be another Ogmus."

"But you are not merely Ogmus," rumbled Kraelin.

"No, I'm not. But they needn't know that. Believe me, Kraelin, I am no threat to you."

Kraelin sighed and looked over at Reizgoth.

To Nina she looked like what she was; young and in need of wise counsel. During their journey back to Hope she and her gran, or rather her mother, had shown Kraelin what had transpired on Tiernan Og since the original dragons' arrival, and of the threat that now faced them. The young queen had taken it all in and listened intently, not venturing an opinion until the story was told. "So that is where my people are," was all she'd said. But Nina realised that she was worried by the story; especially by the implied threat of having another queen in the flight, albeit one in mortal form.

Reizgoth met Kraelin's gaze. "You are queen, Kraelin. Nanapussy is ancient, in both dragon and mortal terms."

"Thank you very much," Nanna Pussy snapped, folding her arms across her chest and glaring at the big red dragon.

"No offence intended, Nanapussy. I merely wished to point out to our young queen that it is highly unlikely that your ageing body would survive the change back to dragon, should you attempt it. The dragons will not take leadership from a mortal, not even one who was formerly dragon. Kraelin is queen, for now and always."

Nanna Pussy wilted at Reizgoth's words. Her shoulders sagged and her face appeared to age before Nina's eyes. Gathering her composure she stood up straight and turned to Kraelin. "He is quite right," she said, her voice barely audible. "Even should I wish to revert to dragon, I could not. You are the queen here, Kraelin. I am not your rival."

Kraelin flicked a concerned glance at Reizgoth, who nodded his agreement. "She speaks the truth," he murmured.

"What will you do when the others return then?" Kraelin asked, fixing Nanna Pussy with an inquisitive gaze.

"Do?" Nanna Pussy laughed. "Why I shall enjoy what little life I have left in this frail old body. Who knows —" she gave Nina a sly wink "— I may even take that old reprobate up on his offer."

"Wild Bill?" gasped Nina, aghast at the thought. "Surely not."

Nanna Pussy shrugged. "I don't see many others coming my way. And once this is all over, you won't want me hanging around and getting in the way."

Kraelin made to speak but was stopped by Reizgoth's barely audible warning. Changing the subject he asked, "Do you have a plan to defeat these blacks?"

"After a fashion." Nanna Pussy smiled weakly. "It rather depends on the abilities of Snorkel, and on us being able to lure the blacks to Hope."

Lure the blacks to Hope? Nina frowned. Whatever would her mother want to do that for? Hope was the last place they wanted them, or so she thought. "Why here?" she asked.

"Because here is where they will be coming, and soon, if

Jophrey has relayed all that he learned. Hope is where we stand or fall." She gave a wry grin. "I, for one, will happily plump for the former."

"And it all depends on the dwarf?" Kraelin asked, her voice tinged with doubt.

Nanna Pussy nodded.

"May the gods preserve us," mumbled the dragon.

"He managed to get us here," Reizgoth pointed out.

Kraelin snorted. "And for that I should be thankful?"

Nina stepped forward and placed her hand on Kraelin's foreleg. "I am," she said, "for if he hadn't brought you I would not have been complete. I realise that now. You are the part of me that was missing. Snorkel will succeed. Have faith."

A smile appeared on the dragon's face. "You say the nicest things," she said. "I, too, am pleased that we are one. If you are convinced he can do what is necessary, then I agree that he should be given the chance."

Reizgoth gave a low, rumbling groan.

Looking up, Nina noticed that he was staring at a point on the other side of the cavern, beyond the Ogmus. "What is it?" she asked. "I can't see."

"The dwarf!" snapped Kraelin, following Reizgoth's gaze. "It would appear that our saviour is barely capable of looking after himself, never mind us."

"Why? What's the matter?" Nina stood on her tiptoes in an attempt to see over the heads of the crowd but it was no use, she wasn't tall enough.

"Matter? He's just been carried into the cavern by his woman; that is what the matter is. And we have to rely on him? Pah!"

"Trust him," urged Reizgoth. "He may have imbibed too much of the demon spirit, but ..." He paused, realising his mistake.

Kraelin rounded on him. "Demon spirit? You mean he is drunk?"

"A little hung over, that is all. He will be fine. I have seen him far worse than this."

Kraelin growled in disapproval. "And that is supposed to make me feel better?"

"Leave it to me," said Nanna Pussy, with iron in her voice. She strode towards the crowd of Ogmus, who for some strange reason were cheering and whistling at something she could not see. "I have not come this far to be thwarted by a drunkard. He *will* succeed, even if I have to pummel him back to life!"

Nina watched her march away, her sympathies with Snorkel. He would not know what hit him when Nanna Pussy got hold of him.

Chapter Thirty

Tobias sat as far away from Volgen as he possibly could without appearing rude. He leaned against the rock wall beside the mouth of the tunnel, staring surreptitiously at the pot-bellied man, who was deep in conversation with Cronan. Tobias still could not believe it. All these years spent loathing the man and his vulgar ways, and he turned out to be his dad. It was a hard fact to stomach.

As he watched a dragonet the colour of summer gold glided down and settled on Volgen's shoulder, making Cronan jump with surprise. Volgen winced as she landed. "Hello, Flame," he said, reaching up to tickle her under the chin.

Flame arched her neck and purred with pleasure.

"She's beautiful," murmured Cronan. "May I?"

Volgen grinned. "Feel free. I'm sure she'll enjoy the attention."

Cronan leaned forward and tickled the dragonet behind her ear hole. "Her skin isn't rough at all," he said. "It's almost like supple leather."

Trimble tugged at Brimble's sleeve and whispered, "It's one of them small dragons, Brimble. Look. With Volgen. Over there. Look Brimble, look!"

Tobias turned his attention to the Beastie Boys, who were sitting between Wild Bill and Wooster. Wild Bill leaned back against the rock, eyes closed, seemingly asleep; while Wooster sat with his head bowed, staring at his clasped hands.

"Can I go see? Can I? Please? I won't scare it. Honest!"

Brimble looked across at Flame and smiled. "Let's all go take a look," he said, rising. "They look kinda cute."

"Woohoo!" Trimble leapt to his feet and raced to where Volgen sat, small puffs of dust rising as he ran. Stopping and standing close by, he watched respectfully, as Flame opened her eyes and regarded him.

"She likes you," said Volgen, grinning at the little man. "And wants to know why you're so small."

"Why's she?" Trimble countered.

Brimble dug him in the ribs with his finger. "Don't be so rude, idiot."

Trimble rounded on him. "I wasn't being rude; I only wanted to know. And who are you calling an idiot?"

Tobias sighed. He could sense yet another Beastie Boy brawl developing.

"Would she mind if we stroked her?" asked Boo, defusing the situation. Flame looked at Volgen, who nodded.

Stretching her neck she bugled six times, each one short and sharp. In moments six dragonets appeared in the tunnel, one red and five blue. Shrieking their welcome they glided down to land beside the Beastie Boys, who jumped back in surprise. Standing up, the dragonets were taller than they were.

Tobias watched in amazement as each of the flying lizards picked a Beastie Boy and waddled towards him.

The red chose Brimble. Sweat beaded on his forehead and a terrified expression appeared on his face as the dragonet moved closer. It grinned, revealing rows of needle-sharp teeth. Brimble's face broke into a smile and he hesitantly raised his hand to tickle it under the chin. "He's called Blooper," he said excitedly.

"Skyskimmer!" shrieked Trimble, throwing himself forward to embrace the blue that stood before him. "I think I love you." Skyskimmer purred with delight, then bugled loud and long.

Wild Bill jerked awake, smacking his head against the wall, but the sight of the dragonets with the Beastie Boys stifled his angry words. Instead he rubbed at his injury as he watched the bonding session that was being enacted in front of him. "Bleedin' hell," he murmured.

One by one the dragonets introduced themselves to the Beastie Boys. Boo was the last to step forward, and then only because the blue dragonet wrapped its tail around him and dragged him closer. His screech of alarm died, replaced by a gasp of awe. "He's called Scratch," he yelled excitedly. Scratch raised his back leg and began to rub at a spot on his side. "Let me," said Boo, reaching over to scratch the offending area.

"It would seem that our little friends are a hit. It is as it should be: dragon and companion. Dragons need companions, no matter how small the beast or the man."

Startled by Wooster's words, Tobias looked up. He was surprised to see tears in his eyes. "Are you all right?" he asked.

Wooster smiled wanly. "Yearnings, Tobias. Seeing all this has made me realise what I gave up to save my kin." He looked at the ground. "I just hope it will all prove worthwhile."

Tobias found himself at a loss for something to say. He could sense depression settling over the man like a dark cloud. "C-can't you turn back?" he asked eventually.

"It is not that easy." He met Tobias's gaze. "It would take the talents of more than I to do such a thing, and I fear that such skill is no longer a part of Ogmus magic."

"But it could be done?"

Wooster nodded. "Yes, it could be done."

"Then I'll do it!" Although not having the faintest idea of what he would have to do, Tobias knew he had to attempt it. If it were not for Wooster he could well have faded away altogether. He had to try.

Wooster's mouth twitched into the semblance of a smile and he shook his head. "Although you are true Ogmus, it would take more than your powers to alter the genetic make-up of this body. Once a dragon has changed, great magic is required to restore it to that which it once was."

The news was deflating, but suddenly an inspirational thought struck him: Snorkel. He was true Ogmus, too. Maybe the two of them could work the magic to change Wooster back. "Snorkel!" he shouted. "We have Snorkel. Surely between the two of us we could manage it."

"Manage what?" asked Wild Bill, drawn to the conversation by the volume of Tobias's response.

"Maybe," said Wooster, his eyes lighting up at the suggestion.

"Maybe what?" demanded Wild Bill.

"Put me down, woman!"

"Not till you better, Norkel. You not well yet. Me carry."

Tobias, Wooster and Wild Bill peered into the gloom of the tunnel at the sound of raised voices. Wide-eyed with astonishment they watched as a woman of more than ample proportions strode into view, a crimson clad figure cradled in her muscular arms.

"Snorkel?" murmured Tobias. He watched as they walked past and entered the amphitheatre.

"Then again …" whispered Wooster, staring dejectedly at the duo.

"You can't carry me in like this in front of everyone," Snorkel cried. "I'll be a laughing stock."

Snorkel turned and glared at the sound of Wild Bill's laughter, but before he could utter a word in his defence a cry of pleasure distracted him. Flying round the cavern he saw Scratch, with Boo sitting astride him, his legs clamped around the dragonet's body and arms gripping its neck. He was shrieking with delight. The other Beastie Boys quickly mounted their own dragonets, and with shrill cries of glee they flew around over the heads of the watching Ogmus.

"Bugger me," murmured Wild Bill. "It's the bleedin' cavalry. And here's the general," he added, spotting Nanna Pussy striding towards them. "And she doesn't seem right pleased."

"Who doesn't?" asked Snorkel, peering myopically into the crowd.

"Nanna Pussy," answered Tobias, rising to his feet.

"Who's she then?" asked Snorkel.

"I think you're about to find out," Tobias said, with a grim smile.

The crowd turned to watch the Beastie Boys and dragonets cavorting around the cavern. They laughed, cheered and pointed, and were oblivious to what was going on in the tunnel.

Unfortunately Snorkel wasn't. "I think you'd better put me down," he whispered out the side of his mouth, noticing the old woman striding out of the crowd towards him. Seeing that Meelan was about to protest he added, "Now!"

Meelan shrugged and let him drop.

Unprepared, Snorkel hit the floor with a thud. "Not like that," he muttered, scrambling to his feet and dusting himself down. He winced and glared at Meelan as the thumping in his head intensified.

"You must be Snorkel!" The tone of Nanna Pussy's voice suggested that she was less than impressed.

Snorkel turned to face her. Although she was not much taller than him, he could sense the aura of power emanating from her. He gulped; the hairy guy was right, she did not seem best pleased. Fighting back the feeling of nausea that the pounding in his head had brought on, he bowed briefly; the last thing he needed was to puke all over her feet. "At your service," he said, a forced smile curling his lips. It faded as Nanna Pussy's glower refused to be budged. "Anything wrong?" he asked.

Standing with her hands on her hips she glowered at him. "Very soon we are going to be attacked by the blacks, and our saviour is so hung over he has to be carried to the battle briefing by his wife. And you ask me if anything is wrong?"

Taken aback by the tirade Snorkel blurted, "She's not my wife," then wilted under her icy glare.

"Come here!"

Snorkel took a step back. "Why?" he asked, fearful of the consequences of obeying her command.

Nanna Pussy sighed. "To see if I can clear your head enough for you to be of any use to us. That's why. Now are you coming or do I have to get you myself?" She folded her arms and tapped her foot on the ground impatiently.

"I'd do as she says if I were you," advised the hairy man.

Glancing round at the amused expressions on the faces that surrounded him, Snorkel knew he was beaten. But what did the woman plan to do? Was she a witch?

'Of a fashion,' a voice whispered in his head.

His jaw dropped in astonishment.

'So do not keep me waiting for too long or I'll turn you into something small and horrid.'

Her voice reminded him of someone he once knew, someone who was equally forceful. Like her, Nanna Pussy did not seem to be someone he would want to mess with.

'I'm glad we've got that sorted,' said the voice in his head.

He stepped forward hesitantly.

"Now you're for it," chortled the hairy bloke.

"Ignore him," said a voice behind him. "She only wants to help."

"Bow your head."

Nervously Snorkel did as he was told, wondering all the while what the old lady was going to do to him. He soon had his answer.

Her gnarled fingers grasped his head in a vice-like grip and he gasped as a multitude of tiny needles lanced through his temples, probing and burrowing deep into his skull. It felt as though an army of hairy caterpillars were holding a party. It was not painful or unpleasant; more disquieting. After a few moments Nanna Pussy dropped her hands and the caterpillars disappeared.

"That should do it," she said, stepping back to inspect Snorkel's face. "You have a bit more colour at least."

Amazingly his headache had gone, as had the bilious feeling. He grinned.

"Come," commanded Nanna Pussy. "It is way past time that plans were made. Your Queen demands your presence." She cast her eyes over the rest of the group. "And you lot."

The man with the hairy face rose to his feet in one fluid motion. "I'll follow you anywhere, my sweet," he said. "Just lead the way."

Nanna Pussy rolled her eyes and walked out into the amphitheatre, seemingly ignoring the man's chuckle.

Snorkel flinched as Meelan strung her arm through his. "Me come too, Norkel. You want carry?"

"I feel fine now." He reached out and patted her belly. "Anyway you're carrying enough. I can walk."

Whistling happily to himself, he followed Nanna Pussy through the crowd and across the heated sand with a spring in his step. He had the girl of his dreams on his arm, he was about to become a father for the first time — that he knew of — and his hangover had been cured. He would listen to their plan and offer some sage advice, then sit back and leave them to it. After all he'd brought them their queen; what else could they want of him?

* * * * *

"You want me to do what?" Standing before Kraelin, Reizgoth, Nanna Pussy and Nina in the middle of the arena, Snorkel could not believe what he had just heard. "Do you realise how much power that would take? I'd be drained for weeks, months, years even. And that is if I could manage to do what you want in the first place."

"You exaggerate," snapped Nanna Pussy.

From her perch on his shoulder pad Draco nodded her agreement, much to Snorkel's annoyance.

"We know you can do it," continued Nanna Pussy. "You managed to get Kraelin, Reizgoth and the dragonets here without any harm being done to yourself."

"Apart from killing off some of his few remaining brain cells with alcohol afterwards, that is," Kraelin snorted.

"Will you leave him be?" rumbled Reizgoth.

"It was his fault," Snorkel retorted, casting Volgen a dark look.

"No one asked you to drink the piggin' brew," muttered Volgen.

"When you two have quite finished!" shouted Nanna Pussy. "We have a plan to agree."

"I agree to it," said Kraelin, brightly.

"And me," added Nina, grinning.

"Yer have my vote," nodded Wild Bill.

One by one the others voiced their agreement. Snorkel wilted at each 'aye'. Things were not turning out quite the way he expected. "Don't I have a say in this?" he asked, knowing what the answer would be.

"No," said Kraelin. "We know you can do it, so why must you prevaricate?"

"I'll help you." Tobias stepped forward. "Just tell me what to do and I'll do it."

Snorkel gave him a grateful smile and shook his head. "I barely know what to do myself, let alone direct anyone else." Realising he had upset the boy he gripped his shoulder. "But thank you all the same."

"You have a different role to play, Terminator." Tobias looked at Nanna Pussy, startled by her softly spoken words. She smiled warmly at him. "I realise now what you must do, and it does not involve defeating the blacks as I had first thought." She glared at Snorkel. "When he has done his part then you must do yours."

"What am I to do?"

"Why, bring back the other dragons, of course. Terminate their enforced exile."

Cheers erupted from the Ogmus who lined the sandy arena. "What on earth are those little fools up to now?" snapped Kraelin, glaring over at the disturbance.

At the other side of the amphitheatre six dragonets and their jockeys raced through the air, much to the delight of the earth-bound onlookers. Responding to the cheering, the Beastie Boys encouraged their mounts to greater efforts as bookies shouted out odds and took bets.

"Get them down, now!" Kraelin commanded.

'I'll stop them.' Draco launched herself into the air and flew towards the racing dragonets shrieking at the top of her voice. The dragonets immediately pulled up, much to the disappointment of the crowd, who groaned and tore up their betting slips, tossing them to the ground in disgust.

Nanna Pussy tapped her lips with her forefinger as she thoughtfully watched the downward spiralling dragonets. "Hmmm. They've just given me an idea." She turned to Snorkel. "Could you ask your dragonet to call them over?"

As he mind-spoke the request to Draco, Snorkel couldn't help but wonder what hair-brained idea Nanna Pussy had come up with now. It would seem that he had left one world of madness to enter another. At least in his old world they'd had decent bars, and right now he could do with a drink. More than one in fact!

Chapter Thirty One

In the comfort of his refurbished meeting room, Lord Blackbishop sprawled in his newly upholstered armchair, his paper slipper encapsulated feet resting on the teak desk and his hands clasped behind his head, eyes closed, trying to ease his troubled mind. For what seemed like the hundredth time he pondered the day's events in an attempt to find the cause of his depression, but its origin eluded him. The initial excitement of the battle had long worn off and a feeling of despondency had settled, darkening his mood. He had sent the other lords to their rooms, as he found their high spirits and doltish games irritating. Why his mood should have changed so dramatically was beyond him. After all, they'd fought a magnificent battle and won; vanquished their enemies. Or, in this case, enemy. Maybe that was what bothered him. He had expected more than one dragon to come through, and one with wings come to that. And where had the queen been? And Snor'kel? It was all too much for his mind to make sense of. In stark contrast, the other lords seemed well pleased with the day's outcome, as did the black dragons. Maybe it was just him.

A light breeze blew through a partially open window and set the torches' flames to dancing. His nose twitched as smoke wafted around the room. He removed a scented handkerchief from his tunic pocket and dabbed at his nose. Sighing, he vowed to instruct the masons to install some form of extraction first thing in the morning. Ever since the fire he'd had an aversion to smoke and flames. Grimacing at the hazy memory, he absently stroked the bare skin above his top lip with his finger and thumb. Perhaps he should grow the moustache again. He kind of missed it now that it wasn't there.

A knock on the door interrupted his musings and he scowled. "Enter!" His voice was harsher than he intended. Lifting his feet from the desk he sat upright in his chair to await the caller.

The door eased open and his apprentice manservant entered, a hesitant smile on his pasty-white features. He stopped inside the threshold, wringing his hands.

Lord Blackbishop felt his mood darken still further. More than anything he wished Wooster would hurry up and return. Aside from missing his unflappable, cultured manner, his old manservant would have known what to do to improve his current mood. Wooster always did.

"What is it, Jives?" Lord Blackbishop snapped, glaring at the unfortunate with his best 'I'm mighty pissed off at being interrupted' look.

"It's Jeeves, my Lord," Jeeves corrected softly, wringing his hands even more and dipping his head.

"Never heard of the man. What's up with him?"

"Pardon, my Lord?" Jeeves stared at him questioningly.

Rolling his eyes Lord Blackbishop rose to his feet, placed his fingertips on the desk and leaned forward. "Was that question too difficult for you? Should I speak more slowly?"

Jeeves shook his head. "No, no, my Lord. I just meant ... That is ... Well ..."

"Yes?"

"Is there anything I can get you? Refreshments, perhaps?"

"But what of this Joves fellow?"

"Joves, my Lord?"

Lord Blackbishop sighed. Was the man such a simpleton that he could not answer a straightforward question? "You interrupted some very important thoughts to ask me about Joves. Correct?"

Nonplussed, Jeeves stood and gaped.

"And then you can't even remember what you wanted to ask me about him. Are you an idiot?" Lord Blackbishop's voice became low and menacing. "Or perhaps you think I am."

What little colour Jeeves' face possessed fled at the suggestion. "N-n-no, my Lord. I would never think such a thing. I merely came to see if you required anything before I retired for the night."

A twisted smile formed on Lord Blackbishop's face. With a snort of amusement at the young lad's obvious discomfort, he leaned back to seat himself in his chair; and missed. With a cry of surprise he landed on the floor.

"My Lord," shouted Jeeves, hurrying forward. "Are you all right?"

Before he could reach him, Lord Blackbishop sprang to his feet and bobbed on the spot, laughing and launching a couple of playful punches. Then he stopped his shadow boxing and began to dust himself down.

"Allow me, my Lord," begged Jeeves.

Lord Blackbishop jumped out of his reach. "Don't touch me," he shrieked. "In fact get out. Get out! Go on. Vamoose, scarper, get lost, get thee hither from my sight!" With each curt word he took a pace toward Jeeves, waving his hands to shoo the lad to the door.

Jeeves whimpered and grabbed at the latch. Pulling the door open he fled, slamming it behind him.

Lord Blackbishop winced at the sound then grinned. "Well that showed him." He slapped his hands together in delight. But it was short lived, as his thoughts turned again to the day's events and his good humour evaporated. Something was not right, but what it was he had no idea. Cursing to himself, he walked over to the window and stared into the darkness beyond, wondering how close Wooster and Jophrey were to returning. Right now he could do with their company. Well, Wooster's at least.

* * * * *

"I don't understand," said Jophrey. "Why can't I come with you?" Despite the darkness, Jophrey saw the tightening around Mandrake's eyes and began to regret labouring the point. The last thing he needed was to upset the dragon. "I'm sorry," he said. "It's just that I want to be there when it all happens."

The huge black dragon lowered his head until it was level with Jophrey's. "I understand. But with this Tobias held firmly in the clutches of the demons, you are our only hope once we have vanquished them and their servants. If you came with us and were ..." He turned away to clear his throat. When he swung his head back round Jophrey saw tears glistening in the dragon's eyes. "We are dealing with agents of the darkness, Jophrey, who do not have morals like we do. They would think nothing of eliminating you if they thought you were truly aligned with us. I suspect that the only reason they did not kill you before was that they thought they could turn you to their cause."

"Never!" snapped Jophrey. "After what those little gimps did to me with their drugged darts, I'd never join them."

Mandrake nodded. "So you see my dilemma?"

Jophrey sighed and looked at the ground, scuffing his foot in the grass. "I suppose so."

"Good boy. You know it makes sense." Mandrake straightened, his towering bulk dwarfing Jophrey.

"But what am I supposed to do while you see off the demons and capture the queen?"

"Do? Prepare for the future, young Lord." Mandrake chuckled. "Because it is not very far away. Now I must join my brothers and plan the attack. They wait on the other side of Wellstown for my arrival."

The dragon spread his huge wings, preparing to launch himself into the air.

"Wait!" shouted Jophrey. "How will I know that you have succeeded?

"You'll know," answered Mandrake, as his mighty hind legs thrust him skywards. "We are linked you and I, Jophrey. Believe me, you will know."

With a flap of his leathery membranes Mandrake powered into the night, the draught from his departure nearly knocking Jophrey off his feet. He ducked as twigs, grass and small stones buffeted him. When the wind had died down he looked up, but Mandrake was nowhere to be seen. He had disappeared into the blackness and was one with the night.

'Wait there for me,' the dragon's voice whispered in his head. *'I will collect you once we have finished what we set out to do.'*

Resigned to missing all the fun, Jophrey turned and made his way back to where he had hobbled Dancer. Why was it he missed out on all the excitement? He so much wanted to be there when the queen was captured, and to see the looks on those hateful midgets' faces when the blacks arrived and flamed them to death.

As he walked back to his horse a thought occurred to him. Why did he have to wait around for Mandrake to pick him up? Surely after the battle the dragon would be too busy organising Hope and the captives to want to come away and collect him. Why not save him the bother?

By the time he reached Dancer he was almost running. The pang of guilt at disobeying Mandrake was firmly quashed by the excitement of actually doing something positive. If he rode through the night he could be at The Forest by daybreak, and well on his way to Hope. That way if Mandrake got delayed coming back for him he would almost be there anyway.

Dancer whinnied a greeting as Jophrey drew near, which was fortuitous as it was so dark he might never have found him without assistance. Whispering pleasantries, he stooped and removed the hobble before vaulting onto the horse's back. Grabbing handfuls of mane he gave a loud "Yeehaa!" and heeled the animal into action. It would be a long, cold ride, but what the hell; it would be worth it. As he rode he conjured images of strange new worlds in his mind; central to them being the magnificent form of Mandrake swooping down over alien landscapes, strange beings rushing out to bow beneath him and the mounted dragonlord.

Jophrey cackled with laughter at the thought. He could picture himself with a golden crown adorning his black flying helmet, accepting homage from conquered worlds.

Dragonlord! It had a nice ring to it.

* * * * *

"Are you sure?" Mandrake demanded.

Spot jumped up and down and bugled, before nodding his head vigorously.

"Show us!" Mandrake ordered.

In the centre of the circle of black dragons, Spot sat down and screwed his eyes shut. He clenched his teeth with concentration.

"It is no use," snapped Vizigoth after a few moments. "I can't see a damn thing."

"TRY HARDER!" roared Mandrake, his patience running out. "OR THE FIRST THING TO GET FLAMED IN THE ATTACK WILL BE YOU!"

Spot squeaked in alarm and cracked open an eye to peer at Mandrake, who was leaning forward glowering at the diminutive dragon. Spot's eye snapped shut and he tried again.

Mandrake sighed. Perhaps it had been a mistake sending Spot to carry out the reconnaissance. Although small and less likely to be seen by the enemy, he was barely above Blackbishop and the other lords on the intelligence scale. Spot had still not managed to convey the location of the entrance to the dragon caves of Hope, and they had been working on their plan for over a candle-mark now. If he did not project the image soon, it would be dawn and the element of surprise would be lost. Mandrake could not risk casualties in the approaching battle; they were too few in number already. Well there was *one* he wouldn't mind losing, he thought, glaring at Spot whose face was still puckered in concentration.

Slowly a fuzzy image began to materialise in Mandrake's head. It took a moment for him to realise that Spot was actually projecting the location of the entrance. A smile formed on his face. At last! The image began to clear and become sharper. "That's it," he murmured in encouragement. The image sharpened and Mandrake groaned.

"YOU IDIOT!" he roared, trying to clear the picture of an erupting volcano, with a roasting calf being turned on a spit over its crater, from his mind. He shook his head and the picture shattered. Leaning forward he glared at the cowering dragon. "You have one more chance! Get it wrong and it will be you roasted over a hot fire with a stick up your arse! Understand?"

Spot gulped and nodded hesitantly. The other dragons chuckled, deep and rumbling.

"And you lot can shut up too!" Mandrake snapped. He glowered at Spot. "Get it right!"

The little dragon scrunched himself up, closed his eyes and tried again; this time with more success.

Mandrake purred happily as the image of Hope Mountain sprang into his mind. Snow-capped and stark, the mountain zoomed into focus, centering on a position two thirds of the way up its southern slope. The cliff face was sheer and vertical, unblemished except for a wide cave entrance. No pathways could ever be cut into the rock to reach it. A dragon entrance; it had to be. As his mind's eye stared at the dark opening, two dragons emerged; one gold and one red. "The Queen," he whispered, his voice filled with admiration. "Our future!"

Deep, low-pitched murmurs added their weight to his reverence. As he watched the dragons fly out, he noticed a figure sitting at the base of the red dragon's neck. He peered closer. "Snor'kel?"

he said, astonished. He had expected a more imposing figure than the one he now observed. Dressed in a powder-blue flying suit and looking as though he were about to vomit, the pot-bellied man looked like anything but a dragon rider; a man gifted with Ogmus magic.

The dragons swooped into focus and Mandrake felt his stomach flutter at the speed. He panicked, realising that they were re-enacting Spot's flaming. "Enough!" he yelled, but it was too late. A huge fireball blocked out the vision. Bright violent light flared in his head and he roared in pain.

So did his brothers.

Multicoloured lights flashed and bounced around the inside of Mandrake's brain. The pain was insufferable and he clasped his foreclaws to his head in an attempt to clear his senses, but to no avail. With a loud roar he collapsed to the ground and thrashed his legs. Eventually the pain subsided and his thrashing grew less frantic. After what seemed like an eternity he felt able to rise, and rolled over to stand on shaking legs. Steeling himself he opened his eyes, containing his anger for the moment when he focussed on Spot; then their little group would definitely be one dragon less. He would tear the little idiot to pieces, then feed the bits to the others.

Through the haze that clouded his vision he could see the other dragons in various states of distress, rolling on the ground as he had been but moments before; but of Spot he could see nothing. His anger grew as he scoured the darkness. Spot had fled!

Rearing up on his hind legs, Mandrake roared his anger to the skies."WHEN WE HAVE FINISHED WITH THE OTHERS, WE WILL COME LOOKING FOR YOU, YOU LITTLE DOLT! THERE IS NOWHERE YOU CAN HIDE THAT WILL BE SAFE FROM US! DO YOU HEAR? WHEREVER YOU ARE WE WILL FIND YOU; AND WHEN WE DO..."

Concealed in the thickest part of The Forest, Spot cowered beneath a huge, spreading chestnut tree, his head buried in his foreclaws. Even though he was leagues away from where he had left the others, he still heard Mandrake's promise of retribution and whimpered with fear.

* * * * *

On the outskirts of Wellstown Jophrey woke to find he was lying on the ground. His dew-dampened clothing clung to his skin, suggesting that he had been there for some time, and his head throbbed. Groaning he rolled over and pushed himself to his knees before rising shakily to his feet. He gently probed at his forehead with his fingers, feeling the bump on his skull. What had happened? The last thing he remembered before blacking out was a bright light that seemed to explode in his head. What had caused it? As he pondered the question he realised he was alone. Something was missing.

Dancer!

With his hand pressed to his injured forehead he peered into the pre-dawn light, looking for signs of his horse, but it had gone. It must have wandered away while he was out cold. He cursed his ill-fortune.

The sun cleared the horizon and pale light bathed the grasslands, sparkling off the wispy mist that hugged the contours of the land. In the distance he could see the rooftops of Wellstown. With a resigned sigh, Jophrey staggered down the track towards the buildings. It looked like it would take a lot longer to reach Hope than he had first thought. As he walked he studied the approaching town, where something in the air caught his eye. He stopped and shaded his eyes, squinting to see what it was.

"And so it starts." He gazed with satisfaction at the dark shapes rising into the sky, appearing as pinpricks against the cloudless, pale-blue backdrop. Behind him he heard the clatter of hooves and turned. "Dancer," he cried, seeing the horse trotting up the trail towards him.

Dancer neighed a greeting.

With a whoop of joy Jophrey ran to the animal. All of a sudden his luck seemed to be changing, and for the better.

Chapter Thirty Two

After Spot's little show it was a silent, morose group that flew through the air towards the distant mountain home of the Ogmus. Even though the early morning sun felt warm and soothing, it did nothing to alleviate the blacks' sour mood. Although not one for giving credence to superstitious nonsense, Mandrake worried that the morning's mishap could be a prelude to things to come. Far below them five black shadows swept silently across fields, hamlets, streams and hills in the classic flying 'V' formation, filling the early risers who saw them with fear. Oblivious to the panic their passing created the dragons flew on, drawing inexorably closer to Hope and their destiny.

On the horizon grey shapes began to rise from the earth, stretching right to the far distant sea and left to the interior of Tiernan Og. Tall, snow-capped and imposing, the mountains loomed ever nearer as the dragons powered towards them. Mandrake felt his mood begin to lighten. Soon it would all be over and they, the blacks, would be masters of not only this world, but others too. Excitement and expectation rippled through the dragons as he broadcast his thought.

Eventually they flew over the River Dragle and Mandrake swung the flight east to follow the river's line, which he knew led to Hope Mountain. Soon they were flying through a tree-lined valley, sheer walls of rock rising on either side, erupting from lush grassland as though driven through from below. The air was colder here and Mandrake felt his muscles lose some of their fluidity. He shivered. Winter was on its way and with it the snows. He hated winter, when cold days and nights thickened dragons' blood and made them sluggish. Once they had completed their mission, he'd ensure that Snor'kel's first task would be to open a wyverhole to a world of perpetual sunlight and warmth.

Something struck him on the snout, the sharp pain making him roar with surprise.

'What is it?' asked Paladin.

'A rock,' said Mandrake, peering up at the cliffs on either side of them. *'It must have fallen down off the mountain.'*

Another cry of pain sounded and Mandrake twisted to see which of them had shrieked. *'What is it, Nazier?'* he asked, when he saw the dragon dipping his head and raising his foreleg to rub at his snout.

'A rock,' the dragon answered, examining the mountainside. *'It must have fallen from up there.'*

Mandrake followed his gaze, but could see nothing. Two rocks? Falling within moments of each other and striking the dragons? He frowned. Coincidence?

Snaggletooth roared. *'One has just hit me,'* he broadcast, rubbing at his injury.

Three rocks? That was definitely not coincidence. With hooded eyes Mandrake scoured the surrounding cliffs, looking for ...

He had no idea what. But definitely something that should not be there. Something caught his eye high above, streaking through the air at an amazing speed. His huge eyes followed the fast-moving shape and his jaw dropped in astonishment. It was a dragon, and it was carrying a rock. He looked more closely. It was too small to be a proper dragon. And was that a tiny man sitting on its back, his legs wrapped under the creature's belly for balance? No, not a man. A low, angry growl rumbled in the base of his throat and he felt heat being generated within. A Pixel!

'Up there!' mind-yelled Snaggletooth, pointing to Mandrake's right.

Mandrake looked across and scowled. There was another one there too.

'And there!' shrieked Peladin.

In all there were six of the tiny creatures, five blues and one red. Each one carried a rock and had a Pixel perched on its back. The Pixels seemed to take great delight in pulling faces at the dragons. One even had the cheek to bare his backside.

Mandrake snorted angrily, a plume of black smoke escaping his nostrils. "FLAME THE LITTLE BASTARDS!" he roared, soaring up towards them.

But he was too slow. With incredible speed the mini-dragons dropped their loads and rocketed away. Once they were a safe distance away they slowed and the riders took the opportunity to taunt the dragons, leering and making obscene gestures.

It was too much for Mandrake. First Spot had nearly turned them into drooling idiots with his mind-blast; now Pixels were taunting them while riding midget, rock-carrying dragons. Urging his brothers on, he powered after them, intent on rending both creatures and Pixels apart. But try as he might they kept ahead of him and he could make no headway. He was tiring fast and knew his brothers would be feeling the same way, especially Nazier, the fat slob.

On and on they chased, swerving round bends, dropping down to just above tree level before soaring up again, but all the while heading towards Hope Mountain. With a wry grimace Mandrake worked out their plan. They intended to tire the blacks out before heading back to the safety of the caverns, where a trap would be waiting. But they had badly underestimated him; he was too clever to fall for that one. Once they had led them to the tunnel, and he would know whether it was the right one or not thanks to Spot, he would call a halt and wait until he and his brothers had rested before he launched the final assault. The demons' desperate plan for survival would fail.

His realisation eased his mood, and he quickly relayed a message to the others telling them to cease the chase once they were near to the tunnel.

The mini-dragons steered a course to the southern face of Hope Mountain. Mandrake grinned. The fools; they did not realise that they were dealing with creatures of intelligence. *'Get ready,'* he commanded his brothers. *'Hold back from the chase,'* he mind-yelled, seeing the mini-dragons heading for the sheer face of the mountain. At the last moment the mini-dragons veered upwards, following the vertical cliff face. Had the blacks been pursuing at full speed, they would have smashed into the rock, not having sufficient space to carry out the same evasive manoeuvre.

Like ferrets down a rabbit hole the mini-dragons and their riders disappeared into the mountain, diving through the wide entrance.

Mandrake rose to hover before the opening, his brothers arrayed behind him holding the 'V' formation. After taking time to inspect the dark maw for evidence of a trap, he slowly edged forward, every sense alert for any sign of an ambush. Nothing appeared to be wrong, but something was still bothering him. What it was, he could not tell. But he felt uneasy.

Suddenly out of the darkness the six mini-dragons and their riders appeared. They turned in the air and hovered with their backs to the blacks, whereupon the mounted Pixels raised their bums and dropped their leggings.

Mandrake's eyes narrowed in rage as his gaze fixed on six, green-tinged full moons. This was too much! How dare they treat the future masters of the world in such an insolent manner. Roaring his outrage, his unease forgotten, he arrowed forward. He was closely followed by his brothers, who nearly collided as they rushed to be first into the tunnel behind him.

At Mandrake's roar the mini-dragons hurtled into the dimly lit tunnel. Throwing caution to the wind, Mandrake and his flight gave chase. For what seemed like an age they careered along the tunnel, veering to left and right, until eventually a long straight brought them out into the open. Mandrake spread his wings and came to a rapid stop in mid-air, ignoring the cries of alarm from behind, his mind trying to make sense of the alien landscape before him.

Rock and desert, rust-red in colour, hot and inhospitable, met his incredulous gaze. In the distance a gigantic mountain belched smoke and flames, and a noise like thunder rolled towards them. High above a huge sun hung in murky skies, an aurora of dust stifling its intense heat.

'Are we inside the mountain?' asked Peladin, gasping for breath as he hovered in the heavy, dust-filled air.

'Does it look like it?' Mandrake snapped, twisting his head round to glare at him. His jaw dropped in horror as he saw what was behind them. Desert, desert and more desert. Of the tunnel there was no sign. It was as if it had never been there. "No!" he shrieked. "NOOOOOOOOO!"

Below them a huge, scaled reptile slowly raised its head and opened an eye. Blinking away grit and sand, it took one look at the beasts hovering in the air above it and added its own voice to Mandrake's. Unlike the dragon's, its roar was one of annoyance at being so rudely awakened.

* * * * *

"Where'd they go, where'd they go?" shouted Wild Bill, ducking as the six dragonets and their riders sped over his head.

Tobias gaped in astonishment as the black dragons winked out of existence before his very eyes. One moment the enormous blacks had been hovering outside the tunnel mouth, seemingly reluctant to enter; the next they were powering after the dragonets, and then — gone! He would never have believed it if he had not seen it with his own eyes.

"To another world!" Nanna Pussy's softly spoken words barely carried to where they stood. "A primitive one, where they can't cause any harm. Well not to others, anyway."

Silhouetted by the shimmering light from the outside world, she stood beside Snorkel close to the wall, some distance back from the tunnel mouth. Her arms were wrapped around the dwarf's waist. He was standing with arms spread, eyes closed and face screwed up in concentration holding open the wyverhole. Tobias could see the beads of sweat running down his face, and his crimson tunic was darkened and damp. Nanna Pussy looked in no better shape. The old lady appeared even older than normal with the strain of adding her power to Snorkel's.

"Your turn," she whispered. Turning her head, her eyes pleaded with Tobias to hurry.

"Go on young 'un," urged Wild Bill, laying a huge hand on Tobias's shoulder and squeezing it gently.

This was the moment Tobias had been dreading. The moment when he had to enter the wyverhole and bring back the others. He felt ill. What if the wyverhole led to the same world that the blacks had been sent to? Then he would be trapped with them and would never be able to get back. If they allowed him to live, that is.

'It doesn't,' Wooster's calm mind-speak advised. *'With Nanapussy's help, Snorkel has altered the co-ordinates for the final destination. It will take you to Midas.'*

Tobias cast Wooster a thankful look and hesitantly walked towards the shimmering veil suspended across the tunnel. Snorkel had already told him that it was a different kind of wyverhole to the one he had opened to bring himself and the dragons through to Tiernan Og. With Nanna Pussy's guidance he had been able to refine the knowledge passed down through generations of Ogmus, so that long detours were a thing of the past. Now he should be able to transport Tobias directly to where he needed to go.

It was the word 'should' that made Tobias nervous.

'Relax Tobias. Just do as I have said and all will be well. You have allies on the other side who are all too eager to return. Just call them by name and they will appear. Trust me.'

Although he had only known Wooster for a short time Tobias did trust him. It did not make him feel any easier about entering the wyverhole, but it helped to know that he would have friends on Midas. As long as that was the world Snorkel was sending him to.

A cool breeze caressed his face as he drew level with Nanna Pussy. He revelled in its feel, and paused to let it wash over him. All the while his gaze remained fixed on the shimmering curtain standing between himself and Midas.

"Go," said Nanna Pussy through gritted teeth. "Even with my aid Snorkel cannot keep the wyverhole open for much longer. You do not have much time, so don't waste it dawdling; get going."

Tobias gave her a nervous glance and gasped. Her face was an unhealthy grey colour and dark rings had formed beneath her eyes. She looked exhausted. As if sensing his concern, Nanna Pussy forced a smile. *'You do not have long,'* her voice whispered in his head. *'Please hurry.'*

Steeling himself Tobias gave a curt nod, gritted his teeth and stepped forward, his eyes fixed on the patch of daylight at the tunnel's mouth. A tingling sensation washed over him as he entered the wyverhole, making goosebumps break out all over his body. In an instant the patch of daylight ahead disappeared, replaced by a brilliance that lanced into his head. He screamed in agony and sank to his knees, hands clasping his temples and eyes screwed tightly shut against the pain.

* * * * *

Concealed in a copse at the base of Hope Mountain, Spot stared up at the rock face where his brothers hovered outside the cave mouth. He'd followed at a discreet distance, hoping they did not see him and flame him before he'd had a chance to make amends for his earlier over exuberance. It wasn't his fault he'd got carried away.

He just wanted to let them know what a good dragon he had been and how he had succeeded in his mission. Unfortunately, in his excitement he'd forgotten the first rule of mind-merge: do not show — tell. And now his brothers wanted to kill him. With any luck they would change their minds once they had captured the queen, and would realise what a good, brave dragon he had been.

Spot stifled his bugle of excitement in the nick of time, a muffled squeak emerging from his mouth instead of a full-throated roar. When his brothers rocketed into the cave, however, he let rip with the loudest roar he had ever produced. Jumping into the air he flapped his wings in excitement and let loose a flame; incinerating a nearby bush and roasting the small wild pig that had been hiding behind it. The enticing aroma of sizzling pork wafted over to him and he sniffed the air. Locating the cooked animal, he snuffled at its charred flesh with relish and licked his lips.

Before he could make the most of his good fortune he felt a presence rip into his very being and snatch something away. What it was he didn't know, but it made him jerk forward, such was its force. He roared with pain and flopped to the ground, lying gasping for breath as he tried to figure out what had been taken. It took him a while, but when he did tears sprang to his eyes. Scrambling to his feet he howled to the heavens for the loss of his brothers, for it was their touch that had been taken. He could no longer sense them at all. They had gone, disappeared, vanished as though they had never existed.

Sitting astride Dancer as he made his way towards The Forest, Jophrey felt the loss at the same moment, although he did not know it for what it was. As they entered the trees he realised and pulled the horse to a stop. *'Mandrake!'* he mind-yelled, praying to the gods that what he'd felt was not the dragon's death.

Silence shrieked back at him.

'Mandrake! What's happened? Where are you?'

'They're gone. All gone. Bad demons kill them. Nasty green men trick them and now they're gone. Spot got no one now. He all alone. Brothers dead.'

'Spot? Is that you?'

After a moment's pause Spot's voice sounded in Jophrey's head. *'Who that? Who calls Spot?'*

'It's me, Jophrey.'

'Funny boy with idiot dad?'

Jophrey sighed. *'Yes.'*

'Spot not alone! Idiot boy with funny dad still here. Where you? Spot come find. Then we flame demons!'

Jophrey vaulted off Dancer and led the horse to the side of the trail, where he left it to crop at the grass. Staring up into the leafy canopy he asked, *'Where are you?'*

'Spot at Hope. He see brothers fly into hole in mountain and then ...'

'Then what, Spot?' Jophrey cried. *'What happened?'*

'They not come back,' Spot answered, his voice heavy with misery. *'Demons kill them. Spot feel them rip from body. They dead!'*

Dead? They were all dead? Jophrey didn't want to believe it. Mandrake couldn't be gone. He just couldn't. Tears filled his eyes, threatening to spill down his cheeks.

'All dead.' Spot whimpered. *'Only Spot left. What Spot do?'*

Jophrey wiped his eyes with his sleeve. Inside he knew that what Spot told him was true. The blacks were gone, killed by the demons. Steely resolve replaced the sorrow that threatened to engulf him. The demons hadn't killed all the blacks; one still survived, and together they would avenge the murders. Together they would pay the demons back for what they had done.

'Come to me,' Jophrey commanded. *'Come and get me. We have plans to make. The deaths of our brothers will not go unavenged. Not while we still live and breathe.'*

'You mean Spot and Jophrey kill demons?'

With sudden clarity Jophrey knew that was exactly what he meant, and he also knew just the place to start looking for answers as to how. *'Yes,'* he said, his voice cold. *'We kill demons.'*

* * * * *

Jeeves knocked on the door of Lord Blackbishop's meeting room, his master's breakfast of a basket of fruit and a jug of water on the tray that was balanced on his arm. He knew his Lord was in there, as his bed had not been slept in and the boy he had left outside the room in case his master needed him had not seen him leave. He tried again, but still no one answered.

"My Lord?" he called. "Are you in there?"

There was no answer.

With a sigh Jeeves decided to take the plunge and grasped the handle, preparing himself for Lord Blackbishop's fury. As he slowly pushed the door open he cringed with expectancy. When no shout of outrage was forthcoming he opened the door fully and entered. The room was empty. Frowning, he walked in and spotted Lord Blackbishop's clothing piled in a heap on a chair, a pair of paper slippers on the floor beneath. Placing the tray on the table, he glanced at the room's three windows, and was relieved to see that they were all firmly closed. After witnessing the mood his master had been in the previous night, he had feared the worst when he'd seen the crumpled clothing.

Then he saw something that demanded further investigation; ash was piled in the slippers. What would someone as fastidious as Lord Blackbishop be doing with piles of ash in his footwear?

Jeeves walked round the desk to take a closer look. He gasped. His master's clothing was filled with fine ash too. Just what had he been up to?

Before he had the chance to ponder the situation further a scream rang out. It sounded like one of the maids. He turned and ran from the room and down the short flight of stairs to the hallway, nearly colliding with the shrieking woman.

Jeeves gripped her by the shoulders and peered into her eyes. "What is the matter? Calm down and tell me." He shook her to stop her sobbing. "What has happened?"

"It's the lords, sir. They're ..."

"They're what?"

The maid's fist flew to her mouth and her eyes widened. "Dead! Turned to ash in their beds, they are. All of them. Dead!" The last came out as a shriek.

Jeeves' thoughts turned to the piles of ash in Lord Blackbishop's clothing, and he realised she spoke the truth. The lords were no more. He did not know whether to laugh or cry.

"Who's dead?" asked Lord Blackhead, scratching at his head and yawning as he emerged from a doorway.

Seeing him, the maid fainted and sagged into Jeeves' arms.

Lord Blackhead gave a knowing smile and winked. "Bit early for that type of stuff, isn't it? Now what's all this shouting about?"

Jeeves lowered the maid to the floor and dipped his head in deference to Lord Blackhead. Straightening he said, "It would appear that you are now the Lord, my Lord."

Lord Blackhead frowned and rubbed at his chin. "Hey?"

Jeeves sighed. And just when he had thought things could not get any worse!

Chapter Thirty Three

Searing pain lanced through Tobias's head and bright specks danced in his closed eyes. He was in agony. Curled into a ball on the hard ground he rocked to and fro in an effort to gain some semblance of control over his senses. After what seemed like an age the specks became less agitated, though his head still pounded. He groaned and scrambled onto his hands and knees. He felt awful. Shivers wracked his body and a cold sweat slicked his skin. He fought the queasiness, wishing with his whole being that his body would heal itself; knowing he had little time to complete his task. To his astonishment his headache vanished and the nausea abated. He realised he had discovered another aspect of his Ogmus legacy. With a sigh of relief he rose to his feet. He eased open his eyes and received his second shock. He had been blinded! Panic set in, but using his newfound skill he attempted to wish back his sight. It didn't work.

Fearful of stumbling into a crevice or losing the location of the wyverhole he stayed where he was, concentrating on his other senses while he tried to slow his fast-beating heart. With his arms outstretched he probed the area around him, but could feel nothing apart from a warm breeze that caressed his flesh and carried with it a faintly familiar metallic scent. His heart hammered against his ribs, sending blood pulsing through his body and making him light-headed.

Taking deep breaths he managed to calm his nerves, but he could still feel the panic lurking inside him, waiting to strike at the first opportunity. Although he sensed the presence of the wyverhole behind him, he knew he did not have long to summon the dragons before it winked out of existence, leaving him blind and trapped on an alien world. Remembering what Wooster had said, he concentrated on calling the others to him.

'Krystchun, Stormflier, Arclund! Winegrath calls you.' He waited for a reply, but none was forthcoming. He tried again. *'Krystchun, Stormflier, Arclund! Winegrath calls you.'*

Still there was no answer. The world around Tobias was silent. There were no birdcalls, animal sounds or noises of any sort. For all he knew he could be standing in the middle of a gigantic hole. The thought made him shudder.

'Who calls us?'

Tobias cried out in surprise as the voice sounded in his head, his heart threatening to burst in his chest. When he'd recovered his composure he stammered, *'W-W-Winegrath.'*

'But you are not Winegrath, so why do you call us?'

It was one of the dragons he was to bring back, of that Tobias was sure. *'Winegrath sent me to guide you back to Tiernan Og. He couldn't come himself and asked me to come in his stead.'*

'How do we know you speak the truth?'

'You know,' answered Tobias, feeling more confident. *'Otherwise you would not be talking to me. But if you require further evidence, Nanapussy sends her regards and begs you to return to the world where you rightfully belong.'*

'Nanapussy? She still lives?'

'Yes. But not for much longer if you do not travel with me now. It is taking all of her power and that of another to hold the wyverhole open. If you do not return soon the hole will close, leaving us forever on Midas. I can already sense the power that holds it open beginning to weaken. Please hurry.'

"But we are already here," a deep voice said.

Tobias flinched and the suppressed panic inside him threatened to make a break for it.

The deep voice chuckled. "We have been here all along. Did you not see us?"

Turning in the direction of the voice, Tobias realised why he had smelt the metallic scent earlier. It was the smell of dragon. "I-I-I cannot see," he spluttered. "I was struck blind when I crossed over."

"It must have been the gold," another voice chimed in; this one more melodious than the first. "See his eyes? He is not used to bright light."

"Do we believe him?" asked a third voice.

"He speaks the truth," said the first dragon. "Anyway, what have we to lose? We have witnessed the lure of Midas turn the others into drooling, mindless creatures devoted to the gold. Would you sooner we stayed and lost our minds? I believe the boy is what he says he is."

"I agree," said the second voice.

"You're the leader, Stormflier," said the third. "Lead on."

Tobias felt a shudder run through the wyverhole. "It closes!" he cried. "We're too late!" He sensed an enormous shape looming over him and huge talons snatched him from the ground. A current of air swept by him, followed by the tingle of the wyverhole as they passed through. The speed of his passage was too much for his body to take and he blacked out.

* * * * *

Like darts from a blowpipe, the six dragonets shot into the amphitheatre, bugling their triumph at the top of their voices. Hundreds of others launched themselves into the air to greet their brothers, chittering and shrieking in welcome. To the Ogmus standing below it seemed like the rocky canopy had come alive. The air above their heads was a fluid mass of wings and bodies, and central to the aerial display were the five blues and the red. On their backs, the Beastie Boys basked in the adulation and doffed their hats in greeting. As if at a silent command, the cavorting dragonets formed a cavalcade in the air and followed their heroes on a lap of honour, circling the great amphitheatre in one long, noisy procession as the watching Ogmus looked on in stunned silence.

"Really!" snorted Kraelin, glaring up in disgust at the preening creatures. "Anyone would think that they ruled here."

Nina giggled and patted the queen's foreleg affectionately. "Let them have their celebration, my Queen."

Kraelin peered down at her and smiled, a merry twinkle in her eye. "For the moment. But if they do not stop that infernal racket soon they will be reminded who is in charge."

Squatting on the sand beside her Reizgoth rolled his eyes and shook his head.

From across the arena there came the sound of cheering. Nina looked over to where the Ogmus were gathered on the rocky surrounds of the sandy basin and smiled. Soon more cheers joined the first and before long five hundred voices were raised in acclaim. The Ogmus jumped up and down in delight, hugging their neighbours and dancing as news of the blacks' demise spread. The dragonets and the Beastie Boys were heroes who had returned from a duel with death, unscathed and in triumph. It was something to celebrate.

Out of the throng strode Volgen, Meelan and Cronan. With smiles on their faces they made their way over to Nina and the two dragons. Draco was perched on Meelan's shoulder, the dragonet's tail wrapped lightly around her neck. Nina's gaze fixed on Cronan. He looked so much happier now that he was back at Hope. It was as though a great weight had been lifted from his shoulders.

"Have we won, my Queen?" Volgen had to shout over the roar of the crowd and the racket from the dragonets to make himself heard.

Meelan pushed past and stood between him and Kraelin. She gave a clumsy bow, then craned her neck to look the queen in the eye. "Norkel? He fine?"

"Who?" Kraelin glowered up at the circling dragonets and appeared to be on the verge of saying something.

'Leave them be, my Queen. They will calm down soon. Please let them enjoy their moment for a little longer,' Nina urged.

Kraelin snorted her disapproval but said nothing. She peered down at Meelan instead. "What is it you want?"

"Norkel?" asked Meelan, a worried look on her face. "He all right?"

"He's fine," answered Nina, having picked up the mental image of Snorkel and Nanna Pussy from Kraelin. She reached out and squeezed Meelan's shoulder. "I'm sure he will be back with us soon."

Meelan smiled gratefully and bobbed her head. On her shoulder Draco lifted a sleep-laden eyelid and yawned.

"See? Draco knows that Snorkel is well."

'Snorkel? Well? That's a matter of opinion.' Nina laughed aloud at Draco's comment.

"Why you laugh?" asked Meelan, her eyes narrowing. Draco winked, closed her eyes and went back to sleep.

"No reason," said Nina, trying to think of an explanation that Meelan would understand.

'They come!' Kraelin projected excitedly, the volume of the dragon's mind-shout making Nina flinch. *'They come!'* Kraelin

blasted again. Stretching her neck she bugled loud and long, silencing both Ogmus and dragonets.

"What's happening?" cried Volgen.

"The dragons!" said Nina, clapping her hands and jumping up and down on the spot. She grinned at Volgen. "They're coming. Tobias has done it!"

Volgen folded his arms across his chest. "I knew he would," he said. "The lad's a piggin' marvel."

An expectant hush descended on the amphitheatre as Kraelin's bugling faded. The Ogmus, sensing the fulfilment of their prophecy, shuffled towards the sandy arena, their eyes trained on the access tunnel. The Beastie Boys and their mounts glided down to land on the sand beside the two dragons, leaving their brothers and sisters to settle on the rocky ledges.

Starting as a barely audible thrumming, the distant whump of wings carried into the cavern. As the volume of the sound began to increase, so did Nina's nervousness. The thumping set her body shaking in time with the beat and made her mouth go dry. By the time the dragons emerged into the amphitheatre she felt quite faint.

Three dragons there were. Two greens and a red; magnificent, huge beasts. They roared as they entered, causing the Ogmus to scream and hug each other in terror and the dragonets to shriek in alarm.

"Piggin' hell!" murmured Volgen, his eyes filling with tears. "There's a whole piggin' herd of them."

"Flight," corrected Reizgoth, shaking his head.

Cronan fell to his knees at the sight, but jumped quickly to his feet again as the hot sand burned his legs.

Nina's hand flew to her mouth when she saw a figure being carried by the red. It was Tobias. Not daring to give voice to her fears, she stared in horror at the limp body.

'He is fine,' Kraelin's voice whispered in her head. *'He sleeps.'*

'Sleeps?' Nina queried, peering up at the queen.

Kraelin shrugged and fixed her attention on the three dragons who were circling the amphitheatre. Exhaling loudly she waddled further out onto the sand, and Nina could sense her impatience. Although she could not hear what the dragon said, she knew that the queen had communicated with them.

After a moment's delay, the three dragons began to descend, slowly spiralling down until they settled on the sand before Kraelin; the red still cradling Tobias in his forelegs.

"That's Tobias," gasped Cronan.

Nina grabbed him by the arm as he attempted to get past. "He's fine," she said, her voice pitched low to avoid diverting the dragons' attention from the queen.

"B—"

Nina gave him a hard stare. With pursed lips Cronan glared back, then he pulled his arm from her grasp and turned to survey the group.

"Is that Tobias?" whispered one of the Beastie Boys.

"He looks dead," said another.

"He is not dead," snapped Nina, rounding on them.

Brimble smiled weakly in apology and glowered at Trimble, who shrugged and draped his arm around Skyskimmer, pulling the dragonet into an embrace. Skyskimmer purred with delight.

As Kraelin conversed telepathically with the three newcomers, the murmur of animated chattering gradually built in volume as more Ogmus and dragonets joined in. Standing beside Nina, Reizgoth fidgeted nervously. Looking at his pensive expression, she doubted whether it had anything to do with the rising tide of excitement. "What's happening?" she asked.

Reizgoth turned his head and regarded her. "They will not accept Kraelin as their queen," he answered, his voice low.

"Why not?" Nina was incredulous. How could they *not* accept her?

"Tobias told them that Nanapussy requested their presence on this world." He shrugged. "So they await her. She was their queen when they were tricked by the blacks and they will not accept another in her stead."

"But that's ridiculous," said Nina. "Nanna Pussy is not dragon, she's ..." She struggled to describe what her gran, or rather her mother, actually was. "Hasn't Kraelin told them?"

Reizgoth nodded. "But it makes no difference. So now we wait. And they argue."

Nina looked across the sand at Kraelin and the three new dragons. She could see the annoyance on Kraelin's face and feel her agitation. It would not be long before the young queen gave vent to her fury, and the three dragons knew it. So did Reizgoth. Having grown ever more agitated as time passed, he had started to edge towards the group, and Nina knew he would die to protect Kraelin should the others turn on her.

What had started out as a great victory for Ogmus and dragon-kind was rapidly turning into a confrontation. And one that had potentially deadly consequences.

* * * * *

Crouched between the two prone figures lying where they had fallen when the wyverhole closed, Wooster pressed his fingers lightly against Nanna Pussy's neck. It was with relief that he felt the flicker of a pulse. Although weak and erratic, it was there. "She lives," he said, withdrawing his hand.

"What about him?" asked Wild Bill, nodding at Snorkel.

"He also lives," said Wooster, checking for a pulse.

Wild Bill puffed out his cheeks and exhaled loudly. "Thank the gods for that." He clapped his hands together. "Right! Grab hold of Snorkel and I'll take her." Stepping forward he made to scoop Nanna Pussy up in his arms.

With amazing speed Wooster's hand shot out and gripped his forearm.

Wild Bill squealed and jumped back, wrenching his arm from Wooster's grasp. Glowering at him he rubbed his injured wrist. "What the bleedin' hell was that for?" he growled.

Meeting Wild Bill's angry gaze Wooster answered, "No one touches Nanapussy except for one of the blood."

Wild Bill sneered. "One of the bleedin' blood? What do yer think yer are? Some sort of secret society?" A suspicious frown formed on his face. "I know what it is, yer dirty great toerag. Yer want her for yerself, don't yer?" He folded his arms across his chest. "Well yer gonna have to get past me first. No one messes with my woman. Understand?"

Wooster sighed. The man was insufferable, and as thick as a very short plank. "I do not intend to *mess* with *your woman*," he answered, speaking slowly in an attempt to try and get through to the man. "As I am one of her kind, it is my duty to carry her." He rose to his feet. "And I shall not let any other touch her while she is incapacitated."

"Like that is it? Well! I got news fer yer, dog-breath. Yer won't be carrying her anywhere." He began to push the sleeves of his long-coat up his arms.

Wooster laughed. "And you intend to stop me?"

Wild Bill nodded grimly and crouched into a fist-fighter's stance. Balanced on the balls of his feet he bobbed and weaved, waving his meaty fists in front of Wooster's face.

With his arms folded Wooster looked on, bemused. The man was deranged. He had to be. Why else would he want to fight when they had just succeeded in their aims?

With a sharp hiss Wild Bill jabbed a right. Wooster swayed to the side, avoiding the clumsy punch with ease. "Will you stop this insanity? It serves no purpose."

"That's what you bleedin' think," snapped Wild Bill, throwing another punch.

Wooster leaned back out of reach.

"Think yer clever, hey?" sneered Wild Bill. "Come on, make a fight of it. Yer win, yer carry her. I win, I carry her. Right?"

"Wrong. I walk!"

"Huh?" Wild Bill paused and stared at Wooster. "How'd yer say that without movin' yer lips?"

"It was me, moron!"

Wild Bill looked down.

"Nanapussy," murmured Wooster, dropping to his knees.

Nanna Pussy cast Wild Bill a stern look and said, "Help me get up, before the fool injures himself."

Her voice sounded weak and Wooster very much doubted that she had the strength to stay standing once she was on her feet.

"I'll help yer," said Wild Bill, rushing forward.

"You will not!" she snapped. She turned to peer up at Wooster. "Lend me your strength," she whispered. "All is not as it should be in the cavern. I fear for our new queen's safety. The others will not accept her."

"Who?" asked Wooster, frowning.

"The dragons."

The colour drained from his face. He knew what the outcome would be if Kraelin pressed her point.

"What yer on about?" Wild Bill asked, scratching at his matted beard.

Wooster ignored him. "As you command," he said, reaching down to help Nanna Pussy to her feet, and infusing her body with strength as he did so.

Nanna Pussy smiled gratefully. "Not command, Winegrath. Never that. I lost that right a long time ago."

"You never lost that right, my Queen," he responded, dipping his head.

"Queen?" asked Wild Bill, his face screwed up in puzzlement. "What's he on about?"

"Make yourself useful and pick up Snorkel," said Nanna Pussy, "instead of wasting time asking stupid questions."

"There's no need to get shirty," he said, his bottom lip stuck out in a sullen pout.

"That is where you are wrong," retorted Nanna Pussy. "Believe me, that is where you are very wrong."

Chapter Thirty Four

The atmosphere in the amphitheatre had changed, Nina could tell. The euphoria of the dragons' return had been replaced by an aura of menace. The dragonets had picked up on it straight away and had been the first to cease their high-pitched chatter. Now even the Ogmus sensed the change in the mood and had fallen silent. They watched the battle of wills being enacted in the centre of the arena without realising what it was, but knowing it was important.

Needing the comfort of another's touch, Nina reached out and gripped Cronan's hand.

"What's happening?" he asked quietly. "Why has Reizgoth gone to join Kraelin?"

"The others will not accept her as their queen," Nina answered, her eyes fixed on the young queen, whose manner was becoming increasingly agitated.

"Why not?"

"They were expecting another," she answered, not wanting to give away Nanna Pussy's secret. Already there were too many people who knew what she once was.

"What's that mean then?" Volgen's voice was full of concern.

"I wish I knew," murmured Nina.

A bestial roar shattered the silence as Kraelin reared on her hind legs and flapped at the air angrily, her neck arched and head pointing at the three newcomers. The threat was obvious to all. The three dragons leapt back and reared, their roars of defiance deafening in the enclosed space.

Seeking to protect his queen, Reizgoth launched himself into the gap between the adversaries, his huge form shielding Kraelin as he snarled a challenge to the three.

"Piggin' hell!" cried Volgen. "There's going to be a fight. Nostra never mentioned anything about that in his prophecies."

The watching Ogmus screamed in terror and started heading for the safety of the tunnels, and soon a full scale exodus was underway. The dragonets, following their basic instincts, also fled, flying above the heads of the Ogmus as they made for the sanctuary of Hope.

"Tobias!" gasped Nina. "The red dragon still has him in his claws! He'll be killed."

"Not if we have anything to do with it!" Brimble shot past on Blooper, heading straight for the dragons, the remaining Beastie Boys following close behind.

"By the gods," muttered Volgen. "The little bastards have some nerve. Er, sorry Miss," he hastily apologised.

Nina was only vaguely aware of Volgen's words, her attention firmly fixed on the six figures arrowing towards certain death. For she felt sure that was what awaited them.

"They'll be killed," Conan whispered, echoing her thoughts.

The dragons were too focussed on each other to notice the dragonets and their riders until they darted between them, the Beastie Boys yelling at the tops of their voices.

Roaring angrily one of the greens lunged forward, his huge jaws narrowly missing the tail of Boo's mount. The dragonet quickly shot out of reach, nearly unseating Boo who cried out in alarm and flailed his arms for balance. Having completed their pass, three dragonets veered right, the remaining three left. Turning sharply they headed back towards the dragons, flying on courses that would take them behind the warring parties. The diversionary tactic seemed to be working and the dragons' attention was drawn to their small adversaries.

With a powerful thrust of his hind legs, the green that had snapped at Boo's mount launched himself into the air to give chase. But his huge form was too large for fast manoeuvring in the confines of the cavern and the dragonets easily avoided his pursuit, ducking and diving as they took turns to loop back and irritate the enraged beast. Down below the green's comrades urged him on, roaring when he got close to catching a dragonet and groaning each time he missed.

Tobias began to come round, the thunderous roars of the dragons rousing him from his state of unconsciousness. "Wh-what's happening?" he asked, his voice weak.

No answer was forthcoming; instead another deafening roar went up. Tobias's stomach lurched as he was moved sharply to the side. He was still being carried by a dragon! He felt panic rising in him. It sounded as though a battle was being fought. Where had he taken them to? Had his loss of consciousness got anything to do with it? *'What's happening?'* he mind-shouted. *'Where are we?'*

'Back on your world,' came the reply. *'But all is not as we were led to believe.'*

'What do you mean? There are no enemies on Tiernan Og, not now that the blacks are vanquished.' Another mighty roar came from somewhere overhead, and Tobias wished that his sight would return so he could see what was going on.

'Nanapussy is not here. Instead there is another who claims to be queen.'

'Kraelin!' said Tobias. *'She* is *Queen.'*

'She is not our queen,' replied the dragon. *'Where is Nanapussy?'*

'Nanapussy is no longer dragon,' Tobias answered. *'I thought you knew that.'*

Before the dragon had the chance to respond, a massive surge swept through Tobias's very being, setting his whole body tingling. With it came a command. *'DESIST!'*

He knew from the quiver that rippled through the dragon that he had felt it too.

'Who calls us?' the dragon thundered.

'It is I, Nanapussy. Now are you going to stop behaving like younglings or am I going to have to come out there and sort you out myself?'

'Nanapussy?' queried the dragon. *'You are not dead?'*

'Of course I am not dead! But if you carry on behaving like idiots you'll begin to wish that I was!'

* * * * *

Tobias sat at the side of the amphitheatre, near to the tunnel leading to Hope's living areas. They had been sitting for the last candle-mark while the dragons, Nanna Pussy and Wooster held a conference in the middle of the sandy arena. Although his sight had begun to return, Tobias could not yet see clearly and the group looked like a fuzzy multi-coloured lump.

"What's happening?" he asked Nina.

"I don't know," she answered. "Kraelin is closed to me. I guess she doesn't want to be overheard."

"Reizgoth is, too," said Tobias.

"What I want to know," broke in Wild Bill, leaning forward, "is how come Nanna Pussy and that nerk Wooster can sit with the dragons and expect them to do as they say."

"They will," said Nina with confidence.

"How can you be so sure? I wouldn't do a damn thing Wooster told me to, so why should the dragons?"

"Because they are dragon," said Tobias. "That's why!"

"Who's dragon?" Wild Bill scratched at his head and took the opportunity to tap his temple with his forefinger and raise his eyebrows at Volgen.

"Wooster and Nanna Pussy."

Wild Bill snorted in disbelief.

"You'll see," said Tobias, unperturbed.

"If you say so, young 'un. If you say so."

"How's Snorkel?" asked Tobias, trying to change the subject. "Has he come round yet?"

Wild Bill glanced over his shoulder to where Snorkel lay on the ground, his head resting in Meelan's lap and a lazy smile on his face. "Who? The ugly old git with the girly red suit?"

Snorkel sat bolt upright, his beard bristling. "Who are you calling an ugly old git?"

Wild Bill laughed. "Yep! Looks like he's come round."

Snorkel glowered at Wild Bill's back and lay back to receive further petting from Meelan.

"Ignore big bear-man, Norkel. You lie here, let Meelan make better. All right?"

"Sure thing, sweetcakes. You make Norkel better." He winced as Meelan gave him a playful punch on the arm.

"Here they come," said Volgen, rising to his feet.

"Who?" asked Tobias, squinting. All he could see were hazy images. It was like looking through honey.

"Wooster and Nanna Pussy. I guess the meeting must be over," answered Nina, standing up and helping Tobias to his feet.

"Well?" asked Volgen when Nanna Pussy and Wooster reached the pensive group. "What's happening?"

"It's sorted," said Nanna Pussy.

"What's sorted?" said Wild Bill.

311

Nanna Pussy met Nina's gaze and smiled. "Kraelin is Queen."

With a squeal of delight Nina clapped her hands and wrapped her arms round Tobias. Slightly awkwardly he returned her embrace.

"Steady on young 'un. Or you'll make an old man jealous."

"So it's over then?" asked Cronan timidly.

Nanna Pussy nodded. "It's over." The glimmer of tears appeared in her eyes. "The dragons are back where they belong."

At her side Wooster cleared his throat. Nanna Pussy turned and gave him a smile of encouragement, gesturing him forward with a flick of her eyes.

Wooster coughed and dipped his head in deference to Tobias. "I would ask a boon, young Master."

Tobias eased Nina away from him, a half smile on his face. "I take it you want to make the attempt?" he asked, knowing what it was that Wooster wanted.

"Attempt what?" Wild Bill muttered, his gaze flicking between Wooster and Tobias.

Wooster ignored him. "I do. I have been too long in this body."

"What the bleedin' hell is the nerk on about?"

"Will you shut up," snapped Nanna Pussy. "Let the man speak."

Wild Bill scowled. Tobias leaned over and whispered quietly in Nina's ear. Giggling, she gave Wild Bill a wink and made her way to where Snorkel lay, passing on her message to him in hushed tones. The dwarf rose to his feet and followed her back, and another whispered conversation ensued. The furrow between Wild Bill's eyes deepened as he leaned forward in an attempt to overhear what was being said.

"Hear anything useful?" Tobias asked, with an air of innocence.

"Not a bleedin' thing," Wild Bill muttered in disgust, smoothing down his long-coat and straightening the lapels.

Tobias winked and clicked his tongue. "Well you'd better just watch and learn then, hey?" Laughing he linked arms with Snorkel and followed Wooster out onto the sand.

* * * * *

A knock on the door woke Jophrey with a start. His eyes flickered open and focussed on the shapeless lump of wax on the table beside his head. Despite the candle having melted away, pale light illuminated the meeting room. It was morning, he realised. He must have dozed off while he was trying to decipher Nostra's insane ramblings.

The knock came again, louder.

Yawning, Jophrey sat up and rolled his head on his shoulders in an attempt to ease the ache in his neck. So much for the promise he'd made himself to sleep in his own bed for a change. This was the fifth night in a row he had spent in his father's meeting room, poring over the verse. But it had been worth it; last night he had found what he had been looking for. "Enter!" he called, knowing who it would be. Leaning back in the armchair, he closed his eyes and clasped his hands behind his head.

"Breakfast is served, my Lord."

Jophrey inhaled, savouring the aroma of freshly baked bread. He opened his eyes and lowered his arms. "That smells good, Jeeves."

Jeeves closed the door with his heel and, crossing the room, placed the breakfast tray on the table. It held a bowl of thick porridge, a small pot of honey and two small bread rolls. "You have been working all night again I see, my Lord." His lips were taut with disapproval.

Jophrey grinned and rose to his feet, snatching one of the rolls from the tray. He tore off a chunk and shoved it into his mouth. It tasted divine. Wiping crumbs from his lips with the back of his hand, he walked over to one of the windows and looked out. "I found it," he said, staring absently into the distance.

"Found what, my Lord?" asked Jeeves.

Early morning was Jophrey's favourite time of day; when pale sunlight spread across the land, bringing with it freshness, vitality and the promise of things to come. He shivered. With winter not far away, the sun gave little in the way of warmth and he was freezing. "The answer, Jeeves." He turned round to face him. "The answer!"

A dark shape plummeted past the window, shrieking as it fell.

Jophrey spun in alarm. "What was that?" he cried.

Jeeves sighed. "Lord Blackhead, at a guess," he replied. "Since you commandeered his dragon he has been working on ways to improve his new invention. He informed me not a candle-mark ago that he was heading up to the tower to try it out. It would seem, however, that the secret of self-propulsion through the air shall remain firmly in the domain of dragons and birds."

Jophrey opened the window and leaned out. Down below a black shape lay splattered on the ground. The figure appeared tiny, but Jophrey could tell it was a man. A very dead man, surrounded by the debris from the wooden wings that had previously been strapped to his back. "No great loss," he said, moving back inside and closing the window.

"My thoughts exactly," said Jeeves, dipping his head.

Jophrey stuffed the rest of the roll in his mouth and returned to the table. He slid Nostra's book round and tapped at one of the last verses to have been written.

Leaning forward, Jeeves read the lines to himself, his eyes flicking down the page. When he had finished, he looked up and met Jophrey's gaze. He smiled. "For once his writings make perfect sense," he said.

"Well?" asked Jophrey.

The smile on Jeeves' face widened. "As you quite rightly say, my Lord, you have your answer."

Chapter Thirty Five

Winegrath launched himself from the ledge at the mouth of the access tunnel; out into the early morning sun, his wings spread wide as he glided down to the lush valley below. Sitting at the base of his neck Tobias revelled in the feeling of flight, as he had done these past four cycles. It seemed like an age had passed since his first fearful steps into the great outside.

The valley floor rushed ever closer and the changes in Hope Valley became more evident. The woodland had been cleared back from the river and a settlement had sprung up on its banks. Cultivated swathes of land spread out from the cluster of timber buildings either side of the narrow blue ribbon, and cows, sheep and goats grazed in the nearby fields. Even at this early hour people were up and about, tending to their fields and animals. Since the defeat of the blacks the Ogmus were thriving and most had taken to living outside again, even though few dared to venture too far from the place they still called home.

Winegrath wheeled to the right to enter the village from the north, downwind from the livestock, the folk that were up and about waving in greeting as the dragon flew overhead.

Dust spiralled up from the dried mud track as Winegrath came in to land. When it had settled, Tobias leaped from his back and brushed particles of dirt from his thick, quilted flying jacket. *'I'll call you as soon as I am done,'* he said, removing his goggles and reaching up to slap the dragon's shoulder. *'I shouldn't be too long.'*

Winegrath snorted. *'That rather depends on his condition.'*

Tobias laughed. *'I'll call you. Now be off. You have a queen to take care of.'*

'Maybe I shall go for a short flight,' Winegrath said, grimacing. *'I could do with some peace and quiet.'* Thrusting upwards with his powerful hind legs, he took to the air.

Tobias closed his eyes and ducked away from the blast of wind-blown grit. When the maelstrom was over, he brushed himself down again and walked up the short flight of steps leading to the entrance of the large two storey building. As always his attention was drawn to the bright red lettering above the doors. Winking down at him were the words, 'Snorkel's Snug', underscored with 'Hope's Premier Piss-up Palace'.

Without bothering to knock, Tobias pushed the doors open and strode inside, his riding boots clunking hollowly on the timber floor. Navigating the haphazard cluster of tables and chairs, he made his way to the bar and plucked a small brass bell off the polished surface. Its bright, cheery note echoed around the room. When no answer was forthcoming he shook it more vigorously.

"We're closed!" a sleepy sounding voice shouted from somewhere upstairs.

Tobias leaned over the counter and looked towards the flight of stairs that led up to the first floor. "Snorkel!" he yelled. "It's almost time!"

"Tobias? Is that you?"

"Of course it's me," he answered. "Who else would knock you up at this time of the morning?"

Footsteps sounded on the timber treads and a pair of hairy legs came into view, a scarlet dressing gown concealing the remainder of Snorkel's body from sight. The dwarf, hair dishevelled and eyes bleary, descended and stood behind the bar. "For a moment I thought it was Wild Bill," he muttered, pushing a hand through his tangled locks.

Tobias laughed. "He and Nanna Pussy are away on one of their trips, so he won't be back until later today. Nina sent Reizgoth to find them and bring them home for the hatching."

Snorkel looked up, his eyes suddenly bright. "How soon?" he asked.

Tobias shrugged. "Like I said, they'll be back later on today."

"Not Wild Bill and Nanna Pussy, the hatching!"

"Oh, that. Any time now." He pursed his lips. "Between Kraelin and Nina the whole place is in uproar. The pair of them are on edge, and they're driving everyone to distraction."

"I know the feeling," Snorkel muttered quietly, his eyebrows twitching.

"Hmmm! How *is* Meelan?" Tobias asked.

"The same as ever. You'd think that after two kids she would be used to this pregnancy lark." He shook his head and grimaced. "But she's as ornery as ever. Women, hey?"

A tight-lipped smile formed on Tobias's face. Despite now being a dragon rider he still had as little luck with women as ever; there had been a few minor flirtations but nothing serious, discounting Mihooda and her ribald comments. It would seem that red hair was not a desirable feature in a potential partner.

Snorkel chuckled. "Don't worry, lad. Your time will come. Then you'll remember the times when you used to be free and single with great affection, believe you me."

Suddenly a loud bugle of alarm shook the building, setting the glasses vibrating and the windows rattling.

"Whatever can that mean?" said Snorkel, his eyes narrowing. Raising the hinged section of the counter, he opened the serving door and stepped from behind the bar. "Best take a look, hey?" he said, striding towards the doors.

Before he reached them a blast of air and dust hammered against the building. "By the gods!" he shouted, ducking behind a table.

The doors burst open and crashed against the wall and Volgen strode in, his face red and powder-blue flying suit crumpled and dirt-streaked.

"What's the matter?" demanded Tobias, noticing the fearful look in Volgen's eyes.

"You have to come back immediately." He glanced at Snorkel and was momentarily rendered speechless as his eyes fixed on the bright red dressing gown. "Both of you."

"Why?" Snorkel asked, frowning. "Is there a problem?"

Volgen swallowed nervously. "You could say that." His gaze flicked between the two men. "There's been a piggin' egg-napping!"

* * * * *

As soon as Winegrath and Stormflier landed in the amphitheatre Volgen, Tobias and Snorkel leapt from their backs. Nina ran across the sand from one of the side tunnels and flew into Tobias's arms. "It's gone," she sobbed. "It's gone!"

Tobias eased her away and looked into her eyes. They were red and puffy from weeping. "Calm down and tell me what happened," he said gently.

Nina sniffed and wiped her eyes with the back of her hand. "The egg," she wailed. "The golden egg! It's been stolen! It must have been taken while we were out bathing last night."

Tobias felt his jaw drop in horror. Although Volgen had said an egg had been taken, he'd never said which one. "Where is Kraelin?" he asked.

Nina stifled a sob as the tears began to fall again. "In with the other eggs. She is overcome with guilt and blames herself for not being here when it happened. She'd ordered the others to tend to her, you see, so the birthing chamber was left unguarded."

"But who would do such a thing? *How* could they do such a thing? It would take at least two men to move the egg; and how would they carry it once they had taken it from the chamber?"

"I think I have the answer as to the who," said Cronan.

Tobias looked at the old librarian, who had arrived unnoticed. Clasped in his hands was a book. "Nostra's Book of Prophecies," he gasped, recognising the large, leather-bound tome.

Cronan nodded. "I found it on my desk in the library." He opened the book and handed it to Tobias. "It had a book-mark at this page. Read it; it needs no translation. The meaning is perfectly clear."

Tobias read the untidy writing, his eyes widening. When he had finished he looked up and met Nina's worried gaze. "Jophrey!" he said. He tossed the tome to the ground, then turned and climbed onto Winegrath's back.

"Where are you going?" cried Nina.

"To find Jophrey," he answered. He turned to Volgen. "Round up the others. We have a thief to catch!"

Stunned to silence by the commanding tone of Tobias's voice, Volgen watched Winegrath take to the air and fly from the amphitheatre. When he had disappeared from sight he murmured, "Who's the piggin' Wing Commander here?"

"I think you'll find that he is," Cronan answered quietly, as he stared into the dark maw of the tunnel. "It was what he was born to be, according to Nostra." Turning to Nina he said, "Shall I tell him or should you?"

On the ground the pages of the Book of Prophecies fluttered in the breeze caused by Winegrath's departure, finally coming to rest at the bookmarked passage. To those that could read the recently added handwritten scrawl, it said:

In the dead of night, when the moon shines bright, a hero shall drop from the air,
On wings of dark stealth, he'll take the queen's wealth, when she leaves those under her care.
Although ye shall look both near and far, no gleam of gold shall there be,
For into strange lands the thief shall have gone, and his name shall be known as Jophrey.

As translated by Jophrey, Lord of the Blacks.

ENDS

Printed in the United Kingdom
by Lightning Source UK Ltd.
127324UK00001B/6/P